Ka[illegible] n drama teac[illegible] writing romance [illegible] women's fiction and all her stories [illegible] demptive power of love. Kate lives in a tiny village in the English Cotswolds with her husband, five children, and an overly affectionate golden retriever.

Cat Schield lives in Minnesota with her daughter, their opinionated Burmese cats and a silly doberman puppy. She is the winner of the Romance Writers of America 2010 Golden Heart® for series contemporary romance. When she's not writing sexy, romantic stories for Mills & Boon Desire, she can be found sailing with friends on the St. Croix River or in more exotic locales like the Caribbean and Europe. You can find out more about her books at www.catschield.net

Kimberly Lang is a Southern belle with a trouble-making streak and a great love of strong heroes and even stronger heroines. A former ballet dancer and English teacher, she now does yoga and writes the kind of books she always loved to read. She's married to her college sweetheart, is mum to the most amazing child on the planet, and shares her office space with a dog named Cupid. Visit her website at www.BooksByKimberly.com

Tempted by the Rock Star

KATE HEWITT
CAT SCHIELD
KIMBERLY LANG

MILLS & BOON

First Published in Great Britain 2019
by Mills & Boon, an imprint of HarperCollins*Publishers*
1 London Bridge Street, London, SE1 9GF

ISBN: 978-0-263-27782-1

0919

MIX
Paper from responsible sources
FSC™ C007454

This book is produced from independently certified FSC™ paper to ensure responsible forest management.

For more information visit: www.harpercollins.co.uk/green

Printed and bound in Spain
by CPI, Barcelona

IN THE HEAT OF THE SPOTLIGHT

KATE HEWITT

To my big brother Geordie,
the real writer of Aurelie's song.
Thank you for always being my (tor)mentor.
Love, K.

CHAPTER ONE

LUKE BRYANT STARED at his watch for the sixth time in the last four minutes and felt his temper, already on a steady simmer, start a low boil.

She was late. He glanced enquiringly at Jenna, his Head of PR, who made useless and apologetic flapping motions with her hands. All around him the crowd that filled Bryant's elegant crystal and marble lobby began to shift restlessly. They'd already been waiting fifteen minutes for Aurelie to make an appearance before the historic store's grand reopening and so far she was a no-show.

Luke gritted his teeth and wished, futilely, that he could wash his hands of this whole wretched thing. He'd been busy putting out corporate fires at the Los Angeles office and had left the schedule of events for today's reopening to his team here in New York. If he'd been on site, he wouldn't be here waiting for someone he didn't even want to see. What had Jenna been thinking, booking a washed-up C-list celebrity like Aurelie?

He glanced at his Head of PR again, watched as she bit her lip and made another apologetic face. Feeling not one shred of sympathy, Luke strode towards her.

'Where is she, Jenna?'

'Upstairs—'

'What is she doing?'

'Getting ready—'

Luke curbed his skyrocketing temper with some effort. 'And does she realise she's fifteen—' he checked his watch '—*sixteen* and a half minutes late for the one song she's meant to perform?'

'I think she does,' Jenna admitted.

Luke stared at her hard. He was getting annoyed with the wrong person, he knew. Jenna was ambitious and hardworking and, all right, she'd booked a complete has-been like Aurelie to boost the opening of the store, but at least she had a ream of market research to back up her choice. Jenna had been very firm about the fact that Aurelie appealed to their target group of eighteen to twenty-five-year-olds, she'd sung three chart-topping and apparently iconic songs of their generation, and was only twenty-six herself.

Apparently Aurelie still held the public's interest—the same way a train wreck did, Luke thought sourly. You just couldn't look away from the unfolding disaster.

Still, he understood the bottom line. Jenna had booked Aurelie, the advertising had gone out, and a significant number of people were here to see the former pop princess sing one of her insipid numbers before the store officially reopened. As CEO of Bryant Stores, the buck stopped with him. It always stopped with him.

'Where is she exactly?'

'Aurelie?'

As if they'd been talking about anyone else. 'Yes. Aurelie.' Even her name was ridiculous. Her real name was probably Gertrude or Millicent. Or even worse, something with an unnecessary i like Kitti or Jenni. Either way, absurd.

'She's in the staff break room—'

Luke nodded grimly and headed upstairs. Aurelie had been contracted to sing and, damn it, she was going to sing. Like a canary.

Upstairs, Bryant's women's department was silent and empty, the racks of clothes and ghostly faceless mannequins seeming to accuse him silently. Today had to be a success. Bryant Stores had been slowly and steadily declining for the last five years, along with the economy. No one wanted overpriced luxuries, which was what Bryant's had smugly specialised in for the last century. Luke had been trying to change things for years but his older brother, Aaron, had insisted on having the final say and he hadn't been interested in doing something that, in his opinion, diminished the Bryant name.

When the latest dismal reports had come in, Aaron had finally agreed to an overhaul, and Luke just prayed it wasn't too late. If it was, he knew who would be blamed.

And it *would* be his fault, he told himself grimly. He was the CEO of Bryant Stores, even if Aaron still initialled many major decisions. Luke took responsibility for what happened in his branch of Bryant Enterprises, including booking Aurelie as today's entertainment.

He knocked sharply on the door to the break room. 'Hello? Miss…Aurelie?' *Why* didn't the woman have a last name? 'We're waiting for you—' He tried the knob. The door was locked. He knocked again. No answer.

He stood motionless for a moment, the memory sweeping coldly through him of another locked door, a different kind of silence. The scalding rush of guilt.

This is your fault, Luke. You were the only one who could have saved her.

Resolutely he pushed the memories aside. He shoved his shoulder against the door and gave it one swift and accurate kick with his foot. The lock busted and the door sprang open.

Luke entered the break room and glanced around. Clothes—silly, frothy, ridiculous outfits—were scattered across the table and chairs, some on the floor. And something else was on the floor.

Aurelie.

He stood there, suspended in shock, in memory, and then, swearing again, he strode towards her. She was slumped in the corner of the room, wearing an absurdly short dress, her legs splayed out like spent matchsticks.

He crouched in front of her, felt her pulse. It seemed steady, but what did he really know about pulses? Or pop stars? He glanced at her face, which looked pale and was lightly beaded with sweat. Actually, now that he looked at her properly, she looked awful. He supposed she was pretty in a purely objective sense, with straight brownish-blonde hair and a lithe, slender figure, but her face was drawn and grey and she looked way too thin.

He touched her cheek and found her skin clammy. He reached for his cell phone to dial 911, his heart beating far too hard. She must have overdosed on something. He'd never expected to see this scenario twice in one lifetime, and the remembered panic iced in his veins.

Then her eyes fluttered open and his hand slackened on the phone. Luke felt something stir inside him at the colour of her eyes. They were slate-blue, the colour of the Atlantic on a cold, grey day, and they swirled with sorrow. She blinked blearily, struggled to sit up. Her gaze focused in on him and something cold flashed in their blue depths. 'Aren't you handsome,' she mumbled, and the relief he felt that she was okay was blotted out by a far more familiar determination.

'Right.' He hauled her up by the armpits and felt her sag helplessly against him. She'd looked thin slumped on the floor, and she felt even more fragile in his arms. Fragile and completely out of it. 'What did you take?' he demanded. She lolled her head back to blink up at him, her lips curving into a mocking smile.

'Whatever it was, it was a doozy.'

Luke scooped her up in his arms and stalked over to the bathroom. He ran a basin full of cold water and in one quick and decisive movement plunged the pop star's face into the icy bowlful.

She came up like a scalded cat, spluttering and swearing. 'What the *hell*—?'

'Sobered up a bit now, have you?'

She sluiced water from her face and turned to glare at him with narrowed eyes. 'Oh, yes, I'm sober. Who are you?'

'Luke Bryant.' He heard his voice, icy with suppressed rage. Damn her for scaring him. For making him remember. 'I'm paying you to perform, princess, so I'll give you five minutes to pull yourself together and get down there.' She folded her arms, her eyes still narrowed, her face still grey and gaunt. 'And put some make-up on,' Luke added as he turned to leave. 'You look like hell.'

Aurelie Schmidt—not many people knew about the Schmidt—wiped the last traces of water from her face and blinked hard. Stupid man. Stupid gig. Stupid her, for coming today at all. For trying to be different.

She drew in a shuddering breath and grabbed a chocolate bar from her bag. Unwrapping it in one vicious movement, she turned to stare at the clothes scattered across the impromptu dressing room. Jenna, the Bryant stooge who had acted as her handler, had been horrified by her original choice of outfit.

'But you're *Aurelie*... You have an *image*...'

An image that was five years past its sell-by date, but people still wanted to see it. They wanted to see her, although whether it was because they actually liked her songs or just because they hoped to see her screw up one more time was open to debate.

And so she'd forsaken the jeans and floaty top she'd been wanting to wear and shimmied into a spangly minidress instead. She'd just been about to do her make-up when she must have passed out. And Mr Bossy Bryant had come in and assumed the worst. Well, she could hardly blame him. She'd done the worst too many times to get annoyed when someone jumped to that rather obvious conclusion.

Clearly she was late, so she wolfed down her chocolate bar and then did the quick version of her make-up: blush, concealer, eyeliner and a bold lipstick. Her hair looked awful but at least she could turn it into a style. She pulled it up in a messy up-do and sprayed it to death. People would like seeing her a little off her game anyway. It was, she suspected, why they were here; it was why the tabloids still rabidly followed her even though she hadn't released a single in over four years. Everyone wanted to see her fail.

It had been a good twenty minutes since she was meant to perform her once-hit single *Take Me Down*, and Aurelie knew the audience would be getting restless. And Luke Bryant would be getting even more annoyed. Her lips curved in a cynical smile as she turned to leave the break room. Luke Bryant obviously had extremely low expectations of her. Well, he could just join the club.

Stepping onto a stage—even a makeshift one like this—always felt like an out-of-body experience to Aurelie. Any sense of self fell away and she simply became the song, the dance, the performance. Aurelie as the world had always known her.

The crowd in front of her blurred into one faceless mass and she reached for the mike. Her stiletto heel caught in a gap in the floor of the stage and for a second she thought she was going to pitch forward. She heard the sudden collective intake of breath, knew everyone was waiting, even hoping, she'd fall flat on her face. She righted herself, smiled breezily and began to sing.

Usually she wasn't aware of what she was doing onstage. She just did it. Sing, slink, shimmy, smile. It was second nature to her now, *first* nature, because performing—being someone else—felt far easier than being herself. And yet right there in the middle of all that fakery she felt something inside her still and go silent, even as she sang.

Standing on the side of the makeshift stage, away from the audience assembled in the lobby, Lukc Bryant was staring right at her, his face grim, his eyes blazing. And worse, far worse, since he *should* be staring at her, was the realisation that she was staring back at him. And some part of herself could not look away even as she turned back to face the crowd.

Luke watched as Aurelie began her routine, and knew that was what it was. She was on autopilot, but she was good enough that it didn't matter. Her whipcord-slender body moved with an easy, sensual grace. Her voice was clear and true but also husky and suggestive when she wanted it to be, like sunshine and smoke. It was a sexy voice, and she was good at what she did. Even annoyed as he was with her, he could acknowledge that.

And then she turned and looked at him, and any smug sense of detachment he felt drained away. All he felt was… *need.* An overwhelming physical need for her but, more than that, a need to…to *protect* her. How ridiculous. He didn't even like her; he *despised* her. And yet in that still, silent second when their gazes met he felt a tug of both heart and… well, the obvious.

Then she looked away and he let out a shuddering breath, relieved to have that weird reaction fade away. Clearly he was overtired and way too stressed, to be feeling like that about someone like Aurelie. Or anyone at all.

He heard her call out to the crowd to sing along to the chorus of the admittedly catchy tune, and watched as she tossed her head and shouted, 'Come on, it's not that old a hit that you can't remember!'

He felt a flicker of reluctant admiration that she could make fun of herself. It took courage to do that. Yet remembering her slumped on the break room floor made his mouth twist down in disapproval. Dutch courage, maybe. Or worse.

The music ended, three intense minutes of song and dance, and Luke listened to the thunder of applause. He heard a few catcalls too and felt himself cringe. They liked her, but part of liking her, he knew, was making fun of her. He had a feeling Aurelie knew that too. He watched as she bowed with a semi-sardonic flourish, fluttered her fingers at her fans and sashayed offstage towards him. Their gazes clashed once more and Aurelie tipped her chin up a notch, her eyes flashing challenge.

Luke knew he'd treated her pretty harshly upstairs, but he wasn't about to apologise. The woman might have been on *drugs*. Now that she had done her act he wanted her out of here. She was way too much of a wild card to have in the store today. She came towards him and he reached out and curled one hand around her wrist.

He felt the fragility of her bones under his fingers, the frantic hammering of her pulse, and wished he hadn't touched her. Standing so close to her, he could smell her perfume, a fresh, citrusy scent, feel the heat from her body. He couldn't quite keep his gaze from dipping down to the smooth roundness of her breasts and the gentle flaring of her hips, outlined all too revealingly under the thin, stretchy material of her skimpy dress. His gaze travelled back up her body and he saw her looking at him with an almost weary cynicism.

He dropped her wrist, conscious that he'd just given her a very thorough once-over. 'Thank you,' he said, and heard how stiff his voice sounded.

Her mouth twisted. 'For what, exactly?'

'For singing.' He hated the lilt of innuendo in her voice.

'No problem, Bossy.'

Annoyance flared. 'Why do you think I'm bossy?'

'We-ell…' She put her hands on her hips. 'You dunked me in a sink of cold water and expected me to thank you for it.'

'You were passed out. I was doing you a favour.'

Her lips curved and her eyes glittered. Everything about her mocked him. 'See what I mean?'

'I just want you to do what you're meant to do,' Luke said tightly. The sooner this woman was out of here, the better. The store opening didn't need her. He didn't need her.

With that same mocking smile she placed one slender hand on his chest so he could see her glittery nail varnish—and she could feel the sudden, hard thud of his heart. He could feel the heat of her hand through his shirt, the gentle press of her slender fingers and, irritatingly, his libido stirred.

'And what,' she asked, her voice dropping an octave, 'am I meant to do?'

'Leave,' he snapped. He couldn't control his body's reaction, much as he wanted to, but he could—and would—control everything else.

She just laughed softly and pressed her hand more firmly against the thin cotton of his shirt, spreading her fingers wide. He remained completely still, stony-faced, and she dropped her gaze downwards. 'You sure about that?' she murmured.

Fury beat through his blood and he picked up her hand—conscious again of its slender smallness—and thrust it back at her as if it were some dead thing. 'I'll have security escort you out.'

She raised her eyebrows. 'And that will look good on today of all days.'

'What do you mean?'

'Having Aurelie escorted out by your security buffoons? The tabloids will eat it up with a spoon.' She folded her arms, a dangerous glitter in her eyes. It almost looked as if she was near tears or, more likely, triumph. 'Your big opening will be made into a mockery. Trust me, I know how it goes.'

'I have no doubt you do.' She'd been ridiculed in the press more times than he cared to count.

'Suck it up, Bossy,' she jeered softly. 'You need me.'

Luke felt his jaw bunch. And ache. He was tempted to stand his ground and tell her to leave, but rationality won out. Too much rode on this event to stand on stupid pride. 'Fine,' he said evenly. 'You can circulate and socialise for an hour, and then leave of your own accord. But if you so much as—'

'What?' She raised her eyebrows, her mouth curving into another mocking smile. 'What do you think I'm going to do?'

'That's the problem. I have absolutely no idea.'

She'd looked so coy and cat-like standing there, all innuendo and outrageous suggestion, but suddenly it was as if the life had drained out of her and she looked away, her expression veiled, blank. 'Don't worry,' she said flatly. 'I'll give everyone, even you, what they want. I always do.' And without looking back at him she walked towards the crowd.

Watching her, Luke felt a flicker of uneasy surprise. He'd assumed Aurelie was as shallow as a puddle, but in that moment when she'd looked away he'd sensed something dark and deep and even painful in her averted gaze.

He let out a long, low breath and turned in the opposite direction. He wasn't going to waste another second of his time thinking about the wretched woman.

Now that the mini-concert was over, the crowd milled around, examining the glass display cases of jewellery and make-up, the artful window dressings. Luke forced himself to focus on what lay ahead. Yet even as he moved through the crowd, smiling, nodding, talking, it seemed as if he could still feel the heat of her hand on his chest, imagined that its imprint remained in the cloth, or even on his skin.

Aurelie turned around to watch Luke Bryant walk away, wondering just what made Mr Bossy tick. He was wound tight enough to snap, that was for sure. When she'd placed her hand on his chest she'd felt how taut his muscles were, how tense. And she'd also felt the sudden thud of his heart, and knew she affected him. Aroused him.

The knowledge should have given her the usual sense of grim satisfaction, but it didn't. All she felt was tired. So very tired, and the thought of performing on a different kind of stage, playing the role of Aurelie the Pop Star for another hour or more, made her feel physically sick.

What would happen, she wondered, if she dropped the flirty, salacious act for a single afternoon, stopped being Aurelie and tried being herself instead?

She thought of the PR lady's look of horror at such a suggestion. No one wanted Aurelie the real person. They wanted the pop princess who tripped through life and made appalling tabloid-worthy mistakes. That was the only person they were interested in.

And that was the only person she was interested in being. She wasn't even sure if there was anything left underneath, inside. Taking a deep breath, she squared her shoulders and headed into the fray.

The crowd mingling in the elegant lobby of Bryant's was a mix of well-heeled and decidedly middle class. Aurelie had known Bryant's as a top-of-the-line, big-name boutique but, from a glance at the jewellery counter, she could tell the reopening was trying to hit a slightly more affordable note.

She supposed in this economy it was a necessary move and, from her quick once-over, it didn't seem that the store had sacrificed style or elegance in its pursuit of the more price-conscious shopper. Ironic, really, that both she and Bryant's were trying to reinvent themselves. She wondered if Luke would make a better job of it than she had.

For three-quarters of an hour she worked the crowd, signing autographs and fluttering her fingers and giggling and squealing as if she was having the time of her life. Which she most certainly was not. Yet even as she played the princess, she found her gaze wandering all too often to Luke Bryant. From the hard set of his jaw and the tension in his shoulders, he looked as if he wasn't having the time of his life, either. And, unlike her, he wasn't able to hide it.

He was certainly good-looking enough, with the dark brown hair, chocolate eyes and powerful body she remembered the feel of. Yet he looked so serious, so stern, his dark eyes hooded and his mouth a thin line. Did he ever laugh or even smile? He'd probably had his sense of humour surgically removed.

Then she remembered the thud of his heart under her hand and how warm his skin had felt, even through the cotton of his shirt. She remembered how he'd looked down at her, first with disapproval and then with desire. Typical, she told herself, yet something in her had responded to that hot, dark gaze, something in her she'd thought had long since died.

His gaze lifted to hers and she realised she'd been staring at him for a good thirty seconds. He stared back in that even, assessing way, as if he had the measure of her and found it decidedly lacking. Aurelie felt her heart give a strange little lurch and deliberately she let her gaze wander up and down his frame, giving him as much of a once-over as he'd given her. His mouth twisted in something like distaste and he turned away.

Aurelie stood there for a moment feeling oddly rebuffed, almost hurt. How ridiculous; all she'd been trying to do was annoy him. Besides, she'd suffered far worse insults than being dismissed. All she had to do was open a newspaper or click on one of the many celebrity gossip sites. Still, she couldn't deny the needling sense of pain, like a splinter burrowing into her heart. Why did this irritating man affect her so much, or even at all?

She heard the buzz of conversation around her and tried to focus on what someone was saying. Tried to smile, to perform, yet somehow the motions wouldn't come. She was failing herself, and in one abrupt movement she pivoted on her heel and walked out of the crowded lobby.

Luke watched Aurelie leave the lobby and felt an irritating mix of satisfaction and annoyance war within him. He didn't particularly want the woman around, yet he hadn't liked the look on her face, almost like hurt, when he'd gazed back at her. Why he cared, he had no idea. He *didn't* care. He wanted her gone.

And yet he could remember the exact blue-grey shade of her eyes, saw in that moment how they had darkened with pain. And despite every intention to stay and socialise, he found himself walking upstairs, back to the break room where he figured Aurelie had gone.

He pushed open the now-broken door without knocking, stopping suddenly when he saw Aurelie inside, in the process of pulling her dress over her head.

'Excuse me—'

'No need to be shy, boss man.' She turned around wearing nothing but a very skimpy push-up bra and thong, her hands on her hips, eyebrows raised, mouth twisted. 'Now you can have the good look you've been wanting.'

He shook his head. 'You're really unbelievable.'

'Why, that's almost a compliment.'

And Luke knew he *was* having a good look. Again. He could not, to his shame, tear his gaze away from those high, firm breasts encased in a very little bit of white satin. Furious with himself, he reached for a gauzy purple top lying on the floor and tossed it to her. 'Put something on.'

She glanced at the top and her mouth curled in a feline smile. 'If you insist.'

She didn't look any more decent in the see-through top. In fact, Luke decided, she looked worse. Or better, depending on your point of view. The diaphanous material still managed to highlight the slender curves that had been on such blatant display. She was too skinny, he told himself, yet once again he could not keep his gaze from roving over her body, taking in its taut perfection. He felt another stirring of arousal, much to his annoyance. Aurelie's mouth curved in a knowing smile.

'I came up here,' he finally bit out, 'to see if you were all right.'

She raised her eyebrows, and he sensed her sudden tension. 'And why wouldn't I be all right?'

'Because—' What could he say? *Because I saw such sadness in your eyes.* He was being ridiculous. About a completely ridiculous woman. 'You seemed troubled,' he finally answered, because he didn't dissemble or downright lie. He wouldn't, not since that moment twenty-five years ago when he'd put his heart and soul on the line and hadn't been believed.

'Troubled?' Her voice rang out, incredulous, scornful. Yet he still saw those shadows in her eyes, felt the brittleness of her confident pose, hands on hips, chin—and breasts—thrust out. She cocked her head, lashes sweeping downwards. 'Aren't you Mr Sensitive,' she murmured, her voice dropping into husky suggestion that had the hairs on the back of

Luke's neck prickling even as his libido stirred insistently. It had been far too long since he'd been in a relationship. Since he'd had sex. That had to be the only reason he was reacting to this woman at all.

She sashayed towards him, lifted her knowing gaze to his. Luke took an involuntary step backwards, and came up against the door. 'I think you're the troubled one, Mr Bossy,' she said, and with a cynical little smile she reached down to skim the length of his burgeoning erection with her fingertips. Luke felt as if he'd been jolted with electricity. He stepped back, shook his head in disgust.

'What is *wrong* with you?'

'Obviously nothing, judging by your reaction.'

'If I see a fairly attractive woman in her underwear, then yes, my body has a basic biological reaction. That's all it is.'

'Oh, so your little show of concern for my emotional state was just that?' She stepped back, and her smile was now cold, her eyes hard.

'You think I was coming on to you?' He let out a short, hard laugh. 'If anything, you're the one who's been coming on to me. I don't even like you, lady.'

She lifted her chin, her eyes still hard. 'Since when did like ever come into it?'

'It does for me.'

'How quaint.' She turned away and, reaching for a pair of jeans, pulled them on. 'Well, you can breathe a sigh of relief. I'm fine.'

And even though he knew he should leave—hell, he should never have come up here in the first place—Luke didn't move. She didn't *seem* fine.

He stood there in frustration—sexual frustration now, too—as Aurelie piled all the clothes scattered around the room into a big canvas holdall. She glanced up at him, those stormy eyes veiled by long lashes, and for a second, no more, she looked young. Vulnerable. Then she smiled—he hated that cold, cynical smile—and said, 'Still here, Bossy? Still hoping?'

'I'm here,' he said through gritted teeth, remembrance firing his fury, 'because you're a complete disaster and I can't trust you to walk out of here on your own two feet. An hour ago you were passed out on the floor. The last thing I need is some awful exposé in a trashy tabloid about how pop princess Aurelie ODed in the break room.'

She rolled her eyes. 'Oh, and here I was, starting to believe you were actually *concerned* about me. Don't worry, I told you, I'm fine.'

Luke jerked his head into the semblance of a nod. 'Then I'll say goodbye and thank you to use the back door on your way out.'

'I always do. Paparazzi, you know.' She smiled, but he saw her chin tremble, just the tiniest bit, and with stinging certainty he knew that despite her go-to-hell attitude, he'd hurt her.

And even though he knew he shouldn't care, not one iota, he knew he did. 'Goodbye,' he said, because the sooner he was rid of her, the better. She didn't answer, just stared at him with those storm cloud eyes, her chin lifted defiantly—and still trembling. Swearing aloud this time, Luke turned and walked out of the room.

CHAPTER TWO

'"BRYANT'S REOPENING HIT exactly the right note between self-deprecation and assurance,"' Jenna read from the newspaper as she came into Luke's office, kicking the door closed behind her with one high-heeled foot. She glanced at him over the top of the paper, her eyes dancing. 'It was a total hit!'

Luke gave a rather terse smile back. He didn't want to kill Jenna's buzz, but he hadn't meant the reopening to be 'self-deprecating'—whatever that was supposed to mean. A quick scan of the morning's headlines had reassured him that the opening had been well received, if not exactly how he'd envisioned, and the till receipts at the end of the day had offered more proof. It was enough, Luke hoped, to continue the relaunch of Bryant Stores across the globe—if his brother Aaron agreed.

He felt the familiar pang of frustration at still having to clear any major decisions with his brother, even though he was thirty-eight years old and had been running Bryant Stores for over a decade. He'd surely earned a bit more of Aaron's trust, but his brother never gave it. Their father had set up the running of Bryant Enterprises in his will, and it meant that Aaron could call all the shots. And that, Luke knew, was one thing Aaron loved to do.

'Getting Aurelie really worked,' Jenna said. 'All the papers mention her.'

'They usually do,' Luke answered dryly. He spun around in his chair to face the rather uninspiring view of Manhattan's midtown covered in a muggy midsummer haze. He did *not* want to think about that out-of-control pop princess, or the shaming reaction she'd stirred up in him.

'Apparently it was a stroke of genius to have her sing,' Jenna continued, her voice smug with self-satisfaction.

'Hitting the right note between self-deprecation and assurance?' Luke quoted. The newspaper had managed to ridicule Aurelie even as they lauded the opening. *Even if Aurelie is too washed up to reinvent herself, Bryant's obviously can.* Briefly he closed his eyes. How did she stand it, all the time? Or did she just not care?

'Maybe you should have her perform at all the openings,' Jenna suggested and Luke opened his eyes.

'I don't think so.'

'Why not?' Jenna persisted. 'I know she's a bit of a joke, but people still like her music. And the newspapers loved that we hired a has-been to perform… They thought it was an ironic nod to—'

'Our own former celebrity. Yes, I read the papers, Jenna. I'm just not sure that was quite the angle we were going for.' Luke turned around and gave his Head of PR a quelling look. He liked hiring young people with fresh ideas; he wanted change and innovation, unlike his brother. But he didn't want Aurelie.

Actually, the problem is, you do.

'Maybe not,' Jenna persisted, 'but it worked. And the truth is that nobody wants the old Bryant's any more. You can only coast on a reputation for so long.'

'Tell that to Aurelie,' he said, meaning to close down the conversation, but Jenna let out a sharp little laugh.

'But that's all she has. Do you know she actually wanted

to sing something new—some soppy folk ballad.' Jenna rolled her eyes, and Luke stilled.

'A *folk* ballad? She's a pop star.'

'I know, ridiculous, right? I don't know *what* she was thinking. She wanted to wear jeans, for heaven's sake, and play her *guitar*. Like we hired her for that.'

Luke didn't answer, just let the words sink in. 'What did you say to her?' he asked after a moment.

'I told her we'd hired her to be Aurelie, not Joan Baez.'

He rolled a silver-plated pen between his fingers, his gaze resting once more on the hazy skyline. 'What did she say?'

Jenna shrugged. 'Not much. We're the ones who hired her. What could she do, after all?'

Nothing, Luke supposed. Nothing except lash out at anyone who assumed she was just that, only that—Aurelie, the shallow pop princess. An uncomfortable uncertainty stole through him at the thought.

Who *was* Aurelie, really?

'That will be all, Jenna,' he said and, looking faintly miffed since he'd always encouraged a spirit of camaraderie in the office, she left. Luke sank back into his chair and rubbed his hands over his face.

He didn't want to think about Aurelie. He didn't want to wonder if there was more to her than he'd ever expected, or worry about what she must have been feeling. He didn't want to think about her at all.

Sighing, he dropped his hands to stare moodily out of the window. Jenna's suggestion was ridiculous, of course. There was absolutely no way he was hiring Aurelie to open so much as a sugar packet for him. He never wanted to see her again.

Then why can't you get her eyes out of your mind?

Her eyes. When he closed his own, he saw hers, stormy and sad and *brave*. He was being ridiculous, romantic, and about a woman whose whole lifestyle—values, actions, everything—he despised. She might have written some soppy new song, but it didn't change who she was: a washed-up, over-the-top diva.

Yet her eyes.

He let out a groan of frustration and swivelled back to face his computer. He didn't need this. The reopening of the New York flagship store might have been a success, but he still had a mountain of work to do. Bryant Enterprises had over a hundred stores across the world and Luke intended to overhaul every single one.

Without the help of Aurelie.

Aurelie bit her lip in concentration as she played the four notes again. Did it sound too melancholy? She had to get the bridge right or—

Or what?

She glanced up from the piano to stare unseeingly around the room she'd converted into a work space. Nobody wanted her music any more. She might be good for rehashing a few of her hit singles, but nobody wanted to hear soulful piano and acoustic guitar ballads. She'd got that loud and clear.

When she'd stupidly mentioned such an idea to her agent, he'd laughed. *Laughed.* 'Stick with what you're good at, babe,' he'd said. 'Not that it's all that much.'

She'd fired him. Not that it mattered. He'd been about to let her go anyway.

Sighing, she rose from the piano bench and went to the kitchen. She'd been working all morning and it was time for a coffee break. She hated indulging in self-pity; she knew there was no point. She'd made her bed and she'd spend the rest of her life lying in it. No one was going to let her change. And, really, she didn't need to change. At least not publicly. She could spend the rest of her life living quietly in Vermont. She didn't need a comeback, despite her pathetic attempt at one.

Just the memory of the Bryant's booking made her cringe. The only reason she'd accepted it was to have a kind of test run, to see how people responded to a new and different Aurelie. And it had failed at the very first gate. The Head of PR who had booked her had been appalled by her suggestion she do something different. *People are coming to see the Aurelie they know and love, not some wannabe folk singer. We only want one thing from you.*

Sighing again, she poured herself a coffee and added milk, stirring moodily. She'd given them the old Aurelie, just as that woman had wanted. She'd given it to them in spades. Briefly she thought of bossy Luke Bryant, and how she'd baited him. Even now she felt a flicker of embarrassment, even shame. All right, yes, she'd seen the desire flaring in his eyes, but instead of ignoring it she'd wound him up on purpose. She'd just been, as always, reacting. Reacting to the assumptions and sneers and suggestions. When she was in the moment it was so incredibly hard to rise above it.

The doorbell rang, a rusty croak of a sound, surprising her. She didn't get visitors. The paparazzi didn't know about this house and the townspeople left her alone. Then she remembered she'd ordered a new capo, and went to answer it.

'Hey…' The word died off to nothing as she stared at the man standing on the weathered front porch of her grandma's house. It wasn't the postman. It was Luke Bryant.

Luke watched the colour drain from Aurelie's face as she stared at him, obviously shocked. As shocked as he had been when he'd found this place, for an old farmhouse in a sleepy town in Vermont was not what he'd expected at all. He'd supposed it was a pretty good cover for someone like her, but it had only taken about ten seconds standing on her front porch to realise this wasn't a bolt-hole. It was home.

'What…' She cleared her throat, staring at him with wide, dazed eyes. 'What are you doing here?'

'Looking for you.'

'Why?' She sounded so bewildered he almost smiled. Gone was any kind of innuendo, any flirt. Gone, in fact, was so much as a remnant of the Aurelie he'd encountered back in New York. He looked at her properly for the first time, and knew he wouldn't have even recognised her if not for the colour of her eyes. He'd remembered those straight off. The woman in front of him was dressed in faded jeans and a lavender T-shirt, her silky hair tossed over one shoulder in a single braid. She wore no make-up, no jewellery. She was the essence of simplicity and, despite the slight gauntness of her face and frame, Luke thought she looked better now than he'd ever seen her in person or on an album cover.

'May I come in?'

'I…' She glanced behind her shoulder, and Luke wondered what she was hiding. Suspicion hardened inside him. All right, the house might be quaint in a countrified kind of way, and her clothes were…well, normal, but could he really doubt that this woman was still the outrageous, unstable pop star he'd met before?

Well, yes, he could.

He'd been doubting it, aggravatingly, ever since Jenna had suggested he book her for a string of openings and he'd refused. Refused point-blank even as he couldn't get her out of his mind. Those eyes. That sense of both sadness and courage. And how she must have come to Bryant's wanting to be different.

That was what had finally made him decide to talk to her. What a coup it would be to have Bryant's orchestrate a comeback for a has-been pop star that no one believed could change.

Although if he were honest—which he was determined

always to be—it wasn't the success of the store that had brought him to Vermont. It was something deeper, something instinctive. He understood all too well about wanting to change, trying to be different. He'd been trying with the store for nearly a decade. And as for himself… Well, he'd had his own obstacles to overcome. Clearly Aurelie had hers.

Which had brought him here, five weeks later, to her doorstep.

'May I come in?' he asked again, politely, and she chewed her lip, clearly reluctant.

'Fine,' she finally said, and moved aside so he could enter.

He stepped across the threshold, taking in the overflowing umbrella stand and coat rack, the framed samplers on the walls, the braided rug. Very quaint. And so not what he'd expected.

She closed the door and kept him there in the hall, her arms folded. 'How did you find me?'

'It was a challenge, I admit.' Aurelie had been off the map. No known address besides a rented-out beach house in Beverly Hills, no known contacts since her agent and manager had both been fired. Jenna had contacted her directly through her website, which had since closed down.

'Well?' Her eyes sparked.

'I'm pretty adept with a computer,' Luke answered. 'I found a mention of the sale of this house from a Julia Schmidt to you in the town property records.' She shook her head, coldly incredulous, and he tried a smile. 'Aurelie Schmidt. I wondered what your last name was.'

'Nice going, Sherlock.'

'Thank you.'

'I still don't know why you're here.'

'I'd like to talk to you.'

She arched an eyebrow, smiled unpleasantly. 'Oh? That wasn't the message you were sending me back in New York.'

'That's true. I'm sorry if I appeared rude.'

'Appeared? Well, I *appeared* like I was strung out on drugs, so what does it really matter?' She pivoted on her heel and walked down a dark, narrow hall, the faded wallpaper cluttered with photographs Luke found he longed to look at, to the kitchen.

'Appeared?' he repeated as he stood in the doorway, sunlight spilling into the room from a bay window that overlooked a tangled back garden. Aurelie had picked up a mug of coffee and took a sip. She didn't offer him any.

'I told you, it doesn't matter.'

'Actually, it does. If you have a substance abuse problem, I need to know about it now.' That was the one thing that had almost kept him from coming at all. He would not work with someone who was unstable, who might overdose. He would never put himself in that position again.

'You need to know?' she mocked. She held her coffee mug in front of her as if it was some kind of shield, or perhaps a weapon. Luke stayed by the door. He didn't want its contents thrown in his face. 'What else do you *need*, Luke Bryant?'

Her eyes flashed and he tensed. He hated innuendo, especially when he knew it held a shaming grain of truth.

'I have a proposition to put to you,' he said evenly. 'But first I need to know. Do you have a substance abuse problem, of any kind?'

'Would you believe me if I told you?'

'Yes—'

'Ri-ight.' She shook her head. 'Why are you really here?'

'I told you, I have a proposition to put to you. A business proposition.'

'It's always business, isn't it?'

Luke bit down on his irritation. Already he was regretting the insane impulse to come here. 'Enough. Either you listen to me or you don't. If you're interested in making a comeback—'

He saw her knuckles whiten around her coffee mug. 'Who said I was interested in that?'

'Why else accept the Bryant's booking?'

She raised her eyebrows. 'Boredom?'

Luke stared at her, saw the dangerous glitter in her eyes, the thin line of her mouth. The quivering chin. 'I don't think so,' he said quietly.

'Why are you interested in me making a comeback?' she challenged. 'Because you certainly weren't in New York.'

'I changed my mind.'

'Oh, really?'

'Look, I'll tell you all about it if you think we can have a civil conversation, but first just answer the question. Do you have a substance—'

'Abuse problem,' she finished wearily. 'No.'

'Have you ever?'

'No.'

'Then why were you passed out in New York?'

Her expression was blank, her voice flat. 'I hadn't eaten anything. Low blood sugar.' Luke hesitated. It hadn't seemed like just low blood sugar. She eyed him cynically. 'Clearly you believe me, just like you said you would.'

'I admit, I'm sceptical.'

'*So* honest of you.'

'I won't have anything to do with drugs.'

'That makes two of us. Amazing,' she drawled, 'we have something in common.'

He thought of the tabloids detailing her forays into rehab. The pictures of her at parties. He really should turn around and walk right out of here. Aurelie watched his face, her mouth curling into a cold smile he didn't like. 'That doesn't mean I've been a Girl Scout,' she told him. 'I never pretended I was.'

'I know that.'

'So what do you want?'

What *did* he want? The question felt loaded, the answer more complicated than he wanted it to be. 'I want you to sing. At the reopening of four of my stores.'

He felt her shock even though her expression—that cold, cynical smile—didn't change. 'Why?' she finally asked. 'You certainly didn't seem thrilled I was singing at your New York store.'

'No, I didn't,' he agreed evenly. 'Bryant Stores is important to me and I didn't particularly like the idea of endorsing a washed-up pop star as its mascot.'

'Thanks for spelling it out.'

'I've changed my mind.'

She rolled her eyes. 'Well, *that's* a relief.'

'The opening was well received—'

'Oh, yes, the papers loved the irony of a store trying to reinvent itself hiring a pop star who can't. I got that.' Bitterness spiked her words, and Luke felt a rush of something like satisfaction. She *was* trying to change.

'People still wanted to see you.'

'The most exciting part was when I almost tripped. People want to see me fail, Bryant. That's why they come.' She turned away and he gazed at her thoughtfully, saw the way the sunlight gilded the sharp angles of her profile in gold.

'I don't want to see you fail.'

'What?' She turned back to him, surprise wiping the cynicism from her face. She looked young, clear-eyed, even innocent. The truth of her revealed, and it gave him purpose. Certainty.

'I don't want to see you fail. Give yourself a second chance, Aurelie, and listen to what I have to say.'

* * *

Aurelie stared at him, wishing she hadn't revealed so much. *People want to see me fail.* Why had she told him the truth? Even if he already knew it, he hadn't known that she knew it. And, worse, that it hurt her. Yet she was pretty sure he knew now, and she hated the thought.

She hated that he was here. She couldn't act like Aurelie the go-to-hell pop princess here, in her grandma's house. Her home, the only place she'd ever been able to be herself. Be safe.

She felt a tightness in her chest, like something trying to claw its way out, finally break free. 'I want you to leave,' she said, and thankfully her voice came out flat. Strong. 'I'm not interested in anything you have to say, or any job you might have for me, so please, *please* leave.' Her voice wasn't strong then. It trembled and choked and she had to blink hard, which made her all the more furious.

Why did this man affect her like this? *So much?* In sudden, fearful moments she felt as if he saw something in her no one else did, no one else even wanted to. What a joke. There was nothing there to see. And, even if there were, he wouldn't be the one to see it. He still probably thought she did drugs.

'I will leave,' Luke said steadily. 'But please let me say something first.'

He stood in the doorway of her kitchen, so still, so sure, like a rock. A mountain. She couldn't get him out of here if she tried. Yet bizarrely—and terrifyingly—there was something steady about his presence. Something almost reassuring. Which was ridiculous because she didn't trust any men, and especially not ones who strode in and blustered and proclaimed, insisting that they were going to rescue you as if they were some stupid knight. All Luke Bryant needed was a white horse and a big sword.

Well, he *had* a big sword. She was pretty sure about that.

And she knew exactly how to knock him off his trusty steed. Men were all the same. They might say they wanted to help you or protect you, but really? They just wanted you. And Luke Bryant was no different.

'All right.' She folded her arms, gave him a cool smile. 'So tell me.'

'I'm overseeing the launch of our stores in Asia, and I'd like to hire you to perform at the reopening of each.'

'So you want me to sing *Take Me Down* at each one? Slink and shimmy and be outrageous?' The thought made her feel ill. She could not do that again. She wouldn't.

'No,' Luke said in that calm, deep voice Aurelie found bizarrely comforting. 'I don't want you to do any of those things.'

'That's what your Head of PR paid me to do.'

'And this time I'm paying you to do something else.'

She felt that creeping of suspicion, and a far more frightening flicker of hope. 'And what would that be, Mr Bossy?'

'To sing your new song. The one I heard while I was standing on your front porch.'

CHAPTER THREE

AURELIE ALMOST SWAYED, and Luke took an instinctive step towards her. Clearly he'd surprised her with that one. Well, he'd meant to. He had to do something to shock her out of that jaded superstar persona she wore like rusty armour. And the fact that he knew it was armour, no more than a mask, made him more certain.

She *was* different.

But how different? And how crazy was he, to come here and suggest they do business together? She might still possess a certain popularity, but he knew he was taking a huge risk. And he wasn't entirely sure why he was doing it.

'Well?' he asked, pushing away those irritating doubts. She had turned away from him, her arms wrapped around herself, her head slightly bowed. Luke had to fight the ridiculous and completely inappropriate impulse to put his arms around her. *That* would really go down well.

Then she lifted her head and turned to face him with an iron-hard gaze. 'You came all the way to Vermont without hearing that song, so that wasn't your original intention.'

'Actually, it was. But hearing it was a nice confirmation, I'll admit.'

She shook her head. 'How did you even know—'

'Jenna, my Head of PR, told me that you'd asked to sing a new composition.' *Some soppy folk ballad* had been her actual words, but Luke wasn't about to say that. And one glance at Aurelie's stony face told him he didn't need to.

'Somehow I don't think you came here on Jenna's recommendation,' she said flatly. 'She hated the song.'

'I'm not Jenna.'

'No,' she said, and her gaze swept over him slowly, suggestively. 'You're not.' She'd dropped her voice and it slid over him, all husky sweetness. Luke felt that prickling on the back of his neck. He hated how she affected him. Hated and needed it both at the same time, because there could be no denying the pulse of longing inside him when that husky murmur of a voice slid over him like a curtain of silk and she turned from innocent to siren. *Innocent Siren*, that had been the name of her first album.

Except there was nothing innocent about her, never had been, he was delusional to think that way—and then Luke saw she was walking towards him, her slender hips swaying, her storm cloud eyes narrowed even as a knowing smile curved those soft pink lips that looked so incredibly kissable.

'So why are you really here, Luke?' she asked softly. He felt his neurons short-circuit as, just as before, she placed one slender hand on his chest. He could feel the heat of her through the two layers of his suit, the thud of his own heart in response.

'I told you—' he began, but that was all he could get out. He could smell her perfume, that fresh, citrusy scent. And her hair tickled his lips. He definitely should have got a handle on his libido before he came here, because this woman made him *crazy*—

'I think I know why you're here,' she whispered, and then she stood up on her tiptoes and brushed her lips across his.

Sensation exploded inside him. He felt as if Catherine wheels had gone off behind his eyes, throughout his whole body. One almost-nothing kiss and he was firing up like a Roman candle.

'Don't—' he said brusquely, pulling away just a little. Not as much as he should have.

'Don't what?' she teased, her breath soft against his mouth, and then instinct and desire took over and he pulled her towards him, his mouth slanting over hers as he deepened her brush of a kiss into something primal and urgent. His arms came around her, his hands sliding down the narrow knobs of her spine to her hips where they fastened firmly as if they belonged there and he brought her against him. He claimed that little kiss, made it his.

His, not hers. Not theirs. Because in some distant part of his brain he realised she'd gone completely still, lifeless even, and all the while he was kissing her like a drowning man clinging to the last lifebelt.

With a shaming amount of effort he pushed himself away from her, let out a shuddering breath. His heart still thudded. 'What the hell was that about?'

She gazed back at him in stony-faced challenge, seeming completely unaffected by something that felt as if it had almost felled him. 'You tell me.'

'Why did you kiss me?'

'Are you trying to act like you didn't want it?'

'I—' Damn. 'No, I'm not.' Surprise rippled in her eyes like a shadow on water but she said nothing. 'I admit, I'm attracted to you. I'd rather not be. And it has nothing to do with why I came here.'

She arched her eyebrows, elegantly incredulous. 'Nothing?'

Luke expelled an exasperated breath. He didn't lie. Couldn't, ever since he'd told the truth in one of the most defining moments of his life and hadn't been believed. He'd been blamed instead, and maybe—

He pushed the thought away. 'It probably had something to do with it,' he admitted tersely. 'But I wish it didn't.'

'Really.' She sounded utterly disbelieving, and he could hardly blame her. From the first moment he'd met her his body had been reacting. Wanting. He knew it, and obviously so did she.

'Why did you kiss me?' he countered. 'Because I admit I might have taken over, but you started it and there's got to be a reason for that.'

'Does there?'

'I think,' Luke said slowly, 'there's a reason for everything you do, even if it seems completely crazy from the outside.'

She let out a little laugh, the first genuine sound of humour he'd heard from her. 'Thank you for that compliment… I think.'

'You're welcome.'

They stared at each other like two wrestlers on either side of the mat. Some kind of truce had been called, but Luke didn't know what it was. Or why he was here. His calm, no-nonsense plan to hire Aurelie for the Asia openings—to change the public's opinion of both her and the store, the ultimate reinvention—seemed like the flimsiest of pretexts after that kiss.

He'd come here because he wanted her, full stop. It really was that simple.

Aurelie stared at Luke, wondered what tack he'd try next. The honesty had surprised her. Unsettled her, because she knew he was speaking the truth and she didn't know what to do with it. She wasn't used to honesty.

Trying for something close to insouciance, she turned away from him, picked up her discarded mug of coffee and kept the kitchen counter between them.

Luke folded his arms. 'So you still haven't told me why you kissed me.'

She shrugged. 'Why not?' That kiss had started out as a way to prove he just wanted one thing and it wasn't her song. But then she'd felt the softness of his lips, his hair, and she'd forgotten she'd been trying to prove a point. She'd felt a flicker of…something. Desire? It seemed impossible. And then Luke had deepened the kiss and she'd felt herself retreat into numbness as she always did.

She took a sip of her now-cold coffee. She shouldn't have kissed him at all. She didn't want to be Aurelie here, in the only place she'd ever thought of as home. She wanted to be herself, but she didn't know how to do that with someone like Luke. Or with anyone, really. She'd been pretending for so long she wasn't sure she could stop. 'Why don't you tell me why you want to hire me for these reopenings.'

'I told you already.'

'The real reason.'

He stared at her, his dark eyes narrowed, lips thinned. He really was an attractive man, not that it mattered. Still a part of her could admire the chocolate-coloured hair, could remember how soft it had felt threaded through her fingers. How hard and toned his body had been against hers. How *warm* his eyes had seemed—

She needed to put a stop to that kind of thinking right now. 'Well? Why?'

'It's more complicated than I'd prefer it to be,' Luke said, the words seeming wrested from him. 'It makes good business sense on one level, and on another…yes.' He shrugged, spread his hands. 'Like I said before, attraction comes into it. Probably. It doesn't mean I'm going to act on it.'

'Despite the fact that you just did.'

'If you thrust your tongue into my mouth, I'll respond. I'm a man.'

Exactly. And she knew men. Still, the extent of his honesty unnerved her. He could have easily denied it. Lied. 'What are you,' she said, 'Pinocchio?'

He glanced away, his expression shuttering. 'Something like that.'

The man could not tell a lie. How fascinating, considering she told dozens. Hundreds. Her whole *life* was a lie. 'So if I asked you anything, you'd have to tell me the truth?'

'I don't like lying, if that's what you mean.'

'Don't like it, or aren't good at it?'

'Both.'

She was tempted to ask him something really revealing, embarrassing even, yet she decided not to. Any more intimacy with this man was not advisable.

'Okay, then. Tell me just what this whole Asia thing is about.'

'I'm relaunching four stores across Asia. Manila, Singapore, Hong Kong and Tokyo. I want you to sing at each opening.'

'Sing my new song.'

'That's about it.'

'That's kind of a risk, don't you think?'

He raised his eyebrows in both challenge and query. 'Is it?'

'How long were you standing on my porch?'

'Long enough.'

She had the absolutely insane impulse to ask him what he'd thought of that song. She'd been working on it for months, and it meant more to her than she ever wanted to admit—which was why she wouldn't ask. 'Why don't you want my usual Aurelie schtick?' she asked instead.

He nodded, and it felt like an affirmation. 'That's what it is, isn't it? A schtick. An act. Not who you really are.'

She didn't like the way his gaze seemed to sear right

through her. She didn't like it at all, and yet part of her was crying out yes. *Yes, it's pretend, it's not me, and you're the only person who has ever realised that.* From somewhere she dredged up the energy to roll her eyes. Laugh it off. 'Of course it's a schtick. Any famous person is just an act, Bryant. A successful one.'

'Call me Luke.' She pressed her lips together. Said nothing. He took a step towards her. 'So will you do it?'

'I can't give you an answer right now.'

'You'd better give me an answer soon, because I fly to the Philippines next week.'

She let out a low breath, shook her head. She wasn't saying no, she just felt…

'Scared?'

'What?'

'You're scared of me. Why?' She stared at him, wordless with shock, and he gave her a little toe-curling smile. 'The honesty thing? It goes both ways. I call it as I see it, Aurelie. Always. So why are you scared?'

She bristled. 'Because I don't know you. Because you practically stalked me, coming to my house here, muscling your way in—'

'I asked. Politely. And you're the one who kissed me, so—'

'Just forget it.' She turned away, hating how much he saw and didn't see at the same time. Hating how confused and needy he made her feel.

'Tell me why you're scared.'

'I'm not scared.' She was terrified.

'Are you scared of me, or of singing?' He took another step towards her, his body relaxed and so contained. He was so sure of himself, of who he was, and it made her angry. Jealous. *Scared.*

'Neither—' *Both.*

'You know you're not that great a liar, either.'

She whirled around to face him, to say something truly scathing, but unfortunately nothing came to mind. All her self-righteous indignation evaporated, and all the posturing she depended on collapsed. She had nothing. And she was so very tired of pretending, of acting as if she didn't care, of being someone else. Even if the thought of being herself—and having people see that—was utterly terrifying.

'Of course I'm a little…wary,' she snapped, unable to lose that brittle, self-protective edge. 'The press lives to ridicule me. People love to hate me. Do you think I really enjoy opening myself up to all that again and again?'

He stared at her for a moment, *saw* her, and it took all her strength to stand there and take it, not to say something stupid or suggestive, hide behind innuendo. She lifted her chin instead and returned his gaze.

'You act like you do.'

'And I told you, every famous person is an act. Aurelie the pop star isn't real.' She couldn't believe she was saying this.

'Then who,' Luke asked, 'is Aurelie Schmidt?'

Aurelie stared at him for a long, helpless moment. She had no answer to that one. She'd been famous since she was sixteen years old. 'It hardly matters. Nobody's interested in Aurelie Schmidt.'

'Maybe they would be if they got to know her.'

'Trust me, they wouldn't.'

'It's a risk you need to take.'

It was a risk too great to take. 'Don't tell me what I need.'

Luke thrust his hands into his pockets. 'Fine. Let me take you to dinner.'

Suspicion sharpened inside her. 'Why?'

'A business dinner. To discuss the details of the Asia trip.'

She started to shake her head, then stopped. Was she really

going to close this down before it had even started? Was she that much a coward? 'I haven't said yes.'

'I know.'

Slowly she let out her breath. She *was* scared. Of singing, and of him. Of how much he seemed to see. Know. And yet part of her craved it all at the same time. Desperately. 'All right.'

'Any recommendations for a good place to eat around here?'

'Not really. There's a fast food joint in the next town over—'

'Anything else?'

'Nothing closer than thirty miles.'

He said nothing, but his thoughtful gaze still unnerved her. This whole thing was a bad idea, and she should call it off right now—

'Tell you what,' Luke suggested. 'I'll cook for you.'

'What?' No man had ever cooked for her, or even offered.

'I'm not Michelin, but I make a decent steak and chips.'

'I don't have any steak.'

'Do you eat it?'

'Yes—'

'Then I'll go out and buy some. And over a meal we'll discuss Asia.'

It sounded so pleasant, so *normal*, and yet still she hesitated. Pleasant and normal were out of her realm of experience. Then she thought of what Luke was offering her—an actual *chance*—and she nodded. Grudgingly. 'Okay.'

'Good.' He turned to go. 'I'll be back in half an hour.'

Thirty minutes' respite. 'Okay,' she said again, and then he was gone.

Luke gave her nearly an hour. He thought she needed the break. Hell, he did too. He took his time choosing two thick fillets, a bag of potatoes, some salad. He thought about buying a bottle of wine, but decided against it. This was a business dinner. Strictly business, no matter how much his libido acted up or how much he remembered that mind-blowing kiss—

Hell.

He stopped right there in the drinks aisle and asked himself just what he was doing here. His brain might be insisting it was just business, but his body said otherwise. His body remembered the feel of her lips, the smoke of her voice, the emotion in her eyes. His body remembered and wanted, and that was dangerous. *Crazy.*

He straightened, forced himself to think as logically as he always did. All right, yes, he desired her. He'd admitted it. But this was still business. If Aurelie's performance at Bryant's gave her the kind of comeback he envisioned, it would create fantastic publicity for the store. It was, pure and simple, a good business move. That was why he was here.

As he resolutely turned towards the checkout, he felt a prickle of unease, even guilt. He'd told Aurelie he didn't lie, but right then he was pretty sure he was lying to himself.

By the time he made it back to the house on the end of the little town's sleepiest street it was early evening, the sun's rays just starting to mellow. The air was turning crisp, and he could see a few scarlet leaves on the maple outside the weathered clapboard house Aurelie called home.

He rang the doorbell, listened to it wheeze and then her light footsteps. She opened the door and he saw that she'd showered—squash *that* vision right now—and her hair was damp and tucked behind her ears. She'd changed into a pale green cashmere sweater and a pair of skinny jeans, and when he glanced down he saw she was wearing fuzzy pink socks. Fuchsia, actually.

He nodded towards the socks. 'Those look cosy.'

She gave him the smallest of smiles, but at least it felt real. 'My feet get cold.'

'May I come in?'

She nodded, and he sensed the lack of artifice from her. Liked it. *Who is Aurelie Schmidt?* Maybe he'd find out.

But did he really want to?

She moved aside and he came in with the bag of groceries. 'Do you mind if I make myself comfortable in your kitchen?'

She hesitated, and he could almost imagine her suggestive response. *You go ahead and make yourself comfortable anywhere, Luke.* He could practically write the script for her, because he was pretty sure now that was all it was: a script. Lines. This time she didn't give them to him; she just shrugged. 'Sure.'

He nodded and headed towards the back of the house.

Fifteen minutes later he had the steaks brushed with olive oil and in the oven, the potatoes sliced into wedges and frying on the stove, and he was tossing a salad. Aurelie perched on a stool, her fuzzy feet hooked around the rungs, and watched him.

'Do you like to cook?'

'Sometimes. I'm not a gourmet, by any means. Not like my brother Chase.'

'He's good?'

Luke shrugged. He wished he hadn't mentioned Chase, or anything to do with his family. He preferred not to dredge those dark memories up; he'd determinedly pushed them way, way down. Yet something about this woman—her fragility, perhaps—brought them swimming up again. 'He's good at most things,' he replied with a shrug. He reached for some vinaigrette. 'Do you have brothers or sisters?'

'No.' From the flat way she spoke Luke guessed she was as reluctant to talk about her family as he was to talk about his. Fine with him.

He finished tossing the salad. 'Everything should be ready in a few minutes.'

Aurelie slid off her stool to get the plates. 'It smells pretty good.'

He glanced up, smiling wryly. 'Are we actually having a civil conversation?'

'Sounds like it.' She didn't smile back, just took a deep breath, the plates held to her chest. 'Look, if you came here on some kind of mercy mission, just forget it. I don't need your pity.'

He stilled. 'I don't pity you.'

'If not pity, then what?'

A muscle bunched in his jaw. 'What are you saying?'

She lifted her chin. 'I find it hard to believe you came all the way to Vermont to ask me to sing. You hadn't even heard that song. It could have sucked. Maybe it does.'

'I admit, it was a risk.'

'So why did you come? What's the real reason?' Suspicion sharpened her voice, twisted inside him like a knife. Did she actually think he'd come here to get her into bed?

Had he?

No, damn it, this was about business. About helping the store and helping Aurelie. The ultimate reinvention. Luke laid his hands flat on the counter. 'I don't have some sexual agenda, if that's what you're thinking.'

She cocked her head. 'You're sure about that?'

He shook his head slowly. 'What kind of men have you known?'

'Lots. And they're all the same.'

'I'm different.' And he'd prove it to her. He took the plates from her, his gaze steady on her own stormy one. 'Let's eat.'

Luke dished out the meal and carried it over to the table in the alcove of the kitchen. Twilight was settling softly outside, the sky awash in violet. Used to the frantic sounds of the city, he felt the silence all around him, just like he felt Aurelie's loneliness and suspicion. 'Do you live here most of the time?' he asked.

'I do now.'

'Do you like it?'

'It'd be a pretty sad life if I didn't.'

He sat opposite her and picked up his fork and knife. 'You're not much of a one for straight answers, are you?'

She met his gaze squarely, gave a small nod of acknowledgement. 'I guess not.'

'All right. Business.' Luke forced himself to focus on the one thing he'd always focused on, and was now finding so bizarrely hard. He wanted to ask her questions about the house, her life, how she'd got to where she was. He wanted to go back in the hallway and look at the photographs on the walls, he wanted to hear her play that song, he wanted—

Business.

'It's pretty simple,' he said. 'Four engagements over a period of ten days. You sing one or two of your new songs.'

'The audience won't be expecting that.'

'I know.'

'And you're okay with that?' She raised her eyebrows. 'Because your Head of PR definitely wasn't.'

'Good thing I'm CEO of the company, then,' Luke said evenly.

'You know,' Aurelie said slowly, 'people want things to be how they expect. They want me to be what they expect. What they think I am.'

'Which is exactly why I want you to be different,' Luke countered. 'Bryant's is an institution in America and other parts of the world. So are you.'

'Now that's something I haven't been compared to before.'

'If you can change your image, then anyone can.'

'Judging by the papers, you've already changed the store's image successfully. You don't need me.'

Luke hesitated because he knew she was right, at least in part. 'I didn't like the way the press spun it,' he said after a moment.

'The whole self-deprecating thing?' she said with a twisted smile. 'Former celebrity?'

'Exactly. I want a clean sweep, home run. No backhanded compliments.'

'Maybe you should just take what you can get.'

He shook his head. 'That's not how I do business.'

She glanced away. When she spoke, her voice was low. 'What if I can't change?'

'There's only one way to find out.' Aurelie didn't say anything, but he could see her thinking about it. Wondering. Hoping, even. He decided to let her mull it over. Briskly, he continued, 'Your accommodation will be provided, and we can negotiate a new rate for the—'

'I don't care about the money.'

'I want to be fair.'

She toyed with her fork, pushing the food around on her plate. He saw she hadn't eaten much. 'This still feels like pity.'

'It isn't.'

She glanced up and he saw the ghost of a smile on her face, like a remnant of who she had once been, a whisper of who she could be, if she smiled more. If she were happy. 'And you can't tell a lie, can you?'

'I won't tell a lie.'

She eyed him narrowly. 'But it's something close to pity.'

'Sympathy, perhaps.'

'Which is just a nicer word for pity.'

'Semantics.'

'Exactly.'

His lips twitched in a smile of his own. 'Okay, look. I told you, I don't pity you. I feel—'

'Sorry for me.'

'Stop putting words in my mouth. I feel…' He let out a whoosh of exasperated breath. He didn't like talking about feelings. He never did. His mother had died when he was thirteen, his father had never got close, and his brothers didn't ask. But here he was, and she was right, he couldn't lie. Not to her. 'I know how you feel,' he said at last, and she raised her eyebrows, clearly surprised by that admission. Hell, he was surprised too.

'How so?'

'I know what it feels like to want to change.'

'You've wanted to change?'

'Hasn't everybody?'

'That's no answer.'

He shrugged. 'I've had my own obstacles to overcome.'

'Like what?'

He should never have started this. The last thing he wanted to do was rake up his own tortured memories. 'A difficult childhood.'

Her mouth pursed. 'Poor little rich boy?'

He tensed, and then forced himself to relax. 'Something like that.'

She lifted her chin, challenge sparking in her eyes. 'Well, maybe I don't want to change.'

It was such obvious bravado that Luke almost laughed. 'Then why write a different kind of song? Why ask to sing it? Why accept the Bryant's booking when you haven't performed publicly in years?'

Her mouth twisted. 'Done a little Internet stalking, have you?'

'I didn't need to look on the Internet to know that.' She shook her head, said nothing. 'Anyway,' he continued in a brisker voice, 'the point is, I've been trying to reinvent Bryant's for years and—'

'What's been stopping you?'

Luke hesitated. He didn't want to bring up Aaron and his constant quest for control. 'Change doesn't happen overnight,' he finally said. 'And Bryant's has a century-old reputation. There's been resistance.'

'There always is.'

'So see? We have something else in common.'

'You want to reinvent a store and I want to reinvent myself.'

Luke didn't answer, because there was an edge to her voice that made him think a simple agreement was not the right choice here. He waited, wondered why it mattered to him so much.

He didn't need Aurelie. He didn't need her to open a store or sing a damn song. He didn't need her at all.

Yet as she gazed at him with those rain-washed eyes he felt a tug deep inside that he couldn't begin to understand. More than lust, deeper than need. Despite having had three long-term satisfying relationships, he'd never felt this whirlpool of emotion before, as if he were being dragged under by the force of his own feelings. Never mind her being scared. He was terrified.

The smart thing to do right now would be to get out of this chair, out of this house. Walk away from Aurelie and all her crazy complications and go about his business, his *life*, the way he always had. Calm and in control, getting things done, never going too deep.

He didn't move.

Aurelie drew a deep breath, let it out slowly. 'Let me play you my song,' she finally said and, surprised and even touched, Luke nodded.

'I'd like that.'

She smiled faintly, that whisper of a promise, and wordlessly Luke followed her out of the room.

CHAPTER FOUR

AURELIE LED LUKE into the music room at the front of the house, her heart thudding, her skin turning clammy. She felt dizzy with nerves, and silently prayed that she wouldn't pass out. The last thing she needed was Luke Bryant to think she'd ODed again.

She paused in front of the piano, half-regretting her suggestion already. No, not even half—*totally.* Why was she opening herself up to this? She didn't need money. She didn't need to sing in public again. She didn't need any of this.

But she wanted it. She actually wanted to share something that was important to her, share it with this man, never mind the public, even as it scared her near witless.

'Aurelie?'

There was something about the way he said her name, so quietly, so *gently*, that made her ache deep inside. She swallowed, her face turned away from him. 'It sounds better with guitar.'

'Okay.'

She reached for her acoustic guitar, the one her grandmother had bought her just before she'd died. *Don't forget who you really are, Aurie. Don't let them turn your head.* But she had let them. She'd forgotten completely. Her fingers curled around the neck of the guitar and, unable to look at Luke—afraid to see the expression on his face—she bent her head and busied herself with tuning the instrument. Needlessly, since she'd played it that afternoon.

After a few taut minutes she knew she couldn't wait any longer. Yet she was terrified to play the song, terrified to have Luke reject it. *Her.* He'd let her down easily because, no matter what he said, she knew he did feel sorry for her. But it would still hurt.

'So has this song got some kind of long silent intro or what?'

She let out a little huff of laughter, glad he'd jolted her out of her ridiculous stage fright. 'Patience.' And taking a deep breath, she began. The first few melancholy chords seemed to flow through her, out into the room. And then she began to sing, not one of the belt-it-out numbers of her pop star days, but something low and intimate and tender. *'Winter came so early, it caught me by surprise. I stand alone till the cold wind blows the tears into my eyes.'* She hesitated for a tiny second, trying to gauge Luke's reaction, but the song seemed to take up all the space. *'I turn my face into the wind and listen to the sound. Never give your heart away. It will only bring you down.'* And then she forgot about Luke, and just sang. The song took over everything.

Yet when the last chord died away and the room seemed to bristle with silence, she felt her heart thud again and she couldn't look at him. Staring down at her guitar, she idly picked a few strings. 'It's kind of a downer of a song, isn't it?' she said with an unsteady little laugh. 'Probably not the best number to open a store with.'

'That doesn't matter.' She couldn't tell a thing from his tone, and she still couldn't look at him. 'Of course, if you had another one, maybe a *bit* more hopeful, you could sing that one too.'

Something leapt inside her, a mongrel beast of hope and fear. A dangerous animal. She looked up, saw him gazing at her steadily, yet without any expression she could define. 'I could?'

'Yes.'

'So…' She swallowed. 'What did you think? Of the song?'

'I thought,' Luke said quietly, with obvious and utter sincerity, 'it was amazing.'

'Oh.' She looked back down at her guitar, felt tears sting her eyes and blinked hard to keep them back. Damn it, she was not going to cry in front of this man. Not now. Not ever. 'Well…good.' She kept her head lowered, and then she felt Luke shift. He'd been sitting across from her, but now he leaned forward, his knee almost nudging hers.

'I can understand why you're scared.'

Instinct kicked in. 'I never actually said I was scared.' And then she sniffed, loudly, which basically blew her cover.

'You didn't have to.' He placed one hand on her knee, and she gazed down at it, large, brown, strong. Comforting. 'That song is very personal.'

Which was why she felt so…*naked* right now, every protective layer peeled away. She swallowed, stared at his hand, mesmerised by the long, lean fingers curled unconsciously around her knee. 'It's just a song.'

'Is it?'

And then she looked up at him, and knew she was in trouble. He was gazing at her with such gentle understanding, such tender compassion, that she felt completely exposed and accepted at the same time. It was such a weird feeling, such an *overwhelming* feeling, that it was almost painful. She swallowed. 'Luke…' Her voice came out husky, and she saw his pupils flare. Felt the very air tauten. This tender moment was turning into something else, something Aurelie knew and understood.

This was about sex. It was always about sex. And while part of her felt disappointed, another part flared to life.

Luke straightened, taking his hand from her knee. 'I should go. It's late.'

'You can't drive all the way back to New York tonight.'

'I'll find a place to stay.' He made to rise from his chair, and Aurelie felt panic flutter like a trapped, desperate bird inside her.

'You could stay here.'

He stared at her, expressionless, and Aurelie put away her guitar, her face averted from his narrowed gaze. Her heart was pounding again. She didn't know what she was telling him. What she wanted. All she knew was she didn't want him to go.

'I don't think that's a good idea,' Luke said after a moment and Aurelie turned to face him.

'Why not?'

He smiled wryly, but she saw how dark and shadowed his eyes looked. 'Because we're going to have a business relationship and I don't want to complicate things.'

She lifted her eyebrows, tried for insouciance. 'Why does it have to be complicated?'

'What are you asking me, Aurelie?'

She liked the way he said her name. She'd always hated it, a ridiculous name given to her by an even more ridiculous mother, but when he said it she felt different. She felt more like herself—or at least the person she thought she could be, if given a chance. 'What do you want me to be asking you?'

He laughed softly. 'Never a straight answer.'

'I'd hate to bore you.'

'I don't think you could ever bore me.' He was staring straight at her, and she could see the heat in his eyes. Felt it in herself, a flaring deep within, which was sudden and surprising because desire for a man was something she hadn't felt in a long time, if ever. Yet she felt it now, for this man. This wasn't about power or control or the barter that sex had always been to her. She simply wanted him, wanted to be with him.

'Well?' she asked, her voice no more than a breath.

Luke didn't move. Didn't speak. Aurelie saw both the doubt and desire in his eyes, and she took a step towards him so she was standing between his splayed thighs. With her fingertips she smoothed the crease that had appeared in his forehead. 'You think too much.'

His mouth curved wryly. 'I think I'm thinking with the wrong organ at the moment.'

She laughed softly. 'What's wrong with thinking with that organ on occasion?' She let her fingertips drift from his forehead to his cheek, felt the bristle of stubble on his jaw. She liked touching him. How strange. How *nice.*

Luke closed his eyes. 'I really don't think this is a good idea.'

'That's your brain talking now.'

'Yes—'

She let her thumb rest on his lips. They were soft and full and yet incredibly masculine. With his eyes closed she had the freedom to study his face, admire the strong lines of his jaw and nose, the sooty sweep of his lashes. Long lashes and full lips on such a virile man. Amazing.

'Shh,' she said softly, and then slowly, deliberately, she slid her finger into his mouth. His lips parted, and she felt the wet warmth of his tongue before he bit softly on the pad of her finger. Lust jolted like an electric pulse low in her belly, shocking her. Thrilling her. Luke opened his eyes; they blazed with heat and need. He sucked gently on her finger and she let out a shuddery little gasp.

Then he drew back, his eyes narrowing once more. 'Why are you doing this?'

She smiled. 'Why not?'

'I don't want you throwing this in my face, telling me I'm just like every other man you've met.'

'I won't.' She knew he wasn't. He was different, just like he'd said he was. And she wanted him to stay. She *needed* him to stay. 'You really do think too much,' she murmured. She stepped closer, hooked one leg around his. She hooked her other leg around so she was straddling him. Then she lowered herself, legs locked around his, onto his lap. She could feel his arousal pressing against her and she shifted closer, settling herself against him.

'That's a rather graceful move,' Luke said, the words coming out on a half-groan.

'All that dancing onstage has made me *very* flexible.'

'Aurelie…'

'I like how you say my name.'

Luke slid his hands down her back, anchored onto her hips, holding her there. 'This really isn't a good idea,' he muttered, and Aurelie pressed against him.

'Define good,' she said, and as he drew her even closer she knew she had him. She'd won, and she felt a surge of both triumph and desire. Yet amidst that welter of emotion she felt a little needle of disappointment, of hurt. Men really were all the same.

He was being seduced. Luke had realised this at least fifteen minutes ago, when Aurelie had first got that knowing glint in her eyes, and even though just about everything in him was telling him this was a bad idea, his body was saying something else entirely. His body was shouting, *Hell, yes.*

He felt as if he were two men, one who stood about five feet behind him, coldly rational, pointing out that he was doing exactly what Aurelie had accused him of doing. Coming here with a sexual agenda, with a plan to get her into bed—

Except she was the one trying to get *him* into bed.

And he wanted to go there.

Still, that cold voice pointed out, sleeping with Aurelie was a huge mistake, one that would cause countless complications for their proposed business trip to Asia, not to mention his personal life. His *sanity.*

The other man, the one curving his hands around her hips, was insisting that he wasn't sleeping with Aurelie, he was sleeping with Aurelie *Schmidt.* The woman who had sung that beautiful, heartbreaking song, who hid her heart in her eyes, whom he'd recognised from the first moment she'd looked up at him.

Yet maybe that was even worse. That woman was confusing, vulnerable, and far more desirable than any persona she put on. And whether it was the pop star or the hidden woman underneath on his lap, he knew it was still a hell of a mistake.

And one he had decided to make. Luke slid his hands up her back to cradle her face, his fingers threading through the softness of her hair. And then he kissed her, his lips brushing once, twice over hers before he let himself go deep and the coldly rational part of himself telling him to stop went silent.

Somehow they got upstairs. It was hazy in his mind, fogged as it was with lust, but Luke remembered stumbling on a creaky stair, opening a door. There was a bed, wide and rumpled. And there was Aurelie, standing in front of it, a faint smile on her face. Luke slid her sweater over her head, unbuttoned her jeans. She wriggled out of them and lay on the bed in just her bra and underwear, waiting, ready.

Except her damn chin was quivering.

Luke hesitated, the roar of his heated blood and his own aching need almost, almost winning out. 'Aurelie—'

He saw uncertainty flicker in her eyes, shadows on water, and then she reached up to grab him by the lapels of his suit; he was still completely dressed.

'It's too late for second thoughts,' she said, and as she

kissed him, a hungry, open-mouthed kiss, he had to agree that it just might be.

He kissed her back, desire for her surging over him in a tidal wave, drowning out anything but that all-consuming need, and he felt her fumble with the zip of his trousers.

'Aurelie…' He groaned her name, felt her fingers slide around him. He pushed aside the lacy scrap of her underwear, stroked the silkiness of her thigh. He slid his fingers higher, kissed her deeper, his body pulsing with need, aching with want. Yet even as his hands roamed over her, teasing and finding, a part of his brain started to buzz.

Distantly he realised she'd stopped responding. Her arms had fallen away from him and she was lying tensely beneath him, stiff and straight.

She let out a shudder that could have been a sob or a sigh, and Luke pulled back to look down at her.

Her eyes were scrunched shut, her breathing ragged, her whole body radiating tension. She looked, he thought with a savage twist of self-loathing, as if she were being tortured.

Swearing, Luke rolled off her. His body ached with unfulfilment and his mind seethed with regret. He'd *known* this was a mistake.

He raked a hand through his sweat-dampened hair, let out a shuddering breath. 'What happened?' he asked in a low voice, but Aurelie didn't answer. Silently she slid off the bed and disappeared into the bathroom. Luke heard the door shut and he threw an arm over his eyes. He didn't know what had just happened, but he was pretty sure it was his fault.

From behind the closed door he heard her moving around, a cupboard opening and closing. Seconds ticked by, then minutes. Unease crawled through him, mingling with the virulent regret and even shame he felt. He hated locked doors. Hated that damning silence, the helplessness he felt on the other side, the creeping sense that something wasn't right. Something was very, very wrong.

He got up from the bed, pulled up his trousers and buckled his belt, then headed over to the door.

'Aurelie?' No answer. His unease intensified. 'Aurelie,' he said again and opened the door.

As soon as he saw her Luke swore.

She stood in front of the sink, one arm outstretched, a fully loaded syringe in the other. Acting only on instinct, Luke knocked the syringe hard out of her hand and it went clattering to the floor.

Aurelie stilled, her face expressionless. 'Well, *that* was a waste,' she finally said, her voice a drawl, and bent to pick up the syringe.

'What the hell are you doing?'

She eyed him sardonically. 'I think the more important question is, what do you think I'm doing?'

He stared at her, confusion, fury and shame all rushing through him in a scalding river. This woman drove him *insane.*

Would you believe me if I told you I didn't? He'd said he would. 'It looks,' he said as evenly as he could, 'like you're shooting yourself up with some kind of drug.'

Her lips curved in that way he knew and hated. Mockery. Armour. 'You get a gold star,' she said as she swabbed off the syringe with a cotton pad and some rubbing alcohol. 'That's exactly what I'm doing.'

And he watched as she carefully injected the syringe into the fleshy part of her upper arm.

Luke felt his hands clench into fists at his sides. 'Why don't you tell me what's really going on here?'

She put the syringe away in a little black cosmetic bag. Luke glimpsed a few clear phials inside before she zipped it up and put it away. She gave a small, tired sigh. 'Don't worry, Bryant. It's only insulin.'

She walked past him back into the bedroom, and Luke turned around to stare at her. '*Insulin?* You have diabetes?'

'Bingo.' She reached for a fuzzy bathrobe hanging on the back of the door and put it on. Sitting on the edge of the bed, swallowed up by fleece, she looked young and vulnerable and so very alone.

'Why didn't you tell me?'

'When should I have done that? When I was passed out on the dressing room floor, or after you dunked me in the sink?'

Slowly he walked into the bedroom, sank onto a chair across from her. He raked his hands through his hair, tried to untangle his tortured, twisted thoughts. 'So when you were passed out in New York, it was because of low blood sugar?' Just like she'd said.

'I forgot to check my bloods before I went.'

'That's dangerous—'

She let out a short laugh. 'Thanks for the warning. Trust me, I know. I've been living with diabetes for almost ten years. I was keyed up about the performance and I forgot.' And then as if she realised she'd revealed too much, she folded her arms and looked away, jaw set, eyes hard.

'Why didn't you tell me earlier? In the kitchen, when I *asked*?'

'You wouldn't have believed me—'

'I said I would—'

'Oh, yes, you *said*.' Her eyes flashed malice. 'Well, maybe you're not such a Boy Scout after all, because I don't think you were telling the truth.'

'It was,' Luke said, an edge creeping into his voice, 'a little hard to believe you were passed out just from lack of food. If I'd known you had a *condition*—'

'And maybe I don't feel like explaining myself every time

something looks a little suspicious,' she snapped. 'If you were passed out, would someone assume you'd done drugs? Were a junkie?'

'No, of course not. But I'm not—'

She leaned forward, eyes glittering. 'You're not what?'

Luke stared at her, his mind still spinning. 'I'm not you,' he said at last. 'You're *Aurelie*.' The moment he said it, he knew it had been completely the wrong thing to say. To think.

She turned away from him, her jaw set. 'I am, aren't I,' she said quietly.

Luke dropped his head in his hands. 'I only meant you've been known to…to…'

'I know what I've been known to do.' Her eyes flashed, her chin trembled. He could always tell the truth of her from that chin. She was scared. And sad. Hell, so was he. *How had they got here?*

He shook his head, weary and heartsick, but also angry. 'What happened back there on the bed, Aurelie? Why did you look like…' He could barely say it. 'Like you were being tortured? Or attacked? Were you trying to prove some point?' Had she set him up, shown him to be exactly what she'd accused, just another man determined to get her into bed? 'Well, I guess you made it,' he said heavily when she didn't answer. 'Congratulations.'

Still she said nothing, just stared him down, and in that silence Luke wondered if things could have turned out any worse.

'Do you still want me to go?' she finally asked. 'To Asia?'

He let out a short, disbelieving laugh. 'Do you still *want* to go? After this?'

She raised her eyebrows, her expression so very cold. 'Why shouldn't I?'

He felt a rush of anger, cleaner than shame. She'd *played* him. Admittedly, he'd let himself be played. He'd been willing to be seduced, had turned it to his advantage. But the fact remained that she'd used him, coldly and deliberately, to prove some twisted, paranoid point. He hadn't had a sexual agenda until she'd sat in his lap.

Liar.

'Yes, you can go to Asia,' he told her wearily. Something good would come out of this unholy affair. 'I'll have my PA email you the details. You need to be in Manila on the twenty-fourth.' With that he stood up and he saw, with some gratification, that her eyes had widened.

'You're going?'

'I don't want to stay and, frankly, I don't think you want me to, either. Like I said, you made your point.'

She stared at him, still swallowed up by her bathrobe, her eyes wide and stormy. Luke felt the shame slither inside him again. 'I didn't come here intending to sleep with you,' he said. 'I swear to God I didn't.'

She said nothing and with a shake of his head he left the room.

CHAPTER FIVE

AURELIE GAZED AT her reflection for the fifth time in the hall mirror of the deluxe suite Luke had booked for her in the Mandarin Oriental in Manila's business district. She'd arrived a few hours ago and was meeting Luke in the bar in ten minutes.

And she was sick and dizzy with nerves.

She let out a deep breath and checked her reflection again. She wore just basic make-up, mostly to disguise the violet circles under her eyes since she hadn't had a decent night's sleep since Luke had walked out of her bedroom ten days ago.

She closed her eyes briefly, the memories making her even dizzier. She couldn't think about Luke without reliving that awful encounter. The condemnation and disgust in his eyes. The *confusion*. And her own impossible behaviour.

She hadn't brought him to her bed to set him up, the way Luke had so obviously thought. She'd been acting out of need and maybe even desire—at least at first. When she'd touched him she'd felt something unfurl inside her, something that had been desperately seeking light. But then it had all gone wrong, as it always did. The moment she was stretched out on that bed she'd gone numb. He'd become just a man who wanted something from her, and he'd get it, no matter what. She'd give it to him, because that was what she did.

Except he hadn't taken it, which made him different from every other man she'd known. Why did that thought scare her so much?

He obviously didn't think *she* was different. She could still see the look of disgust twisting Luke's features, the condemnation in his eyes when he'd opened the door to the bathroom. He thought she'd been doing drugs. And then those damning words, words she felt were engraved on her heart, tattooed on her forehead. Impossible to escape.

You're Aurelie.

For a little while she'd thought he believed she wasn't but now she knew the truth. He might want her to be different on stage, but he didn't think she could really change as a person.

Aurelie with a folk ballad and guitar was just another act to Luke Bryant, a successful one that would help with his stupid store openings.

And as long as she remembered that, she'd be fine. No more longing to reach or be reached. To know or be known. No more giving in to that fragile need, that fledgling desire.

This was business, strictly business, a chance for her to validate her career if not her very self. And that was fine. She'd make sure it was.

Aurelie straightened, briskly checked her reflection for the sixth time. She looked a little pale, a bit drawn, but overall okay. The lime-green shift dress struck, she hoped, the right note between fun and professional. With a deep breath, she left her suite and went downstairs to meet Luke.

The tropical heat of the Philippines had hit her the moment she'd stepped off the plane, and she felt it drape over her once more as she stepped outside like a hot, wet blanket. Luke had texted her to say he'd meet her in the patio bar and she walked through the velvety darkness looking for him, the palm trees rustling in a sultry breeze, the sounds of a vibrant and never-sleeping city carrying on the humid air.

She found him sitting on a stool by the bar, and everything inside her seemed to lurch as she looked at him. He wore a slightly rumpled suit, his tie loosened, and in the glint of the bar's dim lighting she could see the shadow of stubble on his jaw. His head was bowed and he held a half-drunk tumbler of whisky in his hand. She stared at him almost as she would a stranger, for he looked so different and yet so much the same. So *sexy.*

Then he glanced up and as he caught sight of her it was as if that sexy stranger had been replaced by a mannequin. His face went blank, his eyes veiled even as his lips curved in a meaningless smile and he crossed the patio towards her.

'Aurelie.' He kept his gaze firmly on her face, that cool, professional smile in place. He didn't offer her a hand to shake or touch her in any way. Stupidly, she felt his chilly withdrawal like a personal rejection.

No, she would not let this be personal. This was her chance at a comeback, and to hell with Luke Bryant.

'Luke.' She nodded back at him, tried to ignore the painful pounding of her heart. *This didn't hurt.*

'Would you like a drink?'

'Just sparkling water, please.'

Luke signalled to the bartender and ushered her towards a private table tucked in the corner, shaded by a palm tree.

'Trip all right?' he asked briskly. 'Your suite?'

'Everything's lovely.'

'Good.'

The bartender came with their drinks and Aurelie sipped hers gratefully. She had no idea what to say to this man. She didn't *know* this man. And she knew that shouldn't be a surprise.

'So everything is set for tomorrow,' he said, still all brisk business. 'I have a staff person on site, Lia, who will tour you around the store, get you sorted for the performance at three.'

Aurelie stared at his blank eyes and brisk smile and thought suddenly, *You're lying.* So much for honesty. This whole conversation was forced, fake. A lie.

Yet she had no idea what he really felt. Was he disgusted with her, with who he thought she was? *You're Aurelie.*

Or could she dare hope that some remnant remained of the man who had smiled at her with such compassion, such understanding, and seemed to believe she was different?

No, she didn't dare. There was no point.

'That all sounds fine,' she said, and he nodded.

'Good.' He hadn't finished his drink, but he pushed it away from him, clearly done. 'I'm afraid I have quite a lot of work to do, but I'll probably see you at the opening.'

Probably? Aurelie felt her throat go tight and took another sip of water. Somehow she managed a breezy smile. 'That sounds fine,' she said again, knowing she was being inane, but then he was too. This whole conversation was ridiculous. And a desperate part of her still craved something real.

'Fine,' Luke said, and with one more nod he rose from the chair. Aurelie rose too. She hadn't finished her water but neither was she about to sit in the bar alone. So that was it. Yet what had she really expected?

Even so, she could not keep a sense of desolation from sweeping emptily through her as Luke strode away from the bar without a backward glance.

That went well. *Not.* Luke tugged his tie from his collar and blew out his breath. He knew he didn't possess the charm of his brother Chase or Aaron's unending arrogance, but he could definitely have handled that conversation better. He'd been trying to keep it brisk and professional, but every time he looked at her he remembered how she'd felt in his arms, how much emotion and desire she'd stirred up in him, and business went right out of the window.

Maybe it wasn't actually Aurelie who was doing this to him. Maybe he was just out of practice. He hadn't had sex in a while, and he'd always been careful with his partners. A relationship came first with him, always had, because he'd never wanted to be like his father, going after everything in a skirt and ruining his mother's life in the process.

But maybe if he'd indulged in a few more flings, he wouldn't be feeling so…lost now. He'd gone over their encounter—was there really another word for it?—far too many times in his mind. Wondered when it had started to go wrong, and why. Had Aurelie been setting him up, the way he'd believed? Proving her damn point that he'd only come there to get into her bed? It seemed obvious, and yet a gut-deep instinct told him it wasn't the whole story.

He remembered the raw ache in her voice when she'd spoken to him. *I like how you say my name.* The way her fingers had trailed down his cheek, eager and hesitant at the same time, the tremble of her slender body against his. She'd felt something then. Something real.

And then she'd gone so horribly still beneath him and he'd felt as if he were…*attacking* her. He'd never felt so repulsed, so ashamed.

The best thing to do, he told himself now, the *only* thing to do, was to avoid her. Easier for both of them. He'd only suggested this meeting as a way to clear the air, draw a firm line under what had happened. And that at least had been accomplished, even if he still felt far from satisfied in any way.

As he headed back up to his suite, Luke had a feeling the next ten days were going to be a whole new kind of hell.

Aurelie stood to the side of the makeshift stage in Bryant's lobby and tried not to hyperventilate. A thousand people mingled in the soaring space, all modern chrome and glass, so different from the historic and genteel feeling of the New York store.

She'd spent the morning with Lia, touring all ten floors of the store on Ayala Avenue and then running through sound checks and getting ready. And trying not to think about what lay ahead.

What was happening *now*, with the crowd waiting for her to walk out and be Aurelie.

Fear washed coldly through her, made her dizzy. At least she'd checked her blood sugar. If she passed out now, it would simply be from nerves.

'Thirty seconds.' The guy who was doing the sound nodded towards her, and somehow Aurelie nodded back. She was miked, ready to go—and terrified.

She peeped out at the audience, saw the excited crowd, some of them clutching posters or CDs for her to sign. They were, she knew, expecting her to prance out there and sing *Take Me Down* or one of the other boppy, salacious numbers that had made her famous. They wanted her to sing and shimmy and be outrageous, and she was going to come out in her jeans, holding her guitar, and give everyone an almighty shock.

What had she been thinking, agreeing to this? What had Luke been thinking, suggesting it? It wasn't going to work. It was all going to go hideously, horribly wrong, for the store, for her, for everyone, and it was too late to do anything about it.

She closed her eyes, terror racing through her.

I can't do this. I can't change.

She wished, suddenly and desperately, that Luke were here. A totally stupid thing to want considering how cold he'd been to her last night, but just the memory of his voice, his tender, gentle look when he'd said her song was amazing gave her a little surge of both longing and courage.

'You're on.'

On wobbly, jelly-like legs she walked onto the stage. Considering she'd played sold-out concerts in the biggest arenas in the world, she should not be feeling nervous. At all. This was a tiny stage, a tiny audience. This was nothing.

And yet it was everything.

She felt the ripple of uneasy surprise go through the audience at the sight of her, felt it like a serpent slithering round the room, ready to strike. Already she was not what anybody had expected.

She sat on the stool in the centre of the stage, hooked her feet around the rungs and looked up to stare straight at Luke. He stood at the back of the lobby near the doors, but it was a small enough space she could make out his expression completely.

He looked cold, hard and completely unyielding. Their gazes met and, his mouth thinning, he looked away. Aurelie tensed, felt herself go brittle, shiny.

'Give us a song,' someone called out, impatience audible. 'Give us Aurelie!'

Well, that was easy enough. That was who she was. Drawing a deep breath, she started to play.

Luke stood in the back of the lobby waiting for Aurelie to come on, battling a disagreeable mix of anxiety and impatience. He'd been deliberately avoiding her since their drink together last night, had convinced himself that it was the best way forward. Yet, standing there alone, he felt an irritating needle of doubt prick his conscience.

Avoidance had never been his style. Avoidance meant letting someone down, and that was something he never intended to do again. He'd worked hard all his adult life to exorcise the ghosts of his past, to earn the trust and respect of those around him.

Even Aurelie's.

He didn't like the thought of her getting ready for this performance on her own. He knew this had to be pretty terrifying for her. He should have sought her out, offered her—what? Some encouragement?

He knew where that led.

No, it was better this way. It had to be. And it wasn't as if Aurelie actually needed him.

Luke heard the ripple of uneasy surprise move through the audience as she walked onto the stage. She looked vibrant and beautiful in a beaded top and jeans, her hair loose about her shoulders. Then she looked at him, her eyes so wide and clear, and a sudden, sharp longing pierced him. He looked away.

Someone called out, and Aurelie started to play. It took him a few stunned seconds to realise she wasn't singing the song he'd heard in her house back in Vermont. She was singing one of her old hits, the same boppy number she'd sung in New York, but this time to acoustic guitar. She glanced up from her guitar, gave the audience a knowing, dirty smile. A classic Aurelie look, and one Luke already hated. Everyone cheered.

Disappointment and frustration blazed through him. This wasn't what they'd agreed. Why had she changed their deal? Was it fear—or some kind of twisted revenge?

The song ended, and Luke heard the familiar mixture of catcalls and cheers. Nothing had changed. So much for the ultimate reinvention. Aurelie walked off the stage, and even though there were several local dignitaries waiting for him to escort them through the store, Luke turned and walked away from it all.

He found her in the break room she'd been using, just as before, to change. Her back was to him as she put her guitar away, and under the flowing top he could see the knobs of her spine, the bared nape of her neck as she bent her head. Desire and anger flared inside him, one giving life to the other.

'You didn't play your song.'

She turned towards him, her face completely expressionless. 'Actually, I did.'

'You know what I mean.'

'It wasn't going to work. I warned you, you know.'

'You didn't give it a chance.'

'I could tell. Honestly, Bryant, you should be thanking me. I just saved your ass.'

'You saved your own,' he retorted. 'What happened, you chickened out?'

'I prefer to think of it as being realistic.'

Frustration bit at him. 'I didn't hire you to be Aurelie all over again.'

'Oh?' She raised her eyebrows, her mouth curving in that familiar, cynical smile, innuendo heavy in her tone. 'What *did* you hire me for?'

He shook his head, the movement violent. 'Don't.'

'Don't what?'

'Don't,' Luke ground out, 'make this about sex.'

'Everything's about sex.'

'For you, maybe.'

'Oh, and not for you? Not for the saintly Luke Bryant who said he had a business proposition for me and two hours later was in my bed?'

Luke felt his fists clench. 'You wanted me there.' At least at the start.

'I've never denied it. You're the one swimming down that river.'

His nails bit into his palms. This woman made him feel so *much*. 'I'm not denying anything. I never have.' He let out a long, low breath, forced himself to unclench his fists.

To think—and react—calmly. 'Look, we obviously need to talk. I have to go out there again, see people—'

'Do your schtick?' She gave him the ghost of a smile, and Luke smiled back.

'Yeah. I guess everyone has one.' For one bittersweet moment he felt they were in agreement, they understood each other. Then Aurelie looked away, her expression veiled once more, and Luke felt the familiar weary frustration rush through him. 'But we are going to talk,' he told her. 'There are things I have to say.' She just shrugged, and with a sigh Luke turned towards the door.

Aurelie let out a shuddering breath as she heard the door close behind him. She put her hands up to her face, felt her whole body tremble. *Why* had she done that? Acted like Aurelie, not just to a faceless audience, but to *him*?

She'd been reacting again, she knew, to the rejection. It didn't take a rocket scientist to figure that out. Nobody would let her change, so she wouldn't. It was, she knew, a pretty pathetic way of trying to stay in control.

And clearly it wasn't working because she didn't feel remotely in control. She felt as if she were teetering on the edge of an abyss, about to fall, and she didn't know what waited darkly beneath her.

Maybe this whole thing had been a mistake. Trying to change. Wanting to be different. The audiences weren't going to accept it. *Her.* And, no matter how he fussed and fumed, neither was Luke.

Drawing another deep breath, Aurelie reached for her bag. She'd fix her make-up, and then she'd go out and mingle. Smile and chat. She'd get through this day and then she'd tell Luke she was going home. She was done.

* * *

Four hours later the opening was over and Aurelie was back in her suite at the Mandarin, exhausted and heartsore. She'd managed to avoid Luke for the entire afternoon, although she'd been aware of him. Even as she chatted and smiled and laughed, nodded sympathetically when people told her they didn't really like the guitar or the jeans, she'd been watching him. *Feeling* him.

He looked so serious when he talked to people. He frowned too much. He stood stiffly, almost to attention. Yet, despite all of it, Aurelie knew he was being himself. Being real.

Something she was too afraid to be.

She'd been resigned to giving up the rest of the tour and going back to Vermont. Staying safe. Being a coward. Yet four hours later Aurelie resisted the thought of slinking away like a scolded child. Never mind what Luke thought, what anyone in the audience thought or even wanted. She needed to do this for herself.

Yet the realisation filled her only with an endless ache of exhaustion. She didn't think she had the strength to go on acting as if she didn't care when she did, so very much.

Wearily she kicked off her heels and stripped the clothes from her body. She needed a stingingly hot shower to wipe away all the traces of today. She knew Luke had said he wanted to talk to her, but the last time she'd seen him he'd been in deep discussion with several official-looking types. He'd probably forgotten all about her and the things he supposedly needed to say.

Fifteen minutes later, just as she'd slipped into a T-shirt and worn yoga pants, a knock sounded on the door. Aurelie sucked in a deep breath and ran her fingers through her hair, still damp from her shower. A peep through the eyehole confirmed her suspicions. Luke hadn't forgotten about her after all.

She opened the door and something inside her tugged hard at the sight of him, his hair a little mussed, his suit a little rumpled. He looked tired.

'Long day?' she asked and he nodded tersely.

'You could say that. May I come in?'

He always asked, she thought. Always asked her permission. Strangely, stupidly, it touched her. 'Okay.'

She stepped aside and Luke came into the sitting area of the suite. She saw his glance flick to the bedroom, visible through an open door, the wide bed piled high with silken pillows.

Then he turned back to face her with a grim, iron-hard resolution. 'We need to talk.'

With a shrug she spread her hands wide and moved to sit on the sofa, as though she were actually relaxed. 'Then talk.'

He let out a long, low breath. 'I'm sorry about the way things happened back in Vermont. I didn't want it to be like that between us.'

He looked so intent, so sincere, that mockery felt like her only defence. '*Us*, Bryant?'

'Don't call me Bryant. My name is Luke and, considering we almost slept together, I think you can manage my first name.'

She tensed. 'Almost being the key word. That doesn't give you some kind of right—'

'I'm not talking about rights, just common civility.' He sat across from her, his hands on his thighs, his face still grim. 'I'm being honest here, Aurelie—'

'Sorry,' she drawled, 'that doesn't score any Brownie points. I already know you can't be anything else.'

'Just stop it,' he bit out. 'Stop it with the snappy one-liners and the bored tone and world-weary cynicism—'

'My, that's *quite* a list—'

'Stop.' He leaned forward, his face twisting with frustration or maybe even anger. 'Stop being so damn fake.'

She stilled. Said nothing, because suddenly she had nothing to say. She'd defaulted to her Aurelie persona, to the bored indifference she used as a shield, but Luke saw through it all. He stared at her now, those dark eyes blazing, burning right through her. She swallowed and looked down at her lap. 'What do you want from me?' she asked in a low voice.

'I want to know what *you* want from *me*.'

She looked up, surprise rendering her speechless once more. Her throat dry, she forced herself to shrug. 'I don't want anything from you.'

'Why did you want to sleep with me?'

She tensed, tried desperately for that insouciant armour. 'Why not?'

'Well, obviously not because you were enjoying it.'

She lifted her chin. 'How do you know I wasn't enjoying it?'

'I don't know what your experience with men has been, but most of us can tell when a woman is or isn't enjoying sex.' Luke's mouth quirked upwards even as his eyes blazed. 'Generally when a woman enjoys sex, she responds. She kisses you and makes rather nice noises. She wraps her legs around you and begs you not to stop. She doesn't lie there like a wax effigy.'

Aurelie could feel herself blushing. Her whole body felt hot. 'Maybe I thought I would enjoy it,' she threw back at him. 'Maybe you were a disappointment.'

'I have no doubt I was,' Luke returned, his tone mild. 'I confess I was a little impatient. I haven't had sex in quite a while.'

That made two of them. Aurelie swallowed. 'I don't know why we're having this conversation.'

'Because if we're going to work together for the next nine

days, I need to—' He stopped suddenly, shook his head. 'No, that's not the truth. This isn't about forging some adequate working relationship.'

Aurelie eyed him uneasily. 'What is it about, then?'

'It's about,' Luke said quietly, 'the fact that I can't stop thinking about you, or wondering how it all went so terribly wrong in the course of a single evening.'

She had no sharp retort or bantering comeback to *that*. She had no words at all. She made herself smile even though she felt, bizarrely, near tears. 'You are *so* honest.'

'Then be honest back,' Luke answered. 'Did you sleep with me to prove a point? To show me I was like all the other men you've ever known?'

'No.' It came out as no more than a whisper. Lying no longer felt like an option, not in the face of his own hard honesty. 'It was because I wanted to. Because I didn't want you to go and I…I liked being with you.' Her voice came out so low she felt the thrum of it in her chest. She stared down at her lap, wondered why anyone ever chose to be honest. It felt like peeling back your skin.

'Then what happened?' Luke asked, and his voice was low too, a gentle growl, a lion's purr.

She shrugged, her gaze still on her lap. 'Look, I've never enjoyed sex, okay? So don't worry, it wasn't an insult to your manhood or something.' She'd tried for lightness even now, and failed miserably. Luke had fallen silent, and after a few taut moments she risked a glance upwards. He was gazing at her narrowly, a crease between his eyes, as if she was a problem he had to solve.

'Never?' he finally said, and he sounded so quiet and sad that Aurelie had to blink hard.

'I wasn't abused or raped or something, if you're thinking along those lines.'

'But something happened.' It was a statement, and one

she could not deny. Yes, something had happened. Her innocence had been stripped away in the course of a single evening. And she'd allowed it. But since that night she'd never again thought of sex as something to be enjoyed. It was just a tool, and sometimes a weapon, to get what you wanted, or even needed.

'It doesn't matter,' she snapped. 'I don't even know why we're talking about this. Business relationship only, remember?'

'I remember.'

'So.' She straightened, gave him an expectant this-is-your-cue-to-leave look. He ignored it.

'Aurelie.' She wished he hadn't said her name. He said it the way he always said it, deliberately, an affirmation, and it made her ache inside. Stupid, because it was just her name. A name she hated and yet—

When Luke said it, she didn't feel like Aurelie the pop star. She felt like Aurelie the girl who'd grown up wanting only to be loved.

'What?' she demanded, too harshly, because he'd stripped away all her armour and anger was her last defence.

He shook his head. 'I'm sorry.'

She stared at him wordlessly, dread rolling through her, making her sick. He was letting her down. Of course. The concert hadn't worked and he didn't want her Aurelie act, so he was going to tell her to go home. It was over. So much for trying to change.

Four hours ago she'd told herself she wanted that but now she felt the sting of tears. Another failure.

'Well,' she forced herself to say, even to smile, 'we tried, didn't we? Never mind. I knew it was a long shot.' And she shrugged as if it were no big deal, even managed a wobbly laugh.

Luke frowned, said nothing for a long, taut moment. 'What do you think I'm talking about?' he finally asked.

She eyed him uncertainly. 'The concerts, right? I mean… the audience didn't really go for it today—'

'They would have if you'd done what you were supposed to, and sung your song.' He spoke without rancour, but she still prickled.

'They would have gone for it even less.'

'Yet you weren't willing to risk that. I'm sorry for that too. I should have spoken to you before you went onstage. I was trying to keep my distance because—' He stopped, blew out a weary breath. 'Because it seemed simpler. Easier. But I think I just made it harder for you. I'm sorry I let you down.' She didn't answer. This conversation had gone way outside her comfort zone. She had no comebacks, no words at all. 'But I wasn't apologising for the concerts,' Luke continued quietly. 'I'm not cancelling them. I still think you can turn this around.'

'You do?' She felt a stirring of hope, like a baby's first breath, infinitesimally small and yet sustaining life.

'Yes. But I don't want to talk about that.' He gazed straight at her then, and she saw the hard blaze of his eyes, golden glints amid the deep brown. 'I want to talk about us.'

'Us—' The word ended on a breath. She had no others.

'Yes, us. I'm still attracted to you.' Aurelie felt her heart lurch with some nameless emotion, although whether it was fear or hope or something else entirely she couldn't say.

'So it is about sex.'

Luke said nothing for a moment. He gazed out of the window, the sky turning dark, twinkling with the myriad lights of the city. 'Do you know how many women I've slept with?' he finally asked.

'I'm not sure how I would have come by that information—'

'Three.' He glanced back at her with a rueful smile, his eyes still dark. 'Three, four if I include our rather mangled attempt.'

'Right.' She had no idea what to make of that.

'I've had three relationships. *Relationships.* They all lasted months or even years. And the women involved were the only women I've ever had sex with.'

'So you really are a Boy Scout.' She felt incredibly jaded, with way too much bad experience behind her.

'No, I just…I've just always taken sex seriously. It's meant something to me. Emotionally.'

'Except with me.'

Luke was silent for so long Aurelie wondered if he'd heard her. She sought for something to say, something light and wry to show him she didn't care, it didn't matter, but it was too late for that. He'd already seen and heard too much.

'It did mean something,' he finally said, his voice so low she almost didn't hear him. 'From the moment I saw you slumped on the floor from what I thought—assumed—was an overdose. You opened your eyes and I…I felt something.'

'Felt something?' she managed, still trying for wryness. 'What, annoyance?'

'No.' He glanced up at her, and she saw the honesty blazing in his eyes. 'I don't know what it was. Is. But I can't pretend I don't feel something—for you. For the you hiding underneath the pop star persona, the you who wrote that song.'

She swallowed. 'But you didn't even hear that song until—'

'I saw it in your eyes.'

She looked away. 'I never took you for a romantic.'

'I didn't, either.'

Aurelie could feel her heart beating so hard it hurt. She felt dizzy and weirdly high, as if she were floating somewhere up near the ceiling. And she felt scared. Really scared, because she didn't know what Luke was trying to tell her.

She licked her lips, found a voice. 'So what…what are you saying exactly?'

'I don't even know.' He raked a hand through his hair, let out a weary laugh. 'Part of me thinks we should keep this strictly professional, get through the next nine days, and never see each other again.'

'That would probably be the smartest move,' she agreed, trying to keep her voice light even as her mouth dried and her heart hammered and she *hoped.* Yet for what?

'I think it would be,' Luke agreed. 'But here's the thing. I don't want to.'

'So what do you want?' Aurelie whispered.

He stared at her for a long moment, and she saw the conflict in his eyes. Felt it. He didn't want to want her, but he did. 'I want to start over,' he said at last. 'I want to forget about what happened—or didn't happen—between us. I want to get to know you properly.'

'Are you sure about that?' she joked, but her voice wavered and it fell flat.

'I'm not sure about anything,' he admitted with a wry shake of his head. 'I'm not even sure why I'm saying this.'

'Ouch. Too much honesty, maybe.'

'Maybe.' His gaze rested on her. 'But I want a second chance. With you. I want you to have a second chance with me.'

A second chance. Not professionally, but personally. So much more dangerous. And so much more desirable. A chance to be real. Aurelie closed her eyes. She didn't know what to feel, and yet at the same time she felt so much. Too much.

'The question is,' Luke asked steadily, 'is that what you want?'

She opened her eyes. Stared. His hair was still mussed, his suit still rumpled. He had shadows under his eyes and he badly needed to shave. He looked wonderful.

'Why?' she finally whispered.

'Why what?'

'Why do you want a second chance—with me?'

His mouth twisted. 'Is it so hard to believe?'

'You don't even know me.'

'I know enough to know I want to know more.'

She felt a tear, a terrible, treacherous tear, tremble on her lash. 'I would have thought,' she said in a low voice, 'that what you know would make you not want to know more.'

'Oh, Aurelie,' Luke said quietly, 'I think I know what's an act and what's real.'

'How can you know that?' She felt that tear slide coldly down her cheek. 'I don't even know that.'

'Maybe that's where I come in.'

She prickled instinctively, reached for her rusty armour. 'You think you can help me? *Save* me?'

He stilled, went silent for so long Aurelie blinked hard and looked up at him. 'No,' he said with a quiet bleakness she didn't understand. 'I know I can't save anyone.' He smiled, but it still seemed sad. 'But I can think you're worth saving. Worth knowing.'

She swallowed, sniffed. 'So what now?'

'You answer my question.' Words thickened in her throat. She didn't speak. 'Do you want to try again?' Luke asked. His gaze remained steady on her, and she found she could not look away. 'Do you want a second chance, with me?'

She couldn't speak, not with all the words thick in her throat, tangling on her tongue. Words she was desperate not to say. *Yes, but the thought terrifies me. What if you find out more about me and you hate me? What if you hurt me?*

What if it doesn't work and I feel emptier and more alone than ever? What if I can't change?

'Aurelie,' Luke said, and it wasn't a question. It sounded like an affirmation. *I know who you are.*

Except he didn't.

He was still gazing at her, still waiting. Aurelie swallowed again, tried to dislodge some of those words. She only came up with one.

'Yes,' she said.

CHAPTER SIX

LUKE STARED AT Aurelie's pale face, her eyes so wide and blue, that one tear tracking a silvery path down her cheek.

Hell.

He'd come up here to talk to her, to tell her what he'd started out saying, which was that he was sorry for what had happened but they'd keep this whole thing professional and try to avoid each other because clearly that was the safest, sanest thing to do.

Except he'd said something else instead, something totally dangerous and insane. *I know enough to know I want to know more.* No, he didn't. He didn't want to know one more thing about this impossible woman. He wanted to walk away and forget he'd ever met her.

Except that honesty thing? It got him every time. Because he knew, even as he stared at that silver tear-track on her cheek, that he'd been speaking the truth.

He felt something for her. He *did* want to get to know her, even though there could be no doubting she was fragile, damaged, *dangerous*. The possibility of hurting her was all too real—and terrifying.

'Luke?' She said his name with a soft hesitancy that he'd never heard before. She felt vulnerable, he knew. Well, hell, *he* felt vulnerable. And he didn't like it. He raked his hands through his hair, tried to find something to say.

Aurelie rose from the sofa and grabbed a tissue, her back to him as she wiped her eyes, as if even now she could hide her tears.

'Look,' she said, her back still to him, 'maybe this is a mistake.'

Luke straightened, dropped his hands. 'Why do you say that?'

She turned around. 'Because of the look on your face.'

'What—'

'You're looking like you seriously regret this whole thing.'

'I wouldn't say *seriously*.' He'd meant to joke, but she just stared at him hard. He sighed. 'Aurelie, look. This is new territory for me. I'm stumbling through the dark here.'

'You and me both.'

'Have you ever been in a serious relationship before?'

Her eyes widened, maybe with fear. 'Is that what this is?'

'No.' He spoke quickly, instinctively, and she gave him a wobbly smile. They were both scared here, both inching into this…whatever *this* was. 'One day at a time, right?' He smiled back. 'I just wondered.'

She turned away again, her hair falling in front of her face. 'You're asking because of the sex thing, right? Because I didn't enjoy it.'

'That among other things.' *The sex thing.* Yeah, that was something else they'd have to deal with. Something had happened to her, he just didn't know what. And he didn't know if he even wanted to know. His three relationships, he realised, had not prepared him for this. They'd been safe, measured, considered things, and even though he'd had a deep affection for each of the women he'd shared a part of his life with, he hadn't felt *this*.

This tangle of uncertainty and exhilaration, this terror that he could hurt her, that he might fail. What had he got himself into?

'I've been in one relationship,' she said quietly, her face still turned away from him. 'Just one. But it lasted over three years.'

'It did?' He shouldn't be surprised. He might not have seen a mention of such a relationship in the press, but he'd known from her song that she'd had her heart broken. The thought filled him with something that felt almost like jealousy.

She kept her face averted. 'I'd rather not talk about it.'

'All right.' He drew a breath, felt his way through the words. 'But if we're going to…to try this, then we need to be honest with each other.'

She let out a short laugh. 'Well, that's obviously not a problem for you.'

'Actually it is. I might be honest but that doesn't mean I wear my heart on my sleeve. No one in my family talks about emotional stuff.' And he didn't even like admitting *that*. There was a reason for his family's distance, their silence and secrets. A reason locked deep inside him.

Aurelie hunched her shoulders, folded her arms. 'Well, I'm never honest. I don't even know if I can be. I've been on my guard for so long I don't know how to let it down.' She stared at him with wide eyes. 'I honestly don't know.'

'Well, see,' Luke said lightly, 'you were being honest right there.'

She let out a shaky laugh, the sound trembling on the air. Luke felt an ache deep inside. He didn't know everything she'd been through, but he knew it had to have been a lot. And he wanted, on a deep, gut and even heart level, to make it better. To have her trust him. He wanted to redeem her, yes, maybe even save her, and save himself in the process. This time he could make it right.

'Give us a chance, Aurelie.'

'How?'

How to begin? 'We don't have to be in Singapore until the day after tomorrow. Give me tomorrow.'

She eyed him warily. 'One day?'

'One day. One date. It's a start.' For both of them.

'And then?'

'We'll see. We'll take one day at a time and see how we go.' He had a feeling one day at a time was all they could handle. He didn't know what he was asking, what he wanted. This was new territory for both of them.

'One day,' she repeated, as if she liked the sound of it. 'One date.' Luke nodded, felt his heart lift. 'Okay,' she said, and smiled.

Aurelie stood in the lobby of the hotel and tried not to fidget. Luke had told her he'd meet here at nine for their day out. Their *date*.

When had she last had a date?

She couldn't remember, although it wasn't for lack of men. There had, she knew, been far too many men in her life. But she hadn't dated them. The whole concept of a date made her feel like a giddy girl, young, innocent, full of hope.

Ha.

She was none of those things. She might only be twenty-six, but she'd lived enough for three lifetimes. And as for innocent, *hopeful*…Luke Bryant might stir something inside her she'd long thought destroyed, but he couldn't change her and she didn't think she could change herself.

And when Luke discovered that… Swallowing, she forced the fluttery panic down. There was no point thinking about the future. Luke was giving her one date. One day. And by the end of it he'd probably have had enough.

'Ready?'

She whirled around, saw Luke smiling at her. He wore a dark green polo shirt and khaki shorts, and she realised it was the first time she'd seen him in casual clothes. The shirt hugged the lean, sculpted muscles of his chest and shoulders, and the shorts rested low on his trim hips. Her gaze travelled down his tanned, muscular legs to the pair of worn trainers and then back up again to his face, where a surprising grin quirked his mouth.

'Finished?'

She had, Aurelie realised with some mortification, been checking him out. And not in a deliberate, outrageous, Aurelie-like way. No, this had been instinctive, helpless, yearning admiration. Somehow she managed to smile, nod.

'Yeah, I'm done.'

'And do I pass?'

'You'll do.'

He chuckled and placed one hand on the small of her back. She felt the warm, sure press of his palm against her skin and the answering shivers of sensation that rippled out through her body from that little touch.

'So where are we going?' she asked as they left the hotel. A luxury sedan with tinted windows and a driver at the wheel waited for them at the kerb. Luke opened the door and ushered her into the sumptuous leather interior.

'Camiguin.'

'Cami-what?'

He smiled and slid in next to her, his thigh brushing hers. Aurelie didn't know why she was suddenly hyper-aware of his movements, his body. She'd already been naked with this man; he surely shouldn't have this effect on her.

And yet, somehow, he did.

'Camiguin,' Luke repeated. 'A small island province in the Bohol Sea.'

'So we're not taking this car there, I assume?'

'No, we're taking this to the airport, and then a private

plane to Mambajao, the capital city. And then we'll hire a Jeep.'

'Planes, trains and automobiles.'

'It shouldn't take more than two hours, overall.'

'A private jet is pretty classy.'

Luke gave her the glimmer of a smile. 'I can be a pretty classy guy.'

She felt a ripple of something like pleasure at the light remark, the curve of his mouth. She'd spent so much of her time trying to push Luke away and protect herself. It felt amazingly liberating not to do it. To banter without the barbs, to relax into a—

A what? A *relationship*? She didn't do relationships. Luke might go for them, but they didn't work for her. She turned to stare out of the window, told herself this was *one date*. It was nothing. By this time tomorrow they'd probably have decided they'd *both* had enough.

The private jet was waiting for them on the tarmac at Manila's International Airport. Aurelie had taken private jets before, back in her heyday, but she hadn't been on one in over four years and it felt strange. She stood in the main cabin, glancing around at the leather sofas, the champagne chilling on ice, and felt something cold steal inside her.

Luke paused in the doorway, his gaze on her face. 'What is it?'

She glanced up at him, bemused that he would sense her mood so quickly and easily. She wasn't even sure what she was feeling. 'Nothing. Everything's very nice.'

'That's a scathing indictment if I ever heard one.' His gaze moved slowly over her, assessing, understanding. His forehead creased and he nodded. 'I guess you've taken a few of these in your time.'

She shrugged. 'One or two.'

'Does it bring back memories?'

Did it? 'No, just a feeling.'

'Not a very nice one.'

She opened her mouth to deny it, then said nothing. This honesty thing was *tough*. 'Maybe,' she finally allowed, and Luke smiled faintly, as if he knew how difficult she found this kind of talking. Sharing. All of it awkward, awful, painful.

'How have you flown under the radar for so long?'

'By holing up in Vermont.'

'And no one there gives you away?'

'They're a close-mouthed bunch. And they're loyal to my grandmother.' Too late she realised she'd said more than she meant to. Funny how that happened. You started being a little honest and then other things began to slip out. Soon she wouldn't be able to control it.

'Your grandmother? Was Julia Schmidt your grandmother, then?'

'No.' She moved over to sit on the sofa, rubbing her arms in the chilled air of the plane's interior. 'Are we going to get going?'

Luke sat across from her. 'As soon as we're cleared for take-off.' He didn't speak for a moment, just studied her, and Aurelie looked away from his gaze. She heard the plane's engines thrum to life with a feeling of relief. 'Champagne?' he asked, and she nodded, glad he wasn't going to ask any more questions.

It wasn't until he'd handed her a glass and raised his own in a toast that he finally spoke again. 'You know, this second chance thing?' She eyed him warily. 'It doesn't work if you're going to guard everything you say.'

'I wasn't,' she protested, and Luke just arched an eyebrow. She took a sip of champagne, glad for the distraction. 'I told you I'm not good at this.' He said nothing and, goaded, she said a bit sharply, 'It's not like you've been baring your soul.'

'Haven't I?' he asked quietly. He looked away then, and Aurelie felt a strange twisting inside as she thought of his words last night. Words which made a shivery thrill run all the way through her. *I know enough to know I want to know more.*

Did she want to be known?

She took a sip of champagne, the bubbles seeming to fizz all the way through her. Maybe she did. At least for one day. One date. That was safe enough, surely.

'All right.' She set her champagne glass on the coffee table between them. 'What do you want to know?'

Luke turned back to her, bemused. 'You look like you're facing the firing squad.'

'It feels that way, a little bit.'

'I suppose you've always had to be careful about what you say.'

'I haven't always been careful enough.' He acknowledged the point with a nod. There had been several tell-all exposés in various tabloids, all with too much truth in them. Aurelie felt herself start to prickle. 'So what do you want to know?'

'What do you want to tell me?'

She gave a soft laugh. 'Not much.'

'There must be something. Some small, innocuous bit of information that you don't mind imparting.'

She smiled, felt the tension inside her ease, at least a little bit. 'Well…I like bubblegum ice cream.'

'Bubblegum?' His jaw dropped theatrically. 'You have got to be kidding me.'

'It's delicious.'

'It's way too sweet—'

She leaned forward. 'And pink and sugary and with little bits of gum in the ice cream. Yum.'

'Whoa.' He held up a hand. 'TMI.'

A bubble of laughter erupted from her, surprising them

both. He smiled, a real smile, lightening his stern features in a way that made her feel suddenly breathless. His dark eyes glinted gold. She shook her head slowly. 'I didn't think you had a sense of humour, you know.'

'It's a shy creature. It only appears on rare occasions.'

'So it does.' She gazed at him thoughtfully. 'What's your favourite flavour of ice cream?'

'Not bubblegum.'

'We've established that.'

'Probably vanilla.'

'Vanilla?' She rolled her eyes. 'Could you be more boring?'

His mouth twitched. 'Probably not.'

'What's there to like about vanilla?'

'It never lets you down. Other flavours can be so disappointing. Not enough mint in the mint chocolate chip, too many nuts in Rocky Road.'

'I have been seriously disappointed, on occasion, with the lack of cookie dough in cookie dough ice cream.'

'Exactly.' He nodded his approval. 'But vanilla? Never a disappointment. Completely trustworthy.'

Like you are? She almost said the words. And meant them. No snide mockery, just truth. Too much truth. She wasn't ready for that.

'Well.' She shifted in her seat, gave him a breezy smile. 'Now we've broken the ice.'

'Or the ice cream.'

'That was a seriously weak joke.'

'I told you, my sense of humour only appears on rare occasions. Anyway—' he glanced at her as he took a sip of champagne '—can you eat bubblegum ice cream? Or does that send your glucose levels through the roof?'

'Everything in moderation.'

He nodded towards the handbag at her feet. 'I should have asked before, but did you bring everything you need?'

She nodded. 'I have a little kit for testing my blood. It travels easily.'

'When were you diagnosed?'

'When I was seventeen.' She swallowed, remembering those awful early days. At the time she'd just been moving from one event to another, dazed, incredulous, hopeful and yet still afraid.

Too late she realised Luke was watching her face, and she knew he could see the emotions in her eyes. Emotions she'd meant to hide. 'Anyway,' she said, apropos of nothing.

'How did it happen?'

'The usual symptoms. Weight loss, excessive thirst, dizzy spells.'

His eyes narrowed, and she could almost see his mind working. Understanding. 'And the tabloids claimed you had anorexia. A drinking problem. A drug overdose.'

She lifted one shoulder in a shrug. 'That's what they like to do. And in any case I haven't been a saint.' She lifted her chin a notch, tried to smile again, but her heart was thudding hard.

Luke gazed at her steadily. 'Who has?'

'You seem to have been a regular Boy Scout.'

'No, not a Boy Scout.' He rubbed his jaw, a movement that Aurelie couldn't help but notice was inherently sexy. Although, perhaps the sexiest thing about Luke Bryant was how unaware he seemed of his own attractiveness. He moved with unconscious grace, and her gaze was helplessly drawn to the shrug of his broad shoulders, the reassuring squareness of his jaw. Everything about him solid and strong. *Safe.*

'Why haven't you ever talked about your diabetes publicly? Issued a statement?'

She leaned her head back against the seat, suddenly tired. 'It's quite a boring disease.'

'Boring?'

'Much more interesting to let them wonder. So my agent told me.'

'Your agent sucked.'

She let out a surprised laugh. 'Yeah, he wasn't that great. I fired him a couple of years ago.'

'You could have said something since then.'

She opened her eyes. 'Maybe I didn't want to.'

'Why?'

'Because telling the truth and having no one believe you is worse than not telling the truth and having people assume the worst. But I guess you wouldn't understand that,' she finished lightly, 'what with this compulsion to honesty that you have.'

Luke didn't say anything for a moment, yet Aurelie felt him tense, saw something dark flash in his eyes before he angled his head away from her. Had she inadvertently touched on something painful with her offhand remark? 'I understand,' he said finally, his voice low, and she almost asked him what he meant. She didn't, though, because they'd surely had enough honesty for one day.

By the time they arrived in Camiguin Aurelie had started feeling relaxed again. Luke had steered the conversation back to lighter subjects, moving from ice cream flavours to movie preferences and whether she supported the Mets or the Yankees.

'Mets all the way,' he'd assured her solemnly, but she saw a glint in his eyes that made her smile.

They disembarked the plane at the tiny airport and took an island taxi—basically, a rusted-out Jeep—into Mambajao. The capital of Camiguin was no more than a small town of rickety buildings with wooden verandas and tin roofs, the narrow streets bustling with bicycles and fruit vendors and raggedy children darting in and out of everything. It was so different from Aurelie's usual experience of travelling, when she kept to limos and high class hotels and never stepped outside of a severely controlled environment. She loved this. Craved the feeling of possibility and even hope wandering around the dusty streets gave her.

'What are we doing first?' she asked Luke, and he smiled and took her elbow, steering her away from a man on a bike pulling a cartload of pineapples.

'I thought we could pick up some lunch in the market, and then we'll take it out to the falls for a picnic.'

'The falls?'

'The Tuwasan Falls. They're pretty spectacular.'

'You've been there before?'

'I stopped over here the last time I came to Manila.'

She felt a completely unreasonable prickling of jealousy. Had he taken one of his serious *relationships* to this falls? Was this his go-to place for a romantic date in the tropics?

'Alone,' Luke said quietly, yet with a hint of humour in his voice that made her blush. Again. She'd never blushed so much with a man, had never had a reason to. She was Aurelie, she was worldly-wise and weary, beyond shame or embarrassment.

But that act was falling away, flaking off like old paint. What would be left when it was gone? Something good, or even anything at all? She still wasn't sure of the answer.

'Come on,' Luke said, and he guided her to a market stall overflowing with local produce and fish. 'Anything look good?'

Aurelie surveyed the jumbled piles of fruits and vegetables, the pots of noodles and trays of spring rolls.

'Crispy *pata*?' Luke suggested. 'It's deep fried pig's leg.'

She winced. 'I don't think I'm feeling quite that adventurous.'

'It's quite tasty.'

'You've had it before?'

'I like to try new things.'

She pointed to a tray of round yellowish fruit that looked a bit like potatoes. 'What's that?'

'Lanzones.'

'Have you had those?'

'Yes, but you have to be careful. If they're not ripe, they taste horribly sour. If they are, incredibly sweet. You just have to take your chances.' He picked up a fruit, testing its ripeness with his thumb. 'Try it.' The fruit seller quickly peeled the *lanzone* with a knife and handed her a piece. Warily, she bit into it and then, without thinking, spat the piece out into her hand. 'Yuck!'

'Bitter, huh?'

'You don't sound surprised.'

He shrugged, and she hit him in the shoulder. 'You did that on purpose!'

'Try this one.'

'Why should I trust you?' she demanded even as she took the second peeled *lanzone*.

'Because even *lanzones* deserve a second chance.'

Something in his quiet, serious tone made her mouth dry and her heart beat hard. She took a bite, and her mouth filled with the intense sweetness of the fruit. Her eyes widened. 'Wow.'

'See?' He sounded so satisfied, so smug, that Aurelie rolled her eyes.

'Thank you very much for that life lesson. Message received. Everything deserves a second chance.'

'Not everything.' After handing the vendor some coins,

he'd placed his hand on the small of her back and was guiding her to the next stall. 'Just me and the fruit.'

He acted, Aurelie thought, as if he were the only one who'd made a mistake. Who needed a second chance. Yet when she thought of her behaviour at their first meeting—and even their second—she felt as if *she* was the one who needed to change. Who wanted to prove she was different. Not Luke.

She glanced at him, her gaze taking in his stern profile, the hard line of his mouth, the latent strength of his body. What was he trying to prove?

He'd put several *lanzones* into a straw basket he'd bought from another vendor, and they added mango, spring rolls and some local sausage and cold noodles to their purchases. The sun was hot overhead even though the air felt swampy, and Luke bought two bottles of water and some sun hats as well.

'Now to the falls,' he said, and Aurelie followed him to a tin-roofed garage where he conferred with a young man who couldn't be more than sixteen before leading her around to the back where a battered-looking Jeep awaited.

'Your carriage, madam.'

She eyed it dubiously. 'I don't particularly relish breaking down in the middle of the jungle.'

'Don't worry, we're not taking this into the jungle.'

'Where, then?'

'A car park about five kilometres from here. Then we walk.'

'Walk? In the jungle?'

'It's worth it.'

'It'd better be.'

Luke stowed their provisions in the bag, handed her a sun hat, and then swung into the driver's seat. Aurelie could not keep her gaze from resting on his strong, browned forearms, the confident way he manoeuvred the rusty vehicle through the crowded streets of Mambajao and then out onto the open road, no more than a bumpy, rutted track.

The breeze was a balmy caress on her skin, the sun a benediction. In the distance the lush mountains—active volcanoes, Luke had told her—were dark, verdant humps against a hazy sky. Aurelie leaned her head back against the seat and closed her eyes.

When had she last felt this relaxed, this *happy*?

It was too long ago to remember. Smiling, she let her thoughts drift as the sunlight washed over her.

'We're here.'

She opened her eyes and saw that Luke had pulled into a rectangle of gravel and dirt that was, apparently, a car park. Their Jeep was the only car.

She rubbed her eyes. 'I must have dozed.'

'Just a little.' There was something intimate about the way he said it, and Aurelie imagined him watching her sleep. Had she rested her head on his shoulder? Had she *drooled*? More blushing.

'So where is here exactly?'

'Well, nowhere, really.' Luke slid out of the Jeep and reached for their basket. 'But we can follow a path through the jungle to the Tuwasan Falls. It's about a mile.'

'A mile in the jungle?' She glanced down at her leather sandals dubiously. 'You should have told me we were enacting *Survivor*.'

He made a face. 'Sorry. But it's mostly wooden walkways, so I think you'll be okay.'

'If you say so.'

She followed him away from the car park and onto exactly what he'd said—a wooden walkway on stilts over the dense jungle floor. Within just a few metres of going down the walkway she felt the air close around her, hot, humid and dense. Birds chirped and cicadas chirrupped—at least she thought they were cicadas—and she could feel the jungle like a living, breathing entity all around her. A bright green lizard scampered across the walkway, and in the distance some animal—Aurelie had no idea what—gave a lonely, mournful cry.

'Wow.' She stopped, her hands resting on the cane railings, her heart thumping. 'This is…intense.'

Luke glanced back at her. 'You okay?'

'Yes, I guess I just thought, you know, first date, maybe a movie?'

He smiled wryly. 'I know you think I'm boring, but Jeez. A movie? I think I can do better than that.'

'I don't think you're boring.'

'You think I'm the human equivalent of vanilla ice cream.'

She gazed at him, the railings slick under her palms. Her heart was still thumping. 'I do,' she admitted quietly, and it felt like the most honest thing she'd ever said. 'Completely trustworthy.'

Luke's eyes darkened and the moment spun out between them, a thread of silence that bound them together, and tighter still. 'Don't speak too soon,' he finally said, and turned away from her to walk further down the path.

'You mean you're not?'

'I mean you don't trust me yet, and why should you? It's something I have to earn.'

Despite the damp heat all around them her mouth felt dry. She swallowed. 'And you want to earn it?'

He glanced back at her, and his eyes were darker than ever. 'Yes.'

Her mind spun with this revelation. She wanted to tell him that he'd already earned it, that she trusted him now, but somehow the words wouldn't come.

They didn't talk for a little while after that, because the

wooden walkway became decidedly rickety, and then it stopped altogether at the bank of a rushing stream.

Aurelie raised her eyebrows. 'What now, Tarzan?'

'We cross it.'

'Did I mention my leather sandals?'

'You might have.'

'And?'

'I didn't think you were the type to care about shoes.'

She wasn't. 'No, but I'm the type to care about getting my big toe eaten by a giant barracuda.'

He laughed then, a great big rumbling laugh that had a silly grin spreading wide across her face. She liked the sound of his laughter. 'I don't think there are any giant barracudas.'

'No?'

'Only medium-sized ones.'

She pursed her lips, hands firmly planted on her hips. 'Is that your sense of humour appearing on this rare occasion?'

'Oops, it darted away again.' He stepped onto a flattish rock in the stream, the water flowing all around him, and stretched out his hand. 'Come here.'

Cautiously she reached out and put her hand in his. His clasp was dry, warm and firm, and with his other hand on her arm he helped her onto the rock. Their hips bumped. Heat flared.

'This is cosy,' she murmured and he gave a tiny smile.

'That's the idea. Next rock.'

He stepped backwards onto another rock, sure and agile, and Aurelie followed him. She could hear the water rushing past them, felt the warm spray of it against her ankles. In the middle of the stream she looked down and saw a bright blue fish darting very near her toes. She slipped and Luke slid an arm around her waist, balanced her. Easily.

'The secret is not to look down.'

'Now you tell me.'

Another rock, and then another, and then they were on the other side. Luke smiled at her rather smugly, and Aurelie shook her head.

'This is all a big lesson, isn't it? How to Trust 101.'

'Is it working?'

'A little,' she admitted. 'What if I'd fallen?'

'But you didn't.'

'But what if I had? What if you'd slipped?'

'Me? Slip?' He shook his head, then gazed at her, his head tilted to one side. 'Do you think it would have ruined everything?'

Her lips curved. She liked being with this man. 'Not everything. But after the *lanzone*...'

'It was delicious.'

'The second one.'

'Exactly.'

He hadn't let go of her hand, and now he led her alongside the stream, the ground soft and loamy beneath them. Aurelie found she quite liked the feel of his fingers threaded through hers. They walked along the bank, winding their way up through the dense foliage, until Luke stopped suddenly.

'Close your eyes.'

More trust. 'Okay.' She closed her eyes and felt Luke tug on her hand. She took a step. Another.

'Open them,' he said softly, and she did. And gasped in wonder.

CHAPTER SEVEN

'Wow.'

'Definitely worth it, huh?'

She turned from the stunning view of the falls to Luke's rather smug smile. 'I wouldn't say definitely. I think my sandals are ruined.'

'Leather dries.'

'It is amazing,' she admitted and his smile widened. Not so smug, she decided. More like…satisfied. *Happy.*

'Let's find a place for a picnic.' He tugged on her hand again and they picked their way along the rocks until they found a large flat one, warm from the sun and perfect for a picnic.

Aurelie stretched out on top of it as Luke unpacked their lunch, her gaze on the waterfall once more. It truly was a spectacular sight, a crystalline fountain flowing from the fern-covered rocks, falling in a sparkling stream to a tranquil pool fifty feet or more below.

She turned to watch Luke peel a *lanzone* with a knife. He glanced up, smiling, a decidedly wicked glint in his eyes. 'Care to try another?'

'I don't know if I dare.'

'This one's sweet, I promise.' And with that wicked glint still in his eyes he fed her a chunk of the sweet, moist fruit, his fingers brushing her lips as she ate it. The barest touch of his fingers against her mouth sent little pulses of awareness firing through her, flaring deep down. *Desire.* It seemed amazing that she could feel it. Want it—and him. She'd never wanted anyone before, not like that. Not since Pete.

'Tasty,' she managed, and swiped at the droplets of juice on her lips. Her heart rate was skittering all over the place, and all from that simple touch and the feelings and thoughts it had triggered, a maelstrom swirling through her.

'You know,' she said as Luke arranged the rest of their picnic items onto two paper plates, 'I don't really know anything about you.'

'What do you want to know?'

'Something. Anything. Where did you grow up?'

'New York City and Long Island.'

'The Hamptons?' He nodded, and she hugged her knees to her chest. 'I guess you grew up pretty privileged, huh? Bryant Enterprises and all that?' She didn't know much about the Bryant family, but she knew they were rich. Featured in the society pages rather than the trashy tabloids like her. 'And you have a brother, you mentioned?'

'Two.'

'Are you close?'

'No.' Luke spoke mildly enough, but Aurelie sensed a dark current of emotion swirling underneath the words, a tension and repressiveness. She was getting to know this man, and now she wanted to understand him.

'Why aren't you?'

He lifted one shoulder in a shrug. 'The short answer? Because Aaron's an ass and Chase checked out a long time ago.'

'Those are rather nice alliterations, but what does that really mean?'

Luke sighed and sat back, his arms braced on the rock behind him. 'It means my older brother, Aaron, loves to be the boss. I can't really blame him, because my father encouraged it, told him he was going to be CEO of Bryant Enterprises when he was older, and he needed to be responsible, authoritative, et cetera. Let's just say Aaron got the message.'

Aurelie observed the tightening of Luke's mouth, his eyes narrowed as he gazed out at the falls, the sunlight catching the spray and causing it to glitter.

'And Chase?'

'Chase is my younger brother. He was always a rebel, got in trouble loads of times, expelled from boarding school, the whole bit. My father disinherited him when he was in college.'

'Ouch.'

'I don't know if Chase even cared. He made his own fortune as an architect and he hardly ever gets in touch.'

Aurelie hugged her knees. 'That's sad.'

'Is it?' He glanced at her, eyebrows raised. 'Maybe he's better off. When I do see him, he always seems happy. Joking around.'

'Maybe that's his schtick.'

'Maybe.'

'And what about you?' Aurelie asked quietly, because that was what she really wanted to know. 'Where did you fit into that picture?' Luke hesitated, and she knew she was getting closer to understanding. 'Or didn't you?'

'I suppose I was the classic middle child.'

'Which is?'

'Caught between two larger personalities. As we got older we all drifted apart and that seemed easier.'

'It doesn't sound like a very comfortable place.'

'No, I don't suppose it was.' Luke turned to her with a faint smile, although Aurelie could still sense that dark emotion swirling underneath. 'I don't miss my childhood, at any rate. I was shy, awkward, and I even had a stammer.' He spoke lightly, but it didn't matter. Aurelie knew it hurt. 'My father didn't have much time for me, to tell you the truth.' He glanced away. 'He didn't have time for me at all.'

'Sounds a bit like my childhood,' Aurelie answered quietly.

Luke turned back to her, his gaze sharp now, eyes narrowed in concern. 'Oh? How so?'

She swallowed past the ache that had started in her throat, an ache of sympathy and remembrance. She'd never told anyone about her childhood. In the world of celebrity, it held a touch too much pathos to be interesting. 'Well, my mother didn't have much time for me. And my father wasn't in the picture.'

'Who raised you?' That thoughtful crease appeared between his brows. 'Your grandmother?'

'I wish. I only stayed a summer with her, when I was eleven, but it was the happiest time of my life.'

'Then where did you grow up?'

'Nowhere. Everywhere. My mom never stayed in the same place for more than a few months, sometimes a few weeks. She'd get a job in a local diner or something, enrol me in school and find a deadbeat boyfriend. When he started stealing her money or knocking her around, she'd move on, dragging me with her.'

'That's terrible,' Luke said quietly, and Aurelie shrugged. 'I got over it.'

'Julia Schmidt,' he said after a moment. 'Your mother. You bought the house from her, didn't you?'

She nodded. 'When my grandmother died she left it to my mom. I was only seventeen, and I think she hoped it would help my mom settle down.'

'But?'

Aurelie sighed. 'My mom didn't want to settle down. So I bought the house from her for far more than it was worth. I was famous by then, so I had the money.'

'And you finally had a home.'

She blinked hard, amazed at how quickly and easily he understood her. How in this moment it felt good and right and safe, rather than scary.

'It must have been a huge loss when your grandmother died,' he said after a moment, and she nodded.

'I still miss her.'

'And your mother?'

A shrug. 'Around. Who knows? She used to appear every so often asking for money, but now that I'm not in the spotlight any more—at least not for any good reason—she's disappeared.' She sighed and stretched out her legs. 'She'll surface one day, I'm sure.'

'So you really are alone.'

So alone. Although she didn't feel alone right now. She wanted to tell him that, confess just a little of the happiness in her heart that he'd helped to create, but fear held her back. Rejection was still a distinct and awful possibility. There was still so much Luke didn't know.

'What about your parents? Are they around?'

He shook his head. 'Both dead.'

'I'm sorry.' Aurelie gazed at him, saw how he'd carefully schooled his features into a completely neutral mask. 'How did they die?'

'My father of a heart attack when I'd just finished college.' A pause, a telling hesitation. 'My mother developed breast cancer when I was thirteen.'

'I'm sorry. That's terrible.'

He jerked his head in a semblance of a nod, his face still so very neutral. He was holding something back, Aurelie suspected, some pain that he didn't want to share with her. She decided not to press.

'So you're alone too,' she said quietly and after a taut moment of silence Luke reached for her hand.

'Not right now,' he said, and as Aurelie's heart turned right over he tugged her to her feet. 'Let's swim.'

'Swim?' Aurelie eyed the deep, tranquil pool below the falls with a dubious wariness. 'What about the giant barracudas?'

'You mean the medium-sized ones? They're friendly.'

'I didn't bring a swimsuit.'

'I'm sure we can improvise.' She hesitated and Luke added quietly, 'Unless you don't want to.'

Was this another trust exercise? she wondered. She was so used to men seeing her as an object. A trophy. She'd encouraged it, after all. And yet she knew Luke was different, knew he saw her differently.

'Okay,' she said. 'Let's do it.'

Luke led her down a narrow path to the pool. Aurelie tilted her head up to watch the waterfall cascade down the rock, churning foam that emptied into a surprisingly placid pool.

'Good thing you're not shy any more,' she said as Luke tugged his shirt over his head. Then her mouth dried, for the sight of his bare chest was glorious enough to start her heart thumping. His shoulders were broad, his chest powerful and browned and perfectly taut. Washboard abs, trim hips. She was gaping like a fool, and realised it when Luke gave her a knowing grin and dropped his shorts.

He wore boxers, and Aurelie could not draw her gaze away from his powerful thighs. As for what was hidden beneath the boxers…

'Look at me like that much longer and I'm going to embarrass myself,' Luke said, a thread of humour in his voice although she caught the ragged note of desire too. And it thrilled her.

She wasn't sure how it could feel so different from before, when she'd wielded his desire for her like a weapon. Now it felt like a joy. She glanced up and smiled right into his eyes.

'I don't think that would necessarily be a bad thing.'

He nodded towards her pale pink sundress. 'Your turn.'

He'd already seen her naked. He'd seen her in her skimpy Aurelie underwear several times. Yet this felt different too, more honest, more bare. She slid the straps from her shoulders and shrugged out of the dress.

'Sorry. I'm wearing boring underwear.' Just a plain cotton bra and boy shorts. Really, incredibly modest. Yet she felt nearly naked, and her body responded to Luke's heated gaze, an answering heat flaring within her, stirring up all sorts of wants. As well as just a tiny little needle of fear. No, not fear, but uncertainty. Memory.

Luke smiled and turned towards the pool. 'Last one in,' he called, and dived neatly into the water below. Aurelie watched him surface, sluicing the water from his face, clearly enjoying himself. He glanced up at her. 'Is a rotten egg,' he finished solemnly and she laughed. Still didn't move.

'Are you chicken?'

'I prefer the word cautious.' She hadn't swum in anything but a lap pool in years.

'Didn't you swim in a lake or watering hole that summer you spent in Vermont?' Luke called up to her. 'This is no different. In fact, it's nicer because the bottom is sand and rock rather than squishy mud.'

She stared at him, amazed at how much he guessed. Knew. She had swum in a lake in Vermont, a muddy-bottomed pond that she'd spent hours in.

'Come on,' Luke called. 'I'm right here. I promise you can scramble onto my shoulders if a medium-sized barracuda happens by.'

More trust. Funny, how trusting in these silly little things made her start to unbend to the notion of trusting him with the bigger things. Like the truth. No, she'd been honest enough about her past for one afternoon. But this she could do.

Taking a deep breath, she took a running jump into the pool. The water closed over her head and for a moment she remained below the surface, treading water and enjoying the complete stillness and silence until she felt Luke's hands close around her shoulders and he hauled her upwards.

'What—'

'You want to scare me to death?' he demanded, but she saw that telltale glint in his dark eyes. 'I thought you were drowning.'

'I can swim, you know.'

'Maybe one of those barracudas had got you.'

She laughed, but the sound trembled and died on her lips as she saw Luke's eyes darken, his pupils dilate, and she felt the pulse of desire in herself. He still held her by the shoulders, and she was close enough to see the droplets of water clinging to his skin, the enticing curve of his mouth, a mouth that she knew was soft and warm and delicious.

Then Luke let her go, easing away from her, and struck out towards the falls. 'Come see this,' he called over his shoulder, and Aurelie felt a flicker of disappointment. Had she wanted him to kiss her?

Yes, she had.

How novel. How exciting. How disappointing that he hadn't.

With a little shake of her head, she swam over to join him at the waterfall.

'There's a little cave behind the falls,' Luke explained. 'Just swim underneath the waterfall and you'll come up right into it.'

'Okay.'

Luke dived down first and Aurelie followed him, surfacing a few seconds later into a shallow fern-covered overhang, the waterfall a sparkling crystalline curtain hiding them from the world. Luke hauled himself up onto a ledge and extended a hand to her.

They sat side by side in silence for a moment, and to Aurelie it seemed completely relaxed, completely wonderful. She'd never felt so much in accord with another human being before, and she knew she wanted to tell him. Forget the fear. Screw rejection. This was too incredible, too important.

She turned to him with a smile. 'It's amazing. This whole day has been amazing.'

Luke touched her cheek, no more than a brush of his fingers. 'It has been for me too.' His gaze was tender and yet intent on hers, the curve of his mouth so close—

'Luke—' She wasn't sure what she was going to say. *Kiss me,* maybe, because she wanted him to. Desperately. But he didn't. Didn't even let her finish, just slipped off the ledge and swam underneath the falls once more.

With a little sigh Aurelie followed him.

They swam a bit more in the shallows of the pool, splashing, teasing and laughing and finally they got out and returned to the sun-warmed rock to dry.

Aurelie sat there, her arms braced behind her, her legs stretched out, wearing only her underwear. And felt completely natural, no Aurelie artifice or armour. She was, she knew, being herself; she'd been herself for nearly the whole day. There *was* something there, underneath all the posing, and she'd needed Luke to show her.

'So if your mother was dragging you around in pursuit of her deadbeats, how did you actually become famous?' Luke asked after they'd sat in a comfortable silence for a little while.

'At a karaoke night at a bar in Kansas, if you can believe it,' Aurelie answered.

'You sang karaoke?'

'We both did. It was a mother-daughter thing.'

'Ah.'

'What do you mean, *ah*?' she asked, because he sounded as if she'd just said something significant.

'Well, your mother isn't famous, is she?'

'No—'

'I'll bet she wasn't pleased that her teenage daughter—how old were you, sixteen?'

'Fifteen,' Aurelie said softly. 'It was a month before my sixteenth birthday.'

'Young and gorgeous,' Luke stated, 'and about to be famous. And your mother wasn't any of those things.'

Strange, she'd never thought of it that way. She'd never considered that her mother might have been jealous of her. Yet now, looking back on that fateful, life-altering night, she remembered how quiet her mother had been. Of course, Pete had done all the talking, made his promises, told Aurelie she was going to be a star. She swallowed, willing the memories away. It had begun right there, she knew, the destruction of herself. The building up of Aurelie.

'It's hard to remember, isn't it,' Luke said quietly. 'I'm sorry.'

She shook her head, her throat tight. 'In some ways it was the happiest—well, I felt the happiest then than I had in such a long time. But if I'd known, if anyone could have told me—'

'Told you what?'

She swallowed. Here was the honesty that hurt. 'That I'd lose my soul. That I'd sell it, because I didn't even know what I was giving away.'

Luke frowned. 'I suppose fame will do that to you.'

'It wasn't fame. It was—' She stopped because she didn't want to tell him, didn't even know how. 'It was awful,' she finished quietly.

He was silent for a long moment. '"Never give your heart

away,"' he quoted her song softly. 'Is that what happened, Aurelie? Someone broke your heart?'

She swallowed. 'Yes.'

He nodded, sorrowfully understanding. 'Three years is a long time. It must have hurt when it was over.'

She let out a sudden, hard laugh because Luke had completely the wrong idea and she didn't want to have to correct him. 'It felt like forever,' she agreed after a moment. 'But my heart didn't break when it was over, Luke. It broke when it began.'

CHAPTER EIGHT

It broke when it began.

Aurelie had said the words with such flat finality, such aching sorrow, that Luke knew she meant them. He just didn't know what they meant.

'I don't understand,' he said quietly, but she shook her head.

'I don't want to talk about it. I don't want to ruin this perfect day by bringing all that up. And it has been perfect, Luke. Everything.' She gazed at him with those wide rain-washed eyes and Luke felt everything in him twist and yearn.

He'd wanted to kiss her so many times today. When she'd planted her hands on her hips and given him an impish look, when she'd tossed him a teasing glance, when he'd held her in the water and longed to pull her close, their wet limbs sliding over each other, twining around.

Hell, he'd been in a permanent state of arousal, it seemed, for half the day. Yet he'd kept his distance, and he would now, because this wasn't about desire.

It was about trust.

He'd meant what he said about earning it. He'd let her down before, but he wouldn't again. He had, despite his instinct which insisted there was so much more, taken her at face value. Aurelie the go-to-hell pop star. And he'd allowed her to seduce him, allowed himself to give in to his own need because the desire had been so strong. Only when he had seen the pain on her face, written on her heart, and known he'd shown her he was just like all the others, had he been able to stop. Yet he feared the damage had been done.

It broke when it began.

What did she mean? Had some bastard abused her? The sudden strong urge to kill such a man with his bare hands surprised him. Aurelie aroused all sorts of feelings in him, feelings he hadn't had in a long time. He had, he saw now, been skimming through life, never going too deep, using work as an excuse because this—this emotion, this intensity—was frightening. Reminded him of how much you could lose, how much risk and pain was involved in any real relationship.

Not pain for him—he didn't care about that—but pain for her. He didn't want to hurt her, and he was so afraid that he might.

How did your parents die?

For a second, no more, he'd wanted to tell her the truth. Yet honesty only went so far, and that secret was buried so deep inside him he didn't think he could let it out if he tried. He tried not to think about it, yet being with this woman brought his own secrets swimming upwards to the light, just like hers.

They were *both* being real.

'It has been perfect,' he agreed. 'But it's getting late and we've got a mile trek through the jungle as well as a ride in the Jeep and a plane to catch.'

'Back to reality,' Aurelie said, making a face, and Luke reached for her hand.

'Maybe reality won't be so bad,' he said quietly. This new reality, with the two of them in it together. *One day at a time.* Yet what would tomorrow hold?

They walked back to the Jeep in companionable silence,

the jungle lush and vibrant all around them. As they emerged into the sunlight a brilliant blue morpho butterfly fluttered close to Aurelie's face and briefly alighted on her hair. She laughed aloud, and Luke smiled to see her joy. Then suddenly, impulsively perhaps, she leaned over and brushed her lips against his.

He stilled under that little kiss, felt a flare of heat inside, the instant arousal, yet something more. Something precious, because he knew that little kiss hadn't been calculated. It had been an expression of her heart.

'What was that for?' he asked, and she shrugged, smiling.

'Just because I wanted to.' She paused, bit her lip. 'Do you mind?'

Mind? 'No,' Luke said. 'I don't mind at all.'

'Good.'

And that, he knew, was a very good start.

By the time they got on the plane Aurelie was feeling sleepy. She curled up in a corner of one of the leather sofas, and when Luke came and sat down right beside her it felt amazingly natural to rest her head on his shoulder. Luke curved his arm around her, drew her closer so her cheek rested against his chest, and with a kind of wonderful incredulity Aurelie realised that felt natural too. It felt right. She snuggled closer, and by the time the plane took off her eyes were drifting shut.

They got back to the hotel after dark, and Luke walked her all the way to the door of her suite. Aurelie turned to him, felt her heart throw itself against her ribs. Should she ask him to come in? Did she want him to? Part of her did, desperately, and another part still felt that old fear.

She took out her keycard, hesitated and turned to Luke. 'Well.' She swallowed, smiled. Sort of.

Luke smiled back and cupped her cheek. The feel of his warm palm against her skin was both reassuring and exciting. Yet even so Aurelie felt herself tensing. She wanted this, she did, and yet…

'Goodnight, Aurelie.' Luke dropped his hand and turned to walk back down the corridor. Aurelie stared at him in disbelief, a little disappointment.

'You mean you aren't…you aren't going to kiss me?'

Luke glanced back, eyes glinting. 'No.'

'But—'

'You didn't want me to.'

'I did,' she said, but she knew she didn't sound that convincing.

'Maybe,' Luke suggested quietly, 'you didn't know what you wanted. And until you do, completely, I'm not going to touch you.'

Aurelie stared at him, her mind spinning. 'Why not?'

'I think the better question is, why would I?' She had no answer to that one. With one last smile Luke walked down the hallway and left her there, half-wishing he'd kissed her and half-glad he hadn't.

The next morning dawned hot and bright and Aurelie lay in bed, her mind tumbling over the events of yesterday—including Luke's non-kiss—and then suddenly freezing on the realisation of what today was.

Today they travelled to Singapore, and she was giving another concert for the store opening tonight. Swallowing hard, she drew her knees up to her chest and hugged them tight. Somehow she didn't think her fans in Singapore wanted to hear her new song any more than the ones in the Philippines had. Which left her…where?

She avoided the question as she got dressed and ate breakfast, meeting Luke down in the lobby at nine, as they'd agreed earlier. They were taking his private jet to Singapore, and from there going on to the Fullerton Bay Hotel on Marina Bay. They'd check in and go directly to Bryant's.

By the time she'd boarded Luke's jet Aurelie could no longer ignore the fluttering nerves that were threatening to take her over. She glanced at Luke sitting across from her, a sheaf of papers on his lap, his thumb and forefinger bracing his temple. He looked so serious and stern, and yet a lock of unruly dark hair had fallen across his forehead and Aurelie longed to brush it away, to savour its softness under her fingers. She'd been wanting to touch him more and more. Luke was awakening a desire in her she hadn't thought she possessed, and all by *not* touching her.

Yet what would happen when he did?

He glanced up as if aware of her gaze, smiled ruefully. 'You're nervous.'

For a stunned second she thought he'd guessed the nature of her thoughts, then realised with some relief that he was talking about the concert. 'Yes, I am.'

'You'll be fine.'

'You don't know that.'

'True.' He stretched his legs in front of him and put the papers back in a leather case. 'What did you do when you had all those big concerts? To warm up, I mean, and get rid of stage fright?'

Aurelie shrugged. 'Honestly, I don't know. I didn't really have stage fright.'

Luke arched an eyebrow. 'Never? Not even when you played to ten thousand people in Madison Square Garden?'

She laughed, but the sound trembled. 'No, because it was all an act. It wasn't really me, and so I didn't…I didn't really care.'

'And now it's you, and you care,' he finished softly, and she nodded, stared at her hands. Luke covered her hand with his own, twined his fingers through hers. He didn't say anything, didn't offer false promises about how they'd all love her, and she was glad. Silence could be honest too.

Yet her nervousness came back as they landed in Singapore and took a limo to the hotel. Aurelie barely registered the sumptuous suite with its view of the bay from one balcony and the city skyline from the other. All she could think about was how in just a few hours she would walk onto that stage and bare her soul.

Why had she written the damn song, anyway? And why had she ever played it for Luke?

'It doesn't matter what they think, you know,' Luke said. She turned and saw him standing in the doorway of her suite. 'It doesn't mean anything if they don't like it.'

'Doesn't it?'

'No. What matters is what you think of it. How you think of yourself.'

How she thought of herself? She couldn't answer that one. Being herself still felt so new, so strange. She still wasn't sure she even knew who she was.

'We'd better get going,' she said, and slipped past him out into the corridor.

Luke stayed with her as they toured the store, five floors on Orchard Road, and showed her the new café, the glittering beauty hall, the department for crafts and clothing all supplied by local artisans, clearly his brain child.

'Don't you have important people to see?' she asked, half-joking, as he escorted her to the dressing room where she was to get ready. Already people were milling about the marble lobby, waiting for the official opening.

'I'll check in with a few people now, and come back before you go on.'

Aurelie swallowed. Luke had done a good job of distracting her with the tour, but the fear—the *terror*—was now coming back in full force.

'Okay,' she said, still trying for insouciance and failing miserably. He put his hands, strong and comforting, on her shoulders and smiled down at her.

'Forget about the crowd,' he said quietly. 'Forget about me. Sing your song for yourself, Aurelie. You need that.'

Somehow, despite the tears now stinging her eyes, she dredged up a smile. 'I knew this was pity,' she joked, and he pressed his lips to her forehead.

'You can do it. I know you can.'

And then he was gone, and Aurelie sagged against the door, completely spent from that small encounter.

By the time Luke returned half an hour later she was ready—or at least as ready as she'd ever be. She wore a sundress this time, in a soft, cloud-coloured lavender, and cowboy boots. Her hair fell tousled to her shoulders, and she carried her guitar.

Luke smiled. 'You look fantastic.'

She smiled back, wobbly and watery. 'I feel like complete crap.'

'You can do it,' he said, and this time it wasn't an encouragement, it was a statement. He believed in her. More, perhaps, than she believed in herself.

A few minutes later she was miked and ready to go, and then she was on. She heard the hiss of indrawn breath as she walked onstage. Another surprised, perhaps even outraged, audience. She sat on the stool, stared into the faceless crowd. Swallowed. Her heart hammered so hard it hurt, and she felt a blind panic overwhelm her like a fog. She couldn't do this.

Then she felt Luke's presence on the side of the stage, just a few feet away. Strange, impossible even, to feel someone when he didn't move or speak, yet she did. He felt warm, and his warmth melted away the fog. She glanced sideways, saw his steady gaze, his smile. She took a breath. Blinked. And started to play.

Distantly she heard the rippled murmur of confusion as she began to play a song they didn't recognise. Her song. But then the song took over and she knew it didn't matter what anyone in the audience thought. Luke had been right; she wasn't doing this for them. She wasn't doing it just for herself, either.

She was doing it for him. Because he was the one person who had believed in her, more than she'd been able to believe in herself. Already he'd given her back her soul; he'd shown her how to reclaim it. She played the song for him, for her, for *them*.

And when it was over and the last note faded away, you could have heard a pin drop on the marble floor of the lobby. You could have heard the tiniest sigh, because no one did anything. No one clapped.

They didn't, Aurelie knew numbly, know *what* to do with her. How to react.

Then, from the side of the stage, she heard the sound of someone clapping. Loudly. *Luke.* And the sound of his clapping was like the trigger to an avalanche, and suddenly everyone was clapping. Aurelie sat there, her guitar held loosely in one hand, blinking in the bright lights and smiling like crazy. And crying too, at least she was as she walked offstage and straight into Luke's arms.

He enveloped her in a tight hug, his lips against her hair. 'You did it. I knew you could.'

She tried to speak, but there was too much emotion lodged in a hot lump in her throat, too many tears in her eyes. So she did what she wanted to do, what she needed to do. She kissed him.

This wasn't a tentative brush of her lips against his. She kissed him with all the passion and hope, the gratitude and joy that she felt. She dropped her guitar and wrapped her arms around him, and Luke took her kiss and made it his own, kissing her back with all he felt too.

It was, Aurelie thought dazedly, the most wonderful kiss.

The rest of the evening passed in a happy blur. Luke kept her by his side, introducing her to various officials and dignitaries, and for once in her life Aurelie didn't feel like the pop star performing for another sceptical crowd. No, with Luke next to her, she simply felt like herself. A woman whose hand was being held by a handsome and amazing man.

She was, Aurelie thought distantly, halfway to falling in love with him. It didn't seem possible after such a short time, and yet she felt the truth of it inside her, like a flame that had ignited to life. She never wanted it to go out.

And yet what *did* she want? The memory of that passionate kiss by the side of the stage had seared itself into her senses, but she still felt her insides jangle with nerves at the thought of what else could happen. What she wanted to happen…and yet was afraid of, both at the same time.

Despite her wonder and worry about what might happen later, she still enjoyed every minute of the evening spent by Luke's side. A dinner for the VIP guests had been arranged in the conservatory on top of the store, with the lights of Singapore stretched out in a twinkling map on three sides, and the bay with its bobbing yachts and sailing boats on the other. A silver sickle moon hung above them, and she felt the warm pressure of Luke's hand on the small of her back.

'Are you having a good time?'

'Very.' She turned to smile at him. 'You've done an amazing job with all these openings. I've heard a lot of great things about the new design of the store.'

'I've heard a lot of great things about your new song.'

She let out a little laugh. 'If you hadn't started clapping, I'm not sure anyone would have.'

'They would have. They just needed a little nudge.'

'Maybe next time you should hold up cue cards. Flash "Clap" in big letters as soon as I finish.'

'Next time they'll know. There were a lot of media people out there in the audience tonight. Word will get around.'

She drew a deep breath and let it out rather shakily. 'That's a scary thought.'

'Is it?'

'I don't know what the response will be.'

'Does it matter?'

She stared at him, surprised, until she realised it *didn't* matter. She hadn't written or performed the song to impress people or even make them change their minds about her. She didn't even want a comeback. She wanted…this.

Acceptance and understanding of who she was, not by a faceless crowd or the world at large, but by Luke—and by herself. And somehow he'd known that even before she had.

'Come on,' he said, 'I have some people I want you to meet.' And with his hand still on her back he guided her through the room.

Luke watched Aurelie chat and laugh with the CEO of the Orchard Bank of Singapore and felt something inside him swell. He loved her like this, natural and friendly and free. He loved *her*.

The thought, sliding so easily into his mind, made him still even as he attempted to keep involved in the conversation. He was trying to negotiate a new deal with a local clothes retailer to design exclusively for Bryant's. It would be an important agreement, and he couldn't afford to insult the CEO across from him.

And yet…he loved her? After just a few short days? When he still couldn't really say he knew her, not the way he'd known the three women with whom he'd had significant relationships. They'd dated for years, had known each other's peeves and preferences, had run their relationship like a well-oiled machine. And yet now he felt he could barely remember their faces. Had he loved them? Not like this, maybe not at all. He'd been emotionally engaged, certainly, although it hadn't hurt that much when they'd mutually agreed to end it.

But this? Her? It felt completely different. Completely overwhelming and intoxicating and scary. Was that love? Did he want it, if it was?

Did he have a choice?

And could she love him, when there were things he hadn't told her? Failures and weaknesses he hadn't breathed a word about? His insides clenched at the thought. She'd been slowly and deliberately baring herself—her soul, her secrets—while he'd kept his firmly locked away.

Could love exist with that kind of imbalance?

'Mr Bryant?'

Too late Luke realised he hadn't heard a word the man in front of him had said. He swallowed, tried to smile.

'I'm sorry?'

Several hours later Luke found Aurelie laughing with the wife of a foreign diplomat and placed a proprietorial hand on the small of her back. He liked being able to touch her in this small way, even if the ways he really wanted to touch her—had been dreaming of touching her—were still off-limits. He'd told her he wouldn't touch her until she wanted him to, until she was certain, and he knew she wasn't yet. He saw the shadows in her eyes even when she was smiling.

'I'm sorry to steal Aurelie away from you,' he told the woman, 'but we have a full day tomorrow and she needs her rest.' He smiled to take any sting from the words, and the woman nodded graciously. 'Been having a nice time?' he asked Aurelie as they headed down to the limo he had waiting.

'Amazing, actually. I thought it would be completely boring, but it wasn't.'

'That's refreshingly honest.'

She laughed, the sound unrestrained, natural. 'Sorry, I didn't mean to be insulting. It's just I've gone to so many parties and receptions and things and it's always been so exhausting.'

'Another performance.'

'Exactly. But it wasn't tonight. I was just able to be myself.' She shook her head slowly. 'I never thought that playing my song would give me anything but a kind of vindication that I could be something other than a pop star, but it has. It's made me feel like I can be myself...anywhere. With anyone.' She paused before adding softly, 'With you.'

She gazed up at him with those wide stormy-sea eyes and Luke felt that insistent flare of lust. He wanted her so badly. His palms itched with the need to slide down the satiny skin of her shoulders, fasten on her hips. Draw her to him and taste her sweetness.

She must have seen something of that in his face because her tongue darted out to moisten her lips and she took a hesitant step closer to him. 'Luke—'

He didn't know what he might have done then, if he would have taken her in his arms just as he'd imagined and wanted, but then the doors pinged open and a crowd of guests moved aside to let them pass. Luke let out a shaky breath and led Aurelie towards the limo.

They didn't speak in the intimate darkness of the car, but he felt the tension coiling between and around them. Felt her thigh press against his own when the limo turned a curve, and the length of his leg felt as if it had been dusted with a shower of sparks. He heard, as if amplified, every draw and sigh of her breath, the thud of his own heart.

He hadn't felt this overwhelmed by desire since he'd been

about eighteen. He let out another audible, shaky breath and stared blindly out of the window.

They remained silent as the limo pulled in front of the hotel, and then in the lift up to their separate suites on the same floor. Luke took out his keycard; it was slick in his hand. His mouth had dried but he forced himself to speak. To sound as if he were thinking of anything other than hauling Aurelie into his arms and losing himself deep inside her.

'So. Another big day tomorrow.'

'Is it? What's the schedule exactly?'

Was he imagining that she sounded just a little breathless? Her cheeks were flushed, her eyes bright. She tucked a strand of hair behind her ear, and Luke's gaze was irresistibly drawn to the movement, the curve of her ear and the elegant line of her neck.

He swallowed. 'We fly to Hong Kong, spend a day touring the city with some officials and then have the opening on the following day, along with a reception. Then two days' rest and on to Tokyo.'

'Right.' She glanced away, and the lift doors swooshed open. Luke walked down the corridor, conscious, so conscious, of Aurelie by his side. The whisper of her dress against her bare legs, the citrusy scent of her, the way each breath she took made her chest rise and fall.

She stopped in front of the door to her suite, and he stopped too. She waited, her hand on the door, her eyes wide. Expectant. But he'd promised himself—and her—that he wouldn't touch her until she asked. Until no uncertainty remained.

Standing there, he knew that time had not yet come. Unfortunately for him.

'Goodnight, Aurelie.' He cupped her cheek, just as he had the night before, because despite all his promises he couldn't resist touching her, just a little. Aurelie closed her eyes. Waited. It would be so easy to brush his lips against hers, to deepen the kiss he knew she wanted. But it was too soon, and he'd still seen the shadows in her eyes.

With a supreme act of will he dropped his hand from her face. He smiled—at least he thought he did—and walked down the hall towards his own lonely suite of rooms.

Aurelie stepped inside her empty suite and leaned against the door, her eyes closed.

Damn.

Why hadn't he kissed her? He'd wanted to, she knew that. She'd wanted him to, had willed him to close that small space between them, but instead he'd pulled away.

Maybe you didn't know what you wanted. And until you do, completely, I'm not going to touch you.

His words from yesterday reverberated through her, made her think. Wonder. Was he waiting for her to take the lead? To say she had no more uncertainty, no more fear?

Did she?

No. She was still afraid. She'd been telling Luke the truth when she said she'd never enjoyed sex. If she'd been totally honest, she would have told him she dreaded it. Hated it, and yet used it because at least then she had some control.

And now? She wanted sex—sex with Luke—to be something different. Something more. And that terrified her more than another bout of unenjoyable coupling.

She opened her eyes, paced the room, her mind racing. She wanted this. She wanted Luke. And, just like with her song, with the trust, with the intimacy, she knew she needed to push past the fear. For her sake as much as Luke's.

So…what did that mean, exactly? Right here, right now? She ran her now-damp palms down the sides of her dress.

Brushed her teeth and hair, applied a little perfume. And then before she could overthink it and start to get really nervous, she went in search of Luke.

CHAPTER NINE

LUKE YANKED OPEN his laptop and stared at the spreadsheet he'd left up on the screen. Work was as good an antidote as any to sexual frustration. He didn't have any better ideas, at any rate.

Sighing, he raked his hands through his hair, loosened his tie and stared hard at the screen.

Five minutes later a knock sounded on the door of his suite.

Luke tensed. He wasn't expecting anyone, and his staff would call or text him before disturbing him in his private quarters. So would anyone from the hotel. Another knock, soft, timid. He knew who it was.

'Hello, Aurelie.' He stood in front of the doorway, drinking her in even though he'd seen her just a few minutes ago. Her hair looked even more tousled, her lips soft and full. She'd sunk her teeth into the lower one and he could see the faint bite marks.

'May I come in?'

It reminded him, poignantly, of when he'd first come to her house in Vermont. How he'd asked, how she'd been so reluctant to let him in.

As reluctant as he was now, because he knew how weak he was when it came to this woman. 'All right.' He stepped aside, felt her dress whisper across him as she passed by.

'Do you need something?' he asked as he closed the door. He heard how formal and stiff he sounded, and he could tell she did too.

Her mouth quirked upwards and she took a deep breath. 'Yes. You.'

God help him. Her direct look, eyes wide, lips parted, had pure lust racing right through him. He clenched his fists, unclenched them. Breathed deep. 'I don't think this is a good idea, Aurelie.'

'Funny, I think you've said that before.'

'I know. And it wasn't a good idea then, either.' Hurt flashed across her face and she glanced away. 'It's too soon,' Luke said quietly. 'This is too important to rush things.'

She took a step towards him. 'Maybe it's too important to hold back.'

He shook his head. 'I don't think you're ready.'

'Shouldn't I be the judge of that?'

'Yes, but—' He hesitated. Wondered just why he was fighting this so much. Then he remembered the look on her face when he'd rolled off her before, as if she'd been cast in stone. He'd felt…he'd felt almost like a rapist. Sighing, he raked a hand through his hair and sank onto the sofa. 'Why don't you sit down?'

Gingerly she sat across from him. He thought of how he'd first met her, the cold cynicism in her eyes, the outrageous smile, the constant innuendo. She was so different now, so real and beautiful and vulnerable. He was so afraid of hurting her. Of failing her.

It was a fear, he acknowledged bleakly, that had dogged him for most of his life. Twenty-five years, to be precise, since he'd battered helpless fists against a locked door, begged his mother to let him in. Tried to save her…and failed.

This is your fault, Luke.

He blinked, forced the memory away. He hardly ever

thought of it now, had schooled himself not to. Yet Aurelie's fragile vulnerability brought it all rushing back, made him agonisingly aware of his own responsibility—and weakness.

'It's not as if I'm a virgin,' she said, clearly trying to sound light and playful and not quite achieving it. 'Even if you're acting as if I am.'

'In some ways you are,' Luke answered bluntly. 'If you've never enjoyed sex—'

'I'm what? An enjoyment virgin?' Her eyebrows rose, and he saw a faint remnant of the old mockery there.

'An emotional one, perhaps.'

She sighed. 'Semantics again.'

'I don't know what sex has been to you in the past, but it's not anything I want it to be with me.'

A blush touched her cheeks. 'I know that. I want it to be different.'

'How?'

She swallowed. 'Maybe you should tell me what it's been to you in the past.'

Now he swallowed. Looked away. He was so not used to these kinds of conversations. Honesty and emotional nakedness were two totally different things. 'Well, I suppose it's been an expression of affection.' *Coward.* 'Of...of love.'

They stared at each other, the silence taut with unspoken words, feelings too new and fragile to articulate. 'Did you love the women you've been with before?' Aurelie asked in a low voice.

'I suppose I thought I did. But honestly, I'm not sure.' He raked a hand through his hair. 'It didn't feel like this.'

This. Whatever was between them, whatever they were building. Luke didn't know how strong it was, whether a single breath would knock it all down.

'That's what I want,' Aurelie finally managed, her voice no more than a husky whisper. 'I know we've only known each other a short while and I'm not saying—' She cleared her throat. 'I'm not trying to, you know, jump the gun.'

His mouth twisted wryly. 'Aren't you?'

'Well, not the emotional gun. Physically, maybe.'

He shook his head slowly. 'They go together, Aurelie. That's the only kind of sex I want with you.'

He saw the fear flash in her eyes but she didn't look away. 'That's what I want, Luke. That's what I want with you.'

And he wanted to believe her. Yet still he hesitated; they'd only known each other, really, for a handful of days. Intense days, yes, amazing days. But still just days.

'Please,' she whispered, her voice low and smoky, and he felt his resistance start to crumble. Not that there had really been much to begin with. He was honest enough—hell, yes, he had to be—to know that any resistance he'd given had been token, merely a show. He wanted this too.

'Anything that happens between us,' he said, his tone turning almost severe, 'happens at a pace I control.'

She stilled for just a second, then gave him a small smile. 'Yes, boss.'

'And if I think it isn't…it isn't working, then we stop. *I* stop. Got that?'

'Got it.'

Hell. He hadn't exactly set the mood, had he? Yet he wanted her to know he wasn't going to rush things, take advantage. In this crucial moment, he wanted her to trust him. He wanted to trust himself.

He swallowed, felt her gaze, wide-eyed and expectant, on him. He could not think of a single thing to say.

A tiny smile hovered around Aurelie's mouth and her eyes lightened with mischief. 'So what now?'

'Hell if I know.'

And then she laughed, a joyous bubble of sound, and he

laughed too, and he felt them both relax. Maybe it would be okay after all. Maybe it would even be wonderful.

He stood up, held his hand out to her. She took it instantly, instinctively, trusting him already. 'Come on.'

He led her to the bedroom in the back of the suite, two walls of windows overlooking the inky surface of Marina Bay. Aurelie only had eyes for the bed. It was big, wide and piled with pillows in different shades of blue silk. She turned to him and licked her lips, a question in her eyes.

'Let's just relax.' He kicked off his shoes, took off his tie and stretched out on the bed. Aurelie sat on its edge and took off her boots. Gingerly she scooted up next to him, lay her head back on the pillows. Luke laughed softly. 'You look like you're on an examining table.'

'I feel a bit like that too.'

'We're not rushing this, you know.'

'I almost wish you would.'

'Oh?' He arched an eyebrow. 'You think you'd enjoy that?'

Now she laughed, the soft sound trembling on the air. 'Probably not.'

Gently he traced the winged arches of her eyebrows, the curve of her cheek. Her eyes fluttered closed and he let himself explore the graceful contours of her face with his fingertips: the straight line of her nose, the fullness of her lips. 'Tell me,' he asked after a moment, 'what your favourite room is in your house in Vermont.'

'What?' Her eyes opened and she stared at him in surprise. Luke smiled and gently closed them again with his fingertips.

'Your favourite room,' he repeated and continued to stroke her face with whisper-light touches. He felt her relax, just a little.

'The kitchen, I suppose. I always remember my grandmother there.'

'She liked to bake?'

'Yes—'

'And you helped her that summer?'

Her eyes opened again, clear with astonishment. 'Yes—' Gently he nudged them closed once more. She relaxed back into the pillows again. 'I always liked helping her with things,' she said after a moment. 'I suppose because she always liked me to help.'

'You must miss her,' Luke said quietly, and she gave a little nod.

'You must miss your mother,' she said, her voice hardly more than a whisper, and for a second his fingers stilled on her face. He hadn't expected her to say *that*. She opened her eyes, gave him a small smile. 'This honesty thing? You told me it went both ways.'

'Yes.' But he really didn't want to talk about his mother.

'Do you miss her?'

'Yes.' He swallowed, felt his throat thicken. 'Every day.' Gently he traced the outline of her parted lips with his fingers and then slowly, deliberately, dropped his finger to her chin. Rested it there for a moment. 'You know, the first time I met you I knew the truth of you from your chin.'

'My chin?'

'It quivers when you're upset.'

She laughed softly. 'No one's ever told me that before.'

'Maybe no one's ever noticed.' He lowered his head and pressed a kiss to the point of her chin. He felt her still, hold her breath. *Wait.* He lifted his head and smiled. 'I like it.'

'I'm glad.'

He touched her chin once more with his fingertip, and then trailed it slowly down the curve of her neck, rested it in the sweet little hollow of her throat. Stroked. He heard her breath hitch and she shifted on the bed. Luke felt the impatient stirring of his own desire. He'd told her they'd go slowly, and he meant it. Even if it was a rather painful process for him. 'Your skin is so soft. I thought that the first time I met you too.'

'You didn't.'

'I did. I was attracted to you from the moment you opened your eyes. Why do you think I was so ticked off?'

She let out a shuddery little laugh as he continued to stroke that little hollow. 'Because I was passed out and running late, I thought.'

'That was just my cover.' He let his finger trace a gentle line from the hollow of her throat down to the vee between her breasts. And he rested it there, the sides of her breasts softly brushing his finger, and waited.

Her cheeks were faintly flushed now, and her eyes had fluttered closed. He heard her breath rise and fall with a slight shudder and he felt a deep surge of satisfaction. She wanted this. She wanted him. He trailed his finger back up to that hollow, and she opened her eyes.

'This is going to take forever.'

He laughed softly. 'Not forever, I hope. That would kill me.' He let his finger trail back down, brushed the soft sides of her breasts this time, and felt her shiver. 'But long enough.' He pressed his lips to the hollow of her throat and then he slid his palm down to cup the soft fullness of her breast. She tensed for a second and then relaxed into the caress with a soft sigh.

Luke felt a powerful surge of protectiveness. He wanted to do this right. But it was killing him to go so slowly, to take the time he knew she needed. He flicked his thumb over the peak of her nipple and heard her indrawn breath, then another sigh. He smiled and moved his hand lower, onto the taut muscles of her tummy.

She opened her eyes, gazed up at him. 'You're being incredibly patient.'

'It's worth it.'

'You don't know that.'

'I know.' He slid his hand lower, down to her bare knee, and rested it there. Watched her eyes widen in expectation, maybe alarm. He stroked the back of her knee, down to the slender bones of her ankle, and then back up again. A little further up, so his fingers brushed the tender, silky skin of her inner thigh and then down again to the safety of that knee.

She let out a little laugh. 'You're torturing me.'

'Am I?' With his other hand he touched her cheek, the fullness of her lower lip, her chin, the hollow of her throat. Saw her eyes go hazy and dark with desire. She reached her hands up and tangled them in his hair, drew him closer.

'Kiss me,' she commanded, her voice husky, and Luke obliged.

He brushed his lips across her once, twice, and then went deep, tasting her as she tasted him. His hand tightened instinctively on her knee, slid upwards. She parted her legs and he felt her hands go to the buttons of his shirt.

'Too many clothes,' she mumbled against his mouth, and in a couple of quick shrugs—and a few buttons popping—he was free of his shirt, the garment tossed to the floor.

'How about your dress?'

She swallowed, nodded, and he slid the skinny straps from her shoulders. One quick, sinuous tug on the zip on the back and she shimmied out of the dress, kicking it away from her ankles.

Luke gazed at her. He'd seen her in her underwear before, of course, but he still loved to look at her. He let his gaze travel back up to her face, those wide, stormy eyes. 'Okay?' he asked quietly, and she nodded.

Still he waited. She nodded towards his trousers. 'Maybe you should deal with those.'

'Maybe you should.'

She arched her eyebrows, then smiled and nodded. Luke bit down on a groan as her fingers brushed his arousal. She fumbled a bit with the belt and zip, which made it all the more of an exquisite torture. Then she slid his trousers off his hips, and he kicked them the rest of the way. All they were wearing was their underwear, and it felt like way too much clothing to him. He smoothed his hand from her shoulder to her hip, revelling in the feel of her satiny skin. She shivered under his touch and he moved his hand upwards again, cupped her breast and smiled as she arched into his hand.

He kissed her again, deeply, and felt her respond, her arms coming around him, one leg twining with his. He moved his hand lower, across her tummy to the juncture of her thighs. Waited there, feeling her warmth, until she parted her legs and he slipped his fingers inside her underwear, felt her tense and then will herself to relax, arching her hips upwards as his fingers explored and teased her.

He felt his control slipping a notch as her own hand skimmed his erection and their tongues tangled, heard her breathing hitch—or was it his? He was so, so ready for this, and she *felt* ready—

He pressed another kiss to her throat, willed his heart to stop racing. 'Okay?' he muttered against her neck, and felt her nod. He slid her underwear off, kicked off his own boxer shorts. And then he was poised between her thighs, aching with need for her, their bodies pressed slickly together, all of him anticipating and straining towards this—

He looked down and saw she'd gone still, actually *rigid*, with her eyes scrunched tightly shut.

Damn.

It took all, absolutely all of Luke's self-control to stop. He took a deep, shuddering breath and rolled off her onto his back. Stared at the ceiling and felt his heart wrench inside him when he heard Aurelie let out a tiny hiccup of a sob. *What had gone wrong?* And how had he let this happen—again?

'I'm sorry,' she finally whispered into the silence.

'No. Don't be.' He was still staring at the ceiling, still feeling that scalding rush of shame and guilt. He was also feeling incredibly, painfully aroused. 'Let me just take a shower,' he muttered and, rolling off the bed, he headed towards the bathroom.

Aurelie lay on the bed and listened to Luke turn on the shower. She blinked hard and tried not to cry. *What had gone wrong?*

She honestly didn't know. One second she'd been lost in Luke's little touches, aching for his deeper caress—and the next? She'd felt the heavy weight on top of her and his breath in her ear and suddenly, painfully been reminded of the first time with Pete.

Let me...

She blinked hard again, forced the memories back. She did not want to think of them now, to bring them into this moment, this bed.

Drawing a deep breath, she reached for her scattered clothes. She didn't even remember Luke unclasping her bra, but he must have done. It was lying on the floor. She dressed quickly, furtively, afraid Luke would come out of the bathroom—and then what? Was he angry? Frustrated, no doubt, in more ways than one. And knowing Luke—which she did now, she realised—he'd want answers. Answers she didn't want to give, because she knew they wouldn't reflect well on herself.

Sighing, she sat back down on the bed and waited.

A few minutes later Luke emerged from the bathroom, a towel around his hips. Aurelie swallowed dryly at the sight of his chest, broad, browned and shimmering with droplets of water. Just a few minutes ago she'd had the power to touch it at her leisure, had felt that hard, muscular body pressed against hers. Just the memory caused a pulse of desire low in her belly. *How* had it all gone wrong? Could memories really have that much power?

Luke reached for a T-shirt and dropped his towel, oblivious to his own nakedness. Aurelie was not. She swallowed again, felt her heart start to thud. He slipped on a pair of boxers and then sat on the edge of the bed. She tensed, waited.

He smiled wryly, his eyes dark, his hair damp and spiky. She wanted to comb it with her fingers, to feel its damp softness. She folded her hands together in her lap.

'I guess you realise we need to talk.' She nodded, and Luke sighed. 'I'm sorry for the way things happened.'

'Don't be.' It hurt to squeeze those two words out, for her throat had got absurdly tight. 'It's not your fault.'

'It's not yours, either.' She didn't answer, and Luke reached over and placed his hand over her tightly clasped ones, his thumb stroking her fingers. 'Tell me what happened to you, Aurelie.'

'Nothing happened.' She shook her head, impatient with the way he was making her a victim. She'd never wanted pity. She'd made all her choices willingly. She *had.*

'Why, then,' Luke asked evenly, 'did you freeze up at a rather crucial point? Everything was going well, wasn't it?'

She let out a little choked sound, half-laugh, half-sob. 'Very well.'

'And then?'

'I don't know. I just—' She moistened her lips, forced herself to continue. 'I just froze up, like you said. To be honest, you're the only one who's ever noticed.'

'Then you haven't had very considerate lovers.'

'No.'

Luke sighed and squeezed her hand. 'I appreciate that I

may not have earned enough of your trust to tell me what happened to you, because something did. Some experience has made you fear sex and, until I know what it is, I can't help you. And,' he added, a wry note entering his voice, 'I can't make love to you, which is a shame.'

Aurelie lifted her gaze to his. 'We could try again—'

'No.' Luke spoke with such flat finality that she recoiled. 'I don't think you realise,' he added more quietly, 'how it makes me feel to see you beneath me, looking like you're bracing yourself for some kind of torture.'

She blinked, felt the hot wetness of tears behind her lids. She hadn't thought of that. She'd only thought of herself, and how disappointing she must be to him. 'I'm sorry,' she whispered.

'I don't want your apologies. I just want your honesty. But I can wait.'

She sniffed. Loudly. 'So what now?'

'How about we go to sleep?'

Hope stirred inside her, a tiny, fragile bud emerging amidst the mire of desolation. 'Here? Together?'

'That's the idea.' And then, gently, perhaps even lovingly, he pulled her into his arms so her cheek rested against that wonderfully hard chest. She felt the reassuring thud of his heart and closed her eyes. 'I'm a patient man, Aurelie.'

She smiled against his chest, even though the tears still felt all too close. 'That's good to know.'

Yet as she snuggled against him beneath the covers, his arms securely around her, she wondered if she was the impatient one. She'd changed and grown so much over the last few days, but she wanted more. She wanted to be different in *every* way, and especially in this one. Yet with this—this crucial intimacy—she didn't know how to change, or even if she could.

CHAPTER TEN

MORNING SUNLIGHT SPILLED across the bed, created pools of warmth amidst the nest of covers. Aurelie rose on one elbow and stared down at the sleeping form of the man she loved.

Yes, loved. She'd been skirting around that obvious truth for days now, because it was too scary and even impossible to grasp. How could she love a man she'd known for such a short time? And why would she, when she knew what happened when you gave your heart away? You lost not just the heart you'd freely given, but your soul as well. Your very self.

She knew Luke was different. She knew it bone-deep, *soul*-deep, and yet that knowledge didn't stay the tattoo of fear beating through her blood. The memory of how absolutely wrecked she'd been when Pete had finally ended it, and how she'd realised she had nothing, *was* nothing but a shell, remained with her. Infected her with doubt.

She didn't doubt that Luke was different; she feared that she wasn't. Even now a sly, insidious voice mocked that she hadn't changed at all, not in the way that mattered most. She'd give herself to him, body and heart and soul, and he would take it and use it and there would be nothing left. She'd be nothing.

And yet, despite that consuming fear, she still felt that baby's breath of hope, and Luke's steady presence, his arms cradling her all night long, had fanned it into something strong and good.

She wanted to take a chance again. With Luke, and with herself.

He opened his eyes.

'Good morning.' His voice was low and husky, and its warmth flooded through her. She smiled.

'Good morning.'

He shifted so she was cradled once more by his arm, and she rested her head on his shoulder, breathed in the warm, woodsy scent of him. Idly he ran a few strands of hair through his fingers. 'Sleep well?'

'Better than I can ever remember.'

He pulled her just a little bit closer, that primal part of him clearly satisfied. 'Good.'

Aurelie took a breath. And another, because this was hard. *So* hard, and as she took another breath she knew she was already starting to hyperventilate. She let it out slowly, a long, breathy sigh, and Luke's hand stilled on her hair. He was waiting.

'I want to tell you some things,' she began, and deliberately he began stroking her hair again, his fingers sifting through the strands.

'Okay.'

'I think I'm ready to…to do that.' He didn't answer, just kept stroking, and Aurelie closed her eyes. 'Not that it's that big a story. I mean, if you're expecting me to tell you something horrible to explain…well, to explain my behaviour, it wasn't like that.'

'You don't need to make any judgements, Aurelie. I won't.'

She felt her eyes scrunch shut, as if she could block out the truth she was about to tell. 'You might.'

'No.'

'I told you I haven't been a Girl Scout. Some of those tabloid stories—a lot of them—are true.' She spoke almost defiantly now, daring him to be shocked. Disgusted.

'I know that,' Luke answered steadily. He was so steady, even when she was doing her best to push him away and pull him closer both at the same time.

'I have to go back to the beginning.'

'I told you I am a patient man.'

'I know.' And now all there was left to do was begin. At the beginning. 'You remember I told you I was discovered at that karaoke night in Kansas?'

'Yes.'

'The man who discovered me was named Pete.'

'Pete Myers,' Luke clarified, and Aurelie realised that he'd heard of him, of *course* he'd heard of him. Pete was famous. He'd managed several major bands, had judged a couple of TV talent shows. He was practically a household name.

'Right,' she said, and continued. 'Well, Pete was amazing back then. He came up to me, told me he could make me a star. He took my mom and me to dinner, told us his whole plan. How I'd become Aurelie.'

'So he was the one behind your image.' Luke spoke tonelessly, but Aurelie still felt the censure. She stiffened.

'I went along with it. Innocent siren, those were his words.'

'You were only fifteen.'

'Almost sixteen. And I thought it all sounded incredibly cool.' She sighed, hating that already she was having to explain, to justify. Luke's arm tightened around her.

'I'm sorry. Continue.'

'Those first few months were a whirlwind. Pete took us all over, to LA, New York, Nashville. I met with agents and songwriters and publicity people and, before I knew what was happening, I was recording and releasing a single, and it was huge. I felt like I was at the centre of a storm.'

'What about your mother?'

'She disappeared a couple of months after Pete discovered me. I think she realised people didn't really want her around, that she was just getting in the way. When she left, Pete offered to have me stay with him. I was still a minor, and he had to make some kind of legal guardian arrangement with my grandmother—' She stopped then, because her throat had become so tight. That had been the last time she'd seen her grandmother alive. She'd given her the guitar, begged her to stay the same. And she hadn't.

'Anyway,' she continued, trying desperately for briskness, 'Pete was great about it all. He gave me my own floor in his house, treated me like—' the word stuck in her throat '—a daughter. At least, he felt like a father to me. The dad I'd never had. He gave me a lot of good advice in the early days, how not to take any of the criticism to heart, how to stay sane amidst all the craziness. He even remembered my birthday—he got me a cake for my seventeenth.'

'A paragon,' Luke said flatly, and she squirmed in his arms to face him.

'I told you not to make judgements.'

'I'm not. I'm just wondering where this is going.'

'I'll tell you.' She took another breath, let it out slowly. 'I'd been living with Pete for a little over a year. He'd seen me through some tough times—my grandmother dying, being diagnosed with diabetes. He was the one who found me, you know. I'd passed out in the bathroom, and he took me to ER. Stayed with me the whole time, made sure I got the proper treatment and counselling once I was diagnosed.' She felt Luke's tension; his shoulder was iron-hard under her cheek. 'I'm telling you all this just to…to explain the relationship. How close we were.'

'I get it.' His tone was even, expressionless, and yet Aurelie sensed the darkness underneath. And she hadn't really told him anything yet.

'So fast forward to my eighteenth birthday. He took me out to dinner at The Ivy, told me how happy he was that I'd made it, how much he cared about me.' She paused, tried to choose her words carefully. She needed the right ones. 'I look back on that as one of the happiest nights of my life.' Before it had all changed.

She fell silent, the only sound in the bedroom the draw and sigh of their breathing. 'And then?' Luke asked eventually. 'What happened?'

'Pete took me home. I went to bed. I was just changing into my pyjamas when he…he came into the room.' He hadn't, she remembered now, asked to come in. Not like Luke. She still remembered that ripple of shocked confusion at seeing Pete standing in the doorway. Staring at her.

'And?' Luke asked very quietly. Aurelie realised she'd stopped speaking. She was just remembering, and she hated it.

'He told me he loved me. He'd always loved me, and then he…he kissed me.'

'Not,' Luke said quietly, 'like a dad.'

'No. Not like a dad.' She still remembered the shocking feel of his mouth on hers, wet and insistent. The way his hands had roved over her body, with a kind of tentative urgency. He'd been crying a little bit, and he kept begging her. *Let me,* he had whispered over and over again, and she had.

'What did you do?' Luke asked. He was still stroking her hair, still holding her. Aurelie blinked back the memories.

'I let him.'

'Let him?'

'He kept saying that. *Let me.* And I did, because…well, because I didn't want to lose him. He was the most important person in my life at that point, the only person in my life. And, looking back, I can see how I got it wrong. He never wanted to be my dad. I was the one who wanted that.'

Luke's hands had stilled. 'So he…he kissed you?'

'We had sex,' Aurelie said flatly. 'That night. It was, if you can believe it, my first time. That whole innocent siren thing? It was pretty much true.'

Luke swallowed, said nothing. 'I didn't enjoy it,' she continued. She felt weirdly emotionless now, as if none of it mattered. 'I hated it. It felt…well, it felt gross, to be honest. But I knew it was what he wanted and so I made myself want it too.'

'And what happened then? After?'

She shrugged. 'We started dating.'

'Dating?'

'A relationship. Whatever. I was already living with him, so—'

'Are you telling me,' Luke asked, and his voice shook slightly, 'that Pete Myers was your serious relationship? The one that lasted three years?'

'Yes—'

'God, Aurelie.' He sank back onto the pillows and when she risked a look at his face she saw he looked shocked. Winded, as if she'd just punched him. Maybe she had.

'I thought you kind of knew where this was going.'

'Well, when you started talking about Myers, I figured he'd…he'd taken advantage of you somehow. But you'd said you weren't abused or raped—'

'I wasn't.' She stared at him in surprise. 'I told you, he asked.' *Let me.* 'And I said yes.'

Luke stared at her. He still looked dazed. 'You remember when we talked about semantics?'

'Yes—'

'Yeah. That.'

She shook her head. 'I wasn't a victim. If I'd told him to leave, he would have.'

'You think so?'

'I know it. Luke, you weren't there. You didn't see how… how pathetic he looked. I felt sorry for him.' Almost.

'Yeah, I'm sure he could look pathetic when he wanted to. He's also one of the richest, most powerful men in the music world, Aurelie. You don't think he might have been taking advantage of you?'

'Maybe,' she allowed, 'but I allowed it to happen.'

'For three years.'

'It was a *relationship*.' She didn't like the tone Luke took, as if she'd been used. Abused. A victim.

'A secret relationship. I've never seen this mentioned in the press.'

'Pete didn't want the tabloids to trash us. He was being protective—'

'Very thoughtful of him.'

'Don't,' she said furiously. 'Don't make this about me being used by him. I was *not* a victim.'

Luke just gazed at her. 'Go on,' he finally said quietly. 'Tell me what happened.'

'When?'

'How did it end?'

'He ended it. He said it wasn't working, that I was too clingy.'

'Too clingy.'

'Yes. And I was, I can see that now. The fame had started to get to me, and I felt like Pete was the only person who knew who I really was. My mom was still out of the picture, my grandma was dead, and I'd never stayed in one place long enough to get to know anyone.'

'So,' Luke said slowly, 'he was all you had.'

'It felt that way. But he started losing interest and my

music started slipping, the media noticed, and when he finally ended it—' She took a breath, plunged. 'I went off the deep end.'

'You weren't,' Luke said, and she almost heard a sad smile in his voice, 'a Girl Scout.'

'No. I pretty much did what the press said I did. I drank, I did drugs, I partied hard and slept around, and my career tanked.' She swallowed, sniffed. 'So there you have it.'

Luke said nothing, and Aurelie felt condemnation in his silence. She'd done so many things she wasn't proud of, the first one being that she'd given in to Pete that first night. That she'd been so clingy and needy and starved of love, she'd taken what she could get. And then when he'd decided he didn't want her any more, she'd spun out of control because she'd felt so horribly empty.

And she was so afraid of that happening again.

'Which part of all that,' Luke finally asked, 'did you not want to tell me?'

She let out a wobbly laugh, surprised by the question. 'All of it.'

'But which part in particular?' He shifted so he was facing her, his gaze intent, his eyes blazing. 'The part at the end? About how you went off the deep end? How you partied and slept around and lost yourself?'

She squirmed under that gaze, those pointed, knowing questions. 'Yes, basically.' *Lost yourself.* That was exactly what had happened, yet even now she couldn't admit as much to Luke. Admit that she was afraid of it happening again, and worse this time. She'd finally found herself again, thanks to Luke. But what if she lost herself once more because she couldn't handle being in a relationship? Being hurt?

What if he grew tired of her like Pete had, like the whole *world* had?

'And what about sex?' he asked quietly. 'Enjoying it? Why do you think you don't?'

She swallowed, wished he didn't have to be quite so blunt. 'I suppose because of my experience with Pete. I was never attracted to him, and being with him like that for so long… it just killed that part of me.'

'And when I'm with you? And you freeze? Why do you think that is?'

'I don't know.' She felt herself getting angry again. She hated him asking so many terrible questions, stripping her so horribly bare. 'I suppose I remember that first time. It was awful, okay?' Tears sprang to her eyes and she turned her face away from him. '*Awful.* I couldn't breathe. He was so heavy. And it…hurt.' She gasped the last word out, tears pooling in her eyes. If she blinked they would fall, and she couldn't have that. If she let those first tears out, too many more would follow, and she was afraid she would never stop crying.

'What about with other men?' Luke asked quietly.

Aurelie sniffed, her face still averted, her voice clogged with all those mortifying tears. 'They were all pretty much the same. They only wanted one thing from me, and I knew that. I was a trophy. I got it, and I used it because—' She stopped, and Luke finished for her, his voice so soft and sad.

'Because it was better than being used.'

She said nothing. Words were beyond her. She wished she'd never told him, desperately wished she hadn't opened up this Pandora's box of tawdry memories. 'Don't judge me,' she finally whispered, a plea, and Luke shook his head.

'I'm not judging you. Not at all.'

He sounded so weary, so resigned, that Aurelie felt her spirits plummet, and they were already pretty low. He was disgusted by her. Of course he was. How could he not be, after all the things she'd told him? She'd known this would happen. She'd been expecting it. She slipped away from him, rolled out of bed and hunted for her dress.

'I should go back to my room.'

'Why?'

'We're going to Hong Kong today, right? I need to shower and get dressed.' She didn't look at him as she slipped her dress on, tugged on her boots. Her hair was a disaster, but all she needed to do was walk down the hall.

'We're not finished here, Aurelie.'

'I'm finished.'

'You're scared.'

Hell, yes. She glanced up at him, hands on her hips. 'Oh, you think so? Of what?'

'A lot of things, I suspect.'

Luke sounded so calm, so relaxed, and here she was feeling like a butterfly pinned to a board. Unable to protect or hide herself, just out there for his relentless examination. 'Well, I'm not scared,' she snapped. 'But I don't particularly like talking about all that, and since we have a full day I'd like to get on with it. That all right by you?' She spoke in a sneering drawl, the kind of voice she'd used so many times before. The kind of voice she hadn't used with Luke since they'd started on their second chance.

Well, so much for that.

'It's all right by me,' he said quietly and, without another word, Aurelie whirled around and stalked out of his bedroom.

Luke lay on the bed and stared at the ceiling, too dazed to do anything but try and process what Aurelie had told him. *Pete Myers.* A man who had to have been at least fifty when he'd first started with Aurelie. A man who had abused her affection, used her body and her trust. And Aurelie didn't see it that way.

She saw it as a *relationship*. Hell, no.

Sighing, he ran his hands through his hair, pressed his fists into his eyes. He had no idea what to do. He was still so afraid of failing her. Failing her like he had last night, when he'd gone about it completely wrong. He'd been trying to ease Aurelie into love-making gently, sweetly, but he'd been the one in control. Hell, he'd told her that before they even started. *Anything that happens between us, happens at a pace I control... Got that?*

He winced at the memory. He'd thought it would help her, to know they would go slowly, but now he saw how it must have accomplished the opposite. He'd been just another man controlling her, using her body. Luke swore aloud.

He saw now that Aurelie needed to feel in control. To *be* in control. That was, he suspected, why she insisted on believing Pete hadn't taken advantage of her, that it had been a willing, committed relationship—because then it was something she could control.

And last night, in an utterly misguided attempt to help her, he'd quite literally taken all the control away from her. Groaning aloud, Luke dropped his fists from his eyes and stared at the ceiling once more. It was time, he knew, for a third chance. Time to earn her trust once more.

By the time he'd showered and dressed, eaten and answered emails, he was near to running late. He'd knocked on the door of Aurelie's room but there had been no answer and he felt a flicker of foreboding. Was she trying to avoid him? Well, that could only last so long.

His mouth firming into a determined line, he headed downstairs.

Aurelie was waiting in the lobby, dressed in a mint-green shift dress, her hair tucked behind her ears, her arms folded. She was fidgeting and she didn't meet his gaze as he came towards her. Clearly now was not the time to have some kind of emotional discussion, and maybe he needed the time—the break—too.

'All ready?' he asked lightly, and she nodded tensely, her gaze fixed somewhere around his shoulder.

They didn't speak in the limo on the way to the airport, or as they boarded the jet that would take them to Hong Kong. Luke pulled out some papers, thinking to work, but then he decided he wasn't that patient after all.

'Aurelie.' She turned towards him, still not meeting his eyes. 'You're doing a pretty good job of avoiding me even though I'm right here.'

She lowered her head so her hair fell forward in front of her face. 'I don't know what to say to you.'

'Maybe you could tell me what you're thinking.'

'That.'

He sighed and slipped his papers back into a manila folder. 'What else?'

She shook her head, bit her lip. Luke just waited. 'I'm thinking I wish I hadn't told you everything I did this morning.'

'Why not?'

'Because…' she lifted her gaze to his, and he saw the storm in her eyes '…because you think of me differently now, and I can't stand that—'

'I wouldn't say differently.'

'What, then?'

'More sympathetically—'

She shook her head, the movement violent. 'I don't want your pity.'

'It's not pity to be able to understand you—'

'I am not some kind of psychological *specimen*—'

'I never said you were.' Luke felt his temper start to fray. He would *never* say the right thing. 'Aurelie, you're going to tank us right here and now if you keep fighting me like this. I'm just trying to make this *work*.'

She hunched her shoulders, her chin tucked low. 'Maybe it can't.'

'Is that what you want?' he asked evenly, and she didn't answer for a moment. Fear lurched inside him. Already he couldn't stand the thought of losing her.

'No,' she finally said, her voice so low he had to strain to hear her. She sighed and rested her head against the seat, her eyes closed. 'Look, I know I'm making a mess of this. But I told you in the beginning that I don't know how to let my guard down—'

'You've already let your guard down. Now you're just desperately trying to assemble it again.'

She let out a soft huff of laughter and lifted her wry, slate-blue gaze to his. 'That's not working, is it?'

'No. And I don't want it to work.' He didn't know what the future held, and he still felt that old fear, but he did know he wanted to keep trying. He hoped she did too.

She glanced away. 'I don't, either.' She nibbled her lip, and he thought about reaching out to touch her. Comfort her. He stayed where he was. The physical aspect of their relationship would be dealt with later. He hoped. 'I'm scared,' she said softly, still not looking at him. 'I'm so scared of losing myself again. Of losing control, of not being able to change.'

'Every relationship contains an element of loss of control, but that doesn't mean you have to lose yourself completely. A relationship should make you better, stronger. More of yourself rather than less.' He smiled wryly. 'Or so all the chat shows and women's magazines tell me.'

She arched her eyebrows. 'You watch chat shows and read women's magazines?'

'All the time.'

She laughed, and he smiled. Miraculously, it felt okay again. 'Sorry,' she said softly, and he shook his head.

'This isn't about sorry.'

'What is it about, then?'

'Trust. You're still learning to trust me. I'm still trying to earn it.'

'You have earned it, Luke.'

He didn't feel as if he had. He'd let her down too many times already. *You're always letting people down. The people that matter most.*

That sly inner voice mocked him, reminded him of his failures. The locked door, his mother's silence. His own. He was still living in the long shadow of that moment, and he hated it. So much of Aurelie's life had been defined by one man's selfish actions. Had his life been similarly defined? Destroyed?

Could he rebuild it again, now, with her?

'We land in an hour,' he said, trying to smile, and felt his heart lift and lighten when Aurelie smiled back.

Aurelie had never been to Hong Kong before, and even though she'd seen photos she wasn't prepared for the sheer scale of the city, the skyscrapers clustered so close together, right to the edge of Victoria Harbour, piercing the sky.

She still felt raw from the conversation with Luke on the plane. This honesty was a killer. And when she caught him looking at her with a kind of sorrowful compassion, she froze inside. Part of her ached for the understanding he offered, and yet another part scrambled away in self-protection. Did she really want to be understood, all the dark parts of herself brought to glaring light?

He knew the worst, at least in broad strokes. He knew that she'd gone into a relationship—an awful, unhealthy relationship—out of pathetic loneliness and fear, and he understood, if not in the tawdry particulars, how she'd reacted when it had ended. The many, many bad choices she'd made.

And he's still here.

The voice that whispered inside her wasn't sly or cynical for once. It was the still, small voice of hope, of truth. *He's still here.*

She'd told him he'd earned her trust, but she wasn't acting as if he had. She wasn't, Aurelie knew, acting as if she trusted him at all.

Could she act that way? Deliberately, a decision? Was change not so much a wishing or a hoped-for thing, but a choice? An act of will?

'You ready?' Luke called back to her and, nodding, Aurelie stepped from the plane.

The day passed in an exhausting blur of meetings with various important people, touring the city. As if from a distance, Aurelie took in the Peak, the Jade Market, the Giant Buddha. She chatted and smiled and laughed and listened, yet all the while she felt as if she were somewhere else, thinking something else.

Can I do this? Can I act differently with Luke, even when every part of me struggles to protect myself?

After a lengthy dinner with many speeches and toasts, they boarded a yacht for a pleasure cruise in the harbour. Aurelie watched Luke circulate through the guests, and realised with a pang that he looked more relaxed than when she'd seen him in New York or Manila. He looked happy.

Acting differently was a *choice*. An act of will. It had to be. Deliberately she walked across the deck to join him. He stopped his conversation to smile at her briefly, then resumed describing his plan to incorporate more local artists and artisans in the Hong Kong store. He spoke with authority, with a kind of restrained pride, that made Aurelie's heart swell.

She loved this man. She was terrified, but she loved him.

A few minutes later they'd been left alone, and Luke placed his hand on the small of her back as he guided her to the railing. 'Look.'

She looked towards the shore, and saw that the skyscrapers were shimmering with lights.

'It's the Symphony of Lights. It comes on every night at eight o'clock.'

'Amazing.' And it was amazing, to be standing here with this wonderful man, the air warm and sultry, the sky lighting up all around them. She turned to smile at him, felt the smile all the way through her soul. And Luke must have felt it too, must have seen it, because he drew her softly towards him and brushed his lips against hers. A promise. A promise Aurelie intended to keep.

They rode home from the party in a limo, their thighs brushing, the silence between them both comfortable and expectant. Aurelie followed Luke into the lift, up to the top floor where they had separate suites. She stopped at his door, and he looked at her, eyebrows raised.

Aurelie felt her heart beat hard, her mouth dry. She lifted her chin. 'I want to come in.'

Luke rested his keycard in the palm of his hand, gazed at her seriously. She stared steadily back. *This was a choice.* 'We don't have to rush things, Aurelie.'

'I'm not rushing things.'

He gazed evenly at her, assessing, understanding. Then he nodded. 'All right. But I have one condition.' He unlocked the door and opened it, and Aurelie followed him in, her heart thudding even harder now.

'And that is?' she asked when he hadn't said anything, just shed his jacket and loosened his tie.

Luke turned to her, his eyes glinting, everything about him sexy and rumpled and gorgeous. 'My condition,' he said, taking off his tie, 'is that we do this on your terms.'

CHAPTER ELEVEN

'WE...WHAT?' AURELIE blinked. '*My* terms?'

Luke nodded, his eyes still glinting, his mouth curving in a smile even though she could sense how serious he was. 'Yes. Your terms. I've been thinking a lot about what happened before and I realise I handled everything wrong—'

'Everything, Luke? I think that might be a slight exaggeration.'

'Slight,' he agreed wryly. 'But I was the one in control, wasn't I? I told you that from the beginning. I said I'd set the pace, and I'd call it off if I didn't think it was working.'

Warily she nodded, folded her arms. She wasn't sure where he was going with this. 'Your terms.'

'Yes, and they weren't the right ones.'

'Why not?'

'From what you've told me, and from what I know about you, control is kind of a big thing.'

She prickled, resisting any kind of analysis. 'You think?'

'I do.'

She let out a slow breath, forced herself to relax even though every instinct had her reaching for armour, for the defence of mockery. 'Well, who doesn't want to be in control, really?'

'No one, I suppose,' Luke agreed quietly, 'and especially not someone who had no choice about where to live or when to move or what school to go to. Or even, really, how famous she wanted to be.'

She felt that first, sudden sting of tears and shook her head. 'Don't.'

'Why not?'

'Because I can't stand being pitied, I told you that—'

'I know, and that's a kind of keeping control, isn't it? You keep insisting that everything was your choice because if it wasn't you're a victim and you can't stand that thought.'

No, she couldn't, and even though she'd never articulated it to herself, Luke had. Luke understood her—far too well. She managed a very shaky smile. 'These are so not my terms.'

'I know, Aurelie. I'm breaking my own rules here, but I need to say this.' He took a step closer to her. 'As soon as the clothes start coming off, you can call all the shots.'

She let out a wobbly laugh. 'Promise?'

'Cross my heart.' He took another step towards her, reached for her hands. 'What you had with Pete Myers was *not* a relationship.'

Her hands tensed underneath his. 'It felt like one.'

'No, it didn't. You have nothing to compare it with, so trust me on this, okay?'

Trust. It always came down to trust. She blinked, swallowed. Willed herself to keep her hands in his, not to pull away. For once. 'So what was it, then?'

'Abuse.'

'No.' Now she did pull her hands away from his. She turned away from him, wrapping her arms around herself as if she were cold. She was cold, but on the inside.

'How old was he when he first kissed you?'

'Why does the age difference even matter? Plenty of people—'

'Fifty?'

'Forty-nine,' she snapped. 'That doesn't *matter.*'

'It doesn't always matter,' Luke agreed quietly. 'But in this case, when you were young, impressionable, utterly dependent on him—he must have known you thought of him like a father, Aurelie. And he knew you had no one else in the world. He took advantage of you—'

'That doesn't make it *abuse.*'

'I won't argue about semantics. What I'm trying to say is you can't judge any other relationship by what happened with that man. It wasn't healthy or right. Whether you acknowledge it or not, he took all the control away from you, even if you think you let him. Your responses weren't normal because the situation wasn't normal or fair. At all.'

She didn't answer because she had no words. She realised, belatedly, she was shivering. Uncontrollably. She hated everything Luke was saying. She hated it because she knew, in a deep and dark part of herself, that he was right.

And she couldn't stand that thought. Couldn't bear to think so much of her life had been wasted, *used.* She'd been such a pathetic victim.

'I'm sorry,' Luke said softly. 'I'm sorry for what happened to you.'

She didn't answer. Words wouldn't come. She blinked hard and turned around. 'So my terms, right?'

Luke hesitated, his gaze sweeping over her. 'Do you really think this is a good—'

'My terms, you said—' she cut across him, her voice hard '—didn't you? So why are you still trying to take control?'

He stilled. 'I'm not.'

'No?' She took a step towards him, amazed at how angry she felt. Not at Luke, not at herself for once. Yet she still felt it, that hot tide washing over her, obliterating any rational thought. 'All right, then. Here are my terms. Strip.'

He blinked. 'Strip?'

She nodded, her jaw bunched. 'Strip, Luke.'

For a second he looked as if he was going to object. Refuse. Aurelie put her hands on her hips, her eyebrows raised in angry challenge. She could hear her breathing coming hard and fast.

'Okay,' he said quietly, and began to unbutton his shirt.

Aurelie felt a little shiver of disbelief. He was actually obeying her. *She was in control.* She watched, her eyes wide, as he finished unbuttoning his shirt, shrugging out of the expensivc cotton. She loved his chest. Loved the hard planes, the way that broad expanse narrowed to those slim hips.

'Your belt,' she snapped. 'Your trousers.'

His gaze steady on her, he undid his belt. Took off his trousers.

'Socks?' he asked, eyebrows raised, and she felt an almost hysterical laugh well up inside her. She nodded. Luke took off his socks. He only wore a pair of navy silk boxers. He waited, and so did she, because hell if she knew what she wanted now.

'Go lie down on the bed,' she said, and heard the waver in her voice. She wasn't sure about this any more. She'd started out angry and strong but now she just felt confused. Sad too, and dangerously close to tears.

She followed Luke into the bedroom and watched as he sat on the edge of the bed, swung his legs over. Lay down and waited, hands behind his head.

She let out a trembling laugh. 'You look a lot more relaxed than I would.'

'I am relaxed.'

'Really?' She sat on the edge of the bed.

'What do you want, Aurelie?' Luke asked quietly, and she knew, she knew that whatever she said she wanted, he would find a way to make it happen. He'd put himself completely in her hands, and she understood that that was what trust was.

Luke trusted her.

And she wanted to trust him.

'I want,' she said, her voice shaking, 'you to hold me. Just hold me.'

And he did, pulling her gently into his arms. She curved her body around his, craving his solid warmth. And as he stroked her hair she did the one thing she'd never, ever wanted to do.

She cried.

Sobbed, really, ugly, harsh sounds that clawed their way out of her chest and tore at her throat. She wrapped her arms around Luke and he held on tight as she sobbed out all the loneliness and pain and confusion she'd ever felt.

Just when she thought she might get a handle on it, she felt new sobs coming up from deep within her and after fifteen minutes or an hour—she had no idea which—she finally managed to wipe her blotchy face and laugh shakily.

'I'm a complete mess.'

'You're beautiful.'

She laughed again, the sound even shakier. 'You cannot mean that.'

'Don't you know by now I never lie?'

She tilted her head to look up at him and saw the truth shining in his eyes. 'How,' she whispered, 'did I ever deserve someone like you?'

'I could ask the same thing.'

She shook her head. 'I don't see how.'

'You're selling yourself short, Aurelie. You often do, you know.' Tenderly he wiped the damp strands of her hair away from her face, tucked them behind her ears. 'You make me laugh. You challenge and thrill me. You stun me with your talent and your courage. Of course I could ask the same question.'

She shook her head, still incredulous, and tenderly Luke

kissed her eyelids, her nose, and then her mouth. 'I do ask it,' he whispered against her lips and, without even thinking about it, just needing to, Aurelie kissed him back. Softly, yet with intent. With promise.

Luke hesitated, just for a second, but long enough so she whispered, 'My terms.'

His hands stilled on her shoulders. 'Which are?' he asked softly.

'I want to kiss you. And you've got to kiss me back.'

'Thosc are terms I can live with.' She felt him smile against her mouth and then she kissed him again, deeper this time, exploring him in a way she never had before, because she hadn't dared or dreamed of it.

Now she had the time, the desire and most of all the control to kiss him at leisure. In depth. She rolled him onto his back and propped herself up on her elbow, kissing every part of him that she wanted to: his lips, his eyes, the curve of his neck, the line of his jaw. His ear, his shoulder, the taut skin of his chest. She heard him groan softly and she felt a thrill of—no, not power. This wasn't even about power. It was about pleasure and trust and love.

His response made her own need flare deeper, and she kissed his mouth again, deeply, rolling on top of him. Luke placed his hands on her hips to steady her and as Aurelie pressed against him she felt that need flare again, white-hot, burning so brightly she couldn't think for a moment.

'Touch me,' she whispered. 'Touch me back.'

'Where?' Luke whispered, and she felt another thrill of pleasure just at the question.

She took his hand and slid it up along her side, placed it on her breast and closed her eyes. 'There.' And when Luke took that touch and made it his own, his fingers stroking her softness, she let out a shudder. 'And here.' She took his other hand and placed it on her tummy, dared to slide it lower, and another shudder ripped through her as his hands slid under her dress, edged her underwear aside. 'Yes…' She pressed against him as his fingers moved deeper, pleasure shooting like sparks through her whole body. There was a freedom in this, and a wonder. She felt a kind of amazed joy, that she could feel so good, that a man could make her feel so good. That Luke could.

'I want to take off my clothes,' she managed.

'With or without my help?'

She heard a smile in Luke's voice and smiled back. 'With.'

He tugged the zip down her back and she shrugged her shoulders so the dress slid off her. Luke managed the rest, and her bra and panties too. She was naked, and with one swift tug of his boxers he was naked too.

'There.' She spoke on a sigh of satisfaction and Luke smiled as he stretched out next to her.

'Now what would you like?'

She laughed, because it felt so amazing to be asked. 'Hmm…let me think.' She touched his cheek, his jaw, the smooth hardness of his chest. Slid her hand lower to the dip of his waist, and then slowly, wonderingly, wrapped her fingers around the length of his erection. 'More of the same, really,' she whispered, and on a groan Luke kissed her.

They didn't say much of anything any more; she didn't need to give instructions and he didn't need to ask permission. This was what sex was supposed to be, she thought hazily. *Making love.* Moving in silent and loving synchronicity, hands and mouths and bodies, all of it as one together.

And when he finally slid inside her, filling her right up, she felt a sense of completion and wholeness she'd never felt before. Never even known you could have.

Gently, still moving inside her, he wiped the tears that had sprung unbidden to her eyes, kissed her damp eyelids. Aurelie let out a wobbly laugh.

'I'm just so *happy*,' she choked, and Luke kissed her mouth.

'I know,' he said. 'I am too.'

Sunlight streamed through the bedroom windows, touched Aurelie's sleeping form with gold. Smiling, Luke rolled over on his side, smoothed her skin from her shoulder to hip with his hand. He loved the feel of her. Loved the taste of her too, the look of her, and most definitely the sound of her. He loved her, full stop.

It didn't scare him, now that he knew who she was. And who she wasn't. No, it thrilled him and made him incredibly thankful at the same time, because he was pretty sure she loved him too. He'd earned her trust. He'd won her love. He felt a sense of completion and wholeness that came not just from last night, but from finally, wondrously coming full circle after a lifetime of feeling only failure and regret. He'd made this right. He'd made *them* right.

Aurelie's eyes fluttered open and, still hazy with sleep, she smiled. Reached for him with such simple ease that Luke's heart sang. Who would ever have thought that it could be so easy between them? That it would be so wonderful?

'Good morning,' he murmured, and kissed her. She kissed him back.

A little—or perhaps a long—while later, they showered and dressed and ate breakfast out on the terrace overlooking Victoria Harbour.

'Look at this.' He'd been scanning the headlines on his tablet computer and now he handed it to Aurelie. She glanced at the article, her eyebrows rising at the headline: *Aurelie Returns, Better than Ever.*

'That was quick.'

He smiled. 'I knew they'd like the song.'

'That's just one article. There will be others.'

'Does that bother you?'

She handed back the tablet, a furrow between her eyes. 'It doesn't bother me, not the way it used to, when I felt defined by what people wrote or said about me.' She let out a slow breath, and he knew this kind of emotional intimacy was still new for her, still hard. 'It doesn't bother me because I have someone in my life who knows who I really am.' She offered him a tentative smile. 'I never had that before.'

Luke reached for her hand. 'I'm glad you have it now.'

'But I don't want a comeback. I don't want to be famous again.'

'You don't?'

She shook her head. 'Singing in public again was more for me than the audience. I wanted to…to vindicate myself, I suppose. But I don't want to be Aurelie again, not in any incarnation. I've had enough of fame to last several lifetimes.'

He twined his fingers with hers. 'And what if these concerts catapult you back into the spotlight?'

'The spotlight will move off me in a few weeks or months or maybe even days, when I refuse to give them what they want. More concerts, more tabloid-worthy moments. I'm done with all that.'

'You're sure?'

'Yes.' She glanced up at him, worry shadowing her eyes, darkening them to slate. 'Do you mind?'

'Mind? Why would I mind?'

She shrugged. 'I don't know. The fame thing, it's kind of big.'

'To be honest, I'd have a harder time following you around on a concert circuit, but I'd do it if that's what you wanted.'

'And what about what you want?'

'I've got everything I want.' He smiled and squeezed her hand. 'You sing this afternoon, and then we have two days until Tokyo. Let's go away somewhere, just the two of us.'

Her eyes widened, her mouth curving in anticipation. 'Where?'

'I'll surprise you.'

He chose an incredibly exclusive resort on a tiny island off the coast of Hong Kong, the kind of place reporters or paparazzi could never find. The kind of place where he could pamper Aurelie all he wanted and they could revel in each other, in long, lazy days on the beach and long, loving nights in their bed, or the hot tub, or even on the beach again. Everywhere.

The night before they were to leave for Tokyo they lay in bed, the sliding glass doors open to the beach, the ocean breeze rustling the gauzy curtains. Moonlight slid over the rumpled covers, their twined legs. Aurelie was silent, one slender hand resting on his bare chest, over the steady thud of his heart.

Luke brushed his lips against her hair. 'What are you thinking?' he asked quietly, because he sensed something from her that was thoughtful, maybe even sad.

'Just how I don't want this to end. I don't want to go back to real life.'

'I'm not sure I know what real life is any more.' He paused, thinking to say more, then decided not to. He hadn't told her he loved her yet, and she hadn't said it, either. He wasn't afraid of saying those three little words, but he wondered how Aurelie felt about hearing them. This was all still so new, and maybe even fragile. There would be time enough later to figure out how this—*them*—was going to work.

On the plane to Tokyo he reluctantly refocused on work. He hadn't given Bryant's or business a single thought in forty-eight hours, which had to be a record for him. Now he checked his phone and groaned inwardly at the twenty-two texts he'd been sent. Most of them, fortunately, concerned minor matters, but one was a tersely worded command from his brother Aaron.

Wait for me in Tokyo.

Irritation rippled through him. Was his brother actually going to fly all the way to Tokyo to boss him around? No doubt he'd seen some of the press about Aurelie and the openings and wanted to throw his weight around, as he always did.

'What's wrong?' Aurelie asked quietly, and Luke glanced up. Over the last few days they'd become amazingly attuned to one another. Aurelie knew him as well as he knew her.

Not quite.

The thought slid slyly into his mind. She might have completely unburdened herself, but in many ways—crucial ways—he was still buttoned up as tight as ever. He still had secrets, and ones he had no desire or intention to share. She had enough to deal with; she didn't need his remembered pain. He slid his phone into his jacket pocket, glanced away. 'Just work stuff.'

Twenty minutes later they landed in Tokyo.

They took a limo to The Peninsula, the luxury hotel Luke's PA had booked overlooking the Imperial Palace Gardens. The air was crisper than in any of their other destinations, a hint of autumn on the breeze that ruffled the leaves of the trees lining the street.

'I cancelled your hotel suite,' he told her as they checked in. Fortunately there was no message from Aaron, and Luke half-hoped his brother had decided to abandon the trip. He turned to Aurelie. 'I hope you don't mind.'

She smiled, eyebrows raised. 'Why would I mind?'

'You might want a bit of privacy.'

'I think a two thousand square metre suite should provide enough of that,' she answered with a little laugh.

The bellhop led them to the penthouse suite, showed them

all of its rooms and wraparound terrace. When they were alone Luke pulled her into his arms, kissed his way down her throat. He loved the feel of her, the sense of rightness she gave him. 'As much as I'd like to finish what I've started,' he murmured against her skin, 'you have a concert to get to.'

'I know,' she agreed on a sigh of disappointment.

He straightened, bringing her with him so he could look into those slate-blue eyes he loved. 'Are you nervous?'

'No, which is amazing considering how terrified I was a few days ago.'

'You've changed.'

'Thanks to you.' She smiled. 'I know I'm not going to get glowing reviews all around. Someone will hate it, and they'll make sure to let me know.' Her mouth twisted wryly. 'But it doesn't matter. It really doesn't.'

'I'm glad,' Luke said, and with one more kiss because he just couldn't resist he smoothed her hair and dress and they went to get ready for the opening.

Two hours later Luke was standing by the side of the stage watching as Aurelie miked up to go on. She wore a flowing dress of pale green silk with a gauzy overlay, her hair pulled up in a loose chignon. She looked effortlessly beautiful, wonderfully natural. His heart swelled with love.

'What the hell,' a voice snapped out from behind him, 'is she doing here?'

Luke turned around to stare into the furious face of his brother Aaron.

CHAPTER TWELVE

'HELLO, AARON,' LUKE said evenly. 'I think I could ask you the same question.'

Aaron just shook his head. 'What are you talking about?'

'What the hell,' Luke asked mildly, 'are you doing here?'

'Saving your ass. Didn't you get my text?'

'Last time I checked, it didn't need saving.' Aaron opened his mouth but Luke forestalled him with one up-flung hand. 'Be quiet. She's about to start.'

Eyes narrowed, Aaron closed his mouth. Aurelie started to sing, and Luke listened to her smoky voice float through the crowd, hushing even the tiniest whisper. Everyone was entranced, including him.

But not Aaron. The second her voice died away Aaron grabbed his arm. Luke shook it off.

'She goes, Luke.'

Luke turned around. 'What do you mean, she goes?'

'She goes. Now. The last thing Bryant's needs is someone with her reputation linked to it—'

Luke eyed him coldly. 'Aurelie has done wonders for Bryant's image, Aaron.'

Just then she came off the stage, her widened gaze taking in the two of them.

Luke knew he didn't want his brother talking to Aurelie. Aaron had the tact of a tank when it came to getting his own way. 'Just give us a minute please, Aurelie,' he told her, and he heard the suppressed anger in his voice. So did she. She tensed, her eyes going wide before she nodded and, still holding her guitar, walked past them to her dressing room.

'Let's take this somewhere private,' Luke said coolly. 'The *really* last thing Bryant's needs is two of the Bryant brothers coming to blows in front of a thousand guests.'

'Coming to blows?' Aaron arched an eyebrow. 'All over a woman, Luke? Didn't you learn anything from our father?'

'Aurelie is nothing like our father's mistresses,' Luke snapped. Not trusting himself to say another word, he turned on his heel and went upstairs to one of the corporate offices. Aaron followed him, closing the door behind him and leaning against it with his arms folded.

'I appreciate she's probably pretty good in the sack, but she goes, Luke.'

Luke didn't think then. He just swung. His fist connected with his brother's jaw and white-hot pain radiated from his knuckles. Aaron doubled over, righting himself with one hand on the desk, the other massaging his already swelling jaw.

'Damn it, Luke. What the hell has gotten into you?'

'I should have done that years ago,' Luke said grimly. He cradled his throbbing hand. It had felt amazingly good to hit his brother. 'You stay out of this, Aaron. Stay out of my personal life and stay out of the store.'

'The store? The store is part of—'

'Bryant Enterprises. Yeah, I get that. I also get that you've got to have your sticky fingerprints on every part of this empire, even though there's plenty for both of us, and Chase too, if he'd wanted it.'

'Chase,' Aaron answered, 'was disinherited.'

'You could have given it back to him. You knew Dad was just acting out of anger.'

'I wasn't about to go against our dead father's wishes.'

'Oh, give it up.' Luke turned away, suddenly tired. 'Like you've ever cared about that.'

Aaron was silent for a moment. 'You have no idea,' he finally said, his voice flat and strange. Luke turned around.

'No?'

'No. And the fact remains that you might be CEO of Bryant Stores but I'm still your boss, and I say she goes.'

Impatience flared through him at his brother's autocratic tone. 'Have you read the papers? Have you seen the positive press—'

'Yes, and along with the positive press they're raking up every bit of tabloid trash that woman has generated. Do you *know* how many photos there are of her—'

'Stop.' Luke held up a hand. 'Stop, because I don't want to hear it and if we continue this conversation I'll punch you again.'

'This time I'll be ready for it,' Aaron snapped. 'I don't care if you're screwing her, Luke, but she can't—'

'Shut. Up.' Luke's voice was low, deadly in a way neither of them had ever heard before. 'Don't say one more word about Aurelie, Aaron. Not one word.' Aaron remained silent, his mouth thinned, his eyes narrowed. Luke let out a low breath. 'Bryant Stores is under my authority. I've been trying to prove to you for over fifteen years that I'm perfectly capable of managing it myself, but you always step in. You've never trusted me.'

'I don't trust anyone.'

Surprise rippled through Luke; he hadn't expected Aaron to say that, to admit so much.

'Why not?'

Aaron lifted one shoulder in an impatient shrug. 'Does it matter?'

'It matters to me. Do you know how hard I've worked—'

'Oh, yes, I know. You've worked hard for everything in your life, Luke, always waiting for that damn pat on your head. You didn't get it from Dad and you won't get it from me.'

Rage coursed through him. 'That's a hell of a thing to say.'

'It's true, though, isn't it?' Aaron stared at him in challenge. 'You've always been working for other people's approval. Trying to prove yourself, and you never will.'

Luke stared at his brother, realisation trickling coldly through him. He didn't like the way Aaron had put it, but he recognised that his brother's words held a shaming grain of truth. He'd been trying to prove himself for so long, to earn people's trust as if that would somehow make up for that one moment when he'd lost his father's.

'I'll stop now, then,' he said evenly. 'You either step off Bryant's or I do.'

Aaron raised his eyebrows. 'Are you threatening to quit?'

'It's not a threat.'

'Do you know what that kind of publicity could do—'

'Yes.'

'You've worked for Bryant's your whole adult life. You really want to just leave that behind?'

Luke knew his brother was testing him, looking for weaknesses. He wouldn't find any. He'd never felt so sure about anything in his life. 'I'll leave it behind if I have to keep answering to you. I'm done proving myself, Aaron. To you or to anyone.'

Aaron's mouth curved in a humourless smile. 'Well, look at you. All right. I'll think about it.'

Luke shook his head. 'Forget it. I resign.'

'You don't need to overreact—'

'No. But I need to stop working for you. In any capacity. Don't worry, Aaron. I'm sure you'll find someone else to be your stooge.' Luke turned away and he heard Aaron's exasperated sigh.

'It's that woman, isn't it? She's changed you.'

'Yes, she's changed me. But not in the way you think. She's *believed* in me, trusted me, and that's something you've never done. And I don't want that pat on the head, Aaron. I'm done. I'm done trying to earn it from you or anyone.'

With one last hard look at his brother, determination now surging through him, Luke left the office.

Aurelie clutched a flute of champagne and eyed the circulating crowd nervously. She still didn't see Luke or the man she knew must be his brother Aaron. He'd looked just like him, except a little taller and broader, a lot angrier.

She took a sip of champagne, forced herself to swallow. When she'd walked offstage she'd felt the tension between the two men and she'd had a horrible, plunging feeling they'd been arguing about her. No doubt Aaron wasn't pleased about her part in the reopening galas. And as for Luke?

What did he feel?

She realised she didn't know the answer to that question. The last few days had been wonderful, but had they been real? You could probably fall in love with anyone in this kind of situation, out of time and reality. And she knew she must be different from the women Luke had known, those three serious relationships he'd had. Maybe the novelty had worn off. Maybe Aaron had made him realise that she wasn't really a long-term proposition.

'I should congratulate you.' She froze, then slowly turned to face the unsmiling gaze of Aaron Bryant. His assessing look swept her from her head to her toes and clearly found her lacking. 'You've managed to ensnare my brother, at least for the moment.'

It was so much what Aurelie had been thinking, what

she'd feared, that she struggled to form any kind of reply. 'I haven't ensnared anyone,' she finally answered, her voice thankfully even.

'No? It's true love, then, is it?' He sounded so mocking, so disbelieving, that Aurelie stiffened. Didn't say anything, because she wasn't about to give this man any ammunition.

And she didn't even know if Luke loved her. He hadn't said those three important words yet, but then neither had she.

Aaron shook his head. 'Be kind to him when you're finished, at least. He deserves that much.'

Surprise flashed through her. She hadn't expected Aaron to care about Luke's feelings. 'I have no intention of finishing with him.'

'No? Then perhaps he'll wise up and finish with you.' With one last dismissive glance, he turned away.

Aurelie stood there, her fingers clenched around the fragile stem of her flute of champagne, the cold fingers of fear creeping along her spine. She knew Aaron had been trying to get to her, to wind her up or put her down or both. It didn't matter what he had said.

What mattered was her response. It all felt so *familiar*, this encroaching panic, the ensuing clinginess. The terror that Luke would leave her, that she'd be lost without him. She'd lose herself.

She'd changed in so many ways, so many wonderful ways, thanks to Luke. But she hadn't, it seemed, changed in the way that mattered most.

She was going to lose herself again. She felt it, in the hollowness that reverberated through her, a sudden, sweeping emptiness at the thought that Luke might leave her. Maybe she couldn't do relationships after all. Maybe this was what would always happen with her.

Somehow she circulated through the crowd, smiled, nodded, said things, although she wasn't sure what they were. She looked for Luke and caught a glimpse of him across the crowded room.

He was deep in discussion, a frown settled between his brows. Aurelie stared at him for a taut moment and then, without thinking, she turned on her heel and made it to the safety of her dressing room.

She kept her mind blank as she threw her belongings into a bag and grabbed her coat. Her plane left for New York tomorrow, but she could go standby. Hell, she could hire a private jet if she wanted to. And what she wanted in that moment was to escape. To flee to a safe place where she could untangle her impossible thoughts, her encroaching fears, and figure out if there was anything left.

She slipped out of the store, hailed a cab to take her back to the hotel. She was still operating on autopilot, reacting as she always had before, and while part of her knew she should stop, wait, *think*, the rest of her just buzzed and shrieked, *Get out. Get away and save yourself...if there's anything left to save.*

She'd packed her suitcases and was just slipping on her coat when she heard the door to the suite open. Luke stood there, looking tired and rumpled, the keycard held loosely in his hand.

'Someone told me you'd left early—' He stopped, his gaze taking in her packed cases, her coat. He stilled, and the silence stretched on for several seconds. 'What are you doing, Aurelie?'

She swallowed. 'I thought I'd leave a little early.'

'A little early,' Luke repeated neutrally. He came into the room, tossing the keycard on a side table. 'Were you going to inform me of that fact, or were you hoping to slip out while I was still at the opening?'

'I...' She trailed off, licked her lips. 'I don't know.'

He stared at her, his face expressionless, eyes veiled. 'What happened? Did Aaron talk to you?'

'Yes, but that doesn't really matter.'

'Doesn't it?'

'No. I just…I need some space, Luke. Some time. I'm not sure…' Her voice cracked and she took a breath, tried again. 'I'm not sure I can do this.'

'This,' he repeated. 'We never did decide what *this* was.'

Was, not is. So maybe her worst fears were realised, and he was leaving her. Not that it mattered either way. This was her problem, not Luke's.

'And you don't think you could have told me any of this?' he asked, his voice still so very even. 'You don't think you could have shared any of this with me before you tried to bust out of here?'

'I'm telling you now—'

'Only because I came back early!' His voice rose in a roar of anger and hurt that had Aurelie blinking, stepping back. 'Damn it, Aurelie, I trusted you. And I thought you trusted me.'

'This isn't about trust—'

'No? What's it about, then?'

'It's my problem, Luke. Not yours.'

'That's a rather neat way of putting it, considering it feels like my problem now.'

'I'm sorry.' Her throat ached with the effort of holding back tears. 'I just…I can't risk myself again. I can't open myself up to—'

'To being mistreated and abused like that scumbag Myers did to you?'

She felt hot tears crowd her eyes. 'I suppose. Yes.'

Luke let out a hard laugh, the kind of sound she'd never heard from him before. 'And you say this isn't about trust.'

'It isn't,' she insisted. 'This is about what's going on in my own head—'

'You want to know what's going on in my head?' Luke cut her off and Aurelie stilled. Nodded.

'Okay,' she said cautiously.

'I've had a few revelations today. Starting with the fact that I've resigned from Bryant Stores.'

'Resigned—'

'My brother told me I was always trying to prove myself to people, trying to earn their trust. And he was right. I was certainly trying to earn it with you.'

'I know you were, Luke. And you did earn it—'

'Obviously I didn't, if you're trying to sneak away now.' Luke shook his head, his gaze veiled and averted so Aurelie had no idea what he was thinking. 'But this goes back before you. Way back.' He let out a slow breath. 'I told you my mother died of breast cancer, but she didn't.'

'She didn't?' Aurelie repeated uncertainly.

'She killed herself.' Aurelie blinked. Luke stared at her grimly, his gaze unfocused, remembering. 'I was the only one home. I'd come back from boarding school, Chase and Aaron were still at sports camps. My father was on a business trip.'

'What happened?' Aurelie whispered.

'She was hysterical at first. She'd just found out about another of my father's mistresses. He always had some bimbo on the side, which is why I've been a bit more discerning with my own relationships. I saw what it did to my mother. Anyway—' he shrugged, as if shaking something off '—she sat me down in the living room, told me she loved me. I'd always been the closest to her, really. And then she said she was sorry but she couldn't go on, dwindling down towards death while my father flaunted his affairs.' Luke paused, and Aurelie could see how he was gripped by the force of such a terrible memory. 'I didn't realise what she meant at first. Then it hit me—she was actually going to kill herself. She'd gone upstairs, and I ran after her, but the door was locked.' He shook his head. 'I tried to reason with her. I pleaded, I shouted, I even cried. But all I got was silence.'

'Oh, Luke.' Tears stung her eyes as she imagined such a terrible, desperate scene.

'I tried to break the door open, but I couldn't. I *couldn't*.' His voice broke, and Aurelie felt something in her break too.

'I believe you,' she whispered.

'In the end I called 911 but it was too late. She'd slipped into a coma by the time the medics arrived, and she died later that night, from a drug overdose. Anti-depressants.'

Oh, God. So much made sense to her now. She blinked, swiped at her eyes. 'I'm so sorry.'

'So am I. I'm sorry I've let that whole awful episode define and cripple me for so many years. My father blamed me, you see, and so I blamed myself. He said I could have saved her, that I was the only one, that I should have done something. For so long I believed him. I told myself I didn't, but inside? Where it counts? I did. I spent years trying to earn back his trust and respect. His love. And he died without ever giving it to me.' Luke drew a deep breath, met her gaze with a stony one of his own. 'I should have told you this before. I thought it didn't matter, that I'd put it all behind me, but I've been doing the same thing with you, haven't I? I even told you I was. I was trying to earn your trust. I was trying to save you and I can't.'

'I don't want you to save me,' Aurelie whispered.

'Then what do you want, Aurelie? Because I'm done with trying to prove myself. You're either in or you're out. You either love me or you don't.'

Love. She swallowed, her mouth dry, her heart pounding like crazy. 'Luke—'

'I love you. Do you love me?'

Yes. She wanted to say it, felt it buoy up inside her, the pressure building and building, but no words came out. She was still so afraid. Afraid of losing herself, giving up control—

'I see,' Luke said quietly.

'It's not that simple,' she whispered.

Luke stared at her for a long moment. He looked so unyielding, yet a bleak sorrow flickered in the dark depths of his eyes. 'Actually,' he said, 'it is.'

Without another word, he turned and walked out of the room.

The flight back to New York was a blur, as was the drive up to Vermont. Aurelie arrived back at her grandma's house twenty-four hours after she'd left Tokyo. Left Luke, and her heart with him.

She dropped her bags by the door and walked through the rooms like a sleepwalker. She'd only been gone a little less than two weeks, yet it felt like forever. She'd lived a lifetime in the space of ten days. Lived and died.

For she was back exactly where she'd started, where she'd been stuck for years. Alone, hopeless, unable to change.

Just the memory of the hard, blazing look on Luke's face as he asked her if she loved him made her cringe and want to cry. She'd been too much of a coward to admit the truth, to take that leap.

She'd failed him, and failed herself. Fear rather than trust—*love*—had guided her actions.

In her more rational moments she convinced herself that it really was better this way, that Luke would be better off with someone more like him. Someone steady and balanced, who didn't drag a lifetime of emotional baggage behind her.

Yet in the middle of the night when her bed felt far too

empty, when she stared at her guitar or piano and couldn't summon the will to play, when every colour seemed to have been leached from the landscape of her life, she thought differently. She thought she might do anything to get him back, to have the chance to tell him that she loved him and was willing to take that risk, that he didn't have to earn anything because she'd give it all to him, gladly. So gladly.

Two weeks after she'd returned someone rang her doorbell, which was surprising in itself because she received pretty much zero visitors. She opened it, her heart lurching when she saw the familiar figure standing on her front porch.

'Luke—'

'Sorry. I know I must be a disappointment.'

The man in front of her wasn't Luke, but he looked a lot like him. His eyes and hair were a little lighter, but he had the same tall, powerful frame, the same wry smile.

'I'm Chase,' he said, and held out his hand. 'Chase Bryant.'

'You like to cook,' Aurelie said dumbly, because she was so surprised and that was the only thing she could remember. No, there was something else. *Chase checked out.*

'I do make a mean curry.' He raised his eyebrows. 'Luke's been talking about me, huh?'

'A little bit.'

'May I come in?'

He sounded so much like Luke that her eyes stung. Wordlessly Aurelie nodded and led him through the front hall to the kitchen. 'Do you want something to drink? A coffee or tea?'

'I'm good. I know you're wondering why I'm here.'

'I'm wondering how you even know who I am.'

Chase smiled wryly. 'That part's not so hard. The fame thing's a bitch though, I'm sure.'

She raked a hand through her hair. 'Oh. Right.'

'I saw Luke back in New York. He's not looking so good.'

That probably shouldn't have lifted her spirits, but it did. 'No?'

'No. In fact, he looks like crap and I told him so.' Chase paused. 'He told me about you.'

Aurelie stiffened. 'What exactly did he tell you?'

'Not much. And not willingly. I've gone pretty emo since I've become engaged, but Luke's still working on getting in touch with his feelings.'

She laughed, surprising herself because she hadn't laughed for so long. Since Luke. 'So what did he tell you?'

'That it didn't work out.'

'It didn't.'

'Yeah, I kind of figured that one out.' Chase took a step towards her. 'The thing is,' he said, and now he sounded serious, 'I'm in love with this amazing woman, Millie. And I almost completely blew it because I was afraid. You know the whole relationship/love/commitment thing is kind of big.'

'Yeah.' She took a deep breath, let it out slowly. 'It is, isn't it?'

Chase smiled at her gently. 'What exactly are you afraid of, Aurelie?'

'Everything,' she whispered and blinked hard.

'Are you afraid Luke will leave you? Hurt you? Because that was my thing. But maybe yours is something else.'

She glanced down. 'I don't think he'll mean to.'

'But you still think he will?'

She looked up, her eyes filled with tears. 'I'm just so afraid that I can't change.'

Chase tilted his head, regarded her quietly. 'How do you want to change?'

She sniffed. Loudly. 'I was in a relationship before and when it ended I…I was wrecked. Completely wrecked. I spun out of control and I can't stand the thought of that happening again, of losing myself again—'

Chase laughed softly, a gentle sound without any malice. 'Sweetheart, we're all afraid of that. That's what happens when you love someone, when you give everything. If Millie ever left me I'd be lost, completely lost.'

'Then how—'

'Because,' Chase said simply, 'life with her is worth any possible risk. But I'll admit, it took me a while to realise that. And maybe,' he added quietly, 'it will be different this time with you. Knowing Luke, I'm pretty sure it will.'

She sniffed again. Nodded. Because she knew Luke, and he was nothing, *nothing* like Pete Myers. And she was nothing like the way she'd been with Pete. With Luke she was different, new, *changed*.

She *had* changed. Why hadn't she believed it in the critical moment? Why had she blanked and backed away, defaulting to her old self?

She glanced sadly at Chase. 'I think it might be too late.'

He shook his head. 'I was just with Luke. Trust me, it's not too late.'

Two days later Aurelie stood in front of the renovated warehouse that housed Luke's new enterprise. Chase had told her that after resigning from Bryant's Luke had formed his own charitable foundation. She'd been surprised, and also pleased for Luke. He had never seemed like he actually enjoyed working for Bryant's.

And now she was here in lower Manhattan, terrified. Trying to change.

Taking a deep breath she opened the warehouse's heavy steel door and stepped into the building. The space was basically just one cavernous room, with folding chairs and stepladders and sheets of plastic all over the place. A young, officious-looking woman bustled towards her.

'May I help?'

'I'm looking for Luke Bryant—'

The woman's eyes widened in recognition. 'Are you—'

'Yes. Do you know where I can find Luke?'

Her eyes still wide, the woman nodded and gestured towards a door in a corner of the warehouse. Taking another deep breath Aurelie headed towards it.

Luke's back was to her as she opened the door. He was scanning some blueprints. 'Is that lunch?' he asked without looking up.

'Sorry, I don't have any sandwiches.'

Luke glanced up, everything about him stilling, blanking as he gazed at her. Aurelie tried to smile. 'Hi.'

'Hi.'

She couldn't tell a thing from his tone. 'I like the name,' she said, pointing to a sign on the door. *The Morpho Foundation.* 'Reminds me of a really great date I went on, when this butterfly landed in my hair and I kissed a man and it felt like the first real kiss I'd ever had.'

A muscle flickered in Luke's jaw and he dropped his gaze. 'Morpho is the Greek word for change, and this foundation's all about change.'

She swallowed. 'Change is good.'

He glanced up at her, and she saw that something had softened in his face. 'But yeah, it's about the butterfly too.' He paused, and one corner of his mouth quirked the tiniest bit upwards. 'And the kiss.'

It was more than enough of an opening. 'I miss you, Luke. I'm sorry I messed up so badly. I panicked and I acted on that panic instead of trusting you like I should have.'

He shook his head slowly, and Aurelie's heart free-fell towards her toes. 'I messed up too. I should have told you what was going on in my mind. The stuff about my mother. I just hadn't put it all together until that moment.'

'And I was so wrapped up in my own pain and past that I didn't think about yours.' She managed a smile. 'I thought you had it all together.'

'So did I.'

'I'm sorry about your mom,' Aurelie said quietly. 'I can't imagine how hard that must have been.'

'It wasn't easy.'

'I like the idea behind your foundation.' She'd read online that the foundation would be supporting children of parents in crisis. Like a mom with cancer.

'You gave me the idea, actually.'

'Me?'

'I thought about how alone you were, at such a young age. If you'd had one stable adult in your life things might have turned out differently for you.'

She nodded slowly. 'They might have.'

'Anyway—' Luke shrugged '—there's a lot of work to do before this thing is even off the ground.'

'Still, I'm glad you're doing it.' They both lapsed into silence then, and Aurelie's heart started thudding. Again. She'd thought they were getting there, working towards one another, but Luke still looked terribly remote. He didn't move towards her even though she desperately wanted him to. She wanted him to take her in his arms and kiss her, tell her it was all going to work out.

She wanted him to do all the work.

And suddenly she got it. This wasn't about Luke having to prove himself or earn anything from her. She gave it all freely, because she knew this man, and she loved and trusted him so much.

'I'm sorry for walking out on you in Tokyo,' she said. Luke didn't answer. 'You thought I didn't trust you and I can see how you would think that. How it looked that way. But the truth is I didn't trust myself. I was protecting myself, because I was so afraid of feeling like I did before. Out of control. Lost.'

'You'd only feel that way if I left you, if I let you down.'

'No. I never thought you'd let me down. I just…I saw you looking tense and angry with Aaron, and I knew he was probably telling you to forget me—'

'And you thought I'd listen?'

'No. But just the possibility had me panicking, and that scared me. I felt out of control already, and I didn't want that. But the thing I've finally realised—at least I'm starting to—is that love *requires* a loss of control. A giving of trust. And I was fighting against that because it still scared me.'

Luke was silent for a long moment. 'And now?' he finally asked.

'I'm still scared,' Aurelie admitted. 'I wish I wasn't, but I am. This is all terrifying for me, and I'll probably panic again. But I know I'm miserable without you, and I want to make this work. I want to be with you…if you still want to be with me.' Luke didn't say anything, and so she kept speaking, the words tumbling from her mouth, her heart. 'I know I'll mess up again, and I'll probably even hurt you. We'll hurt each other but I won't run away and I'll keep trying to change. It's a process.' She pointed to the foundation's sign. 'A metamorphosis takes a little time, you know.'

'I know. You're not the only one who needs to change.'

She swallowed, made herself say the hardest and most vulnerable words of all. The most changing. 'I love you, Luke.'

He didn't speak and Aurelie felt dizzy with nerves. Maybe she needed to check her blood sugar. 'Say something,' she managed, 'or you might have to dunk me in the sink a second time.'

Luke didn't say anything, though. He just crossed the room in two long strides and pulled her into his arms before he finally spoke. 'I love you too,' he said. 'So much. I'm sorry I ever walked away from you.'

'I'm not,' Aurelie answered, 'even though these last few weeks have been hell. I needed to be the one to walk *to* you for once.'

'Well, now neither of us is going anywhere,' Luke muttered against her throat, and then he was kissing her and Aurelie felt dizzier than ever. Dizzy with joy.

* * * * *

LITTLE SECRET, RED HOT SCANDAL

CAT SCHIELD

For my daughter,
who keeps me current on
all things pop culture.

One

After telling the sound engineer to take a break, Nate Tucker lay down on the couch in the control room of West Coast Records' LA headquarters. Closing his eyes, he listened to the playback of the song he'd just recorded. Over the years he'd trained his ears to pick up every nuance of a performance. His mind then went to work adjusting the frequencies, boosting or cutting EQ, feathering in a touch of reverb to improve the natural sound.

Nothing, however, could fix what Nate was hearing in his own voice. Proof that he'd pushed too hard on the final leg of his twelve-month tour.

He'd hoped that three weeks of rest might have allowed his vocal cords to fix themselves, but his reduced range and the hoarseness that plagued him weren't going away. The vocal cord surgery he'd scheduled for tomorrow was unavoidable. Nate's curses echoed through the room. One more damned thing he didn't have time for.

Since returning to his home in Las Vegas after touring all over the world with his band, Free Fall, he'd been inundated with work. Thank goodness he'd been able to do some songwriting while on the road, because he was all out of space and energy to compose for Free Fall's next album. Maybe that wasn't such a bad thing. With his voice out of commission he wasn't going to be singing anytime soon.

His phone began to ring. Nate checked the screen before levering himself off the couch. In the last three days he'd made a half dozen calls to Trent Caldwell, his business partner and friend. In addition to being partners in Club T's, the premier Las Vegas nightclub that Nate, Trent and Kyle Tailor owned, Nate and Trent were partners in Nate's label, Ugly Trout Records in Las Vegas, as well as West Coast Records, the company Trent had recently bought from his family.

Dropping into the control booth's comfortable leather chair, Nate silenced the music pouring from the speakers and answered the call.

"It's about time you checked in." Nate wasted no time with pleasantries. "Where have you been?"

"Savannah starts shooting next week, so I took her and Dylan to a spa hotel up in Washington." Trent sounded more relaxed and happy than ever. Being engaged to the love of his life obviously agreed with him. "We both turned off our phones for a few days."

Ever since Trent had rekindled his romance with his former lover and found out he was a father, he'd become a whole new person. Nate understood the transformation, after what had happened between him and Mia. It was easy to be cynical and even suspicious about stuff like that until it happened to you.

"Sounds nice." Really nice.

Envy shot through Nate. It wasn't like him to want something another man had. He already had fame and wealth. They didn't drive him. Nate loved what he did and didn't really care if he made tons of money. The music mattered.

And then he'd watched his friend and business partner fall hard for Savannah, and suddenly making music wasn't enough anymore.

"I got your messages about the meeting with Ivy Bliss," Trent said. "Have you lost your mind?"

"What do you mean?" Nate knew perfectly well what Trent was referring to, but decided to pretend he'd been motivated purely by business.

Ivy Bliss was a former child actress turned pop princess with an impressive four-octave range. Five years ago she'd signed with West Coast Records and released two albums. They'd done okay. Thanks to the label's poor management, the production work on the albums hadn't been stellar and the release dates had been pushed back so many times that fans had lost interest.

That was before Trent and Nate had taken control of his family's label the previous month. They intended to turn the record company around and make it a huge success. Ivy Bliss's new album was a great place to start.

But that wasn't the reason Nate had reached out to Ivy's manager-father about producing her new album.

"You did nothing but complain about her the entire eight weeks she was on tour with you."

"Oh, that."

"Oh, that?" Trent mimicked. Nate could hear a baby babbling in the background. "Just a second." There was a pause. "Dylan, Daddy's on the phone with Uncle Nate. Do you want to sing him your new song?"

Nate couldn't ignore the growing ache in his chest

as he listened to Dylan jabber along with his father's soft singing. Ever since Nate had decided on a career in music, every bit of his energy had been focused on writing, performing and producing. Now, he enjoyed all the money and success he'd dreamed about and yet something gnawed at him.

"That was terrific," Nate said when the song was done.

"He's barely a year and already starting to say a few words."

"Have you been teaching him the signs I showed you?" Nate had learned American Sign Language as a kid so he could communicate with his hearing impaired mother, and had taught Trent a few signs Dylan could use to communicate, for words such as *more*, *done*, *eat*, *play*, *finish* and *tired*.

"Yes, he's really taking to it. Now, back to Ivy. Why would you want to produce her new album?"

Nate sighed. "I don't need to remind you that she's a huge talent and poised to break out. She just needs one great album."

"She's a twenty-five-year-old nightmare."

"Yes, well…she's not that bad." Nate winced at the bald lie.

Seven years earlier, when she was seventeen and starring in a Broadway musical after her show on KidZ Channel was canceled, she'd gotten Nate's phone number and for four months she'd sent him impassioned texts and sexy pictures of herself. At first he'd responded with polite rebuffs and then silence. At last he'd contacted her father and warned him that this wasn't going to play well if it got out. All contact stopped.

"She's a little silly and spoiled," Nate continued, "but superstars can get that way sometimes."

Trent ignored his friend's self-deprecating jab. "Why don't you point her toward Savan or Blanco?" Both had worked with her on collaborations with other artists and produced hits.

Nate didn't need to remind Trent that Ivy Bliss had a reputation for being "challenging" in the studio. She didn't take suggestions, and criticism sent her into hysterics. Neither of the producers Trent mentioned would want to work with her again.

"I'm doing this for West Coast Records." Another lie. There were a couple dozen guys who could produce the heck out of Ivy Bliss and make an album that would rocket to the top of the charts.

"I'm not buying it." Trent hadn't made a major success of every one of his business ventures by being dense. "Wait a second, are you into her? Damn. That's crazy, but my sister said you fell for someone on the tour. I never in a million years thought it was Ivy Bliss."

"It wasn't." With a shudder, Nate changed topics before Trent could press further. "The other reason I called is that I'm going in for surgery tomorrow."

"Surgery." Trent's tone sharpened. "What's wrong?"

"I've got these polyps on my vocal cords." He tried to keep the tension out of his voice. The situation was serious, but he didn't want to make a big deal out of it. "I need to get them removed."

"That sounds bad."

"It's outpatient surgery. A couple hours max. I just wanted to let you know that I'm going to be out of commission for a few days."

"Do you want me to take you?"

"And do what?" Nate injected as much sarcasm as he could into the words to hide how embarrassed he was at his mounting anxiety. "Hold my hand? Please."

"Fine." Trent sounded doubtful. "But if you need anything, just let me know."

"Sure."

An hour after hanging up, Nate strode into the conference room for his two o'clock meeting with Ivy Bliss. Only it wasn't Ivy and her manager-father who awaited him, but Mia Navarro, her twin sister and personal assistant. His heart raced across the room toward her. Nate plunged after it for two strides before coming to a stop. What did he think he was going to do? Wrap her in his arms and crush her against his chest? Whisper that the last three weeks had been a living hell without her? That he ached to hear her voice and sulked without her smile to brighten his day?

She'd made her choice and it hadn't been him.

"How have you been?" He searched her face for some sign she'd suffered as he had, lingering over the circles under her eyes and the downward turn of her mouth. To his relief she didn't look happy, but that didn't stop her from putting on a show.

"Things have been great. Ivy's been busy with appearances on *The Tonight Show* and *Ellen*. She's stoked about being asked to perform at the AMAs on the twentieth. And of course she's really excited about working with you."

Nate reined in his impatience, unable to believe that he was nearly back to square one with Mia. He'd spent weeks chatting her up on the tour, afraid if he pushed too fast that she'd retreat into the persona of personal assistant to Ivy Bliss. Many times he'd asked himself why he was working so hard to draw out someone who didn't want to be noticed. Then she'd smile at him and make his entire day.

If only he could convince her to leave Ivy… Mia had

more to offer the world than just being her famous sister's flunky. For one thing, she was a ridiculously talented songwriter. When he'd discovered that she had written all the songs her sister had recorded and that she'd been denied credit on the albums, he'd been seconds away from storming into Ivy's hotel room and demanding she go public with the truth.

Mia had been mortified. She'd claimed to be okay with the lies and Nate could understand letting the error stand for the first album, but not the subsequent one. As someone who nurtured artists, he'd been appalled by what had been done to Mia by her own family, and saddened by how she'd been bullied.

"I didn't ask how your sister is doing. I asked about you."

"I'm fine. Never better." Mia could go on for hours talking about Ivy, but when it came to talking about herself, she was fond of two-word sentences.

"Tell me the truth." He was asking after her welfare, but what he really wanted to know was if she'd missed him at all. It seemed crazy that he'd known her for less than three months and in that time she'd become like breathing to him.

"I'm great. Really."

"What have you been doing since the tour ended?"

Mia shrugged. "The usual."

Meaning whatever occupied Ivy was what Mia had been doing. As her sister's personal assistant, she lived and breathed Ivy Bliss, pop princess.

"I hope she gave you a little time off."

"Ivy was invited to a charity event in South Beach and we extended our stay a couple days to kick back and soak up some sun."

Ivy demanded all Mia's time and energy. That Nate

had been able to spend any time at all alone with Mia during Ivy's eight-week stint on his tour was nothing short of amazing. They'd sneaked around like teenage kids. The danger of getting caught had promoted intimacy. And at first, Nate had found the subterfuge amusing. It got old fast.

For a while Nate wondered if he'd initially been drawn to Mia because he felt compelled to rescue her from her sister's clutches. When Mia was around Ivy, she was a quiet mouse in the corner, fetching herbal tea, being ready with Ivy's favorite snack, loosening her tension with a quick shoulder massage. And it had bothered Nate that Ivy treated Mia like an employee instead of a sister. She never seemed to appreciate how Mia's kind and thoughtful behavior went above and beyond the role of personal assistant.

"I don't like the way we left things between us," Nate declared, taking a step in her direction.

Mia took a matching step backward. "You asked for something I couldn't give you."

"I asked you to come with me to Las Vegas. I wanted to spend more time getting to know you."

"It was all happening was too fast. We'd barely known each other two months." She'd delivered the same excuse three weeks ago and it rang as hollow now as it had then. "And I couldn't leave Ivy."

"She could've found another assistant." He'd said the same thing the morning after the tour ended. The night after she'd stayed with him until the sun crested the horizon.

Their last stop had been Sydney. Following his final encore, Nate had made sure Ivy was busy and then stolen Mia away to a romantic hotel suite overlooking the harbor. They'd sipped champagne, toasted each other, laughed and made love for the first time. But as sunlight filled the room Mia was on the phone with Ivy, making excuses for where she'd been.

"I'm not just her assistant, I'm her sister," Mia said, now as then. "She needs me."

I need you.

He wouldn't repeat the words. It wouldn't do any good. She'd still choose obligation to her sister over being happy with him. And he couldn't figure out why.

"Your sister is a spoiled brat." Frustration and impatience got the better of him. "The only reason I agreed to work on her album is because of you."

Mia's beautiful brown eyes went round with shock, and although her mouth dropped open, no words emerged.

Her phone rang, interrupting the heavy silence between them. "It's Ivy." She looked almost relieved by the interruption. "I should get this."

Nate had grown weary of her sister coming between them. He crossed his arms over his chest and let sarcasm slide into his tone. "By all means, take it."

To his surprise, she put the phone on speaker. "Hey Ivy, I'm with Nate right now and you're on speaker."

After a short pause, Ivy's soprano voice came over the line. "Hi, Nate. Has Mia apologized for me missing the meeting and asked if you could meet for a drink later to chat about my album?"

Mia winced and wouldn't meet his gaze.

"Not yet," he answered.

"Then I'll ask." He could hear the seductive pout in Ivy's tone. "Please come by my house at eight."

He understood the invitation for what it was and barely restrained a growl. "If you wanted to talk about your album, you should've come by today."

Mia's large dark eyes went round with concern. *"Don't upset her,"* she told him in sign language.

Nate pretended that he hadn't seen the plea. While on tour they'd discovered they both knew how to sign. Something he'd used to overcome her reluctance to talk to him. That they'd shared a secret language had drawn them together.

"Didn't Mia explain that I had a conflict? I'm meeting with a representative for Mayfair Cosmetics. It's all hush-hush, but they're looking for the new face to represent their beauty line."

"Can you meet for dinner?" Mia signed, her eyes worried.

Nate reined in his temper, reminding himself the reason he'd offered to work with Ivy was so he could spend time with Mia and hopefully convince her to pick him over her sister this time.

"How about I make a reservation for dinner at eight," Nate said.

"Sure. Dinner would be wonderful."

"I'll text Mia with the details and this time you'd better show up." While Mia stared at him in horror, Nate reached out and disconnected the call. "Studio time costs money. I have a dozen artists I'm currently working with. If Ivy's not going to show up ready to work, then she needs to find a different producer for her album."

"Oh, no, please. She's counting on working with you." Mia was breathless and anxious. "I'll make sure she's where she needs to be exactly when you say."

"Promise?"

He held out his hand, impatient to revisit the feel of her. From the first Mia had appealed to him. She was as natural and competent as Ivy was artificial and flighty.

But it was that electric charge that sizzled through him when they touched that he craved.

Her eyes were solemn and earnest as she placed her palm against his. "Promise."

Mia hoped Nate wouldn't notice the way her fingers trembled as they shook hands. In those delightful seconds, Ivy Bliss faded from Mia's mind. There was only this tall, charismatic man with eyes the color of storm clouds.

For as far back as she could remember, Mia had been invisible. Why would anyone pay attention to the ordinary-looking child standing beside and a little behind the beautiful, charismatic, talented Ivy? And the difference between the twins had only intensified when Ivy had gotten a role in a television series and gone on to Broadway and a pop music career. Mia had become the quiet shadow at her elbow.

And then she'd met Nate. Never in a million years could Mia have believed that someone as talented and charismatic as the lead singer of Free Fall would notice she existed, much less be attracted to her. He'd seen her as a distinct individual with interests and goals. That was pretty heady stuff. No wonder she'd tumbled head over heels for him. What woman with a pulse wouldn't have?

Then the tour ended and the real world overcame the fantasy one she'd dwelled in for two months. She'd had no choice but to turn down his offer to go with him to Las Vegas. Nate had been so angry with her that last morning in Sydney. He'd accused her of leading him on. It struck her as impossible that a nobody like her could be anything more than a momentary distraction to someone as incredible as Nate Tucker.

Given all that he'd accomplished in the music industry, it amazed Mia that he was only thirty-one. An accomplished singer/songwriter and producer, he'd had six Grammy nominations for producing and won two. His band had been nominated for twenty-nine assorted awards and won eight, including several Grammys and an AMA award for favorite pop/rock band/duo/group.

"Are you okay?" he asked, peering at her.

They were still holding hands. Mia's cheeks heated as she released her grip. "Sorry." She took an awkward step back and bumped into one of the chairs surrounding the large oval conference table. "I was just thinking how lucky Ivy was for getting to work with you."

The dimple flashing in Nate's scruffy cheek vanished. "Mia, about what happened in Sydney—"

"You don't need to go there," Mia said, forcing lightness into her voice. "It was a crazy tour. So much fun. I won't ever forget it."

"That's not what I meant and you know it."

"Please, Nate." She longed to surrender to the intense glow in his eyes and fall into his arms. "You need to focus on Ivy. And so do I. She's really freaked out about this new direction in her career. I told her you were the best producer in the business and that together you would make platinum."

"I couldn't care less about her or her album. I'm only doing this so I can spend more time with you."

His words sent a spear of yearning through her, but Mia shook her head. "Don't say that. Ivy needs this album to be great." Maybe if she had a hit Ivy's insecurity would stop consuming her, and Mia could begin to live her life far from her demanding twin.

"How long are you planning to keep on being her lackey? Don't you want to be free to explore what makes you happy?"

"Of course." And she would have that life if Ivy's new project catapulted her into the big time. "And someday I'll have that chance."

"For your sake I hope someday is soon." The intensity in Nate's gaze made her shiver.

"I have to get going," Mia said, although now that she'd seen Nate again, the last thing she wanted to do was leave. "You'll text me the details about dinner tonight?"

"Yes."

As Nate escorted Mia to the lobby, she noticed he didn't touch her again.

"It was good seeing you," she murmured awkwardly. She wanted to throw herself into his arms and declare how much she'd missed him. But that would only make the problems between them worse.

Mia maintained a firm grip on her impulses. The connection they'd share on tour had been packed up and put away with the instruments, lights and sound equipment. Sneaking around behind Ivy's back had been necessary and exciting, but it wasn't something Mia intended to do any longer.

While on tour Ivy had been distracted by the traveling, flirting with Free Fall's single band members and blowing up social media for her fans. In Las Vegas, she would be completely focused on her music and on Nate. Mia wouldn't have any opportunities for time alone with him.

Ever since Ivy learned that she was going to work with Nate, she'd been more agitated and demanding than Mia ever remembered her being. Mia wasn't a fool. She understood why Ivy was so reluctant to give her space. Heaven forbid Mia would get a life and walk away.

After leaving Nate, Mia was halfway through the errands she was running for Ivy when her phone began to play Ivy's latest hit, her special ring tone. Mia held off answering for several seconds. But she'd already ignored a bunch of Ivy's texts, and her sister would have a fit if she didn't pick up now.

"OMG. Where have you been? I've texted you, like, a dozen times." Ivy's voice poured from Mia's smartphone, scattering her thoughts to the wind. Behind closed doors the sweetheart pop star became a demanding diva. "I've been dying to hear all about how excited Nate is that we're working together."

"Sorry I didn't respond." In fact, she'd been lost in thought and hadn't heard the alerts. "Traffic was crazy and there was an accident..."

"If you were sitting in traffic you should have called." Ivy barely gave that a second to sink in before continuing, "Whatever. Tell me. Tell me."

"Of course he's excited to be working with you."

"What did he say exactly?"

"That you're going to make the best album ever." It was lame, but her sister would freak if Mia shared what Nate had actually said. "But listen, Ivy—"

Her sister's squeal interrupted her. "I knew it. He is into me."

"I'm sorry. What?" Mia almost rear-ended the car in front of her when the driver stopped abruptly to avoid hitting an SUV that cut him off.

"Nate. He's into me." Ivy sounded quite pleased with herself. "I told you how he was hitting on me on tour."

"Nate hit on you?" Mia's stomach clenched in dismay at Ivy's words. "When was that?"

When it came to her sister, Mia was like one of Pavlov's dogs. She panicked at the first sign that her sister was scheming. Ivy made an art form out of keeping the focus on her. Even before Ivy became famous she knew how to manipulate a situation to suit her and often Mia received the full brunt of the backlash. Since then Ivy had pulled several stunts to stay in the spotlight. Mia had learned to keep her head down.

"All the time. How did you not notice?"

"Sure. Of course." Mia was glad her sister couldn't see her expression.

"And I never told you, but that last night in Sydney..." She let the confession hang in the air to build suspense.

"What about it?"

"We were together."

A curse shot from Mia before she could stop herself. "Sorry, I almost hit the car in front of me. This traffic is—"

"Whatever. Did you hear what I said?"

"About you being with Nate that last night in Sydney?" Mia was torn between a laugh and a groan. Good thing she'd already put her romance with Nate behind her. Now that Ivy had decided she wanted him, any hint that Mia had feelings for him would be disastrous.

"I should've told you."

Mia's voice was uncharacteristically sharp as she asked, "Why didn't you?"

"You don't need to be such a bitch. I'm sorry I didn't say something sooner, but I wasn't sure if what we had was going anywhere."

"And now?" Mia turned into the parking structure closest to the stores she needed to hit.

"Ever since I found out he asked to work with me on my new album, I've been convinced what we have is the real deal." Ivy sounded at the same time dreamy and triumphant. "When will you be getting back to the house?"

"I'm heading to Rodeo Drive to take care of the stuff you wanted me to return." Ivy loved to shop, but she could be fickle when it came to liking things once she got them home. "It shouldn't take me more than half an hour."

As self-absorbed as Ivy could be, when it came to her twin, she liked knowing everything Mia was up to. It had gotten to the point where Mia gave up on having secrets of her own. Or that's the way it had been until Nate came along. That they shared the ability to sign had enabled Mia to have something all to herself that Ivy couldn't barge in on and take over.

Mia realized she'd been counting on this album to launch her sister, hoping that it would be enough of a distraction to allow Mia to escape.

Was that how she viewed Ivy? As someone Mia needed to run away from? The relationship between Mia and her sister hadn't always been so strained. Until the last three or four years, when Ivy's career really took off, Mia and Ivy had been as close as two people who shared the same womb for nine months could be.

If anything demonstrated how much Mia craved a chance to get out of Ivy's shadow, it was her clandestine flirtation with a man her sister had shown an interest in. And now Mia realized that despite the way she'd left things that last morning in Sydney, a part of her hadn't given up on pursing a relationship with Nate.

In the beginning she'd simply enjoyed Nate's charismatic presence. Not only was the lead singer of Free Fall a musical genius, he had killer dimples that rendered her speechless, and the sort of lean muscles that made her all too aware of her vulnerable heart, unsteady knees and tendency to blush.

At first she hadn't taken his attention seriously. Fate had seen to it that Ivy was granted all the beauty and most of the talent. Most people outside their family didn't even know Mia and Ivy were sisters, much less twins. Ivy had taken their mother's maiden name because she liked the way it sounded, and Bliss worked great for marketing.

And then one day Nate had been backstage while Ivy rehearsed. She'd stopped the sound check and was shrieking at the drummer for messing with the tempo. Across the ten feet separating them, Mia saw the gesture Nate made, and amusement must have shown on her face because he snagged her gaze and winked.

Mia had signed, asking him if he knew what that particular gesture meant, and he signed back that he absolutely did. For the duration of Ivy's sound check, they'd discovered through sign language that each had a hearing-impaired family member. That day something unexpected had happened to Mia. She'd made an unlikely friend. And in the weeks that followed, it became more.

Ivy broke into her thoughts. "Can you stop and get me a coffee on your way back? You know how I like it."

Keeping up with Ivy's demands required Mia's full attention. For most of her life that hadn't bothered her. But ever since Nate had come along and actually noticed her, not as Ivy's twin or her assistant, but as a desirable woman, Mia spent more and more time thinking about a life away from Ivy.

"Sure." Now all she needed to do was find a way to explain to her family that she wanted to strike out on her own. And that was not going to be easy. "I know exactly how it needs to be."

Two

As soon as Mia left the studio, Nate got on the phone with Trent's sister. Melody had been on the tour with him as the opening act for Free Fall the entire twelve months.

Because he knew her as not only a fantastic songwriter and singer, but also as the little sister of his best friend and business partner, when she'd asked what was going on between him and Mia, he'd told her. Melody didn't like the way Mia was treated by her sister any more than he did. She'd grown up with a father who liked to bully people and had a particular sensitivity to such treatment.

Once she'd been clued in to what was going on, Melody had helped keep Ivy distracted so Nate and Mia could have as much uninterrupted time together as possible. At first Nate wasn't sure if Mia had any idea how Melody was helping them, but she'd caught on quickly. Mia and Melody shared a talent for songwriting and during the hours they spent collaborating became good friends.

The difference in Mia when Ivy wasn't around showed Nate how unhappy Mia was being her sister's personal assistant. Yet whenever he broached the subject of leaving her sister's employment to do something for herself, he hit a brick wall.

"You told your brother I met someone while on tour?"

"I might have mentioned that you were a bit distracted." Melody responded carefully, but there was laughter in her tone.

Nate closed his eyes and rubbed his temple. Melody had a romantic nature and succumbed easily to simple gestures of affection, like the dozen handwritten notes her boyfriend, Kyle Tailor, had tucked amongst the clothes in her suitcase. She'd discovered them halfway across the country and been over the moon that Kyle had done something so romantic.

Unfortunately, the strain of separation for so many months had led to trouble in their relationship. Nate blamed himself. If it weren't for him, Melody never would've gone on tour. He'd been the one who persuaded her to leave behind the anonymity of songwriting and to join him onstage. She had a fantastic voice and deserved to shine.

Fortunately, Kyle didn't blame him. If he had, it might have put a strain on their business partnership in Club T's.

"He thinks it's Ivy." Nate spent the next minute listening to Melody's laughter. "It's not funny."

"Oh, it is. Why does he think that?"

"Because I suggested I produce her next album. It's the only way I could think of to spend more time with Mia. She's determined we're over."

"I think that's fantastic. The girl has a killer voice and needs a producer who can showcase it. Besides, no one but you can stand up to that father of hers and make sure her next album kills it."

"I'm flattered that you think so." Nate's tone was as dry as the Mohave Desert.

"So how did the meeting go?"

"It didn't. Mia showed up without her sister and father. Apparently they were taking a meeting with someone from Mayfair Cosmetics. They're considering Ivy as their next spokesmodel."

"Are you kidding? They stood you up? Don't they realize who you are?"

"Obviously someone they can skip a meeting with." Nate thought about his stern words to Mia about her sister and regretted taking his frustration out on her. It wasn't her fault how her sister and father behaved. "I'm taking them to dinner tonight. Hopefully, they'll show up this time. I'm going to be out of commission for a few weeks starting tomorrow."

"Out of commission? What's going on?"

"I'm going in for surgery on my vocal cords."

"What? When did this come up?"

"I started noticing a problem on the tour, but we were so close to the end, and I didn't want to cancel any shows." In part because to do so meant shortening his time with Mia. Their relationship heated up a lot in the last two weeks and he wouldn't have missed that for anything.

"This is serious. Why didn't you say anything to me? Does Trent know?"

"I told him earlier today."

"Is he taking you to the surgery appointment?"

"He's out of town. I have a car scheduled. It'll be fine."

"No it won't. I'll get on a plane and be there to take you back to the hotel."

"That's not necessary. You need to stay in Vegas and work on your album. I've given you a deadline, remember?"

"A couple days isn't going to matter one way or another."

"Humor me." Letting anyone baby him was not in his nature. "It's outpatient surgery. I'll be in and out in a few hours."

"Why do you have to be so strong all the time? It wouldn't kill you to accept help once in a while." Melody let loose an exasperated sigh. "You are so stubborn."

After a childhood spent bouncing from one backwater town to another, Nate had learned to take care of himself. Sometimes his dad would be gone for months, sent all over the country to whatever oil fields needed his expertise the most. If the job required an extended stay, he might bring Nate and his mom along. Nate's dad never cared if this meant his son had to fit in at a new school or that his wife would have to take whatever job she could to make ends meet.

"I could say the same of you." Nate knew of only one way to get Melody off this particular subject. "How are things between you and Kyle? Have you talked yet?"

"Did you know that Trent hired Hunter to DJ twice a month at Club T's?"

"He mentioned something about it. I told him it was a bad idea."

Hunter Graves was Melody's ex-boyfriend. Several months ago he and Melody had run into each other in a New York City club. As they were leaving, to keep from getting separated while passing through the raucous crowd outside, Hunter had taken Melody's hand as they headed to a waiting car. The paparazzi had snapped several pictures of the couple and the media had ruthlessly promoted its theory that the former lovers had reunited.

Back home, while Kyle hadn't really believed Melody was cheating on him, he hadn't appreciated seeing the woman he loved hand in hand with her ex. And the months of separation had created tension for the couple, making Kyle even more reactive.

Melody sighed in Nate's ear. "And to answer your earlier question, Kyle and I have exchanged several texts, but we haven't sat down to talk."

"Don't you think that should happen soon?"

"I'm afraid if we have the talk we'll just end up fighting and the subject of us being over will come up."

"Kyle hasn't come to Las Vegas and taken over temporary management of Club T's because he's ready to give up on you two."

"He's here because Trent's in LA with Savannah and the club needs a manager." Melody's voice had a ragged quality that tore at Nate's heart. "Sorry," she muttered. "I really hope you're right about him, but I can't stop feeling like he's going to use what's happened between us since that photo came out to rationalize that we're not really meant to be together."

"He's not going to do that," Nate said. "Especially after he finds out what's really going on."

"What do you mean by that?" Melody sounded more wary than confused.

"You forget how hard it is to keep secrets on tours."

"You and Mia managed."

"That's because the only one we had to keep in the dark was Ivy, and in general she's so preoccupied with herself that she isn't sensitive to what's going on around her." Nate circled back to Melody's problem. "When are you going to tell Kyle he's going to be a father?"

"Damn. Who else knows?"

"Both Dan and Mike commented that you were looking a bit off and mentioned that their wives had both been sick like that when they were pregnant."

"Why did they tell you?"

"Because you're like my little sister and I've made it pretty clear all along that anyone who messed with you would get their ass kicked by me."

Melody huffed out of a breath. "I can take care of myself."

"Aww, that's cute," he mocked. "But you really can't. You are too sweet for your own good and people take advantage of that."

The same could be said of Mia. And his mother. Nate recognized he had a pattern when it came to women. He didn't actively seek out those most in need of protecting, but he did tend to gravitate to the ones who had a hard time sticking up for themselves.

"And you don't let anyone take care of you," Melody countered. "Case in point, tomorrow's surgery."

"Okay, we've both poked at each other's shortcomings long enough," Nate said with a laugh. "I'll shoot you a text tomorrow after it's done and let you know how it went."

"I'm not kidding about coming to LA to sit at your bedside."

"And I appreciate the offer, but I'd rather you take care of things there." He paused before delivering his final bit of advice. "Talk to Kyle. He's going to be thrilled."

"I will. Good luck tomorrow."

"Thanks."

After talking with Melody, Nate made a reservation for four at WP24, Wolfgang Puck's contemporary Asian restaurant on the twenty-fourth floor of the Ritz-Carlton. He selected this particular restaurant knowing Mia would love the downtown LA views and the blackberry soufflé with key lime ice cream for dessert. Once that was done, he texted her the details and then headed to grab a late lunch with his former buddy whose music career had nosedived six years ago, thanks to a drug problem, but who was making a small comeback.

Nate didn't return to his hotel until nearly six. He spent the time before dinner Skyping with his mother and letting her know in rapid ASL about the surgery the following day. At least he wouldn't have to worry about being able to communicate with her over the next two to three weeks while he was on total voice rest. If only the rest of his clients understood sign language, he might be able to maintain his work schedule with barely a hitch.

At a little before eight, Nate stepped off the elevator on the twenty-fourth floor of the Ritz-Carlton and approached the hostess. His pulse kicked up as he looked around for Mia, but he didn't see her or her family. The hostess confirmed they'd not yet arrived, and escorted him to a table by the windows. When the waiter arrived, Nate ordered a vodka on the rocks with a twist of lime. Normally he'd wait until his party showed up, but he expected Mia and her family to be late and they didn't disappoint them. What he hadn't expected, however, was Mia's absence.

Nate stood as Ivy approached. She wore a strapless emerald dress that clung to her slim body and brought out the gold flecks in her brown eyes. Her five-inch heels put a sexy sway in her stride.

"Nate," she cried in delight as if they were the best of friends. "It's so wonderful to see you."

They hadn't gotten along particularly well on the tour. She'd made demands on everyone from the roadies to the tour manager, and some of her requests had been ridiculous. The amount of time Nate had spent running interference hadn't sat well with him. And he had a particular distaste for how she treated Mia.

"Hello, Ivy," he said, pushing down his annoyance at how he'd been stood up earlier. "Good evening, Javier." He reached out his hand to Ivy's father, a handsome dark-haired man trailing in the pop star's wake. One member of the party was missing. "I made the reservation for four. Will Mia be joining us?"

Ivy settled into the chair beside his. "She wanted to come, but what's the point?"

The annoyance that flared in his gut was familiar. Everything about this spoiled narcissistic brat made him long to hand off her album project to another producer, but his whole purpose in working with Ivy was to have time with Mia.

"The point is I invited her."

"I thought the point of this meeting tonight was to discuss Ivy's album," Javier said, coming down on his daughter's side. "Mia's presence is unnecessary."

"Of course." Giving in was exceedingly painful. Nate could only imagine the conversation that had kept Mia away, and his heart ached that she'd received yet another slight from the people who should have had her best interests in mind.

The waiter approached before Nate could say anything more. Ivy ordered champagne and Javier ordered a gin and tonic.

"I've heard the food here is quite good," Javier said.

Ivy rolled her eyes. "If you like Asian."

Nate was pretty certain no matter which restaurant he'd chosen Ivy would've found something wrong with it.

Without Mia's presence, Nate had no desire to linger over the meal. As soon as they'd ordered he cut straight to business. "I have some ideas for how to proceed with your new album."

"I want to go in a completely different direction," Ivy said, cutting him off before she even heard what he had to say. "I'm not going to write my own music this time. I'd like to record some of Melody Caldwell's music. I heard what she was working on during the tour and I think it suits me."

While Nate agreed, he was dismayed that Ivy had no plans to record her sister's songs. Few people knew Ivy didn't write any of her own music but claimed credit for what Mia composed. Nate had discovered this during the tour and couldn't believe Mia let her sister get away with it. He suspected that part of the reason Mia stayed with Ivy and acted as her assistant was to have her music heard by millions. Did Mia know that Ivy was cutting her out? Would this at last be the catalyst that encouraged Mia to sever the bonds with her sister and strike out on her own?

"I can see if Melody would be open to working with you."

"Why wouldn't she?" Javier demanded. "Having Ivy Bliss record her songs would be a good career move for her."

"Currently Melody is working on an album of her own. A song list hasn't been finalized and I can't promise what will be available for you until that happens."

"I have several songs I'm interested in. I'll have Mia

send her a list in the morning. I'm sure Melody will understand that I can do them justice."

"Perhaps you and Melody could collaborate on some new stuff," Nate suggested, hoping the offer made Ivy squirm. "I've worked with her on several songs she's recorded. I think you two would enjoy collaborating."

He smiled through the patent lie. If Melody caught wind of what he'd just offered, she'd probably kill him. Nate doubted anyone on the planet enjoyed working with Ivy Bliss.

"I'm afraid my daughter will be too busy to write any music this year. This afternoon she signed a deal to become the new face of Mayfair Cosmetics. This will entail many media appearances beginning a month from now. We'd like to get in and get her album recorded as soon as possible."

So they expected him to clear his schedule? Nate wasn't surprised. And he would not be bullied. "I'm afraid the next month will not be good for me. Let's look at something after the first of the year?"

"Ivy is doing a movie in January."

Once again Nate reminded himself that the reason he'd agreed to produce the album was to have time with Mia. And then something occurred to him. It was brilliant, and he kicked himself for not coming up with it sooner.

His lips slid into a genuine smile. "Perhaps we could work something out. I'll need to rearrange my schedule and would appreciate having Mia's help to pull it off."

"Mia's help?" Ivy frowned. "What could she possibly do for you?"

"She understands sign language, doesn't she? I could use her as a translator."

Javier frowned. "A translator?"

"I'm going in for vocal cord surgery tomorrow and won't be able to speak for at least three weeks. I can sign and Mia can relay my instructions."

"Couldn't you find someone else to help with that?" Ivy demanded. "An actual interpreter?"

No one else but Mia would do. "Mia knows the music industry and will understand what I'm saying."

"Daddy?" Ivy's dismay was palpable.

Nate fixed Javier with a flat stare. "Surely you can spare her for a month if it means getting Ivy's album done."

Javier glanced at his daughter. "W-well," he stammered. "Of course. If that's what we need to do."

Nate gave a satisfied nod. "It absolutely is."

Mia sat in a chair beside the window of her bedroom in Ivy's house and stared at the front lawn. An hour earlier she'd watched her father's Mercedes retreat down the driveway, and still couldn't believe that she'd been forced to stay behind. More than ever her role as Ivy's personal assistant grated on her.

Though Mia felt trapped by her responsibility to Ivy, she knew that her sister carried an even heavier burden: the weight of their parents' expectations. Mia barely remembered a time when her sister didn't sing. She recalled their modest house in San Diego, where the twins had shared a bedroom with their older sister, Eva. Their mother had homeschooled all three girls, which offered the flexibility for Ivy to audition anytime an opportunity presented itself. And their parents were able to buy a bigger house when Ivy signed a contract for a new TV show on the KidZ Channel. While she wasn't the star, in the show's four-year run Ivy had demonstrated star potential, which had led to her landing a role in a

Broadway musical and eventually a record deal with West Coast Records.

With each rise in her career, the family home got bigger and better. Their father had quit his job with the post office to manage Ivy when she signed with KidZ Channel. Ivy became his whole focus.

Which brought Mia to tonight, and the business meeting her father and sister were attending with Nate. And just as her presence hadn't been needed at the Mayfair Cosmetics meeting earlier that day, Mia wasn't included now.

She wondered if Nate's choice of WP24 had been for her benefit. She'd mentioned how she'd always wanted to try the restaurant, but that had been a couple months ago. Had Nate remembered?

Mia's stomach grumbled, reminding her she hadn't eaten anything since noon. Even though her appetite was nonexistent, her body still needed fuel. Time to stop brooding and scrounge up something for dinner. Ivy's housekeeper usually cooked some chicken in case Ivy felt like supplementing her junk food diet with something healthy.

After pulling out the fixings for a salad and chopping up a chicken breast, Mia splurged with an extra tablespoon of ranch dressing. Too bad she gained weight simply by looking at French fries. As she headed into the den to watch some TV and hopefully take her mind off what was going on at WP24, she reminded herself that Nate had appreciated her full breasts, small waist and round hips.

Both Mia and Eva took after their mother with their dark brown hair and eyes, pale skin and curvy bodies. Ivy was built like their dad, lean and sinewy, but she had their mother's hazel eyes, smoldering charm and singing ability. Sharon Bliss had been an opera singer in her youth, but happily traded a career on the stage for being a wife and mother when she got pregnant with Eva.

Mia had barely sat down when her cell phone rang. She smiled when she saw that the caller was Melody. "I feel as if I haven't talked to you in ages. How are you doing?" she said by way of greeting.

"I'm doing great. Working on my album."

"How many songs are you up to now?"

Melody was a prolific songwriter with a powerful voice and distaste for the spotlight. The two women had become close while on tour. Mia didn't realize how much she missed having a friend until she and Melody had clicked.

"I don't know," Melody said. "Maybe around fifty. They're not all good, but many of my favorites are the ones with the biggest flaws. How am I supposed to choose between them?"

"I know the feeling. Some of my best stuff will never be heard." Until she'd gone on tour, only her family knew that she—and not Ivy—was the author of Ivy's hit tunes. Then she'd met Nate and Melody, and both of them had figured out her secret. Or maybe she hadn't tried very hard to conceal it. Both were such talented songwriters that Mia couldn't resist the urge to talk to them about their process.

To preserve the illusion that Ivy was writing her own songs, Mia was always careful to work when no one was around. But sometimes a tune got into her head and she caught herself humming it. The same thing happened with lyrics. It was why she always carried around her journal.

The notebook contained bits and pieces of songs and

snippets of lyrics. It also included doodles and miscellaneous thoughts. She filled one every six months or so.

"Nate could help you with that. I'm sure he'd be happy to work up some demos with you that you could shop around the industry. You never know what might get picked up."

"Actually, he's already offered."

"And what are you waiting for?"

Mia hadn't explained to anyone the real reason she stayed at her sister's side despite the way she was treated like hired help instead of family. It wasn't Mia's story to tell and she knew neither Ivy nor her parents would appreciate the information getting out. Not that Melody or Nate couldn't be trusted with yet another of her secrets.

"I'm not waiting for anything. It's just that I barely have enough time to write, much less create demos." But with Ivy scheduled to record her album at Nate's Ugly Trout studios in Las Vegas, perhaps she would have time to do something for herself for a change.

"Speaking of Nate, did you know he was going in for throat surgery tomorrow?"

"No." Mia's heart gave a worried thump. "I knew he was struggling while we were on tour, and that he pushed through because he didn't want to cancel any shows, but we haven't spoken much since the tour ended."

Nate had made it perfectly clear that he wanted to continue the relationship. As intoxicating as their affair had been, Mia knew it was only a matter of time until their paths diverged. He wanted her to choose him over Ivy, but she just couldn't leave her sister. Would the time ever be right? It was the question Nate had posed that last morning in Sydney. Mia had no clear answer.

"I'm worried about him. He's using a car service to get to and from the doctor's office tomorrow, and he doesn't have anyone staying with him at the hotel to help him after the procedure. I was wondering, since you are in LA, if you could check on him."

"Of course." It was something a friend would do and they'd parted on reasonably good terms. Why hadn't he said anything to her when they'd met earlier?

Mia ran through what she would say to her sister tomorrow about taking care of Nate, and decided she would simply tell her that she needed some time off. It wasn't as if Mia got to take vacations like a regular person. All the time she spent around Ivy was work, even when she was technically off. They might head to the Caribbean or the beaches of Europe together for a little R & R, but it wasn't as though Mia got to party all night, drink too much and sleep in.

"Do you know what clinic he's going to?" Mia asked. "And what time the surgery is?"

"No. I'm assuming that he's using Dr. Hanson. He's the best vocal cord surgeon in LA. Nate mentioned the appointment is first thing in the morning."

"How about where he's staying?"

"He usually gets a suite at the Four Seasons Beverly Hills when he's in LA. It's close to West Coast Records' offices."

"I know it well. Ivy stayed there while renovations were being done on her house."

"One more thing. Don't tell Nate you're coming. You know how he hates accepting help."

"I've got it covered. He'll never know what hit him."

"You're a doll," Melody said. "I've been sick, thinking about him all alone after the surgery."

"Don't worry," Mia said. "I'll take excellent care of him."

"I know you will. And he might never admit it, but I think he'll be really glad to have you there."

Three

The morning of his surgery Nate's thoughts were running on a hamster wheel, getting him nowhere. Not being able to talk for several weeks was going to make communicating with his clients a challenge. Although he'd asked for Mia's help from her father and sister, he hadn't approached her about acting as his voice for the next three to four weeks.

It wasn't that he couldn't hire an assistant with ASL experience, although it might be tricky finding one on such short notice. He also wasn't worried that the studio was booked solid and people were counting on him. He dreaded getting turned down by Mia again.

Pushing all that to the side, Nate left his suite and headed to the elevator. When the car arrived at his floor, a young couple with a baby stroller were already inside. Nate stepped to the side of the elevator and gazed from the infant to the happy parents. Almost against his will, his thoughts turned to Mia.

During those days with her on tour, for the first time ever, he'd contemplated what it would take to balance life on the road with a family. With the amount of touring Free Fall had done for the first few years when they were making a name for themselves, Nate hadn't even considered settling down.

Promoting an album meant grueling months on the road. It wasn't the sort of thing where you dragged a wife and kids along. Well, some people did. But unless it was the right sort of relationship, traveling from one end of the country to another put a lot of strain on a couple.

And then he'd met Mia. She was used to long months of touring and being away from home. As Ivy's personal assistant, she was on the go constantly. In fact, he wasn't entirely sure if she had a home of her own. He'd easily pictured them working together in the studio and then going out on tour. If they had a baby, the whole family would travel. It had been an appealing fantasy.

The elevator opened on the lobby and the couple with the stroller exited. Nate's mood, already battered by his anxiety about the surgery, took another hit. Damn, he was tired of being alone.

Suddenly every muscle in his body ached. He hadn't felt a sweeping depression like this in ten years. Back then he'd fought off the darkness with pills, booze and sex. None of it had helped, but for a while he'd been able to forget.

Nate stepped into the lobby, calling himself all kinds of coward and idiot for trying to handle things on his own. He was always the first one to lend a hand if someone needed it. Why did he have such an awful time accepting help?

Shame. Admitting that he wasn't strong enough to protect his mother when he was a kid or conquer an addiction to drugs when he was in his early twenties had led to both situations becoming worse. If he'd reached out for help, maybe his mom wouldn't have been nearly beaten to death by his father and he wouldn't have ended up burning bridges in the music business.

Nate headed across the hotel lobby and outside to where a car should be waiting to take him to the doctor's office. He'd turned down Trent's and Melody's offers to help, and he wasn't feeling great about his decision. But he hated being a bother. Trent was out of town with Savannah and Dylan. Melody was in Las Vegas. And while his mother would have happily flown in from Dallas to baby him for a few days, Nate didn't want to put her out. The surgery was delicate, but not overly invasive, and he was perfectly capable of taking care of himself.

And then the most amazing thing happened. A familiar brunette got up from a chair near the front door and started walking in his direction. Her appearance was so unexpected that he rubbed his eyes to determine if he was hallucinating. If so, she was the most beautiful, wonderful, perfect figment of his imagination he'd ever experienced.

"Mia?"

"At last," she said, gliding into step beside him. "I was worried that I'd missed you. How are you doing?" She peered up at him as the lobby doors opened with a whoosh and fresh air poured over them. "Are you nervous?"

"What are you doing here?"

"I'm here to take care of you." She gave him a stern look. "Why didn't you tell me you were having surgery?"

His first impulse was to tell her he didn't think it would matter to her. But that was a crappy response. He also hadn't thought she'd be available since her sister kept her so busy.

Instead he asked, “How did you know?”

“Melody told me. She said you didn’t have anyone to help you after the surgery and she was worried.” The look Mia shot him was pure accusation. “And so was I.”

“I’ll be perfectly fine.”

“Ridiculous. A doctor won’t release anyone going under anesthesia unless they’re being picked up and watched over by a responsible adult. So, I’m going to sit in the waiting room while you have your surgery. And then I’m going to bring you back here. Tuck you in. And keep watch over you.”

All that sounded like pure heaven. Having her fuss over him for the next few hours would speed his recovery along.

“You don’t need to wait,” he told her as they settled into the back of the town car. “The procedure could take up to six hours.”

“I’m staying.” Her tone was firm. “I brought stuff to read.”

“Thank you.” Such simple words didn’t convey his full emotions. He was so damned glad to have her with him. But she smiled as if she understood.

Nate didn’t feel much like talking on the way to the clinic, so they sat in companionable silence. The surgery was the most terrifying thing he’d ever faced and that included the night his sixteen-year-old self had gone up against his drunk, knife-wielding father.

Singing was more than just Nate’s livelihood. It was how he’d comforted himself as a kid in an abusive home and the way he communicated who he was to the world.

No matter how successful he became as a producer and songwriter, he’d give up every penny he had to be able to perform on stage. This was something he hadn’t realized until he was faced with the grim prospect of throat surgery.

When the nurse came to take him into the back, Mia gave him a reassuring smile. It was her face that filled his thoughts as he was wheeled to the operating room and injected with something to put him to sleep.

And when he woke what seemed like seconds later—in post-op, he guessed, based on the dim lighting and hushed silence—her name was the first thought that popped into his head. He floated in post-surgery haze, happy that she was waiting to take him back to his hotel As the residual anesthesia wore off, Nate lifted fingers to his throat, but the discomfort was all on the inside. Had the surgery been successful? He wouldn't know for several weeks, maybe months.

A nurse came to check on him and asked yes-or-no questions he could answer by nodding or shaking his head. She reiterated what the doctor and all the nurses before her had drilled into him: no talking of any kind for two to three weeks and minimal use of his voice after that. He'd start working with a vocal coach in a month, which would be a new experience. In all the years he'd performed, Nate had never had any formal training. He just got up on stage and let 'er rip.

They wanted him back in three days for a checkup, after which he could return to Las Vegas to continue healing. The nurse recommended Throat Coat tea with honey and gave him a prescription for pain meds.

"Your throat will probably grow more uncomfortable as the day goes on. Drink lots of fluids and remember, no talking."

Nate nodded. He might suck at taking advice on most things, but this he intended to follow to the letter. He couldn't imagine losing the ability to sing and perform.

While he had songwriting and producing to fall back on, the energy that came at him from a packed stadium was a high he craved.

From post-op they sent him back into the waiting room, where Mia was still waiting, and gave him a glass of water. It slid down his throat without too much irritation and he grew hopeful.

"Are you okay?" Mia asked, giving his hand a gentle squeeze. "Let me know when you're ready to head to the car."

He nodded.

The trip back to the hotel was a blur. When they arrived at his suite, Nate fumbled out his key card and tried to focus on getting it into the slot. He wanted to curse, but knew better than to speak. And then, Mia plucked the key from him and within seconds the door swung open. He took a step forward and his head picked that second to swim. With his reflexes not quite back to normal, he swayed and made a grab for the doorframe just in time to prevent himself from pitching forward.

Her arm went around his waist to steady him. "I've got you," she said, but she wasn't as calm and collected as she sounded. Her brown eyes looked huge in her pale face.

"I'm okay, really."

She looked so appalled that he almost laughed, but he knew better than to make a sound.

"You okay?"

She gave a husky laugh. "I'll be better once you're in bed and resting."

"I knew you'd been dying to get me back into bed." His dry smile didn't help ease the tense line between her brows. And then, becoming more serious, he signed, "*It means a lot that you're here.*"

He wanted to follow it up by asking how long she could stay, but again sensed the answer wouldn't make him happy. For now, he'd enjoy her company and take what time with her he could get.

"I'm sorry things between us didn't work out..." She was prevented from saying more by his fingertips against her lips.

He didn't want to talk about the failure of their relationship or argue about Mia's inability to escape her sister's demands. His arms ached to hold her. At the moment he didn't have energy to do more than sit on the couch with her snuggled against him, though.

"Come." He patted the cushion beside him.

"You should go to bed."

"I'm not tired."

For an instant he worried she might call him on that, but then she joined him on the couch.

"At least lie down."

He obliged by shifting until he lay on his back, his head in her lap. She ran her fingers through his hair. The soothing caress made his whole body ache. Damn, but he'd missed her. How many times in the last month had he relived those precious few hours they'd spent together that last night in Sydney? Over and over the memories tumbled through his mind as he recalled every touch and kiss. The ravenous hunger with which they'd come together that first time. The ache in his chest as the sun lifted above the horizon. The glorious, joyful goddess he'd held in his arms, who faded before his eyes as the morning grew brighter.

He'd sworn then that he would have her. All of her. He intended to do whatever it took to make her happy. Only she would have none of it. None of him. She didn't understand what it meant to be selfish. To demand happiness. Her family had molded her into someone who put her needs after everyone else's.

He closed his eyes and enjoyed the silence. With Mia he'd learned to appreciate being quiet, for it allowed him to be fully in the moment. Almost immediately, however, Nate found himself drifting off, and fought to stay awake. He'd learned during those long weeks on tour to savor every minute with Mia, because all too often their secret rendezvous were interrupted. But with what he'd gone through earlier today, his body craved sleep.

The next time he woke the suite was dim. His head remained cushioned on Mia's lap. He rubbed his face and sat up.

"What time is it?" he signed.

"Six. How are you feeling?"

"Sore."

"I'll get you some water." She got to her feet and headed for the wet bar consisting of a mini-fridge behind a white panel door. When she returned and handed him a chilled bottle, she asked, "Do you want to take something?"

He shook his head. Although the pain in his throat required medication to take the edge off, he didn't like the way the drugs made him feel. Early in his career he'd gotten caught up in the highs and lows of the music scene and had partied too hard. He'd relied on booze and pills to jack him up and mellow him out. And then there had always been girls. They were relentless. He'd signed boobs and butts. He'd taken two to bed and woken up with a third. And all this had happened before Free Fall had their first hit.

Then one morning, Nate had woken up with a thick head and a sick feeling in his gut that had nothing to do with how much he'd consumed the night before. There was a fist-size dent in his hotel room wall and a descriptive expletive written in lipstick on his bathroom mirror. He remembered being angry, but not why. It had been perfectly clear, however, that he'd struck out in anger. Just like his old man used to do.

Nate didn't have any luck tracking down the girl he'd brought back to his room. She'd just been one of the faceless hangers-on who liked to party after the concerts. He'd been twenty-three and the wake-up call had changed his life. He took a break from the band and returned home to Las Vegas, where he'd spent the next twelve months writing music.

It hadn't been an easy time. For the first two months neither the words nor the music would flow. The urge to lose himself in alcohol or drugs had been a constant nagging presence. Much of the songwriting he'd done to that point had been while he was under the influence. He was afraid he didn't know how to write any other way. At that time his mom had still been living in Las Vegas. Being around her kept him from backsliding. He had only to look at her to remember how his father had gone after her with fists and eventually a knife.

At long last the music came more easily. The words took a lot longer. What he wanted to say came from his pain and his isolation and his sense of failure. These were not easy places to visit. He'd never really come to terms with the young boy who'd been too afraid to defend his mother. While a rational part of him knew it was ridiculous to expect a kid to take on a drunk, belligerent adult with a murderous temper, Nate knew there were things he should have done.

Like tell someone. His teacher. A cop. Anyone who could help. His mom had never learned to read lips and had had a hard time communicating. Nate became her voice from the time he could speak. But when it counted, he hadn't spoken for her.

"Are you hungry?" Mia asked. "I can heat up some soup. I brought you some of my famous chicken broth. And I have Throat Coat tea with honey."

Nate gazed up at her in bemusement. If this was what it felt like to be the beneficiary of Mia's nurturing, no wonder Ivy kept her sister on such a tight leash. How wonderful to have someone so focused on your every need.

I could get used to having you around all the time, he thought, but instead signed. *"I'm hungry."*

He hadn't noticed his empty stomach until Mia mentioned the soup. The thought of eating something she'd prepared with her lovely hands made him smile.

"What?" she asked, taking in his expression.

"I can't believe you're here."

"Well, don't get used to it," she teased, heading to the fridge once more. "You only get me for three days."

She busied herself pulling out a plastic container and ladling soup into a bowl. The suite had only the bare minimum of supplies—a coffeemaker, cups and a microwave, in addition to the small refrigerator—but somehow Mia presented a lovely tray with silverware, a linen napkin and even a tiny vase with a daisy in it.

"All this for me?" he signed as she placed the tray on his lap.

"Eat what you can. And there's vanilla and caramel gelato for dessert if you think you can manage it."

Instead of joining him on the couch, she sat in a chair nearby and watched him like a hawk as he tasted the soup. "Is it okay? Not too bland?"

"It's delicious."

"You should be able to switch to thicker liquids and

soft foods tomorrow. Maybe some creamy cauliflower or broccoli soup?" He'd once told her he hated any sort of pureed vegetable, and wondered if she was taking perverse pleasure in his situation. When he scowled at her, she laughed. "Macaroni and cheese?"

"Better." And then, since he had her full attention, he added, *"It means a lot to me that you're here."*

Mia drew her knees to her chest, making herself as small as possible. He would have no idea how much his heartfelt words meant to her. Actually, it wasn't his words as much as the look in his eyes that warmed her from the tips of her fingers down to her toes. In the weeks they'd spent apart, she didn't remember ever feeling so alone and empty.

"We promised to be there for each other always," she reminded him, proud that she sounded so steady. He couldn't know what a struggle it was for her to keep from throwing herself into his arms and confessing how miserable she'd been without him. "What sort of friend would I be if I let you go through this alone?"

She knew Nate had trained himself to catch all sorts of subtle nuances in a singer's voice: pitch, strain, emotion. And he could do the same with her. While on tour, it had been pretty obvious that she'd been an open book to him. And he'd capitalized. If it had been another man, Mia might have worried that she was being manipulated into falling into bed. But Nate was a straight arrow. Not one person in the industry had anything but glowing comments about him, personally or professionally.

"We did promise." He gave her a lopsided smile. *"Which brings me to something I spoke to your father about last night. How would you feel about acting as my translator for the next month until I get my voice back?"*

How would she feel? Thrilled. Honored. Slightly terrified. Spending an extended amount of time with him, she was bound to let slip that she was massively crazy about him. Would she have the strength to stick by her original decision if once again he demanded she choose between him and her sister?

The way things were with Ivy at the moment, Mia couldn't leave her. But the opportunity to sit beside Nate while he worked his magic on Ivy's album was worth the risk.

"You talked to my father about this?"

"I wanted to make sure you couldn't use your sister as an excuse to turn me down."

Mia made a face at him. "And both Ivy and my dad were on board?"

"Your sister wasn't thrilled, but she understands in order to have me work on her album in a time frame that fits with her schedule, I'm going to need your special skills."

This arrangement seemed perfect. Ivy would get her album recorded. Mia could keep an eye on her and at the same time spend hours and hours with Nate. A month. It wasn't a lot of time, but it was more than she'd ever expected to have with him after they'd parted in Sydney.

"When do we start?"

"I'm heading back to Vegas on Tuesday after I check in with Dr. Hanson."

"I haven't had a chance to ask. How did your dinner with Ivy and my dad go last night?"

"Did you know your sister wants to record some of Melody's songs?"

"No." Ivy had been acting weird since the tour ended. She'd become more demanding than ever, driving Mia half mad with her quicksilver moods and indecision. And now this. "I guess I shouldn't be surprised. Melody is a talented songwriter and Ivy wants to work with the best."

"I tried to talk her out of it. What you composed during the tour was fantastic."

"She thinks my songs are what are preventing her from moving to the next level." Mia picked at a button on her blouse. "What if she's right? Maybe trying something new will get her that superstardom she craves."

"And what about you?"

"What about me?"

"Are you ready to take your career to the next level?"

"I don't think there's a level above personal assistant." Mia shot Nate a wry grin. But his question had merit.

What did she want to be doing ten years from now? The thought of continuing to cater to her sister's every whim made her stomach churn. Mia supposed their father wouldn't want to manage Ivy forever. Mia could step into that role. Did she want to? If she was honest with herself, she'd admit that more than anything else she wanted to write music.

"I was thinking more in terms of songwriting."

"It's not the easiest way to make a living."

"You might need to combine it with something else to support yourself. Like producing."

"Do you know how many female producers there are in the industry?"

Nate shook his head.

"Neither does anyone else," Mia said with a touch of reproach. "Because the number is so small no one bothers to keep track. But it's around 5 percent."

"How do you know that?"

"When *1989* won the Grammy for album of the year, Taylor Swift talked in her acceptance speech about empowering women and how we should take credit for our own success."

Mia had been sitting alone in Ivy's house, watching the show and feeling a little sick to her stomach at how she hadn't fought for songwriting credit on either of her twin's albums.

"Afterward," Mia continued, "she was criticized for how few women she'd had working on her album. Nineteen people, excluding Taylor, worked on *1989*. Of those, only two were women. That means 11 percent of the production team were female. That's double the percentage of women in the industry."

"Women are underrepresented. How do you feel about changing that? Do you want to?"

"I won't lie and say I've never thought about it. I've been creating beats since Ivy recorded her first single. I know what I would have done to make the song better. Although I've sat in on every one of Ivy's studio sessions, most of what I know about the technical side is from watching other people."

"Is that a yes or no?"

"That's a hell yes, for spending several weeks sitting beside you and learning the ins and outs of what makes you such a fantastic producer. Beyond that I can't say what will happen."

Nate gave a satisfied nod and didn't try to push for anything more. Mia was glad for both their sakes. He'd been so frustrated with her that last morning in Sydney when she dug in her heels and refused to even consider taking time off from her sister and spending it with him. She hadn't seen the point in furthering their relationship when it was all bound to come to an end.

She might have given him a different answer if Nate had been the sort of guy who wanted something casual and would be happy to walk away at any point. If she could've sneaked away here and there for a long weekend with him they might still be involved.

But that wasn't the sort of guy he was. At least not with her. He'd been pretty clear from the start that she was special to him. While he hadn't minded keeping their blossoming romance a secret during the tour, everything had changed after they'd made love. He'd wanted to see her openly and as often as possible.

Ivy would freak if she ever found out Mia and Nate were involved. Especially now that she had some crazy idea that she and Nate were destined for each other. Mia wasn't ready for the upheaval it would cause for her family.

"How's your throat?" She cleared away his tray and brought him some gelato.

"It's great."

But she could tell from the tension in his facial muscles that wasn't true. "Where are your pain meds?"

"I don't want to take them."

Mia was torn. As much as she hated seeing him endure the pain, she had selfish reasons for being glad he'd refused to take the drugs. "Let me get you some water. Everything I've read advises staying hydrated."

She handed him a full water bottle and he signed his thanks. For no good reason, Mia's eyes prickled with sudden tears. Damn this man for turning her into a sappy mess with a simple thank-you. Not trusting her voice, and since saying "you're welcome" wasn't done in American Sign Language, she responded by signing *"no problem"* before turning away.

Despite his short nap earlier, Nate seemed tired, so after watching television together for an hour, she shooed him toward the bedroom. He caught her hand and, before she knew what he intended, dropped a kiss in her palm.

"Are you going to stay?" he signed, his lips curved into a hopeful smile.

The entreaty in his gray eyes messed with her pulse. She'd come prepared to spend the night, but hadn't intended on forcing her presence on him.

"I can."

He wrapped his arm around her waist and drew her against his solid body. Lean muscle shifted beneath her fingertips as she put her hand on his upper abdomen to keep a little space between them.

"On the couch," she added with a shaky laugh.

He shook his head and then tipped it to the side and put his free hand against his cheek to sign *"bed."* Her toes curled at the thought of lying beside him while he slept, listening to his even breathing, tormented by his powerful frame mere inches away. If they shared a bed there was no way she was going to get any sleep tonight.

Every time she shut her eyes she relived that night in Sydney. Sneaking kisses in out-of-the-way places during the early stages of their secret tour romance had been wildly exciting, but nothing had prepared her for the intensity of his mouth on her breasts or the surprising way his muscles shivered beneath her questing fingers.

The memory of making love with him hadn't grown the least bit fuzzy with each week that passed. Nor had her feelings for him dulled. For the last month and a half she'd thrown herself into everything that could take her mind off Nate for even a fraction of a second. Sticking close to Ivy made this pretty easy. And late at night Mia wrote music. Heartbreaking songs of love and loss that belonged on a country music album. They weren't the pop styling of Ivy Bliss.

"Go to bed. I'll be in after I call Melody and let her

know you're okay. I sent her a text while you napped earlier, but she'll want some details."

He kissed the top of her head and stepped back. *"Don't be long."*

"Tyrant."

"This is nothing. Wait until you see me in the control booth."

Mia called Melody and gave her an update on how Nate was doing, and shared that she'd be translating for him for the next month so he could keep his production schedule.

"What a great idea. I know Nate signs because his mother is deaf. How did you learn?"

"My older sister, Eva, lost her hearing when she was two." While Mia and her mother were fluent, Ivy and their father never learned to sign beyond some basic words.

"You haven't talked about her much. Does she live in California?"

"Chicago. She's a psychiatrist and a lot of her patients are hearing impaired." Talking about Eva made sadness swell inside Mia. With her sister so far away and both of them so busy, she didn't get a chance to see her as often as she'd like.

"How did Nate know you could sign?" Melody jumped in and answered her own question before Mia could say a word. "That's how you two communicated when Ivy was around."

Heat crept into Mia's cheeks. "Sometimes."

"I never did understand why you and Nate were so determined to keep your relationship a secret."

"Things like that get complicated around my sister."

"I mean that crush she had on him was, like, seven years ago. And it's not as if he encouraged her. Nate said he deleted every one of her texts."

"Wait..." Mia shook her head and tried to assimilate what Melody was saying. "Ivy had a crush on Nate?" Why hadn't he ever mentioned this to her?

"I thought you were glued to her every second of every day."

Mia rolled her eyes. "Now I am. Seven years ago I was finishing high school, like every other normal eighteen-year-old, while my twin sister was singing and acting on Broadway." That had been around the time when Mia's life stopped being normal. "Tell me what happened?"

"Apparently she got ahold of his phone number and sent him a bunch of texts, telling him how much she loved his music and begging him to come visit her in New York. Didn't Nate tell you?"

"No." Why not? Was that why Ivy had gotten so excited about the prospect of working with Nate? Because she'd had a crush on him a long time ago? "Did he go to New York?"

"Ohmygod, no. He wasn't interested. She isn't his type. He said he had to talk to your dad before it stopped."

Was this a contributing factor to why Mia had had to rush to New York and take a GED exam instead of graduating with her class?

"You should ask Nate about it," Melody continued.

"I will. And speaking of Ivy, Nate said she wants to record some of your songs." Mia was relieved no grief sounded in her tone. Although she was sad and disappointed that Ivy no longer wanted to record her songs, the fact that Ivy and their father had made the decision and not bothered to tell her was what really hurt.

"Which ones?"

"I have no idea."

"I guess I'd better decide which songs I want for my

album or Ivy will snap up all my best stuff." Melody laughed, but there wasn't much humor in it. "Tell Nate I'm thinking about him."

"Will do."

After Mia hung up, she picked up her overnight bag and headed into the bedroom. Nate was propped up on the pillows, his eyes alert and intense. Mia tried to keep her gaze from lingering on his bare torso, but his broad shoulders and muscular arms awakened her hormones and stirred up her desires. His lower half was hidden by the sheet and she prayed that he was wearing pajama bottoms.

"I'm going to change," she murmured awkwardly, heading into the bathroom.

"I've seen—" he began signing, but she was through the door before he could finish. One nice thing about his inability to speak was that all she had to do to get in the last word was not look at him.

She took her time changing into pajamas. She wasn't primping, but hoping that he might fall asleep while waiting for her.

He hadn't. And as she stepped into the bedroom and saw the glint in his eye, she wondered if either of them would feel rested come morning.

Four

"Sexy," Nate signed, grinning as Mia's expression contorted into chagrin.

She dodged his mocking smile and glanced down at her bright blue sleepwear. "What did you expect?"

If she thought covering herself from chin to ankle was going to distract him from her luscious body, she'd underestimated her appeal. Then he sighed. Isn't that what she always did? Undervalued her worth.

"Something see-through and short."

"Ha. I didn't ask what you wanted." She set her bag on the chair next to the window and circled the bed like a wary alley cat confronted by a rival tom. "You're here to recover and I'm here to make sure you get lots of rest."

"Boring."

"I suggest you appreciate the peace and quiet. You're going to have my sister in your recording studio for the next month."

"Come here." He motioned her closer. *"I don't want to talk about your sister."*

Mia crossed her arms over her chest and shook her head. "Why didn't you tell me Ivy had a thing for you seven years ago?"

If Nate could've made a noise, what would've come out of him was a groan. *"Because it was seven years ago. And no big deal."*

"You rejected my sister. Do you seriously think she lets things like that go? She's still mad because Jimmy Reynolds picked me to be his buddy the day we went to the zoo in second grade."

Nate had little trouble believing Ivy couldn't let things go, but surely Mia was exaggerating about her sister holding a grudge because of a second-grade field trip.

Mia threw up her hands. "No wonder she was so cool to you on tour."

Had Ivy been cool? He must've looked puzzled because Mia asked, "You didn't notice the way she flirted with everyone except you?"

He shook his head. In fact he hadn't noticed much about Ivy at all. His attention had all been focused on Mia.

"It explains a lot," she said. "And now she thinks because you want to work with her that you're interested."

Nate wasn't particularly worried. He was a professional and would treat her as such. *"I'm only interested in you."*

Mia's color was high as she approached the bed. "You can't be interested in me. We've been through this already."

"And it didn't end the way I wanted to." He paused to read her expression. *"I don't think it ended the way you wanted, either."*

"What I want hasn't mattered since I was seventeen years old."

"Why?"

She waved her hand, batting his question away. "It's a complicated family thing. Ivy isn't as strong as she appears. She needs me to be there for her."

For how long? The rest of her life? Mia had so much to offer. If only she'd stop hiding behind her sister.

"When you say she needs you to be there for her," Nate began, bringing up something he should've probably saved for another time. *"Does that include making excuses for her when she doesn't feel like doing something?"*

To his mind, Ivy could stand to concern herself with something more than her immediate needs and desires. Maybe she'd grow up a little if she took some responsibility. He wasn't sure that Mia was doing her sister any favors by shielding her.

Mia pressed her lips together and held still for a long moment before offering up a long sigh. "Yes."

He made a rude gesture.

As always Mia was quick to make excuses for her sister. "She's an artist and artists are sensitive."

Nate wanted to point out that he was an artist, as well, and that didn't stop him from dragging his ass out of bed when he was exhausted or showing up on time and ready to work even when he didn't feel like writing or singing or being interviewed.

"That's not going to cut it in my studio. My time is money."

Mia's resistance crumbled. "I know. I'll warn her about that."

"Come here."

This time she didn't resist. Once he had her beneath

the covers, he slid down until he lay flat on his back. The urge to reach across the foot of space separating them on the mattress and touch her overpowered him, but she shook her head, as if she could read his intentions.

"We can't."

"You want to."

"Yes," she whispered, even as she shook her head. "But I can't." And then she turned onto her side and put her back to him with a mumbled good-night.

He signed his response, knowing she couldn't see it, and rolled onto his side away from her before temptation had him rolling her onto her back and covering her mouth with his. Not that he had the energy to make love to her. Damn it all. It figured that he'd get her back into bed when he couldn't capitalize on it. On the other hand, she wouldn't be here at all if not for his surgery.

Nate drifted off to sleep, keenly aware that bare inches separated his back from Mia's. However, at some point during the night, they both shifted, and when he woke up she was nestled beside him, her softness warming his left side, her cheek pillowed on his chest. His arm was around her. He'd buried his nose in her sweetly fragrant hair.

From her deep, even breathing he decided she was still asleep, so he kept perfectly still and savored the moment. Outside, the sun was kissing the balcony railing. Nate closed his eyes and pretended that he still had hours and hours to enjoy having his arms around Mia.

He guessed it was no more than twenty minutes later when she woke. Her body tensed as she became aware of their position, and almost immediately she began to disentangle herself. He tightened his fingers.

"How long have you been awake?" she asked, resisting his hold for several seconds before her muscles went limp once more.

He signed *"twenty minutes"* with his right hand and then placed his fingers beneath her chin to shift her head back. Their eyes met as he lowered his lips to hers.

She sighed into his mouth and he deepened the kiss, tracing her lips and teeth with his tongue until she let him in. His heart ached as her fingers stroked his cheek before latching on to his hair to pull him closer. She groaned against his mouth. Her morning kisses were sweet, with just a hint of sexy. Since he couldn't tell her how amazing she tasted or how soft her lips were, he did his best to let her know with his fingers against her cheek and neck.

"I don't think this is what the doctor ordered," she half moaned as he worked his lips down her throat. With a breathless laugh, she ducked away from the hand he'd slipped beneath the hem of her pajama top and half rolled, half shimmied off the bed.

"I was told not to speak. He said nothing about sex."

"I'm sure you were told not to exert yourself."

Her color was already high and his wicked grin drove the brightness in her cheeks even higher. She caught her lip between her teeth and stared at his bare chest for a long moment before shaking her head.

"I'm going to make you some Throat Coat tea and order you a smoothie for breakfast."

Nate watched her go before rolling out of bed and heading into the bathroom for a shower. When he came out, a bottle of water awaited him on the countertop by the sink. Mia was serious about keeping him hydrated. He dressed and headed into the living room, wondering how he was going to keep himself occupied and his hands off Mia for the next couple days. Idleness wasn't something he did well. If he wasn't working in the studio, he was writing music or promoting the band.

"I don't suppose you want to share what you've been working on lately with me?" he signed after breakfast.

"I have a couple beats I recorded the other day. When Ivy decided she wanted to change things up a bit, I started playing with some synthpop sounds." Mia frowned slightly. "Of course, that was before I learned she wants to record Melody's music."

"Let me hear."

She pulled out her phone and scanned through until she found the track she was looking for. When she played it for him, his eyes widened. It was very different from anything Ivy had done. Perhaps a little too different for the pop princess?

"Has Ivy heard this?"

"I can read your mind," Mia said with a self-conscious sigh. "I know it's different from her usual stuff. And no, I haven't played any of this for her."

"I know a couple singers who might be interested in what you have there." Nate paused and gave her a second to digest that. *"I can give them a call. Or send them a text,"* he amended.

"I'll think about it. It's all pretty rough at the moment."

"Maybe when we get into the studio you can play around with it some more."

"Maybe." She gave a noncommittal shrug. "By the way, I mentioned to Melody that Ivy is interested in recording some of her music, so she can prepare."

"I'm sure she appreciated the heads-up."

Mia's phone buzzed and she glanced at the screen. From her grimace, Nate assumed it was her sister calling. She got up and took the phone out to the small terrace.

"Hi, Ivy, what's up?" Mia stood with her back to him, but it didn't prevent her voice from carrying back into the suite. There was a pause, during which she paced from one end of the terrace to the other. "I can't, because I'm out of town. I drove up the coast for a couple days."

She turned in Nate's direction so he signed at her.

"Liar."

"Shut up." And then she sat on one of the chairs and leaned her forehead on her hand. "Dad hasn't talked to me about the direction for your new album."

Nate wondered what it would take for Mia to come clean about their relationship. What was the harm in explaining that she'd spent last night helping him out after his surgery? The dynamic between the sisters continued to baffle him.

"Of course I understand that you want to work with Melody Caldwell. She's incredibly talented." A long pause, then, "No, I'm not upset. I just needed a break… from LA. Can we talk about this later?"

When Mia hung up with her sister, she blew out a big breath.

"What did she want?"

"For me to run some errands."

"Your talents are wasted on your sister."

"It's more complicated than that." But she didn't defend her situation as adamantly as she'd done in the past. "She really does need me."

Not wishing to spoil their limited time together with an argument, Nate held out his hand and gestured Mia toward him. There would be plenty of time in the next month for them to discuss her future and for him to convince her to leave her sister and stay with him.

"Come play more of what you've been working on."

* * *

A week after Nate's surgery, Mia found herself in the lobby of Ugly Trout Records with her sister and father. The spare, utilitarian space was like Nate. Unpretentious and purposeful. There was a beige leather sectional beneath the company logo rendered in copper on the wall. On the opposite wall six guitars hung in a neat line. It wasn't designed to impress executives or big name stars. Musicians came to Las Vegas to record and work with Nate. His stellar reputation was all the promotion the label required.

Mia followed Ivy and their father through the glass door that led from the lobby into the empty conference room. They were late and Mia grimaced, wondering how upset Nate was at the moment.

"I'm surprised he isn't here to greet us," Ivy said, pulling a small mirror out of her purse to check her appearance yet again.

"Me, too, especially since we're fifteen minutes late."

Ivy shot her a dirty look. "What's gotten into you all of a sudden?"

Mia bit the inside of her cheek and reminded herself that this session would not go well if Ivy was upset. "It's just that I promised Nate we would be here right at ten." The second she used "we" Mia knew she'd screwed up.

"He's expecting *me*."

"Of course." Mia used her most soothing tone. "But you need me to translate what he's saying."

Ivy went back to checking her appearance. "If you think this makes you special, it doesn't. Remember that it's me he asked to work with."

Because he wants to spend time with me. But Mia didn't dare speak the truth out loud. Ivy wouldn't believe her. She barely believed it herself. Why was someone as talented and successful as Nate Tucker interested in a nobody like her?

A couple minutes later Nate, Melody and two men entered the room. The very air seemed to change with Nate's presence and Mia's eyes were glued to him as he came around the conference table to shake hands with Ivy. The rest of his team followed suit. When all the introductions had been made, Nate's gaze sought Mia.

He raised an eyebrow before signing. *"Let's get started, shall we?"*

Mia translated, and for a while the only sound in the room was her voice as she followed Nate's hands. He spoke about Ivy's previous two albums with West Coast Records and how the songs had been great, but the production had been rushed on both.

When Ivy had originally been signed by the label, the company had been run by Siggy Caldwell, Trent and Melody's father. In the past month, Nate and Trent had purchased the failing record company and planned to restore it to its former glory.

"We're going to develop a better marketing strategy for releasing her music this time," Nate signed.

"I'm glad to hear that," Javier Navarro said. "The delays in releasing her last album really hurt the sales."

"Trent and I agree."

"I've been dying to work with you and Melody," Ivy said. "When can I get into the studio?"

Nate glanced toward Melody. *"Studio C is open right now. Why don't you two run through a few songs. I want to give Mia a tour and introduce her to some people she'll be working with this next month."*

Ivy's eyes narrowed. "I thought she was going to translate for you."

"She is."

"Then why does she need a tour?"

"Your sister showed an interest in sound production and she's going to need to learn what I'm talking about in order to make people understand what I'm asking for."

"Whatever."

When Melody led Ivy and Javier out of the conference room, Mia turned to Nate. A blend of resignation and anxiety caused her chest to tighten. Conscious of the production assistants that remained in the room, Mia signed, *"You and I working together is going to make her crazy."*

"I don't care."

"I do. And you're not the one who has to live with her."

"You don't have to, either."

"Please tell me we're not going to have this discussion every day for the next month."

"It's not my fault that your sister misunderstands our relationship."

"By 'our relationship' do you mean yours and mine or yours and hers?"

"Both." Nate's eyes were liquid silver as his gaze settled on her lips. *"Now let's go find an empty studio so I can kiss you."*

"You are nothing but trouble," she declared.

The next four weeks were going to be heaven and hell. As much as it delighted her to be working so closely with Nate, keeping him at arm's length was going to be a nearly impossible task.

"When it comes to you I am very determined." He put his palm on her back and nudged her toward the door.

Just that fleeting touch sent her pulse skyrocketing. A nagging twinge in her chest bloomed into a sharp dig, but she smiled through it. Three days ago she'd woken in his arms and for a few minutes her world had been perfect. But the reality was that they couldn't be together. He wanted something that was impossible for her to give right at this moment. And she couldn't bring herself to hope that he'd wait around long enough for Mia to be reassured that her sister was strong enough to go it alone.

Mia's hands shook as Nate escorted her into a control room. She was relieved to find it occupied. On the other side of the glass, a group of studio musicians were jamming. The intensity of their concentration broke as the song came to an end. Smiles and high fives were shared all around.

Nate signed and then pushed a button. Mia stared at him until he made a gesture and she realized he wanted her to speak.

"Sounds good. This is Mia," she translated, then waved. "She's going to be my voice for the next month."

"You should keep her on permanently," a bald, barrel-chested guy with a goatee called out. "She sounds way better than you ever did."

"Looks a lot better, too."

Once the sound engineers introduced themselves, Nate indicated the door across the hall, which led to another control booth. In the studio a young man rapped to an intricate beat that Mia recognized as something Nate had been fooling around with during the tour.

"You wrote that."

He nodded before introducing her to the guy manning the booth. His name was Craig.

"*Moving on.*"

Nate opened the door to another studio and gestured her inside. The control booth on the other side of the glass was empty. The studio held a set of drums, a couple keyboards and several guitars.

As expected, he spun her around and pinned her against the door. He'd promised to find them an empty studio where he could kiss her, and he'd delivered. She didn't resist as his lips found hers and he stole her breath away. Damn. The man knew how to kiss. His tongue traced her lips until she parted for him. She expected him to deepen the kiss, and when he continued nipping and nibbling her lips, she was the one who pushed up onto her toes and took the kiss to the next level.

Both of them were breathing hard and flushed when he stepped back and signed.

"Feel like fooling around?"

"Depends…" She tucked the hem of her shirt back into her pants and drew the word out, wondering what Nate had in mind.

"Give me a taste of what you've been working on. Just play around a bit with some of it and see what happens."

"I can play some of the melodies." Mia glanced at the instruments.

"And the lyrics."

This wasn't what she was accustomed to. Usually she recorded all her demos using her laptop, alone in her room with a keyboard, synthesizer and a guitar. She was free to make mistakes, and stop and start if things didn't work. She often danced around, as if that somehow could make the creative juices flow.

Nate was watching her closely. *"Okay?"*

She gave a reluctant nod. While on tour, Mia had written several songs inspired by her growing feelings for Nate.

She sat down at the keyboard, but with Nate watching, her mind was blank.

"Can you maybe go sit over there?" She indicated a stool behind her. "You're making me nervous."

"Why? You've played your songs for me before."

"That was messing around. This is your studio and you've kinda put me on the spot."

"Fine."

With him out of her line of sight, the music came rushing back. Mia set her fingers on the keys and played a chord. The notes filled the space, a comfortable cushion for her emotions. She stopped worrying what Nate might think and just set her songs free.

They were two ballads. Some of her best work. Not only had her romance with Nate infused her lyrics with deeper emotion, his musical genius had encouraged her to innovate. To say she was proud of them was an understatement.

But the songs were too personal. Mia had been speaking the truth of her heart. And as she finished playing, she realized she'd written them for Nate. Suddenly, she was very glad Ivy wouldn't record them. To hear her sister sing those lyrics before Mia had even come to terms with what they meant to her would have been awful.

As she turned to face Nate, she found herself holding her breath. His thoughtful expression gave her no clue to his opinion. At last she couldn't take it anymore. "Well?"

"I'd like to run both of those past the guys. Free Fall might be interested in recording one or both."

Mia couldn't stop the tears that flooded her eyes. It was the nicest thing he could've said to her. Nate got to his feet and took several steps in her direction, but she waved him off.

"I'm fine."

"I can't guarantee anything."

"I know." She gave a shaky laugh and wiped moisture away from the corners of her eyes. "It's just such a thrill that you'd even consider..." She trailed off and regarded him suspiciously. "This isn't a bribe to get me to sleep with you, is it?"

His mouth popped open, but he caught himself just in time and signed instead. *"If only I was that devious."* He headed for the door and motioned her out.

The last studio they entered was occupied by Melody and Ivy.

"How's it going?" Mia translated for Nate.

"She likes this one." Melody cued a demo. As her voice poured from the speakers, Melody caught Mia's gaze and gave her head the smallest of shakes.

"I thought you were looking to take your next album in a new direction," Nate signed. *"That's similar to what you did on your last two albums."*

"I don't want to be too different. The fans have certain expectations."

"What about 'Love Me More'?"

Melody cued another song and Mia immediately saw where Nate was going with his suggestion.

An unhappy line formed between Ivy's brows as the chorus started. Mia recognized the warning signs and glanced toward their father, but his expression was thoughtful.

"You'd kill this," Melody agreed.

The song would take Ivy in a whole new direction. It was less sexually charged, more empowered and upbeat. Her sister had mad dance skills and enjoyed moving around the stage. Recording music like this would demonstrate that Ivy could do more than just pout and smolder as she sang.

Unfortunately, Ivy was comfortable pouting and smoldering, and as much as she claimed she wanted to grow as an artist, she retreated back into the same old tricks, where she felt safe.

"Let's give it a try," Mia translated for Nate.

"Now?" Ivy's eyes widened. She hadn't come prepared to record anything. Usually she took weeks and weeks to rehearse a song before she entered the studio. Not only was she a perfectionist, she hated looking foolish.

"Let's see what we can do."

"I don't know the song."

"We'll take it slow."

When Mia repeated what Nate had signed, Ivy shot daggers at her. Mia recognized that Ivy wanted her to speak up on her behalf, but a thousand trifling slights and mistreatments held Mia's tongue. Ivy had claimed Mia's songs as her own on the last two albums and now she wanted a new sound. This was it. Mia glanced between her father and Nate while the tension built in the room.

Finally, after seeing that everyone expected her to agree, Ivy nodded reluctantly. "I'll give it a try."

"Wonderful."

Melody handed her the sheet music and Ivy shot Mia one last scowl before leaving the control booth for the recording studio. When Ivy stood in front of the mike, Nate cued a track and let the music play. Ivy listened for a while and then began to sing. Her vocals were soft and sexy like what she was used to performing and not at all what Nate was looking for.

He signed and cued the mike.

With a silent groan, Mia translated. "Don't be afraid to let go. This is a girl telling a boy to really love her. Get in his face about it."

Nate's eyes were on her as she finished speaking. One corner of his mouth twitched as their eyes met.

Ivy started again. Mia could tell her sister was tense

and uncomfortable. At the halfway point of the song she quit. "This isn't working."

"I'm the producer. Why don't you let me judge what is and isn't going to work. Just sing," Nate signed. Mia translated, painful reluctance in her voice.

She was going to pay for this later.

Five

Nate almost felt sorry for Mia as she told her sister what he wanted. He understood the dynamic between them well enough to know that Mia was miserable relaying his suggestions for Ivy's performance. And Ivy was equally unhappy to receive them. But it had to be good for Mia to be the one in command for a change, even if only by proxy.

And in truth, as the hour went on, Mia's manner grew more confident and Ivy's interpretation of Melody's song evolved into what the songwriter had intended. It wasn't perfect, but it was a start.

"That's much better," Mia translated. "Why don't you come in here and listen to the playback."

"How did it feel to boss your sister around?"

"I wasn't. All I did was tell her what you said."

"Not word for word."

Mia rolled her eyes. *"Did you want her to storm out or keep singing?"*

"What are you two talking about?" Javier asked, breaking into their silent conversation.

"Sorry." Mia shot her father a rueful look. "I'm use to signing with Eva and I forgot that Nate can hear."

"Nice save."

"Nate was just saying how happy he is to be working with such a talented singer." Mia smiled in a way that dared Nate to argue.

As if he could. For all she caved to her sister's domineering ways, Mia had spunk and backbone. During the next four weeks, Nate intended to figure out why she let Ivy push her around, and to do whatever it took to steal her away.

"I enjoyed kissing you earlier."

Ivy entered the booth and sat beside her father on the couch.

"I enjoyed your singing." Obviously rattled, Mia blurted out the awkward translation. She pointed at Nate. "That's what he said."

"That's not what I said. By the way, you're blushing. How long do you think you can keep our relationship a secret?"

"Stop it," she signed back. *"And what relationship?"*

"The one where I tear your clothes off every chance I get."

Although he wanted to stare at Mia and see how his declaration affected her, Nate nodded to the sound engineer, who queued the playback. Beside him, Mia radiated heat, but without glancing at her expression, he didn't know if she was struggling with annoyance or lust.

Ivy's voice filled the space. She'd sung along with a simple piano track that Melody had recorded for the demo. Nate heard the potential in what Ivy could do with the song and the hairs on the back of his neck rose in reaction. It was a good sign. Whether she believed it or not, the music suited her voice. The question remained whether she could get behind the words and sell it.

A collective sigh filled the control booth when the last notes tapered off. Nate nodded in satisfaction and pinned Ivy with his gaze. The woman was ridiculously talented. Pity she was such a diva.

Javier looked pleased with what he'd heard. "I think that's a keeper."

"I'd like to record the other song we discussed earlier, as well," Ivy said, obviously not willing to concede quite yet.

Nate wasn't about to negotiate with the pop princess. He looked at Melody. *"Give her the music for those five songs we talked about."* When Mia translated what he'd said, he turned to Ivy.

"Take the rest of the week and get a feel for the songs. I want you back in the studio on Friday. We'll work on all of them."

"You're only giving me three days. That's not enough time," the pop princess squeaked, shooting a panicked look toward her father.

Javier shrugged. "If we want to get the album done in a short amount of time, you're going to have to commit to working hard."

Nate could almost hear Ivy's thoughts. She didn't want to work hard. She wanted to shop and party and boss her sister around.

Nate began signing again. "You have three days to learn five songs. They don't have to be perfect," Mia translated. "But you do need to have a feel for them."

"Fine." Ivy tossed her head and made her way to the door.

Before Mia could follow on her sister's heels, Nate

caught her by the arm, stopping her. *"Want to be my date to the AMAs?"*

Free Fall had once again been nominated for favorite pop/rock duo or group, an award they'd won two years earlier, and favorite pop/rock album. The competition was especially stiff this year and he didn't expect they'd win. Having Mia sitting beside him would take the sting out of the loss.

"The AMAs?" Mia breathed, beaming at his invitation.

Ivy had reached the hall, but when she heard her sister speak, she whirled around. "What about the AMAs?"

Mia's delight dimmed. "Nate asked me to go with him."

"Why? To translate?"

Nate could tell she was about to lie to her sister once again. He caught her hand to get her attention and shook his head in warning. *"Tell her the truth."*

"As his date."

"Your date?" Ivy looked scandalized as she fixed Nate with her stare. "That's not possible."

"Why not?" Mia translated for him.

The pop star set her hand on her hip and thrust out her lower lip like a toddler. "Because she's my assistant."

And he was sick of the way Ivy treated Mia. *"She's also your sister,"* he signed, but Mia didn't immediately translate.

Both Nate and Ivy glared at her as she stood frozen in mute silence, gazing from one to the other. She deserved so much better than to be at Ivy's beck and call. What was wrong with the entire family that everything revolved around Ivy and her damned career?

"That means she'll already be there," Mia said at last, playing diplomat and not translating his exact words.

The last bit of Nate's patience was draining away. *"Don't let her bully you."*

"But it's Mia," Ivy stated, as if that would convince Nate to change his mind.

He nodded.

Mia finally found her own voice. "I'd love to go."

She spoke softly, but her eyes glowed. In moments like these she was more beautiful than her twin.

"But I need her backstage. I'm performing and presenting."

"You'll have Yvonne to help with your changes and makeup," Mia said. Now that she'd accepted his invitation, she appeared unwilling to back down. It was a nice change from the way she normally catered to her sister's every whim.

"She doesn't own anything that she can wear to an award show," Ivy said to Nate. Clearly, she wasn't giving up.

As a featured artist, Ivy would have her choice of gowns sent over by designers eager for the publicity. Mia didn't have that sort of celebrity and Nate doubted she had the pull to arrange her own red carpet gown.

"I have a stylist in LA who can hook you up," Nate signed. *"I'll give her a call."* He sighed. *"Send her a email."*

"That would be great," Mia breathed, without bothering to translate.

Her reverent expression left Nate wondering how often anything good came her way. It spurred him to work even harder to make the entire event something Mia would want more of. She'd spent far too much time being invisible, not thinking she deserved her moment in the sun. Getting her used to being treated like a celebrity was a step forward in his plan to wrestle her away from her sister.

"I'll make the arrangements. Don't let her talk you out of going with me."

"I won't." And then to Ivy she said, "We'd better head out if you want to make your massage appointment." And as her sister stormed away down the hall, Mia gave Nate one last glance and signed, *"Thank you."*

Mia carried the cup of Throat Coat tea into Ivy's bedroom. Their father had rented a five-bedroom house with a pool in a gated community for the month Ivy would be recording at Ugly Trout. It had been a week since meeting with Nate at the studio and whatever progress her sister was making with Melody's songs was negated by the fact that when Ivy wasn't at the studio, she was either out shopping or partying with her friends Skylar and Riley, who'd shown up from LA.

The appearance of those two raised Mia's concern. The party girls, whose only source of income was their sketchy modeling careers and fashion blog, weren't good for Ivy, who was far too prone to be distracted from what she'd come to Las Vegas to do. Mia had convinced their father to chase them out of the house early that morning so Ivy could work on the songs Nate wanted her to record, but from the pile of high-end shopping bags on the floor at the foot of Ivy's bed, he hadn't persuaded them to leave town.

The fact that her sister wasn't trying on her latest purchases or even admiring what she'd bought told Mia something was wrong. The curtains were drawn over the sliding glass door that led out to the pool. It took a second for Mia to spot her twin. Ivy had pressed herself into a corner of the room, her knees tucked against her chest like a small child trying to make herself invisible. Tears streamed down her face and Mia's heart crashed to her toes.

"What's the matter?" She set the teacup on the bureau and went to sit before her sister. "I brought you some tea. Why don't you try to drink some."

Ivy stared right through her. "I can't do it. Nothing feels right. They're all expecting me to do something amazing and none of it is me." Ivy blinked and her eyes gained focus. She met Mia's gaze. "When we were on tour, I heard the songs Melody was working on and they sounded so wonderful. I want wonderful, but it's not happening."

"That's not true. I've been there, listening to you record. Everything you do is wonderful," Mia assured her sister, speaking from the heart. So often lately when she complimented Ivy it was because her sister expected the praise. But when Ivy was like this, when her demons crowded in, it was easy for Mia to give her twin every bit of support she had in her.

"Dad's expecting me to go platinum with this album, so it has to be perfect."

Mia had always thought having their father manage Ivy's career added extra pressure for her to succeed. In the same vein, if it hadn't been Daddy calling the shots, Ivy's image might be different. Mia was pretty sure her twin never would've had plastic surgery at seventeen and probably wouldn't have become addicted to the painkillers that almost killed her.

"Don't worry about Dad or Mom or what anyone else thinks."

No matter how well Ivy did, she always wanted to do better. And when she wasn't recognized, which was what had happened with this year's American Music Award nominations, things went downhill fast.

Since mid-October, when the nominations were announced and Ivy's name hadn't appeared anywhere, Mia had been scrambling harder than ever to keep her sister happy. As ambitious as she was beautiful and talented, Ivy had grown positively obsessed with making her next album grittier, sexier, more over-the-top than anything she'd done so far.

Mia thought her sister was on the wrong track. It was why Ivy and Nate were butting heads. If Ivy wanted to be taken seriously as an artist, she needed to become more authentic rather than a caricature of the personality she'd become.

"Make music that's in your heart," Mia continued. "Let it speak to who you are."

Ivy's lips curved into a sad smile. "What if I don't know who that is?"

"You'll figure it out. Just believe in yourself."

"Is that what Nate is telling you to do?"

Mia hesitated before answering. Nate was a treacherous topic for her to discuss with Ivy. "It's the message of every positive affirmation ever written. Believe in yourself. Do what you love."

"Are you doing what you love?"

"Sure."

"I mean with me."

"You're my sister. I love being with you."

"I bet you'd love it more if you were with Nate."

Mia sensed the mines beneath her feet, and stepped carefully. "I've enjoyed working with him at the studio. I'm learning a lot. It's something I could see myself doing in the future."

It was the closest Mia had come to sharing her aspirations with Ivy. That she'd dared to confess something so personal terrified her. Ivy didn't like change and might view her twin's dream of having her own career as a threat.

"I wasn't talking about working at the studio. I was talking about Nate himself. You like him." Ivy's voice had taken on a coolness that made Mia shiver. "You like him a lot."

With a shaky laugh that wouldn't fool anyone, Mia said, "Everybody likes Nate."

"But everybody's not sleeping with him." Ivy's eyes glittered in the dim light. "You know he's using you, right?"

"I'm not sleeping with him." How many times had she lied to Ivy to keep her sister in the dark about Nate? A hundred? More? When was she planning to stop? Mia's chest tightened. She was barely able to draw breath enough to defend Nate. "And he's not like that."

"Did you do it because you knew I liked him? Have you been saying bad things to him about me? Is that why he criticized everything I did in the studio? I'm trying really hard to make him happy, but nothing makes him look at me the way he looks at you."

How did Nate look at her? "We're colleagues," Mia said. "That makes things easy between us. With you he's pushing so he can get the best possible song. It might seem like he's not happy, but he thinks this will be some of the best work you've done."

But Ivy wasn't listening to her. Mia had seen that look before. She got up and went to Ivy's purse. Her sister noticed what she was doing and protested. Mia ignored her and started digging through the bag, unsurprised when she came up with a small bag of pills.

"Who gave you these? Skylar or Riley?"

Ivy stuck her lower lip out and stared mutinously at Mia. "Give me those. It's none of your business."

"What's the matter with you?" Sorrow and rage collided inside Mia's chest. "I thought you were done taking prescription meds. Damn it, Ivy."

"I just need something to take the edge off after being in the studio all day. It's exhausting and the pressure… You just don't understand."

"I understand that you almost died because you were taking this stuff."

Mia took the bag into the bathroom and dumped the contents into the toilet. When she turned, her sister was glaring at her from the doorway.

"You had no right." Ivy's voice slashed at her.

Discovering a bag of pills in her sister's possession both angered and frightened Mia. "I'm your sister and I love you. I'm always going to do what's best for you. Even if you hate me for it."

"It's your fault, you know. The reason I have the pills. You haven't been around for me lately."

"I'm with you all day at the studio and when you're working with Melody on the songs you're planning to record." Mia was having trouble catching her breath. She hated conflict and usually gave in to whatever Ivy wanted, but not when it came to her addiction. "The only time I'm not around is when you go out with Skylar and Riley. They're bad news, Ivy."

"They're fun." Ivy scrubbed the tears from her cheeks and shook her head. "I can't have any fun without you being all over me. You used to be fun. We used to hang out."

"That's not my fault." Mia's temper flared at the unfair accusation. It hurt that the two of them had stopped spending time together as sisters and friends. "You're the one who treats me more like an employee than your sister."

"You left me to go to high school."

Mia regarded Ivy in dumb silence. "You were in a show on Broadway. I wanted to be normal." Because she'd been just an average kid with no particular talent or ambition.

If Ivy had never become a pop star, Mia might have ended up like Eva, in a job she loved far from the music industry with its bright lights and soul-crushing pressure to make it big.

"You don't think that's what I wanted?" Ivy's pupils were like pinpoints, something Mia had learned to watch for. "To go to school with my friends and just worry about passing a chemistry test or what boy might think I'm cute?"

"So why didn't you say no?" Though Mia asked the question, she already knew the answer.

"You think it's because I love all the money and fame."

"I do. Ever since we were kids you always needed to be the center of attention."

"It gets old. Sometimes all I want is to be invisible."

"So quit."

"And do what?" Ivy glared at her. "I don't write music like you do. All I have is my voice and this body."

Mia wished her sister could look beyond show business. "What about going to college. You could get a degree. Or you're passionate about fashion. Start a clothing line."

"Sure." Ivy gave a bitter laugh. "Like Dad would let me quit singing and acting to become a fashion designer."

"You don't have to quit. Do both. See how it goes."

For the first time in what felt like forever Mia saw the old Ivy peering out at her. She impulsively took her sister's hands. "Why don't we take Saturday and go do something fun? Just you and me. Like when we were kids and we used to sneak off to the park."

"I'm flying to LA with Skylar and Riley tomorrow to meet with the guy who is going to manufacture their line of purses."

"Tomorrow?" Why hadn't she been told any of this? "But you're scheduled in the studio tomorrow. When are you coming back?"

"I don't know. Skylar and Riley really need my help."

"And by help you mean they want you to invest money." If Mia had disliked Skylar and Riley before, the discovery of the pills made things so much worse.

"I don't care what you think." Ivy glared at her. "I'm going."

"Then I'll go with you." If Ivy was taking painkillers again, Mia really couldn't afford to let her sister go back to LA without her. "I'll message Nate and explain everything."

Well, not everything. She'd shared a lot of her secrets with him, but couldn't tell him her fears about Ivy without explaining about Ivy's near death overdose.

"Sure, whatever. But do it somewhere else. I'm tired and I just want to sleep."

"Then you're not going out tonight?"

"Geez, Mia. It's only seven. Nothing gets going around here until at least midnight." And then Ivy lay on her bed and buried her face in a pillow.

After covering her with a throw, Mia took the now cool cup of tea and went to her bedroom to Skype with Nate. To her surprise, he was fine with the change of plans. He told her he'd head up to LA as well to meet with Trent, and would arrange for Ivy to do a bit of recording at West Coast Records with a producer friend of his so they could keep the schedule moving forward.

By the time Mia signed off an hour later, she was feeling a whole lot better. Nate had that effect on her. But her equanimity lasted only until she went to check on Ivy and found her sister's room in an uproar of rejected outfits, but otherwise empty.

Mia hesitated just a minute before starting a systematic search through Ivy's room. The last time her sister had given into her addiction, she'd squirrel away pills in all sorts of places. Mentally crossing her fingers that she wouldn't find anything, Mia began going through Ivy's drawers and closet. After forty-five minutes of searching, she'd unearthed no contraband, but that didn't mean Ivy couldn't hit up Skylar or Riley tonight.

Mia would have to keep a close eye on her sister to avoid a repeat of the relapse that had happened three years ago, while Ivy was on her first concert tour. Mia had been in LA working on a demo for one of the songs Ivy hadn't wanted to record. Preoccupied by the opportunity to have a career as a songwriter, Mia hadn't been paying attention to her sister and Ivy had started taking pills again.

Sometimes it seemed that every time Mia tried to grab something for herself, Ivy found a way to spoil it. Which explained why keeping quiet about her relationship with Nate was so important. But at what cost? The question roused a host of emotions ranging from frustration to guilt. She'd already lost Nate to her sister's demanding personality.

Was she planning on sacrificing her entire future to it, as well? How long could she live in Ivy's shadow before dissatisfaction with her situation turned love into animosity? Choosing her sister over Nate had been hard the first time, even though she'd known him only a short while and could dismiss their fling as a tour romance. But now that she was working with him every day and accepting his help to develop her music, she was discovering richer layers to her feelings for him. Not sexual or even professional, but a complicated stew of romance, friendship and respect.

He was a brilliant musician and a wonderful man. When the time came to choose, how was she going to give him up again?

Six

Nate glanced Mia's way a hundred times during their drive to Santa Monica, where they were having dinner with Trent and Savannah. She looked beautiful in a navy-and-white abstract print sundress, paired with sandals and wavy beach hair. For a dramatic evening look, she'd applied eye shadow and red lipstick. He couldn't keep his eyes off her.

As he pulled into the parking lot, Mia gave the restaurant a doubtful look. "Are you sure this is a business meeting?"

He nodded, playing innocent when she frowned. He knew what she was thinking, but it wasn't really a double date. Just a quiet dinner with two couples, at a seaside restaurant with lots of good food and wine. Nope. Not a double date at all.

"It seems a little..."

He fitted the car into a parking spot and cut the engine. *"Out-of-the-way?"*

"I was thinking more in terms of romantic."

"Now that you mention it, I see what you mean. But I didn't pick it. Trent did. I think it might be date night for him and Savannah. That's not a problem, is it?"

"Sitting across the table from a newly engaged couple won't bother me a bit."

"Good. I wouldn't want you to get any ideas."

Mia shook her head. "I wouldn't dream of it."

They were fifteen minutes early for the reservation, but the hostess seated them at a wonderful table overlooking the Santa Monica pier and the ocean. The sun had already dipped below the horizon and the sky was saturated with rich gold, red and deep blue.

"Tell me more about Trent and Savannah." Mia's eyes held a wistful glow as she turned from the view. "Start with why they both have the same last name if they're only engaged."

"Savannah is Trent's former sister-in-law."

Mia's eyes widened adorably. "That has to be a tricky situation."

"It's quite complicated. They've known each other since Savannah was a kid. She came to live with her aunt, who happened to be the Caldwells' housekeeper, after her mom died and her father couldn't take care of her. From what Melody tells me, Savannah had a thing for Trent for a long time. When she went off to model in New York City he went out to visit her and they began to..." Nate paused and thought for a moment. *"Date."*

"Why the pause?"

"I don't think Trent realized how he felt about her until after they broke up and she married his brother."

"So why did she marry him? To get back at Trent?"

"That's not her style. She was pregnant and Rafe

wanted a legitimate heir to carry on the Caldwell name. He was dying when he married her, but no one knew."

"How old is her son?"

"Just turned a year. And the boy is Trent's. How that happened is also complicated, but let's just say Trent was a huge idiot for ever letting her go."

"Did Trent know about the baby before she married his brother?"

Nate shook his head. *"I think if they'd been able to talk to each other when she found out she was pregnant they might have saved themselves a lot of heartache."*

"Why didn't she tell him?"

"That would be a good question to ask her. I don't honestly know."

\"I'm glad Trent and Savannah found each other again." Mia paused while Nate ordered a bottle of pinot grigio from the waiter. "I don't remember Trent being a part of West Coast Records when Ivy signed with them. How long has he been involved? It's his family business, isn't it?"

"That's another complicated thing. Trent and his father never got along, so he wasn't involved in the record label. His brother, Rafe took over when their father retired, and mismanaged an already floundering company."

"My dad told me there were rumors that artists weren't being paid. That never happened with Ivy, but she was one of their bestselling artists."

"Trent brought in auditors to look over the books. There was some embezzling on top of everything else. Hopefully, within the next six months everything will get straightened out and people will be paid what they're owed."

The waiter brought the wine, and as it was being

poured, Trent and Savannah arrived at the table. Quick introductions were made and the newly engaged couple sat down.

"You two are early," Trent said, his gaze sliding between Nate and Mia.

"They didn't have a baby to get ready for bed," Savannah said.

"How is your throat?" Trent asked. "Are you speaking yet?"

Nate shook his head and glanced at Mia.

"I'm his voice."

Savannah's eyes widened. "How does that work?"

Nate demonstrated. *"I want to lick every inch of your body."*

"He just said you look lovely and asked how your son is."

"I don't think that's what he said." Savannah laughed. "You just turned bright red. Did he say something naughty?"

Trent cocked his head and regarded his smirking business partner. "So are you two…?"

"Lovers?" He nodded.

"No."

Nate had little trouble conveying his feelings on that situation. *"Not at the moment."*

Savannah grinned. "This feels a little bit like watching a silent movie without subtitles."

"We're being rude," Mia said, shooting Nate a severe look.

"Tell them the truth. It won't go anywhere."

She gave a big sigh. "Nate and I became romantically involved while on tour, but nobody knows that."

"Because?" Savannah prompted.

Nate began to sign, but Mia ignored him. "I work

for my sister and she wouldn't be happy if I was dating Nate."

"Because?" It was Trent who prompted this time.

Mia looked as if she wished the floor would open up and swallow her. "My sister can be a bit needy."

The sign Nate made needed no translation.

"So you're not allowed to date?" Savannah asked. "That seems a bit much."

"It's not that I can't date." Although from what she'd told Nate, her sister had a knack for ruining every chance at romance that came Mia's way. "It's more that I don't have much time for a life outside my work."

"Mia is a fantastic songwriter. I found out on tour that she wrote all the songs Ivy claimed to have written from her first two albums." Nate finished signing and gave her a hard look until she translated his words.

Trent gave her an equally hard look as he listened, but there was regret in there, as well. "You weren't given credit? How did that happen?"

"I don't know," Mia said. "When the first albums came out I wasn't mentioned at all. When I asked my dad about it, he said it was a group decision. They thought it looked better if Ivy was writing her own music instead of some nobody."

From the throb in Mia's voice, the slight continued to pain her.

"If it was something that happened because of my family's mismanagement of the West Coast label, I would be happy to set the record straight."

"No." Mia added a head shake for emphasis. "It would cause too much upheaval. My family would never forgive me if word got out."

Trent nodded. "If anyone understands how complicated family and business can be it's me. You have my word that this stays here."

"Thank you."

Mia gave Trent a wobbly smile and it hit Nate hard. He wanted badly to be able to make everything right for her, but she'd never let him. The best he could hope would be to get her away from Ivy so that her future looked brighter.

They dined on the fresh catch of the day and went through several bottles of wine. Trent, Savannah and Mia carried the conversation. Nate enjoyed his forced muteness and spent most of the dinner watching Mia's confidence bloom beneath his friends' attention.

"Dessert?" Nate asked as the waiter cleared the plates. He wanted to prolong the night as long as possible.

Savannah looked regretful. "I wish we could, but we promised the sitter we'd get home by ten."

Nate turned to Mia, but she was shaking her head. *"How about a walk on the beach?"*

She glanced out the window at the dark water. He knew she loved the ocean. They'd sneaked off to the beach a couple times while touring Australia. He would've liked to steal her away for some snorkeling along the Great Barrier Reef, but the schedule had been too tight for that sort of excursion.

"A short one. If I'm too late Ivy will wonder why."

After settling the bill the two couples separated in the parking lot. Mia maintained her smile as she stripped off her sandals and put them in the car. The temperature had dipped into the upper fifties, but the breeze blowing off the Pacific was light.

Nate took her hand and they made their way toward the sand. As they crossed the broad expanse, he revisited how easy it was to be with Mia. She had an ability to stay tranquil no matter how crazy the people around her became. No doubt it was a trait she'd cultivated in dealing with her sister's demanding ways.

Mia didn't expect conversation or feel compelled to fill silences with chatter. Even before his surgery, they'd spent long silent hours enjoying each other's company, physically connected by the touch of her foot on his thigh or his shoulder against hers, or at opposite ends of a room, content to occupy the same space.

If it weren't for Mia's peculiar attachment to being her sistcr's assistant, he could've delighted in having found the perfect woman. Instead his patience was worn to the thinness of onion skin by his constant need to resist the craving to pull Mia into his arms and kiss her. He was tired of pretending his interest in her was professional.

Fingers knitted together, they walked at the water's edge, heading away from the bright lights of the Santa Monica pier. The quarter moon gave them enough light to see by. Nate stopped and used Mia's momentum to turn her into his arms. Sliding his hand into her hair, he cupped her cheek and brought his lips to hers.

She tasted of the peppermint candy she'd snagged on the way out of the restaurant. When he licked at her lips, they parted for him, and he swept his tongue against hers, stealing her breath and the last bit of the candy disk. He'd always been good with words when it came to writing music, but this rush of emotion that hit him whenever he put his arms around her smothered his ability to form cohesive thought.

"I have a few more hours before Ivy will be home," she murmured against his cheek as he grazed his lips down her neck. She trembled as he nipped her skin. "Feel like going back to your hotel? I'm dying to be alone with you."

* * *

Nate didn't bother signing his answer. He grabbed her by the hand and pulled her toward the car. Mia laughed at his eagerness. It matched the impatience burning in her chest. Why hadn't she said something sooner? They'd wasted fifteen minutes on this walk.

Nate had one hand on the steering wheel and caressed her shoulder with the other while he drove. There was little conversation on the trip back into the city. It gave Mia time to think about what was to come and to work herself into a fine state of frenzied anticipation.

At the hotel, Nate turned his car over to the valet. When he would've put his arm around Mia for the walk through the hotel lobby, she shook her head.

"We can't be seen together like that," she cautioned, thinking what would happen if a picture got out of the two of them linked romantically. "I don't want to show up on social media and invite speculation."

"I think you overestimate my star power."

Mia rolled her eyes. The man had no idea how incredible he was. "I think you underestimate it."

"I'm pretty low-key off tour. And I don't really have one of those faces that everybody knows."

"Are you kidding? You're gorgeous." She covered her mouth with her hand and laughed self-consciously. "I don't know why I'm embarrassed admitting that to you. You already know how I feel."

"I'm not really sure I do." Nate frowned down at her for a long moment.

They joined several other hotel guests in the elevator and got out on the twelfth floor. He took her hand and brought it to his lips. The way he watched her turned her bones to mush. She spent so much time hiding how he made her feel. It was a relief to let her emotions shine.

His eyes widened. *"I never thought I'd see you look at me like that again."*

"I've been fighting this for two months," she murmured as they walked toward his suite. "It's been hell wanting you and knowing—" Her voice broke. The last thing he deserved was to hear her say again that she'd chosen being there for her sister over him.

His fingers tightened against hers as he slid the key card into the electronic lock. As soon as they crossed the threshold he kicked the door closed, gathered her into his arms and kissed her. Mia sighed against his mouth, her lips parting to welcome the plunge of his tongue. She filled her fingers with his soft wavy hair and held him close.

I love you. The words reverberated in her mind, but she didn't dare say them out loud. As much as she wanted him, wanted this, she couldn't commit to anything beyond this night. Soon she would have to consider Nate's place in her life. This connection between them had grown so fast and Mia wasn't accustomed to recklessly throwing herself into any situation. And then there were the doubts that rose after Ivy voiced her opinion about Mia not belonging in the limelight by his side.

Mia took Nate's hand and drew him toward the suite's bedroom. He deserved someone beautiful and confident to walk the red carpet and make other public appearances with him. Mia was too used to hiding in the background, and she knew he wanted to partner in everything private and public. But with his hands sweeping down her spine, his palms sliding over her butt cheeks to lift her against his hard body, it was hard to think about all the reasons she wasn't right for him.

"I'm going to do all the talking for you tonight," she told him, panting as his lips found the sensitive skin on the side of her neck. "You just tell me what to say and I'll say it."

There was a mischievous glint in the depths of Nate's gray eyes as he made an okay sign. He snagged the hem of her dress and skimmed it up her body. The cool air struck her overheated skin and Mia shivered. For a couple seconds the cotton material tangled in her hair as it went over her head and she was blinded. The loss of her sight awakened her sense of smell and she breathed in Nate's familiar scent of soap and aftershave.

Immediately she was transported back to that night in Sydney. She'd been a little intimidated by the discrepancy between their levels of sexual experience and what he might expect of her. And then she'd forgotten to be nervous as his mouth traveled over her body and he introduced her to pleasure she'd never known. After having nearly two months to relive that night over and over, Mia was more than ready to do to him all the things she'd been dreaming about.

His shirt followed her dress to the floor. Once his gorgeous chest was bared to her eyes, she went after his pants with a vengeance. Teeth gritted in concentration, she worked his belt free and had her hands on his zipper when he stopped her.

"What are you doing?" She tugged, trying to free herself from his grip. "I need you naked."

Nate set his forehead against hers and brought her hands to his lips. His breath puffed against her skin as he feathered kisses across her knuckles. Then he turned her in his arms and shifted so they were facing the mirror.

"Before we do this, I want you to know it's never been just about sex for me."

"I know." She relaxed against Nate's strong torso. The hard ridge of his erection nudged against her backside and she resisted the urge to rub against him. "But can't we talk about this later?"

"Now. It's important you understand how much I need you in my life. This isn't something I'm doing lightly. Can you say the same?"

"If you're going to ask me to choose you right now, I can't. Is it possible for you to accept that I care about you and want this to work between us? I'm not leading you on, but I need time to sort everything out."

"You're asking me to be patient."

"And I know it's a lot. You're so wonderful and I don't want to hurt you."

"I wish I could tell you I will make it easy on you, but I'm a selfish jerk who wants you all to himself." He met her eyes in the mirror and gave her wolfish grin. *"Now repeat after me..."* He began simultaneously signing and caressing her body to act out his words.

"I love your breasts and the way your nipples go hard when I touch them," she translated, quaking in reaction to his touch. "Nate, you're killing me with this."

He stopped signing long enough to pop the clasp of her strapless bra. Mia watched it slide off her breasts and hit the floor. Next he skimmed his fingers beneath the elastic of her panties and sent those plunging to the floor, too. Mia stepped out of them. Although she was no stranger to her naked body reflected in the mirror, seeing Nate's large hand fanned over her stomach was an erotic image she'd never forget.

"Keep going."

"I can't wait to taste you." A vivid blush dotted her cheeks as she repeated what Nate had signed. "I love how sensitive you are. It makes me crazy to hear you moan."

He trailed the tips of his fingers along her neck and into the hollow of her throat, all the while watching her in the mirror. She half closed her eyes as each of her senses demanded her attention. The silky drag of his lips across her shoulder competed with the tantalizing view of his fingers circling her belly button before skimming downward.

"Nate." His name was a plea as she shifted her hips, seeking the promise of greater pleasure beneath his hands. "Yes."

"Yes, what?"

"Am I ready for you?" she repeated, her voice a husky moan. "The answer is yes."

He laughed, a brief huff of air against her neck. *"I'm ready for you, too. Can't you feel it?"* He rocked his hips forward and drove his erection against her.

"Then what are you waiting for?"

She dropped her hand to his thigh and slid her palm along the sinewy length. His muscles bunched and jumped beneath her touch.

"I like taking my time with you," Mia repeated, watching as he lifted his fingers to her breasts and brushed the aching tips. She arched her back. "Later you can take your time. Now I want you to make me come."

"My pleasure."

While one hand cupped her breast, the other slid between her legs and dipped into the heat generated by his tantalizing caresses and sexy words. He touched her with tender confidence, sliding his finger around the sensitive nub until she quaked and groaned.

"Oh, yes. There."

He knew exactly what turned her on.

With his hands otherwise occupied and his voice out of commission he had no way to convey how he was feeling, but Mia could guess from the wonder that bloomed across his features and the ragged nature of his breathing.

"Kiss me," she pleaded. Although it pained her to pull his hands from between her legs, she needed his mouth on hers.

She turned to face him and his hands slid into her hair, fingers pressing into her scalp as he tilted her head and brought his mouth to hers. She gasped at the joy and welcomed the plunge of his tongue, meeting it with her own. Her toes curled at the shudder that ran through him when her hands smoothed over his back and down his spine.

During their night together on tour, Nate had proved to be very vocal in bed, crooning encouragement and telling her how she tasted and felt. She could tell his need to remain silent was very frustrating, because his hands tracked over her bare skin with feverish longing.

Mia broke off the kiss and pushed him to arm's length. "Pants off. Now."

With a snappy salute, Nate made short work of his zipper and sent his trousers sliding down his legs. Mia didn't wait for him to take care of his boxer briefs. Her fingers were already on the waistband, yanking them down to free him. His breath was ragged as his fingers formed the sign for a curse word, making Mia smile.

"Get ready," she said. "You haven't yet begun to swear."

She dropped to her knees before him and took him into her mouth before he had a chance to realize what she intended. She closed her eyes to savor the warm, smooth skin stretched over his rigid erection. His hips jerked as she rolled her tongue around him and smiled as his fingers bit down on her shoulder. It must be killing him to remain silent. As much as she didn't want to cause damage to his voice, she knew the fight to stay quiet would only enhance the tension building in him.

He double tapped her shoulder, indicating he wanted

her attention. She lifted her gaze and met his eyes, letting him see how much she enjoyed what she was doing to him.

"You're killing me."

In answer, she took him deeper, using her hand at the base of his erection to provide sensation along the full length of his shaft. She thought about all the things they hadn't done that first night, and not getting to do this for him had been her biggest regret.

The tension in his body built as she worked her mouth on him, but even as his pleasure soared, he broke free and pulled her to her feet. For a long moment he held her cradled against his chest, her ear atop his pounding heart. When he seemed to get himself back under control, he pushed her to arm's length and signed, *"When I come it will be inside you."*

She shivered and took his hand, walking backward toward the bed. Nate reached into the nightstand and pulled out a condom. He brushed her hands aside when she tried to help him. With him otherwise occupied, she let her fingers drift over the taut muscles of his shoulder and biceps.

Once he finished putting on the protection, he turned to her and pointed to the bed. *"Up you go. I'm going to make love to you now."*

"That sounds about perfect."

She shifted onto the middle of the mattress and he stalked right after her, his hot gaze raking over her.

"You are so beautiful." His fingertips grazed her breast, circling the puckered tip.

"So are you." The words were barely a whisper as he closed his mouth over her nipple and sucked hard.

She gasped, the sound escaping her like a half cry as his tongue flicked the sensitive bud. She skidded her fingers along his cheeks and down his shoulders to his back. Muscles bunched and loosened beneath her touch as she investigated each rib and bump in his spine. How often had she watched him move around the stage, his long lithe body filled with such energy and emotion, and wondered what it would be like to be up against his rock-hard abs, a heartbreak away from those mobile, smiling lips?

And then she had been. After one of the shows, Nate had drawn her into a dressing room and kissed her. It was like being embraced by a power line. All the hyped up energy he'd received from performing had translated into a passionate kiss. It had been crazy magic.

He grabbed her hand and now pulled it to his mouth. His eyes captured hers as if asking for permission. Her voice was gone so she nodded.

"I want all of you. Right now. As deep and hard as you want it. Fast or slow," she finally said.

Nate closed his eyes and set his forehead against hers. He gave her the sweetest kiss on the corner of her mouth. *"I don't deserve you."*

You deserve so much better than me. She didn't dare speak the words for fear it would ruin the moment. Instead, she framed his face with her hands and brought his lips to hers. They kissed and passion overwhelmed them once more. He shifted to lie between her spread legs. Once again his fingers drifted between her folds and found her wet and aching. A shudder raged through him as he slid a finger inside her, making her moan. Mia's hips lifted off the bed.

She grabbed his wrist, intent on doing…something to satisfy the tension building inside her. Her gaze flicked to his face and she found him watching what he was doing to her. Her heart tripped and stopped at the level of joy mingling with lust in his expression. And then she was over the edge, her hips bucking as she rode the release Nate had brought to her body.

She barely noticed when he guided himself into position, but as she experienced the last spasms of her orgasm, Nate drove his hips against hers, filling her.

Seven

Air hissed between his teeth as he stopped moving. He was now fully seated inside her and he took a second to appreciate the moment with this spectacular woman. Mia's internal muscles clenched around him as aftershocks reverberated through her. He stroked strands of hair off her cheek and peered at her flushed face and passion-dazed eyes. She was beautiful and sweet. And all his.

She blew out a breath and lifted her gaze to his. He saw a hint of the shyness that always intrigued him. As if she couldn't quite believe he'd noticed her.

As if that was possible.

He raised his eyebrows in a silent question.

"I'm perfect. You're perfect. This—" Mia purred as she ran the soles of her feet along Nate's thighs "—is perfect."

It was all he needed to hear. He began to move, pulling out slowly, before driving back in, loving the way her breath caught and her lashes fluttered. Two months without her was two months too long. Already he could feel pleasure tighten in a frantic ache that pulled him toward completion.

"Harder," she begged. Her nails dug into his back. The tiny pain shot straight to his groin. "Yes," she moaned as he picked up speed. "Like that."

Staying silent during sex was way more frustrating than anything he'd experienced in the last two weeks since his surgery. Curses flooded his mind as he sank into Mia's tight, hot body over and over. He wanted to tell her how good she felt. How she was unlike any woman he'd ever known. Instead, he kissed her, letting his mouth speak in other ways.

His orgasm was close, but he needed her to go first. As their breath rushed together in frantic pants, he slipped his hand between them and cupped her. She uttered a soft cry that sounded like a garbled version of his name and then threw her head back. Her muscles clamped down on him hard and she was going over the edge.

Nate kept himself from climaxing long enough to watch her, and then he couldn't hold it back any longer. He buried his face in her shoulder as his body exploded in pleasure. His lips moved, forming her name against her skin as he gave one final thrust and spilled himself inside her for what felt like endless seconds.

As he became aware of the room again, Nate rolled onto his side, taking her with him.

"Incredible," he signed.

"You can say that again."

He made the sign a second time and she laughed. Brushing aside a damp strand of hair, he made another sign. *"Stay."*

She shook her head. Already he could feel her starting to disengage.

"I can't."

He fought down his disappointment. *"An hour more?"*

When she gave a reluctant nod, he brought his lips to hers. It wasn't much time, but enough to make certain that the next time he asked her to stay, she'd have a much harder time refusing.

Club T's was in full swing when Ivy and three of her besties were escorted past the line of attractive twenty-somethings waiting by the velvet ropes for their chance to get in. Mia trailed behind the group, anonymous and forgettable in a sleeveless black dress that skimmed her curves but left everything else to the imagination. In contrast, Ivy wore a red sequin romper with a plunging neckline that showed off her long legs, toned by hours of dance rehearsals and yoga.

The group bypassed the dance floor and headed straight for thc VIP area. The DJ was cranking great tunes and with Ivy preoccupied for the moment, Mia let herself fall a little behind.

Their private table was set up with bottles of vodka, champagne and assorted mixes. Flanked by her entourage, Ivy slipped into the booth. There was enough space between the couches and the table for the women to rock their hips to the music and fling their hair extensions around. Ivy was in high spirits, yelling that she loved every song that played.

Mia perched on the far end of the couch, suddenly overwhelmed. By the concussive beat. The dazzling light show. The hyped-up customers all around them, whooping, dancing and sucking up all the oxygen. Dizziness consumed her. Mia closed her eyes, wishing she were somewhere tranquil and quiet.

Someone shook her shoulder. Mia's eyes opened and she spied Ivy bent over the table and frowning at her.

"Did you order this?" Ivy demanded, pointing to the bottles. "It's Grey Goose. I wanted Belvedere."

"You always drink Grey Goose," Mia said, feeling very much like screaming.

"Not lately." Ivy rolled her eyes. "You never pay attention."

"I'll go find someone and get it fixed." Mia was glad for the chance to escape. "Be right back."

With the mixes disguising the taste of the liquor, Mia doubted whether Ivy could distinguish one type of vodka from another. Most often she made demands to remind everyone that she was the celebrity. Mia was probably one of the few people who recognized she did it out of insecurity.

And Ivy was feeling all too anxious at the moment. She was fighting the direction Nate wanted for her album and the stress had sent her running for the comfortable fog of prescription meds. This meant Mia needed to be more vigilant than ever. She just needed to get Ivy through the album and then her sister would calm down.

Mia headed to the first floor in search of a waitress and cleared up the vodka situation. She was standing on the edge of the dance floor, wondering if it would be possible to locate Nate in the crowd, when an arm came around her waist, startling her. Mia tensed, intending on twisting away, when a familiar cologne danced past her nostrils. She glanced down as Nate's hands moved.

"Relax. I've got you."

A thousand butterflies took flight in her stomach as he drew her into the crowd on the dance floor. Twisting, grinding bodies surrounded them, driving Mia against Nate so they had no choice but to touch. He turned her so her back rested against his chest and his hands could roam over her.

"I can't." But her words were lost to a groan as his lips trailed along her neck and his hot breath spilled across her skin. "Ivy and her friends are just…over…" She sucked in a jagged breath as his thumb grazed her nipple.

"Damn, I've missed you."

Me, too. She didn't bother with the words. Her muscles trembled as he grazed his hands up her sides and over her ribs, telling him everything he needed to know.

Earlier the music and crowd had bothered her. But away from Ivy and her friends, Mia wanted to get lost on the dance floor for an hour or two, gyrating with the rest of the crowd to the bass-heavy music until her feet had blisters on top of blisters and she was drenched with sweat. How long had it been since she'd done something fun or crazy just for herself?

Two days.

She shut her eyes, blocking out the million-dollar light show, and whisked back in time to the hotel suite and Nate's naked body sliding against her skin as they made love. Placing her hands over his, heat blazing in her cheeks, she pressed him closer.

His familiar scent wrapped around her and she filled her lungs until her chest ached. Nate's body aligned with hers was perfection. It banished her loneliness, stripped away her inhibitions and demolished her dependability until she became someone else. Someone who excited her. Someone filled with poignant emotions of such perfect joy that they terrified her.

That was why she'd broken off with Nate when the

tour ended. She couldn't be two people. She had to choose. In the end, she'd shied away from embracing the daring, impulsive woman she became around Nate and retreated back into the familiar territory of being Ivy's highly efficient, but mostly ignored PA.

Hips swaying in sync, Mia and Nate rocked to the music pouring over them, but all she could hear was the sound of her heart crying in joy. Nothing made her happier than being with Nate. But her life had never been about being happy. It had been about obligation, selflessness and patience.

Sleeping with Nate while in LA had been foolish and reckless, but she wouldn't trade it for anything.

Against her side, her purse buzzed, jolting Mia back to responsibility. She offered up a huge sigh and tugged Nate's hands away from her body. Turning, she signed.

"I have to go."

She made a fist with her right hand to form the letter *A* and then circled it clockwise against her chest twice. Her apology did little to ease the irritation that tightened his lips into a relentless line. Green and amber lights played over his face, highlighting his unhappy expression as he signed a rude response.

"Ivy will wonder where I am."

"I don't care."

"I know."

She grabbed his wrist and dragged him off the dance floor. She thought to leave him near the bar and return to Ivy, but he was on her heels as she ascended the stairs to the VIP section. At the top, Nate was hailed by a pair of tall men, Kyle Tailor, the third partner in Club T's, and Hunter Graves. In the last five years Hunter had become increasingly in demand as a DJ and a producer.

"You have company." Mia indicated the two tall men heading their way. "I should get back to Ivy."

"In a second. Come translate for me."

Before she could refuse, Nate caught her hand and towed her to meet the two men. Mia had never been formally introduced to either of them, but thanks to Melody she knew the story behind Kyle's annoyed frown.

Kyle was the first to speak. "Hey, Nate."

Hunter Graves stuck out his hand with a broad grin. "Good to see you. Kyle was just showing me around. This place is great."

Kyle checked his phone. "I have to take care of something," he said, sending a meaningful glance Nate's way, obviously eager to get away from the DJ. "You don't mind taking over for me, do you?"

As Kyle retreated down the stairs, Nate shook Hunter's hand and glanced at Mia as he indicated his throat.

"He had throat surgery," Mia said. She put out her hand. "I'm Mia Navarro, his translator."

"You're more than that," Nate signed, while she and Hunter shook hands.

"Nice to meet you," Hunter said. "I can't wait to get up there and spin for this crowd." He indicated the DJ booth that overlooked the dance floor. "They're on fire."

"We're glad to have you here," Mia repeated.

Hunter's eyes widened as he gazed from her to Nate and back again. "You weren't kidding about the translating. That's cool. Your own secret language."

"It's been handy having her around the studio these last few weeks."

Mia translated what Nate signed, and then added her own two cents. "His handwriting is terrible. I don't know what would've happened if he'd been forced to write down everything he wanted to say."

Hunter laughed and Mia could see why Melody had been hung up on him for so long. His engaging grin made it easy to smile back. Nate nudged her with his elbow and she shot him a questioning glance.

"Stop flirting with him."

"Did Trent mention to you that I'm interested in booking some time in at Ugly Trout?" Hunter asked, his keen gaze missing little of their exchange.

Nate nodded.

"I've got a couple artists I've started working with and thought it might be good to have them come to Vegas while I'm here."

"Speaking of artists," Mia said, "Ivy's here tonight. Why don't we head over there and you can say hi." Mia glanced at Nate as she finished speaking and sent a mischievous grin his way.

There'd been a very brief flirtation between Hunter and Ivy a year earlier. Hunter might be the perfect anecdote for Ivy's stress. If nothing else, he'd be a good distraction. Although Hunter liked to play as hard as he worked, he was an advocate for clean living. Maybe reconnecting with him would convince Ivy to send Skylar and Riley packing.

"It would be great to see her," Hunter said. "Lead the way."

As he gestured for Hunter to follow Mia, Nate could tell she had something up her sleeve. By the time he reached the table, introductions were being made and Ivy's girlfriends fell over themselves swarming the DJ. Not only was Hunter charismatic and good-looking, but his net worth was in the high seven figures, making him a player worth pursuing.

Ivy didn't seem to be as impressed, but she was the

star and, as always, wanted everyone to know it. But when Hunter gave her his best wicked grin, she thawed and patted the cushion beside her.

Mia signed an explanation. *"They had a brief thing and I think she still likes him."*

Now Nate understood. *"So he's a distraction?"*

Her smile was all the answer he needed and it gave him an idea. Maybe having Hunter in Las Vegas was going to be a good thing, after all. Having him spend time with Ivy might kill two birds with one stone.

The friction between Nate and Ivy in the studio meant that recording the album wasn't going smoothly. He could put it down to artistic differences, but more likely she'd picked up on his disgust for the way she treated Mia, or any number of the other things that irritated him about her. Whatever the cause, the chemistry between them was all bad.

Nate had heard nothing but good things about Hunter as a producer, and he suspected the DJ would love an opportunity to work with Ivy. Maybe he'd have better luck dealing with the pop princess. And if Hunter was reluctant to tackle Ivy's album, maybe he'd be interested in her personally. She was beautiful and talented enough to appeal to him.

And that was the second reason to push them together. Weeks earlier Trent had signed Hunter to a one year contract as a DJ with Club T's, which meant Hunter was going to be spending a lot more time in Las Vegas. While he promised to be a huge draw on Sunday nights, Nate was worried this might further disrupt Melody and Kyle's relationship.

A year earlier Melody had been dating Hunter. They'd been together eighteen months and she found him lacking in the commitment department.

Kyle was Trent's best friend since high school and had always treated his buddy's little sister like family. After listening to Melody complain about her relationship woes, Kyle insisted that if Hunter thought he had competition, he would stop taking her for granted.

At some point during their six-week ruse, both of them got caught up in their pretend romance. But it wasn't until Hunter came to his senses and realized he was about to lose Melody that she and Kyle admitted to each other that they'd fallen in love.

For a while things were going great between them. But then Melody had gone on tour with Nate and the separation had taken its toll on the fledgling romance. Melody and Kyle were committed to making the long-distance thing work right up until Melody got caught by the paparazzi coming out of a New York City club hand-in-hand with Hunter.

The whole incident had been innocent enough. He'd taken her hand to keep from being separated in the crush leaving the club, but there was too much history between Melody and Hunter for Kyle to dismiss the episode.

Seeing that Ivy was utterly absorbed in the DJ, Nate caught Mia by the arm and drew her away.

"Where are we going?" she asked, as he guided her toward the stairs once more.

"Somewhere I can put my hands all over you."

"I really shouldn't be gone for very long."

"Hunter will keep her busy. Let's you and I find a private spot and make out."

She glanced back over her shoulder. "Twenty minutes. No more."

He could definitely work with that. Nate led her through the club to a discreet door that opened into a nondescript hallway. Mia blinked in the sudden brightness of the florescent lighting.

"Where are we going?"

"Somewhere we won't be interrupted." He pulled out his phone and shot Kyle a quick text, warning his business partner that he was going to use Trent's office for a private meeting and didn't want to be disturbed.

While Nate had mentioned to Kyle that he was seeing someone, he hadn't revealed that it was Mia. It wasn't that Nate was keeping her a secret—Melody and Trent knew—but the friendship between the two men was strained because of what was happening between Kyle and Melody.

Nate hadn't exactly taken sides, but Melody was one of his favorite people and she wasn't the one behaving like an idiot. The way Kyle had reacted after her New York club incident with Hunter made Nate feel less than friendly toward his business partner.

Relationships weren't always easy—Nate could attest to that with what was going on between him and Mia—but when you loved someone, you should trust them. And from what he was seeing of Kyle, the guy was worrying more about guarding his heart than opening it to Melody.

And that was the last thought Nate intended to have on that subject for the next hour. He ushered Mia in and closed and locked the door to Trent's office, sealing them inside the space. He didn't bother to turn on the overhead lights. One wall of floor-to-ceiling monitors, tuned to various locations around the club, provided enough light to highlight the wet bar, Trent's neat desk and, most important for Nate's purposes, a comfortable couch.

"Now that you have me here," Mia said, dropping her purse on an end table, "what do you plan to do?"

Was she kidding? He swooped her into his arms and deposited her on the couch. His lips found hers even as her fingers skimmed his suit coat off his shoulders. Fortunately, he wasn't wearing a tie and she was making quick work of the buttons on his dark gray shirt. He barely restrained a groan as her palms slid over his abs and skated around to his back.

As much as he enjoyed that her skill as a translator kept her at his side, he really wanted his voice back so he could tell her all the delicious, wicked things he intended to do to her. Although he could easily spend the near future indulging in one slow, drugging kiss after another, he was afraid they might interrupted by yet another summons from Ivy.

He kissed his way down her neck and across her shoulder. The dress she wore zipped up the back and he cursed himself for not taking it off her before he got her onto the couch. He slid his hand up her bare thigh, hearing her gasp as he hooked his fingertips into her panties and gave a tug. With a little help from her, he got her underwear off. Then she eased the hem of her dress upward until she'd exposed her lower half.

Smiling at the gorgeous picture she made, Nate settled his shoulders between her thighs and pressed his mouth against her. Everything about the moment was perfect, from the way she tasted to the sweet, mewling sounds of pleasure that escaped her lips as he pushed her to the edge of desire and held her there.

She clutched and released his hair as her thighs began to tremble and her back arched. She sighed his name on a ragged breath as he slid two fingers inside her and made her climax. Her hips lifted as she came, body tensing as her release crashed over her. As always he marveled at the power and duration of her orgasm. The only thing he enjoyed more than watching her come was being with her when it happened.

Mia went limp beneath him. "That was just…wow." She panted. "Give me a second and I'll return the favor."

Nate grinned as he stripped off his clothes, slipped on a condom and returned to the couch. Mia had been watching him the whole time, grinning like a satisfied cat.

"You are gorgeous, do you know that?" she murmured as he lay flat on his back and repositioned her so that she straddled him.

"So are you, but I like you better naked." He reached behind her and managed to unzip her dress. In seconds it was on the floor. Her bra followed. He traced her breasts with his fingertips and smiled. *"Much better."*

She lifted her hips and closed her hand around his erection. Nate hissed between his teeth, but before he could react further, she'd settled herself over him. While stars exploded in his vision, Mia leaned forward and kissed him, with such tenderness Nate's heart nearly stopped.

"No," she corrected him, sucking his lower lip between her teeth. "This is much better."

"I stand corrected."

With a husky laugh, she began to move. And suddenly they had no further need for words.

Eight

Five days following that epic night with Nate at Club T's, Mia decided she couldn't put off taking a pregnancy test any longer. While it wasn't unusual for her to miss an occasional period due to stress, or if she was doing a lot of traveling with Ivy, it was over two months since that night in Sydney and time she pulled her head out of the sand.

Part of Mia recognized the old adage that what you don't know can't hurt you. Until she took the test, she didn't have to think about the future. But each day she delayed, the worry consumed her more, and she couldn't decide if her queasy stomach was morning sickness, plain old anxiety or a little of both. Today, however, she'd decided to stop procrastinating.

It was the morning of the AMAs and Ivy was scheduled for a video interview at eight thirty. As soon as her twin slapped on the headphones, Mia made a break for the door. In ten minutes she'd bought the pregnancy test and returned to the television studio. Although taking the test in the bathroom there wasn't ideal, it was better than taking it at home.

She now had ten more minutes until Ivy would be done. Fortunately, she had a full bladder and the test took only three minutes to show results.

She sat on the toilet to wait. Head down, eyes closed, Mia sorted through her tangled emotions for a bright thread of certainty. How did she want things to turn out?

Pregnant? Joy at the possibility filled her like a crystal-pure note perfectly sung. But almost immediately anxiety rose up in her, drowning out the happy emotion. If she was pregnant, her life as she knew it was over. Nothing could possess her to keep being Ivy's assistant, and when Ivy found out who'd fathered her child, Mia would probably find her relationship with her sister over, as well.

And what if she wasn't pregnant? She'd feel a mixture of relief and disappointment. Everything would be easier. She wouldn't have to change a single thing about her life.

But was that really what she wanted? How long did she think she was going to be Ivy's assistant? Was she going to be forty or fifty and still following her sister around? Fetching for her. Putting up with her insecurities. With no husband and children and few friends.

Tears welled up in her eyes. She fought them off by taking several deep breaths and stabbing her fingernails into her palms. A baby would change everything. She could make a case for choosing her child over her sister. The guilt her parents heaped on her shoulders would lose its power.

Three minutes had never felt longer. Mia watched the seconds tick by on her cell phone; she'd started the stopwatch as soon as she took the test. While the seconds ticked off, she stayed in the stall, too afraid to stand in the bathroom proper and get caught with a pregnancy test in her hand. Not that anyone would know who she was or care what she was doing. Sometimes being invisible was nice. But there was that tiny chance that someone would be interested in what was going on and that information could leave the bathroom and cause her a lot of trouble.

When the time was up, Mia found herself unable to look at the test. She sat with it in her lap, the indicator facing downward. She didn't need to look to see the answer. She already knew. She was pregnant. Her phone buzzed, scaring her. She dropped the test. It clattered to the floor and landed faceup.

These days the tests were easy to read. No more questionable results. Depending on which one you chose, there was a line, the word *yes* or the word *pregnant*. In Mia's case it was "pregnant." She swallowed a hysterical laugh. Her whole life had just changed inside the bathroom of a TV station.

No, that wasn't quite true. Her whole life had changed the day she'd met Nate.

Mia had about thirty seconds to absorb the reality of her situation before the bathroom door opened and two women entered with a gust of animated chatter. She recognized the voices and quickly snatched the pregnancy test off the ground and dropped it into her work tote. She would just have to dispose of it later, when no one was around. Opening the stall door, Mia stepped out.

Skylar and Riley were standing at the sink, touching up their already flawless makeup. The key to being one of Ivy's friends was to be beautiful without being too beautiful. No one was allowed to outshine Ivy Bliss.

That had never been a problem for Mia. She barely

had enough time in the morning to shower and brush her teeth. Maybe apply a little eyeliner. A slash of neutral lipstick. Tucking her hair behind her ears, she'd don her uniform of black skinny pants and some sort of blouse. Her only jewelry was a pair of diamond studs she got for her sixteenth birthday.

"What are you two doing here?" Mia asked as she exited the stall. She stepped to the sink to wash her hands, avoiding eye contact with either of Ivy's friends.

"We're here to spend the day with Ivy and help her get ready for the AMAs."

"She doesn't need your help." Mia didn't make any effort to hide her impatience and didn't care if she sounded rude. She'd had enough of these two. "Ivy has a team of professionals to get her ready."

Skylar pouted. "She wants us."

"She told us to come," Riley echoed.

Mia wasn't sure what to believe, but didn't get a chance to argue further because the bathroom door opened and Ivy walked in. She glanced from her two friends to Mia and frowned.

"What are you doing in here?" she demanded. "I've been looking for you all over."

"I was explaining to these two that you don't need them around today."

Ivy pouted. "I invited them."

"You need to focus on tonight." Mia eyed Skylar. "They will just distract you. Come on. Jennifer is going to be at the house in an hour for your massage and Yvonne and her team are coming by at eleven."

"In a second." Ivy headed toward one of the stalls. "Can you go get the car? My feet are killing me in these shoes and I don't feel like walking all the way out to the parking lot."

"Fine."

Mia didn't want to argue with her sister. She was too excited about her own plans for later that day. Nate had pulled out all the stops to make her AMA experience special. He'd arranged for her to have a hotel suite where he was staying, and his stylist would be there at two o'clock with a designer dress and all the trappings to get Mia award-ceremony ready.

Ten minutes later, after Mia had fetched the car and picked up her sister, they were heading back to Ivy's house. "How did the interview go?"

"It went okay. Didn't you stay to watch?"

"I had a quick errand to run."

Ivy yawned. "I'm dead. Can you stop and get me my usual with three shots? I need a pick-me-up."

"Sure." Mia resisted the urge to talk her sister out of such a massive caffeine hit. If Ivy was ever going to start taking care of herself, Mia would have to stop making all her decisions for her.

She drove to Ivy's favorite coffee shop near her house, parked and grabbed her wallet out of her tote. "Anything else?"

"One of those scones with the raspberry."

"The white chocolate one?"

Ivy nodded and Mia headed off. Thanks to the long line, it took her fifteen minutes to get back to her sister.

"They didn't have any of the white chocolate so I got you one with orange and cranberry." Mia set the coffee cup in the drink holder and held out the bag containing the pastry.

Ivy took it without looking up from her phone. She was idly scrolling through pictures and acted as if Mia hadn't spoken. The change of mood wasn't unexpected. Ivy hated being kept waiting for anything.

And then as they pulled up in front of the house, Ivy spoke. “I’m going to get Hunter to produce my album.”

“What?” Mia glanced at her sister in confusion. “Are you sure that’s a good idea? I mean, he’s had some success, but at the same time he’s still pretty new to that side of the business. And the label is expecting Nate to be involved.”

“I don’t like the direction Nate is taking my album. I want to do things my way.”

Often when Mia dealt with Ivy she felt as if she stood between a rock and a hard place. Part of her job was to keep Ivy happy. The other part was more difficult. She needed to keep her sister’s career on a strong trajectory. That meant keeping the label happy.

“Of course you do. But at the same time you have to consider the best for your career.”

“You don’t think I know what’s best for my career?”

“Sure. Of course.” Mia decided retreat was the best option.

Ivy got out of the car, and once she was in the house, headed straight to her room without saying another word. After checking in with the housekeeper, Clara, Mia grabbed her overnight bag and left. She was too excited about her own plans to stick around and let Ivy’s drama spoil the rest of her day.

Mia had booked a spa appointment for herself as a special treat. She’d planned for a facial, pedicure and manicure to get her in the perfect mood for the festive event. It was rare for her to get so much uninterrupted time to herself, and several hours later she felt both relaxed and refreshed as she headed to the suite Nate had booked and put herself into his stylist Patricia’s capable hands.

Although Mia had watched Ivy get ready for dozens

of award shows and thought she knew what to expect, when she saw her dress for the first time she nearly started to cry.

"That's the most beautiful thing I've ever seen."

Patricia smiled at her and Mia wondered what she must be thinking of this silly girl Nate had asked her to dress for the event.

"I'm glad you like it. When Nate described you to me, I knew immediately this dress would be perfect for you. There's so much going on with the wildflower print that I think we should keep your styling simple."

Patricia directed the hairdresser to sweep her hair back into a sleek bun. A smoky eye shadow and rose lipstick accentuated Mia's features. By the time they were done even Mia believed she looked presentable enough for the red carpet. Not that she would be walking with Nate. She'd put her foot down on that score. He had his bandmates to speak for him. Her appearance at his side would only lead the media to ask questions.

"You look fantastic," Patricia said as Mia finished slipping into sparkling sandals and straightened so the stylist could assess her total look. "I know several stars who would kill to have that cleavage."

Mia's fingers coasted over her still-flat belly as she stared at herself in the mirror. The neckline of the gown plunged to her waist, yet somehow managed to look elegant rather than sexy. Mia guessed it was due to the delicate sprays of sequin-accented wildflowers that covered the skirt and halter-style top.

"I'm pretty sure I'll never wear anything so beautiful again." The dress fit as if it had been made for her and had required only a few minor alterations. "What time does it turn into fairy dust?"

Patricia laughed. "So I'm your fairy godmother?"

"You had to work some serious magic to get me looking this good."

"You underestimate how beautiful you are. I suppose it's hard to feel pretty when you're constantly comparing yourself to Ivy Bliss."

"I don't compare myself," Mia said without a hint of bitterness. "Everyone else does that for me."

"I know one person who doesn't. Nate. You are his star."

Mia's cheeks heated at Patricia's knowing grin. Because she doubted the stylist would believe anything she had to say to the contrary, she said nothing at all.

Twenty minutes later she was in a car heading for the venue. She'd followed Ivy's day on social media and saw that her sister was excited about her look for that evening. She'd teased bits of the dress all day for her fans. It was a toss-up which Ivy loved more, fashion or performing. She talked all the time about starting her own clothing line and sketched ideas in her free time.

Determined to bridge the gap developing between her and Ivy, Mia texted her twin to ask if she liked her gown, but received no reply.

She decided to go early in order to slip past the media while they were still in setup mode. Her decision turned out to be sound, but she was surprised at how many people wanted to talk to her. Unlike the commotion caused when Ivy and other big stars walked the carpet, Mia was able to take her time with several of the reporters she knew. If they were surprised to find her walking the red carpet on her own, they made no mention of it.

Once she was inside the theater, several producers Ivy had worked with in the past approached her to chat. Apparently word had gone around that Mia had been working with Nate these last few weeks. Most everyone wanted to know if she was writing as well as producing. She kept her answers vague, but by the time she reached her seat, she felt as if she belonged.

It was a heady sensation, but one she reined in almost immediately. So what if she belonged? It wasn't as if she was free to pursue her dreams. Not as long as Ivy needed her. Yet Nate's question continued to plague her. How long was she planning to keep her life on hold so she could watch over her sister? Ivy was a grown woman, no longer a fragile seventeen-year-old girl getting a taste of stardom for the first time.

Besides, in seven months, Mia's priorities would undergo a massive change. She fanned her finger over her stomach. Pregnant. A chill raced through her at the thought of how everyone around her would react to that news. She imagined her parents would be disappointed in her for not being married. Despite having a daughter who pranced around half-naked onstage, they were conservative when it came to family values. Mia was afraid of how Ivy would react. She hoped her twin would be happy for her, but Ivy rarely liked it when good things happened to Mia.

And how would Nate react? What was going on between them was fun and exciting, but it was also new and undefined. They'd known each other only a few months and weren't exactly dating. To go from lovers to parents without all the stuff in between would be a huge leap. But there wasn't any question in Mia's mind that it was one she was ready to make. So when did she tell Nate?

Tonight was too soon. When Ivy's album was done? Mia shook her head. At the rate things were going, with her sister lobbying to switch producers from Nate to Hunter, getting the recording finished by the end of November wasn't going to happen.

Tomorrow they were heading back to Las Vegas. Thursday was Thanksgiving and she and Nate had talked about spending the day together, cooking a special dinner for Trent, Savannah, Melody and hopefully Kyle. She would tell Nate then.

Blinded by the flash of dozens of cameras, Nate squelched his irritation as he walked the AMAs' red carpet with the other members of Free Fall. Although he'd convinced Mia to accompany him to the event, he'd been unable to persuade her to walk beside him past the gauntlet of paparazzi and press. Nor had he caught a glimpse of her to see how Patricia had styled her. The curiosity was killing him.

Behind them Ivy posed and vamped for the cameras. Tonight she'd abandoned her signature high ponytail for a sleek side bun that complemented her romantic red ball gown with its tiers of gauzy layers. The halter top bared her back and shoulders, but offered full frontal coverage. Fabric roses circled the high neck and waist. The deep scarlet tint showed off her light olive skin and caught every eye.

Nate put on his easy grin and posed with his bandmates. They took selfies and signed autographs for their fans. It was great to step away from his role as front man and let the other guys answer the interviewers' questions. All the while his mind was on what awaited him at the end of the red carpet.

After what felt like a ridiculous amount of time, but was only about a half an hour, they entered the theater and headed to their seats. He saw a woman sitting in one of the seats assigned to Free Fall, her brown hair knotted at the nape of her neck. All Nate's tension fell away as he reached the row and realized it was Mia. While his heart thundered in his ears, he suddenly realized he'd half expected her not to show.

She stared straight ahead with fixed concentration, as if by holding herself perfectly still no one would notice her. She was completely mistaken. For starters, she was wearing the exact opposite of Ivy's gown. This dress boasted a deep V that bared Mia from throat to waist, yet somehow managed to look elegant rather than overly sexy. Nate realized it was the gown's off-white background and the sprays of vivid printed flowers with their hints of sparkle that gave the dress a feminine vibe.

Her expression softened as she saw him approach. Nate's pulse hitched at the relief in her eyes. Or maybe it was just how perfect she looked. And smelled. This last he noted as he sat beside her and brushed her cheek with his lips.

"You look gorgeous," he signed, not trusting his voice. Although he'd been cleared by Dr. Hansen to talk a little, he'd grown accustomed to communicating with her in ASL.

"You look pretty great yourself." She glanced past him at his other bandmates and gave them all a sweet smile. "Are you guys nervous?"

"Nah." Mike, their keyboard player, had his arm wrapped around his smiling wife.

Their base player, Dan, was riding solo tonight. His very pregnant wife had opted to cheer from home. "Hell, yeah."

"Sort of." This last came from their drummer, Brent, who had a stunning blonde in a sequined mini on his arm.

Mia laughed, the sound light and musical. "I would think you guys are old pros at this. How many Grammys have you won?"

Nate took his seat as he listened to Mia banter with his

bandmates. Sitting beside her, he was a little surprised at his light-headedness. The weight he'd been carrying all afternoon lifted. He took her hand, lacing their fingers together, and brought it to his lips.

The theater was filling with musicians. They were fifteen minutes away from the start of the show. Beside Nate, Mia was a bundle of restless energy.

"Did you see Ivy?" she asked.

"She was behind us on the red carpet."

"How did she look?"

"Beautiful as always. She was wearing a red dress."

Mia nodded. "I saw bits of it on Instagram. The style is a departure for her and I think she was both excited and a little nervous about wearing it."

Nate was slightly surprised she'd let him tuck her arm through his. Then he realized, given the way she was looking around at all the celebrities, she probably hadn't even noticed the intimacy between them.

The same couldn't be said for him. He was hyper-aware of every little thing about her, from her muted squeal when Taylor Swift walked past to her soft gasp when Luke Bryan winked at her. Given how often she must have seen these people at other award shows, her starstruck behavior amused him. She was like a kid at Disneyland for the first time.

"It's different sitting in the audience among them," she explained when she caught him grinning at her. "I don't have to be professional."

By professional he sensed what she meant was invisible. She'd learned how to bottle up all her emotions, good and bad. He'd realized this when they first met on tour. They'd hung out for almost three weeks before he realized she liked him the way he liked her.

Excitement hummed in her slim body. "I don't think I could ever get used to this."

"They're all just people, like me and you."

"You're not just people. You're Nate Tucker." She stated his name as if that explained everything.

"I'm just a guy."

She shook her head as if he could never understand. Her voice was soft as she spoke. "I still have a hard time believing you ever noticed me."

Conscious of their surroundings, he resisted the urge to sweep her into his arms and kiss her soft lips. *"Let's go find a quiet corner and I'll notice you plenty."*

Even now after everything they'd shared, she still blushed when he stared at her intently. That she'd somehow maintained such innocence while immersed in show business craziness continued to enthrall him.

"I'm glad you came tonight."

"Me, too." But there was a hint of hesitation in her answer.

She was still worried about Ivy. Nate was of two minds. Part of him was irritated at the hold her sister maintained over her. The other part sympathized with Mia. He knew firsthand the effect of being bullied by family. His father hadn't treated his wife and child as though they mattered to him. On a good day he'd settled in front of the television with a whiskey and ignored them. On a bad day he'd led with his fists.

Music began to play, signaling that the show was getting under way. Mia relaxed and snuggled a bit closer. Had she been worried that her sister might stop by and make a scene? What was it going to take for Mia to get out from beneath Ivy's thumb?

It was nice for a change to not have to worry about performing. The only time he needed to leave Mia alone was a little over an hour and a half into the program, when Free Fall presented the award for Favorite Male Country Artist. He stood to the side while Dan and Mike took turns reading off the nominees. While the winner thanked family and fans, Nate shared a smile with Mia. She looked so perfect sitting there, her eyes bright, her gaze all for him as she waited for him to come back to her.

All of a sudden he couldn't wait for the show to be over so he could take her to the after-party and spend some time with her in his arms on the dance floor. Since she was officially his date, Mia couldn't possibly usc her sister's presence as an excuse to keep him at bay the way she'd done on the tour.

But he'd underestimated Ivy.

When the pop star stepped onstage to perform, something was definitely off with her. Nate doubted most people would notice, but he'd watched her rehearse and perform for weeks while on tour. She was a beat behind the music and she was walking through her complicated choreography. Mia sat forward in her chair, her expression tightening with concern.

"What's wrong with her?"

Mia shook her head, but he knew her well enough to know when she wasn't telling the truth.

"Is she drunk?"

Mia's gaze was glued to Ivy. Nate wasn't sure if she'd even noticed his questions, until she shook her head again after a minute.

"Maybe high." Mia set her fingertips against her mouth and blinked rapidly. The bright glint in her eyes was from tears. "I need to get backstage and be there for her."

"Then we'll both go." He wasn't letting Mia run off without him. She might never come back.

"You can't leave in the middle of the ceremony."

But she could. It was her way of highlighting the difference in their status. She was a lowly, anonymous assistant, while he was a celebrity. Nate was getting tired of it.

"Contact your dad. He's her manager. Let him deal with her."

Mia bit the inside of her lip, looking concerned at his insistence. "I'll call him when I get backstage."

Nate cursed long and viciously in his head. Leave it to Ivy to upset her sister just when Mia was having fun. Nate reached for her hand, but Mia pulled it out of reach before he made contact.

"I'll be back in a little while."

Then, as the performance ended and the crowd politely applauded, Mia slipped away. And Nate wondered if he'd see her again before the evening was over.

Nine

It was a little after midnight when Nate returned to his hotel suite without his date for the evening. He wasn't surprised that Mia hadn't reappeared after heading backstage to check on her sister. At least she hadn't left him hanging. She'd sent him several texts as she assessed the situation and waited for her father to show up and take charge of Ivy.

Now, his cell phone pinged and his screen lit up with a text.

I'm back at the hotel. Sorry about what happened tonight.

The tightness in his chest eased as he texted her back, letting her know that he was also at the hotel and asking her to come to his suite. It was time he and Mia had a serious conversation about what was going on between them and where he saw their relationship going. He needed to know where she stood.

A soft knock sounded on his door. When he opened it, Mia stood in the hallway holding a pint of his favorite ice cream and two spoons.

"What's that for?"

"Girls always eat ice cream after a big disappointment."

He wondered which disappointment she referred to: the fact that Free Fall didn't win their category or that her sister had ruined his evening.

"I'm not a girl. And I don't care that we lost." He plucked the ice cream from her hand and gestured her in.

"I am a girl and the ice cream is for me. I just thought I'd share." She swiped at the container, but he moved beyond her reach.

He set the ice cream on the coffee table and sat down on the couch. *"It's my favorite. And what do you have to be bummed about?"*

"You're mad at me."

"I'm not."

"Liar." She followed him and sat down cross-legged, facing him. "I'm sorry I ruined our night."

"You didn't. Your sister did."

"I shouldn't have left you."

In five minutes she'd managed to dispel his annoyance and arouse his sympathy. Here he'd been feeling sorry for himself, and she was the one who'd had to disrupt her evening to take care of Ivy.

"How come you didn't tell me your sister has a drug problem?"

The question had been burning up his thoughts since he'd realized what's going on.

"She doesn't have a problem."

Mia's evasion annoyed him. It wasn't just that she was keeping a whopping huge secret from him. Ivy's career was something Nate and Trent were investing time and money in. If there was a problem, they needed to know.

"You don't think I can see what's going on? You forget, I've been there."

Mia wouldn't meet his gaze. "I know, but you got clean and Ivy can, too."

"Who knows about this?"

"Just my immediate family."

"How long has this been going on?"

"It started when she had plastic surgery at seventeen. She got hooked on the painkillers. She was on Broadway at the time and I was finishing up my senior year of high school in LA. No one knows this but my parents and me, but she almost died after overdosing." Mia looked miserable. "That's when it was decided I should become her assistant so I could keep an eye on her."

"But it's been eight years." At least this explained Mia's dedication to her sister. *"How long is everyone expecting you to sacrifice your life for Ivy?"*

She didn't answer his question. "She doesn't always make good choices. I've been worried about her spending so much time with Riley and Skylar. They are far more likely to drag her into trouble than they are to keep her out of it."

"How bad are things with her?"

"She's been mostly clean since what happened in New York."

"Mostly?"

Mia winced. "Except for a setback a couple years ago."

"She seemed fine on the tour."

"She was. It's the album. She's really struggling. But I don't know what happened tonight. Usually she loves performing."

Nate had a pretty good idea. *"It's because you're here with me. Your sister loves to spoil things for you."*

"That's not true." But she didn't sound or look convincing.

When Mia offered nothing else, he asked another question. *"Does your father know what's going on?"*

"Before. But not this time around."

"You should tell him. He's her father." Nate thought that Javier needed to act like her father for a change and put his manager role on the back burner. "This could ruin more than just her career."

Mia dropped her gaze to her hands. Misery radiated from her. The tour had offered Nate plenty of chances to observe the family dynamic and he sensed more at work here that Mia wasn't saying.

"What?"

"They'll blame me." She leaned forward and dug her spoon into the ice cream. "That's not true. I don't mean that." But it was obvious that was exactly what worried her. "It's just that I'm supposed to keep an eye on her. And I've been distracted." The sly smile she shot him wobbled at the edges.

His heart broke. *"Why do you let them do that to you?"*

"Because she's my sister and I'm…"

"Responsible for her?"

He'd never had a brother or sister and didn't understand the connection these two had. To make matters worse, Ivy and Mia were twins. Granted, they were fraternal rather than identical twins, but still, sharing a womb with someone for nine months must take the bond to a whole different level.

"Where does it end?" Hopelessness overwhelmed him as he suddenly realized his plan to disengage Mia

from her sister had been doomed from the start. *"When do you get to live your life?"*

"I don't know."

His mother had stayed with a bully too long and she'd ended up beaten and bruised on too many occasions. Mia wore her wounds on the inside.

On the other hand, he wasn't sure if Mia was ready to leave her situation. Shucking off her family's expectations couldn't be easy. He'd seen firsthand the pressure Javier exerted on both his daughters.

"Have you asked yourself what you owe her?"

"I know you don't think I owe her anything," Mia said. "Maybe I don't. I just know if I leave and something happens to her again, I would never be able to forgive myself."

That sort of emotional blackmail was nearly impossible to walk away from. Nate wished he could somehow make her understand what they were doing to her. Or maybe she did. Maybe the way she coped was to pretend it didn't bother her.

More than anything Nate wanted to protect her from herself. He'd be her champion if she'd let him. But he couldn't force her to get out of the bad situation she found herself in. Unlike when he'd stepped between his parents and wrestled the knife away from his father, the danger to Mia wasn't tangible. But that didn't make it any less dire.

"How much longer can you keep it up? Following Ivy around. Keeping her out of trouble. Catering to her every whim. When do you get to live your life?"

He'd posed this same question several times on tour. Each time Mia had given him the same answer.

"It's what I need to do right now. Once Ivy's new album drops and it's a sensation, I'll have more options."

Her eyes pleaded with him to understand. "I promised my parents to watch out for her. She doesn't take good care of herself. That leads to people taking advantage of her. Like Riley and Skylar are doing right now."

"You say you're going to leave after this album launches, but what if she needs you more than ever?"

That Mia didn't answer immediately told him a lot.

"You know I'm in your corner, right?"

"I do." But she didn't look at him.

For a moment he felt as if she didn't want him to be in her corner. As if having him on her side created a whole new set of problems for her. How was that possible?

"Where does this leave us?"

"I just need some time to sort things out."

"How much time?" He had to head back to Las Vegas tomorrow, but hated the idea of leaving her behind in LA.

"My parents are sitting down with Ivy tomorrow. I'll know more then."

"Are you coming back to Las Vegas?"

"I promised I'd help with Thanksgiving dinner." She gave him a wan smile. "We can talk then."

The morning after the AMAs, Mia drove Nate to a checkup with Dr. Hanson and then to the airport. As delighted as she'd been to hear that Nate's progress was good and he was able to start speaking again, she would miss being his voice. That he'd needed her to translate for him was a great excuse for why she was spending so much time with him. Now, she'd have to come clean about their relationship and face Ivy's displeasure.

When Mia got to her sister's house, she saw their mom's car parked in the driveway. Mia approached the front door with a sick feeling in her stomach. Her mother stood in the foyer as Mia entered the house. As Ivy's career had taken off, Sharon Navarro had changed from an average housewife and mother who'd homeschooled her three daughters and shopped discount stores for her clothes to a designer-label-wearing middle-aged woman with large diamonds at her ears and on her fingers. Despite what must have been a harrowing night worrying about Ivy, she looked as if she was ready for lunch at a fancy restaurant.

In contrast, Mia felt disheveled and gritty despite the shower she'd shared with Nate that morning. "What are you doing here?" she asked, hoping nothing worse had happened to her sister overnight. "Is Ivy okay?"

"She's fine. Where have you been?"

"At the hotel. I told Dad last night where I was going. I needed to return the dress."

"And you stayed?"

Although they'd spent the night together, talking and making love until dawn, she couldn't help but feel as if Nate had put a wall up between them. He wanted her to leave Ivy and be with him. Mia thought that's what she wanted, too. So why couldn't she just walk away? Because Ivy needed her? How long was she going to use that as an excuse? Especially now that she was pregnant.

"I knew Dad was here. Ivy didn't need us both." Mia's tone contained a touch of belligerence. "I had a whole night planned." To her own surprise, she sounded like Ivy, petulant and frustrated.

"Do you mean to tell me you went to the after-parties after dropping your sister off here?" Mia's mother looked appalled.

"No, of course not. I just wanted to point out that I had my own plans for the evening that didn't involve my sister getting high and making a fool of herself on live television."

"Mia," her mother admonished. "Your sister works so hard and is under such pressure."

Fury rushed through Mia's body as she thought of her high hopes for last evening. It was supposed to her magical night. Her chance to appear in public with Nate and behave like a couple. To dance and mingle and have fun while not giving her sister a single thought.

"She spoils everything," Mia countered.

"She supports all of us."

"Well, maybe I'm tired of being supported by her. Maybe it's time I started supporting myself."

When had her level of resentment risen so high? How had she not noticed that each day of acting as her sister's assistant grew harder than the one before? Nate's constant pointing out how badly Ivy treated her didn't help.

Mia's mother retreated a half step beneath the rush of her daughter's emotional tirade. "You can't turn your back on her sister. She isn't strong enough to do this on her own."

"I'm not turning my back on her." All the energy drained from her. No matter what she said or did, Mia was never going to win this battle. It all came down to guilt. Responsibility. "She's my sister and I love her. But my life revolves around her and I want a little something for myself."

"You mean your songwriting," Mia's mother said. "I'll speak to your father. Maybe there's room on Ivy's next album for a few of your songs. And this time you should get the credit."

"That's not what I mean." But Mia could tell her mother wasn't listening.

Her fingers shifted to her abdomen and the child that

lay there. Now wasn't the time to get into this with her mom. She needed to talk to Nate first.

But right now, Mia needed some sleep. The past twenty-four hours had been a roller coaster of highs and lows, all of which had taken every ounce of Mia's energy.

"Can we talk about this later?" she said. "I'm exhausted. Are you going to stick around for a while?"

"No. I have a meeting at the foundation."

Sharon Navarro ran the Ivy Bliss Foundation, a program that promoted hearing health and helped low-income children with hearing impairments. It was a charity near and dear to her heart because of her eldest daughter's hearing loss at age two.

"Where is Dad?"

"Your father's meeting with Trent Caldwell about Ivy's album. It looks as if she's going to finish recording it with Hunter Graves." Mia's mother picked up her purse. "He'll come by afterward."

"Then I guess it's just me keeping an eye on her." Again.

"I don't understand what has gotten into you lately. You used to be happy for your sister's success."

"I still am. But she's become such a different person. There are times when I don't recognize her anymore."

"She's a star," Mia's mother said, as if that explained everything.

Overwhelmed by defeat, Mia watched her mother depart before shuffling toward her bedroom. She shut the door behind her and glanced around the space. Besides the clothes in the closet, barely anything in the room belonged to her. Mia dropped her overnight bag on the floor and flung herself on her bed, where she lay on her back, staring at the ceiling. Her eyes were dry despite the lump in her throat.

She didn't remember ever feeling so alone. And yet, what about her situation had changed? Acting as her sister's full-time personal assistant and keeper had kept Mia from forming lasting friendships, and interfered with every man she'd ever tried to date.

Except now, Mia had been given a glimpse of what her life could be. A career as a music producer. Friendships with Melody, Trent and Savannah. A relationship with Nate. Motherhood.

Mia closed her eyes. Ready or not, everything was going to change.

Nate was surprised when the person picking him up at the Las Vegas airport was Kyle and not Melody. As he slid into the passenger seat of Kyle's bright blue BMW convertible, he glanced at his business partner and thought he looked as exhausted and miserable as Nate felt.

"I didn't expect to see you," Nate said.

"Melody asked if I could get you. Seems she had a small window to get Hunter's input on her album—" Kyle's eyes widened. "Hey, you're talking again."

"My doctor gave me the go-ahead to start using my voice, but I'm not supposed to overdo it. So you and Melody are finally talking?"

"If by talking you mean she sent me a text saying she was stuck at the studio and would I pick you up, then yeah."

Nate winced at the other man's bitterness. "You two have got to sit down and chat. Why don't you come for Thanksgiving." Nate had extended the invitation to Kyle once already and been turned down. This time, he decided to push harder.

"I don't want to spoil the day for you guys."

"You won't." The only thing that could spoil the day for Nate was if Mia found a reason not to show. "The longer you and Melody keep up whatever it is you're doing, the harder it's going to be to reconcile."

"What if we're not meant to be together?"

Kyle's question hit at the heart of what Nate himself had been grappling with these last few weeks. And after last night, he was more convinced than ever that when the time came, Mia was going to bolt the same way she had that last morning in Sydney.

And what then? What was he planning to do without her? He couldn't bear to think about it.

"You and Melody love each other," Nate said. And in less than six months they were going to become parents, whether either of them was prepared or not. "You'll find a way to work it out. Just remember why you fell for her in the first place."

"But I've really messed up. I pretty much accused her of cheating on me with Hunter."

Nate could appreciate his friend's predicament. Kyle was a well-known player. Before realizing he was in love with Melody, he'd dated lots of women and committed to none of them.

"Have you asked yourself why?"

"Many times. It's the way Melody and I got together. She was trying to make Hunter jealous. I keep thinking maybe she picked the wrong guy."

Nate didn't think this was the heart of Kyle's troubles. It seemed more likely that he was afraid to give himself over to the intense feelings Melody aroused in him. Nate got it. Falling in love was a big, scary deal. As he was discovering.

"You don't really believe that?"

"That picture of them together in New York. She looked so happy with him. It's been months and months since she's been like that with me..." Kyle's voice trailed off and silence reigned in the car for a while. "And now he's here and working at your studio," he finally added. "I'm sure she's spending tons of time with him. He's going to win her back," Kyle grumbled. "If he hasn't already."

"So that's it then?" Nate's tone was harsh. He wanted Kyle to man up and fight for the woman he loved. "You're giving up?"

"I didn't say that."

"It sure as hell sounds like it."

Kyle opened his mouth but no words came out. Nate would love it if the only problem between him and Mia was a stupid misunderstanding about a photo of her with an ex-boyfriend.

"You're both acting like a couple of idiots," Nate declared. "Things between you might have moved fast, but that's no reason to freak out. Stop being so dense. Tell her you love her and make her believe it."

For a long time Kyle didn't say anything. Then, as he turned the car onto Nate's street, he said, "Thanksgiving, huh? What time should I be there?"

"Dinner's at five, but you're welcome at any time. Trent and Dylan are coming early for the Vikings-Lions game. Savannah and Melody plan on coming midafternoon."

"Can I bring anything?"

Nate grinned. "Just your best behavior. Mia and I will provide the rest."

Twenty minutes later, after switching to his own car at home, Nate was pulling into the studio parking lot.

The receptionist greeted him with a wave when he went inside. He popped into a couple different control booths to see how things were going. He found Melody on the couch in studio C with Hunter at the boards.

When she spotted him, Melody jumped up and rushed across the room to throw her arms around his neck.

"Thanks for sending Kyle to pick me up."

"Sorry about the switch, but Hunter had a free hour to help me out. Hey, you got your voice back." Melody beamed at him. "But you shouldn't overdo it."

"I won't." Natc turned to Hunter. "How's it going with her album?"

"She's got a lot of great songs here. We'll just have to whittle it down." The look he gave Melody sent a wave of apprehension through Nate. "It might take a while."

Maybe Kyle had reason to be concerned, after all. Not because Melody was falling for her ex-boyfriend, but because Hunter had a very possessive look in his eye when he gazed at her. As if he might be planning to work damned hard to win her back.

"Not too long, I hope," Nate said. "I'd like to have it ready to go by the beginning of next year."

"I'll put all my energy into making that happen." Hunter shot Melody a fond look. "But now I've got to get going. Dinner later?"

"Ah, sure."

"I'll pick you up at six."

When Hunter left the control booth, Nate turned on Melody. "What the hell is going on between you two?"

"Nothing. We're just friends."

"And Kyle?"

Melody toyed with her phone. "Kyle and I need some space."

"That's the last thing you need. Have you forgotten that you two are going to be parents? When do you plan to tell him about the baby?" Nate saw the excuses gathering in her eyes and shook his head. "I've invited him for Thanksgiving. You'll be surrounded by family. We'll all be there to support you. Plan on telling him then."

"But that's only three days away."

"The sooner the better."

"So tell me what happened with Ivy at the AMAs last night. She looked out of it."

"Apparently she's been addicted to painkillers on and off for the last eight years and recently suffered a relapse. Mia stayed behind in LA while they figure out the best way to handle things."

"Trent is meeting with Javier today." Melody's features wore a worried expression. "Do you think he'll postpone her album?"

"The way things have been going, it might be a good idea to push it out until later next year. She needs to focus on getting clean again." Nate thought about his plunge down the rabbit hole of drug and alcohol abuse and didn't envy Ivy for what she had to look forward to. "I'm off to get some work done." He leaned over and kissed Melody on the forehead. "Give what I said about you and Kyle some thought before you head off to dinner with Hunter tonight, okay?"

Melody nodded and Nate left to make some music and figure out what he was going to do about Mia next.

Early Tuesday afternoon, Mia was in her bedroom at Ivy's LA house, sorting through recipes and planning the shopping list for her Thanksgiving dinner with Nate and his friends when the door burst open and Skylar plunged into the room with Riley on her heels.

Since she'd returned from dropping Nate at the airport the day before, Mia had either been holed up in her room to escape the thick tension filling the house, or popping in every couple hours to check on Ivy. So far, her sister hadn't shown much interest in anything besides binge watching *Pretty Little Liars* on Hulu.

"You bitch!" Skylar shrieked, her wild eyes fixed on Mia.

"What?" Mia stared at her dumbfounded, unsure what Skylar and Riley were doing in Ivy's house, much less Mia's room.

Ivy must have let them in. Why couldn't she understand that she was supposed to cut all ties with these two? They were the ones who'd been supplying her with the prescription drugs. Mia jumped off her bed as Skylar advanced toward her.

"You have some nerve," Ivy's friend said in a threatening tone.

Mia glanced from Skylar to Riley. "You need to leave. Now."

"We're not going anywhere," Riley piped up. "We know it was you."

Mia shook her head. "It's not just me. My father wants you to stay away from Ivy, too." But she could tell the two women weren't listening to her.

"Haven't you sponged off your sister long enough?"

These two were the most clueless women on the planet. "Sponged? Do you have any idea what I do for Ivy?"

"Well, you don't write her music. That's for sure."

Skylar's words made Mia go cold. Everyone who knew the truth behind Ivy's songwriting worked awfully hard to keep it hidden. Neither one of these two was trustworthy enough to be told such a damaging secret.

"Of course not," Mia said calmly, while her heart thundered.

"Then why did you tell the media that Ivy didn't write any of her songs?"

"I didn't." Mia was besieged by panic. Such a disclosure would devastate Ivy. "I wouldn't do that."

"Sure you would," Riley said.

Skylar nodded. "You resent her."

"I don't." But she could hear the lie in her voice.

She did resent Ivy, but not for the reasons these two thought. Mia didn't care that Ivy had been gifted with all the looks and talent. Up until the last few years, when Ivy had started behaving more and more like a diva, Mia had been happy to be her assistant and do whatever she could to bolster her twin's career.

"Sure you do." Riley exchanged a look with Skylar. "You have a thing for Nate."

"We all noticed."

"But he doesn't know you're alive. He wants Ivy. So you decided to discredit her by lying to the media and saying you're the one who writes her music."

It was on the tip of Mia's tongue to argue that she did write all Ivy's music, but too many years of living with that secret kept her silent now. "I need to talk to Ivy."

Mia started toward Ivy's bedroom, but Riley stepped in her way.

"She doesn't want to talk to you."

Irritation flooded Mia, loosening her tongue. "If you want to talk about people who sponge off my sister, look in the mirror." Imbued with strength she didn't know she possessed, Mia pushed past Riley and headed toward her sister's bedroom. She had to explain.

Ivy was standing by the open sliding glass door that led onto the pool deck, Mia's song journal in her hand.

Mia stopped halfway into the room as Ivy turned her tear-streaked face in her direction.

"I didn't tell anyone about the songwriting," Mia said, her voice clogged with emotion. "I swear."

"Not even Nate?"

"He figured it out all on his own." Mia advanced toward her sister, but Ivy went outside, maintaining ten feet between them.

"You're such a liar." Ivy held out the notebook. "I read this. It's all about him."

Mia's song journal was morc than just a place for her to jot down music and lyrics. She also used it as a diary, and although she'd never used Nate's name, many of the entries had described incidents that made it pretty clear who she was talking about.

"I'll bet you couldn't wait to tell him," Ivy continued. "You probably thought he'd be into you if he thought you were a songwriter."

"I swear I didn't tell him." But in her heart, she knew she'd wanted him to figure it out. And maybe she'd helped that along. "It was just that I wrote songs with Melody on the tour and you never showed any signs that you wrote, too. He got suspicious."

"What other bad things have you been telling Nate about me?"

"I haven't said anything."

Ivy gave a bitter laugh. "I see the way you moon over him. He's never going to be interested in you."

"Why do you care how I feel about Nate?"

"I don't." But it was obvious that she was bothered. "I just hate to see you make a fool of yourself over someone who is so out of your league."

"Nate doesn't see himself that way." The instant the words were past her lips, Mia wished them back.

"He should."

Without warning, Ivy launched Mia's song journal through the air in the direction of the pool. Mia watched in horror as hundreds of hours' worth of angst and love hit the water with a splat and began to sink.

"My journal." An anguished cry broke from her as she rushed forward. She stood at the edge of the pool with her hands over her mouth, unable to believe her sister could have done something so cruel. "What the hell, Ivy?"

Her twin glared at her. "Now there's no proof who wrote those songs."

"You forget that I have years' worth of those journals. Every one of them proves you've been taking credit for my songs. Are you planning on destroying those, as well?"

"Yes."

"Why are you doing this? All we have to do is release a press statement that confirms you write your own songs."

"Why did you have to ruin everything?" Ivy demanded.

"I didn't do anything."

"It's all your fault. Every bit of it." Tears streamed down Ivy's cheeks. "I can't look at you anymore."

"Ivy, why don't you calm down and let's talk about this." Her sister's behavior was scaring Mia. She started to put her hands on Ivy's arms in an effort to connect with her, but her twin threw her off and backed up.

"There's no need to talk. I hate you. I want you out of this house and out of my life. I'm sick of having you telling me what to do and where to go."

"I only do that because I'm your assistant." Mia's frustration was continuing to build; she was at her breaking point. "It's my job to keep you on schedule."

"Well, I'm sick of it. I don't need you."

"What are you saying?"

"I'm saying I don't want you around anymore. Get the hell out of my house."

Ten

Tuesday night after a lonely dinner by himself, Nate sat in his living room with his guitar for company and came to terms with just how miserable he was being a bachelor. He was sick of coming home to an empty house and sleeping alone in his big bed. Sexy Skyping with Mia last night had been more frustrating than fun. He needed her here and now. Tomorrow couldn't come soon enough.

His phone buzzed. Hoping it was Mia calling, Nate reached for it. "Hey, Trent."

His business partner got right to the point without preliminaries. "Someone leaked that Ivy doesn't write her own songs."

"What?"

"Was it you?"

"No." Nate cursed, half wishing he had done it. But Mia would never have forgiven him. "When did this happen?"

"This afternoon. I just found out."

"This afternoon..." Why hadn't Mia called to tell him? She had to know. "Have you spoken to Javier?"

"Not yet. I thought, given your connection to Mia, that we should talk about how you'd like the label to handle things."

While Nate appreciated his friend's consideration, he had absolutely no idea what would be best for Mia. "I think West Coast Records should come out saying we have no knowledge of this."

"But is that true?" Trent sounded tense and weary. "I don't have any idea what sort of unscrupulous business practices the label was engaged in with my father or brother at the helm."

Where was Mia?

Was she corralled with her family as they strategized damage control? Ivy must be near hysterical. First there was the misstep at the AMAs on Sunday. And now this. But why hadn't Mia called or texted?

"What if you make a personal statement that you had no knowledge of the situation and that you will investigate and correct whatever mistakes were made."

"That feels a little bit like we're throwing Ivy under the bus." Trent's tone was neutral, giving Nate no idea which way he was leaning. "Bottom line—do you want Mia to get credit for the songs or not?"

"Let me talk to her. Can you give me a couple hours?"

"I'm not going to rush into anything. Tomorrow morning is soon enough."

Nate hung up with Trent and dialed Mia. He wasn't surprised when he got her voice mail. After leaving a message, he began to pace. Not more than five minutes later, his doorbell rang. Expecting to find Melody on his doorstep, he was shocked to see Mia.

"I was on my way here when I got your message." She looked miserable as she stood outside his front door.

He reached for her hand and pulled her inside. "Are you okay?"

"No." Mia pressed herself against his chest and mumbled her next words into his shirt. "She thinks I did it."

"You didn't, did you?"

Mia pushed away and glared up at him. "Absolutely not."

Of course not. He wasn't even sure why he'd asked. "But now that the truth is out there, Trent and I will back you one hundred percent."

"She threw my journal in the pool. There was almost six months' worth of ideas and melodies." Her small frame shook. "And she fired me as her assistant."

Nate tightened his arms around her and buried his face in her hair. It was probably best that she couldn't see his face at the moment because the news that her sister had fired her pleased him. He knew she wouldn't agree that it was the best thing for her.

She pulled out of his arms and wiped at her eyes. "I can't believe she did that."

He drew her from the foyer and into his living room. Her expression was blank, her gaze turned inward as he settled her on the couch. Once she was tucked against his body with her head resting on his shoulder, he gave a contented sigh. Her life might be falling apart, but in the depths of her despair, she'd come to him.

"I don't know what happened," she murmured after a long, long time. "One second I was working on a shopping list for Thanksgiving dinner, the next Skylar and Riley are bursting into my room and accusing me of being the one who told the media I wrote all Ivy's songs. And when I told Ivy that I wouldn't have done that, she didn't believe me." Mia's breath came in unsteady gasps as she relayed her tale. "She was half out of her mind, saying all sorts of crazy things that made no sense."

"She'll realize it wasn't you."

"I don't think she'll ever believe that. She threw me out. I don't know what that means. I've always lived with her."

This was sounding better and better by the second. "You can move in here," he said, keeping his voice as calm and gentle as possible. Mia was vulnerable. He didn't want to spook her. "Maybe this will all work out for the best," he began. "It'll be a fresh start."

"A fresh start?" She echoed the words as if she were tasting some strange and suspicious dish. "It's not over."

"I thought you said she threw you out and fired you."

"She didn't mean it."

"What if she did?" Nate intended to capitalize on this turn of good fortune. "You could come work for me. Live in Las Vegas." *Be with me.*

It was the same offer he'd made to her in Australia. The one she'd turned down without giving it a second's consideration.

"I could." Her shoulders slumped. She shook her head. "But this isn't how I wanted things to happen."

"What did you want?" Nate couldn't stop his expression from turning grim. "Her blessing? She was never going to give you that."

"I know, but this seems so abrupt. It's like she hates me. Knowing how important my song journal is to me, she ruined it. That's six months of work. Gone."

His eyebrows went up; he couldn't help it. "You forget you have the demos you made." What he'd heard was pretty fantastic. "And you'll write plenty more songs."

She made a face at him. "You make it sound so easy."

Taking him by surprise, she set her hand on his cheek and brought her lips to his in a sweet, poignant kiss. "Besides, those songs were special. They were about us. How I feel when I'm with you."

Nate's heart gave a mighty thump. For a second he lost the ability to breathe. "How do you feel?"

"Like I exist."

"You've always existed to me."

"I know."

When he'd left LA yesterday morning, he'd promised himself to keep his distance until she was ready to commit to being in a relationship with him. That vow went up in smoke as she eased closer and sifted her fingers through his hair.

He had no words to deny her and no willpower to push her away. Letting his eyes close, he absorbed her breath on his skin and the gentle sweep of her lips against his. She touched him tentatively, as if she expected rejection at any second. Even if he had the strength to push her away, he'd never be able to do it. She soothed the places inside him damaged by his father's abuse and the years he'd spent drowning in forgetfulness. Until she came along, he'd filled the gnawing emptiness first with reckless amusements, and then music.

That he couldn't hold on to her, couldn't convince her his need was greater than her sister's, had nudged him close to the dark places he'd once lost himself in. Good thing he was no longer a stupid twentysomething. He might have sought the oblivion of those earlier days in his career before he'd hit rock bottom and cleaned himself up.

"About what you said to me the other night," she said. "Nate, there's something you should know—" she began, but he shook his head, cutting her off.

"Don't talk."

If they started a conversation he wouldn't be able to take her in his arms and show her how much she meant to him. Standing up, he scooped her off the couch and headed for his bedroom.

"Are you sure?" she asked, when her feet touched the floor beside his bed.

"Very sure."

He lowered his lips to her soft neck and breathed in her clean fragrance. Her fingers coasted down the front of his shirt, unfastening buttons as they went. Anticipation coiled in his gut below where she laid her palms against his skin. He shuddered, eager to revisit the heat of her body sliding against his.

"Tonight it's just you and me." And the beginning of everything.

Mia stood in Nate's kitchen, surrounded by the leftovers from their Thanksgiving dinner, and smiled in blissful contentment. In the family room, Nate, Kyle and Trent sat on the couch in front of the big screen television watching football. It was the third game of the day and Mia wondered if men ever grew tired of watching a bunch of beefy guys pass, run and tackle.

"What can I do to help?" Melody slipped into the kitchen and gazed at the packed countertops.

"I've got this," Mia said with a wistful smile. "But if you'd hang out and keep me company, that would be great."

"But you did all the cooking," Savannah said as she passed with her infant son in her arms. She placed the boy in his father's care and returned. "You shouldn't have to clean up, as well."

"I'm happy to do it. Today was one of the best Thanksgivings I've ever had." She pulled out plastic storage containers and began making meals that she intended to send home with everyone.

She'd made enough food for twenty people and what they hadn't finished was way more than she and Nate could eat by themselves.

"I agree," Melody said. "Last year Nate and I were on the road. Kyle and Trent went to Miami." She paused and glanced at Savannah. "Did Rafe make you spend the holiday with Siggy?"

"Unfortunately." Savannah shuddered.

Mia remembered hearing how Melody and Trent's father was a terrible bully who treated Trent like the black sheep of the family for no good reason.

While the two women began sharing tales of Caldwell Thanksgivings past, Mia worked methodically to restore order to the kitchen. Listening to their stories of family dysfunction eased some of her angst. Although she'd called her parents and Ivy to wish them a happy Thanksgiving, not one had picked up.

It seemed impossible that after everything she'd done for Ivy her family could believe she was responsible for the leak. And with each hour that went by, it seemed as though Nate was right about her being permanently fired as Ivy's assistant.

No more demands for coffee or frivolous errands. No more being awakened at three in the morning when Ivy returned home from partying with her entourage, and having to fix waffles or quesadillas, depending on what her sister was in the mood for. Mia still wasn't accustomed to the peace and quiet that came from not being her sister's assistant any longer.

It was nice playing house with Nate. Her gaze traveled toward the couch and lingered on the three men. Was this what a normal Thanksgiving was like? A house filled with great friends, good food and football.

"Oh, I know that look," Savannah said with a wistful sigh.

Melody chuckled. "Do you recognize it every time you look in the mirror?"

"I recognize it from when you and Kyle first started dating." Savannah eyed her sister-in-law. "Don't you think it's time you two stopped playing games and started acting like you're in love once again?"

"Have you told him?" Mia kept her voice low.

Melody shook her head. "I was supposed to today, but there never seemed to be an opportunity."

"We all gave you plenty of chances," Savannah pointed out.

It had been easy to isolate the pair several times over the course of the day, but neither Melody nor Kyle seemed at ease with each other. Three times Mia had watched them engage in awkward conversation before separating. Each time her heart had ached for the pair.

With Savannah gently pressing Melody about her urgent need to talk to Kyle, Mia's own mouth went dry. She'd made a similar promise to herself about telling Nate that he was going to be a father. With all the drama surrounding Ivy, and the frantic meal preparations, it had slipped Mia's mind.

She sipped from her water bottle to alleviate her sudden cotton mouth. Anxiety made her stomach churn. As soon as she told Nate he was going to be a dad, her life would completely change.

Together they would have to decide how to move forward. Mia's hands shook. Despite his declaration that he wanted them to be together, there was a huge difference between building toward a committed relationship and becoming parents.

Well, there was nothing she could do until everyone was gone. Melody was staying at her brother's house while she worked on her album at Ugly Trout Records, and had ridden with them. When Kyle offered to give her a ride home, Mia and Nate exchanged a satisfied look.

It took an hour for Savannah to pry Trent away from the game. Dylan was sacked out in his father's arms and she declared it was time to head home and put him to bed. As the door closed on Savannah, Trent and Dylan, Nate turned to Mia.

"And then there were two," he said, his smile conveying both tenderness and desire.

Mia couldn't resist the invitation in his eyes. She lifted herself onto her toes, but just as her lips made contact with his, her phone buzzed in her back pocket and she instinctively flinched.

"Ignore it," Nate said, gathering her into his arms for a proper kiss that left her gasping for breath and aching for more.

She wrapped her arms around his neck and trembled as he slid his palms beneath her shirt and up along her rib cage to her breasts. Her nipples turned to hard buds as electric impulses sizzled and snapped along her nerve endings.

Her phone buzzed a second time. Nate dragged his mouth from hers and cursed.

"It might be my family," she said, hope tugging at her voice. "Let me check."

"Sure. I'll meet you in the bedroom."

She blew him a flirtatious kiss and went into the family room to shut off the television and close the sliding glass doors that led out to the pool. As she walked, she pulled her phone out and keyed her message app. To her disappointment, the text hadn't come from her family, but Yvonne, Ivy's stylist. The dire message had her clicking on the attached link. A second later, she gasped at what appeared.

For the last forty-eight hours Mia hadn't had time to pop on to social media to see what her sister had been up to. And it had been a relief to be completely disengaged from all the Ivy drama. Nor had she felt any guilt, mostly because of the way her twin had behaved since the truth had come out about Mia's songwriting.

Now, however, all it took was a single Instagram post and she was right back in the thick of the craziness. Mia stared at the picture on her screen. It was a photo of the contents of a very familiar tote. Hers. Including the positive pregnancy test. Also hers.

When had Ivy taken the picture? The answer came at once. The morning of the AMAs, after the television interview. Ivy had asked Mia to get her some coffee. She'd left her tote behind.

Mia's skin turned to ice. All this time her sister had known? Why hadn't Ivy said anything? Suddenly Mia couldn't breathe.

"Mia?" Nate's voice came from the direction of the master bedroom.

"I'll be there in a second."

Her attention returned to her phone. Suddenly, the screen lit up with her mother's number, but Mia doubted she was reaching out to wish Mia a happy Thanksgiving. She let the call go to voice mail and blocked all incoming calls. Then she went back to staring at the picture.

Before she spoke with anyone, she and Nate needed to have a conversation. Ivy's bid for attention on social media had highlighted that Mia's secret was out of the bag. Was it in retribution for her belief that Mia had spilled Ivy's own secret? If so, why not announce that Mia was pregnant?

Because this created a huge buzz. One that might distract everyone from the songwriting scandal and create confusion about the authenticity of all the latest Ivy Bliss stories.

"Mia?" Nate sounded closer.

She'd sat down at the breakfast bar when the room started spinning. Now she looked up and spied him standing a few feet away.

"Sorry," she murmured, struggling to focus, with her thoughts in turmoil. "Did you say something?"

"I asked if you're okay. You've gone awfully pale."

"I'm…"

It was time to tell Nate that she was pregnant. In truth, she'd already delayed too long. The words were on her lips. She just needed to get them out.

"I'm…"

About to be very, very sick.

When Mia rushed out of the room, Nate picked up the cell phone she'd left behind and looked at the photo on the screen. A positive pregnancy test lay nestled atop a wallet, a familiar shade of lipstick and a teal-colored journal, which was probably the one Ivy had ruined when she threw it into the pool. His brain was slow to process the tableau.

What was Mia doing with a pregnancy test in her purse? From down the hall came the sound of retching. Answers from that quarter weren't going to come as soon as he liked. Nate glanced at the text below the photo. It was not Ivy's feed, but that of her friend Skylar. Nowhere in the description was Mia's name mentioned. The photo was teased with Ivy's name and…his.

Now Nate understood Mia's abrupt flight from the room. Fury exploded inside him. Did she seriously in her wildest imagination think he'd ever touched Ivy? That he would do something so cruel to her? Was this why she'd been acting so strange lately? How long had she thought this of him? Obviously, she'd known her sister was pregnant since before they'd gone to the AMAs. Why hadn't she asked him about it? That she had so little faith in him cut Nate to the core.

And what of Ivy? Nate doubted this little stunt had been accomplished without her approval. She'd never tolerate such betrayal from her posse. He couldn't imagine what this would mean for Mia. Would she see herself even more firmly bound to her sister? Or could this be an opportunity for her to break free of her family?

Before he could ask that question, he needed to sort out what was going on in Mia's head. Nate headed down the hall and found Mia on the floor in his master bathroom. She sat with her back to the soaker tub, knees drawn up to her chest, arms wrapped around her legs. Although she'd doubtless heard his approach, she didn't look up from the floor when he stopped in the doorway.

"Are you okay?"

"No." Despite her stricken expression, the word came out with a sarcastic twist. She pushed to her feet and crossed to the sink. After splashing water on her face, she reached for her toothbrush.

"You know I never slept with Ivy." He paused, waiting for her reaction, and when none came, he continued, "I never touched her, never even looked at her in that way."

Mia closed her eyes and didn't respond. Did she not believe him? Was that really possible, given everything they'd been to each other? Nate joined her at the sink and met her gaze in the mirror. Her only acknowledgment was a slight frown before she bent down to rinse the toothpaste from her mouth.

"Why don't you believe me?"

"I do." A tear trickled down her cheek. Air hissed between her teeth as she dashed it away. "But the fact is, it is your baby."

Nate couldn't believe what she was saying to him. "That's both ridiculous and impossible."

Mia turned to look at him at last. "The piece of the puzzle that you're missing," she said, her voice breaking on the words, "is that the pregnancy test doesn't belong to Ivy."

"If it doesn't belong to her, then…" The impact of understanding was like trying to walk through a closed glass door. He bounced off the invisible surface, his whole body rattled by the impact. "You're pregnant?"

"Yes." She nodded as if for emphasis.

Shock reverberated through him like thunder. "How long?"

"Sydney."

"I meant how long have you known?" A voice in the back of his mind told him this was the best thing that ever happened to him. But it was a quiet reminder, easily drowned out by the anger that licked through him because she'd kept this a secret. "It had to be before Ivy threw your journal in the pool. I saw it beneath the pregnancy test."

"The morning of the AMAs."

"Why didn't you say something?"

Her eyes widened. "It was a huge event for you. I didn't want to ruin…"

When she bit her lip and didn't finish, he jumped in.

"Why would you think finding out I was going to be a father would ruin anything?"

She frowned at his aggressive tone. "I didn't plan this. I didn't want you to think I was trying to trap you."

"Trust me, that's the last thing I'd ever think." He gave a bitter laugh. "In fact I'd be overjoyed if that had truly been your motive. At least then I could count on you and me being together."

She didn't immediately respond to his accusation, but a hot burst of color flared across her cheekbones. "That's unfair."

"Is it? You still haven't explained why you didn't tell me as soon as you realized you were pregnant."

"I was scared, okay?"

"Of what? Me?"

"Of everything changing."

"What's so horrible about that?"

"You just don't understand."

But he did. She'd rather remain in her sister's shadow, where she thought it was safe, instead of taking a chance with him.

"When are you going to stop hiding behind Ivy?"

"Hiding? That's not it. You know how she is. What she's struggling with. Every time I'm not there for her something terrible happens."

And there was the core of their problem.

"You can't be your sister's keeper forever." Nate lowered his voice as he fought for calm. "She's never going to take responsibility for herself if you and the rest of your family don't stop enabling her."

"I can't have this conversation again." Mia's lower lip quivered. She caught it between her teeth and pushed away from the sink.

Nate was on her heels as she reentered the master

bedroom and made a beeline for the door. He caught her arm and spun her around to face him. "Where are you going?"

"I need some time to think."

"You've had months and months to think. What you need to do is make a decision about us."

She crossed her arms over her chest. "You don't think I know that?"

He stroked his palms up her arms to her shoulders, but made no move to draw her close. "We are having a baby." He emphasized each and every word, hoping to penetrate the wall of stubbornness she erected around herself. "I intend to be in my child's life. And not in a long-distance sort of way." He didn't mean to sound so angry. He loved her. He wanted to be with her. To marry her and raise their child together. Instead he'd declared a challenge, bordering on a threat. "I've asked you to stay in Las Vegas with me. You haven't said yes. So, what's it going to be, Mia?"

"I want to." Her eyes pleaded with him through the tears. "You want me to choose between you and Ivy. I can't do that."

"Are you going to choose between our baby and Ivy?"

He might as well have hit her. She reeled backward two steps and stared at him in dismay. "That's not fair. Our baby comes first."

Our baby. He liked the sound of that. But what about him? Was she going to choose him?

"Look, I'm sorry." It was inadequate, but he made the apology sincere and heartfelt. "Let's sit down and start again, only calmer this time."

Her hands shook as she dragged them through her hair. "Okay."

She let him guide her toward the bed. They settled

onto the mattress with their backs against the headboard and said nothing for a long time.

"I'm sorry." She set her head against his shoulder and reached for his hand.

"For what?"

"This is not at all how I wanted you to find out that you were going to be father."

"It's not how I expected it to happen, either." He gave a soft chuckle. "Actually, I'm not sure I have any idea what I expected."

"Are you really okay with this?"

"So okay." He threaded their fingers together and gave a gentle squeeze. "It's pretty amazing, in fact. Every time my dad came after me when I was a kid I thought about what being a father entailed. Not everyone is cut out for it, but I knew I'd work twice as hard at it to make up for the hell my dad put me through."

"You're going to make an amazing father. We'll figure out everything. I just need some time to talk to my family. It's pretty obvious from the way Ivy is acting out that dealing with her is not going to be easy."

"You don't have to do it alone. Let me be there for you when you go talk to them." He knew better than to suggest he go with her to confront Ivy. Mia knew how to handle her sister better than anyone.

But to announce a false pregnancy on social media and name him as the baby's father was beyond disturbing. Nate swallowed an I-told-you-so. As much as he wanted to reiterate his opinion on how the entire family's pandering had created the monster that was Ivy Bliss, Mia needed his support, not his criticism.

"Don't be mad," she began, trying for a smile and not succeeding. "I really think I need to go explain things to my dad on my own. Having you there will just complicate the whole situation."

Nate shrugged off his disappointment. He'd like to be at her side, presenting a united front to her father. For support and because he worried that she'd cave to her family once again. "I'll let you handle your family, but I'm telling you right now that I'm calling my publicist and having her deny that your sister and I have had or are having any sort of relationship."

The last thing he intended to do was get into a social media pissing match with Ivy. At least she'd had the sense not to post a picture or the caption herself. She would have plausible deniability.

Suddenly, he was sick to death of talking about Mia's sister. "For the next twelve hours we are not going to talk about a certain pop star. Can you do that?"

"I don't know. I'm not sure I've ever gone that long without talking about her." A cheeky grin spread across Mia's face. "Actually, now that I think about it, there were a couple nights I'll never forget with a handsome guy."

Damn if his pulse didn't kick up a notch. She had the most amazing effect on him. It was what he kept coming back over and over despite how much her obligation to her sister irritated him. But they would worry about her sister later. Right now, it was all about Mia. He eased her back against the headboard and slid his fingers into her hair. She sighed in delight and tilted her face to receive his descending mouth.

Eleven

The next morning, Mia packed a bag and let Nate drive her to the airport to catch a ten o'clock flight to LA, where Ivy and their father were meeting with Trent about the album and their interest in having Hunter Graves produce it instead of Nate.

To her surprise, she hadn't received a single call or text from her family. No doubt they were all in crisis mode over the Instagram post. Mia wondered how her sister was coping with the fallout. Nate had done as he'd promised and released a statement through his publicist. And then he'd watched her fidget as the night stretched on with none of her family reaching out to her.

Was she crazy to resent being shut out after everything she'd sacrificed for her sister and her career? And then she realized how foolish that sounded. None of her family were avoiding her; more likely they just hadn't bothered to bring her into the loop. Resentment flared.

As he pulled to a stop at the terminal, Nate put his

hand on hers and gave a reassuring squeeze. "Are you sure you don't want to just forget about coming clean with your family, and stay with me?"

With each minute that passed she felt less confident about going alone to LA, but she'd put off telling her family about Nate and her pregnancy long enough.

"I appreciate your offer, but I think it will go better if I talk to them in person." She exited the car and waited while Nate pulled her suitcase out of the trunk. "I'll call you later."

But as Mia headed to the counter to check in and drop off her luggage, she was overwhelmed by a mixed bag of emotions. Annoyance. Dread. Her relationship with Nate had been a secret she'd kept to herself for almost four months. Loving him had given her greater joy than anything she'd ever known, and yet she'd hidden her happiness for fear of it being taken away if the truth came out.

It was something she hadn't explained to Nate. He'd assumed that she was afraid of moving forward because her identity was trapped in her sister's shadow. After she'd told him about Ivy's near death experience thanks to the painkillers, he'd been more understanding about the burden of responsibility she felt toward her twin. But he resented that she couldn't leave her sister to make mistakes and face consequences.

Well, Ivy was on her own right now and look what had happened. Hunter Graves was probably going to produce her next album, and while the man was nearly as talented as Nate, Hunter's vision for her music was in line with Ivy's own. They weren't going to record a breakout album. If Ivy had only listened to her…

Mia cut off the thought. Nate was right. She was too caught up in her sister's career and life. Even now, with things so strained between them, even though Ivy had fired her, Mia remained emotionally invested in what her sister was doing.

When it was Mia's turn to step up to the counter, instead of presenting her ticket to LA, she checked to see if there was a flight to Chicago. Suddenly, more than anything, Mia craved some advice from her older sister, Eva. She didn't pause to wonder whether Eva would be happy to see her. Many times in the last five years Eva had also questioned her dedication to Ivy, and as much as they loved each other, Mia's stubborn refusal to leave her twin had led to some tense discussions between Eva and her. Despite this, Mia knew Eva would welcome her with open arms.

After successfully switching her ticket and getting through security, Mia raced to catch her flight and emailed her sister about the surprise visit, mentioning the post on Instagram and offering a brief explanation about the trouble she and Ivy were having. Normally Mia didn't involve Eva in her Ivy issues because she knew how Eva would respond, but Mia wanted her sister's expert opinion.

She had to shut her phone down before Eva replied. Most likely she was in the middle of a session with one of her patients. As a deaf psychiatrist, Eva had a unique niche: almost two thirds of her patients were hearing impaired.

Once she landed in Chicago, Mia exited the airplane and headed for O'Hare's baggage claim. The plan after she collected her luggage was to take the blue line downtown and then the purple line north to her sister's condo in Evanston. The trip would take around an hour and a half. But as Mia entered the baggage claim area she saw a familiar face and sped toward her older sister.

She was so overwhelmed by surprise and relief, she forgot to sign as she blurted, "What are you doing here?" It was the last sentence she uttered before sobs overtook her. Eva's unexpected appearance and the relief of not having to wait two more hours to hug her pulled the cork from the bottle containing Mia's turbulent emotions.

Eva didn't ask questions; she merely wrapped her arms around Mia and let her release all the pent-up sadness that had been building for the last few months. When Mia got herself back under control she realized Eva had coaxed her out of the flow of people and toward the wall. With the initial rush of her tears slowing to a trickle, Mia gave her sister a watery smile.

"What are you doing here?" Mia repeated the question out loud as she wiped her eyes. Eva could read lips and also speak. The sisters usually communicated in a combination of both. "I was going to take the train to your office."

"I canceled my last two appointments," Eva signed. *"You didn't seriously think I was going to let you take the train."*

It seemed impossible that Mia had more tears to shed, but as she and Eva walked arm-in-arm to the baggage claim, Mia's cheeks remained wet. Her initial outburst had lasted long enough for the luggage to make its way from the belly of the airplane to the terminal. Mia collected her suitcase and followed her sister to short-term parking, where she'd left her car.

Because it was impossible for them to have a conversation while Eva drove, they sat in the parking lot long enough for Eva to ask several questions.

"Have you spoken to Ivy and asked her what she was thinking?"

"No. I was afraid what I might say."

"Have you talked to Mom and Dad?"

Again Mia shook her head. "I'm also afraid of what they'll say."

"Do you want to tell me what happened now or wait until we get to my condo?"

"I'll wait."

While Eva drove, she shared with Mia bits of what had been going on in her job. Although Eva preferred to sign, she'd also learned how to speak. She'd had to in order to communicate with their father and sister, neither of whom had learned more than the most basic of signs. Mia knew this hurt Eva, but she was a pragmatist. Which was why she'd left California to pursue psychiatry. Her life in Chicago was the sort of normal Mia craved.

"Are you hungry?" Eva signed as they waited at the bottom of the freeway ramp for the light to turn green. *"We can go to a restaurant and you can tell me what's going on. Or we can go home."*

Mia grew confused by something in her sister's manner. An evasiveness so unlike Eva that Mia grew immediately suspicious. She had to wait until the next stoplight to ask her question.

"What's going on at home?"

"I thought you might be more comfortable talking without anyone around."

"At a restaurant?" Mia eyed her sister intently. "What's at home that you don't want to bring me there?" Not for one second did Mia think it was anyone from their family, and she knew Nate wasn't aware she'd taken a detour. "Jeremy? Did I interrupt your evening? I'm so sorry."

"Nonsense. I haven't seen you in six months." She shot Mia a wry grin. *"Him I see all the time."*

Eva had been dating Jeremy for the last year. He was a

pediatric doctor at Evanston Hospital. They'd met when she'd done her residency there and had been friends for several years before deciding to give dating a try.

Joy flooded Mia. If anyone deserved to be happy it was Eva. "It's gotten serious then?"

The joy shining in Eva's eyes was answer enough. *"We're living together."*

"Wow."

A spike of envy drove through Mia's heart. She didn't resent her sister's happiness, but it shone a light on her own failure to grab the brass ring. Mia's eyes went to Eva's bare left hand as her sister rubbed her ring finger in an unconscious gesture.

"Are you engaged?"

Eva nodded but looked pained. Mia flinched as the subtext hit her in the chest.

"How long?"

"Six weeks. We wouldn't be living together otherwise."

Eva had been engaged for six weeks and had kept it secret from her family. Or perhaps *secret* wasn't the best word. Their parents, Ivy, even Mia, were so focused on Ivy's career that there wasn't room for anything else.

"Where is your ring?"

"My purse."

Mia opened her sister's purse and dug the diamond ring from a zippered interior pocket. She drew it out and handed it to her sister, who slipped it on. "I'm sorry I didn't know."

The stoplight turned green and Eva started the car forward.

"My fault. I should have told you."

But it wasn't Eva's fault. With their lack of interest and support, her family had failed her. It was almost as if once Eva went off to college and then moved to Chicago to do her psychiatric residency she'd been forgotten. Maybe that wasn't completely fair. Mia and their mom flew out to spend long weekends with her a couple times a year. And Eva tried to get back to the West Coast at least once a year, either around the holidays or when Ivy took a break from promoting, recording or touring.

But there was no avoiding the fact that the Navarro family revolved around Ivy and her career.

"Why did you keep it from me?" Even as she asked the question, Mia knew the answer. "Because of what happened to me? Did you think I wouldn't be happy for you because I've royally screwed up with Nate?"

Eva shook her head and Mia saw how her sister's situation was similar to her own. They'd both kept the men they loved from their family in order to savor the joy for as long as possible. It wasn't as if anyone would actively disapprove, but their family had a knack for spoiling things without trying.

"I want to tell him congratulations. Let's go to your condo."

But it turned out that Eva was wrong about her fiancé being at home. He'd left a sweet note explaining that he'd gone out for drinks with his buddies and would catch dinner and be back late. That left hours and hours for the sisters to talk and for Mia to unburden herself.

She started by explaining about how she and Nate had discovered their mutual connection through sign language and then described their secret rendezvous and their one night together in Sydney.

"Very romantic," Eva signed with a hearty sigh.

"And stupid. Looking back, I regret hiding what was happening."

"But you knew Ivy would spoil things."

Mia had known that. *"Why is she like that?"*

"Insecurity. She thinks everyone is happier than she is."

"With all her beauty, fame and success, how is that possible?"

Mia hadn't yet come clean with Eva about being pregnant, and before she could, Jeremy returned home. Mia rushed to congratulate him on convincing the best girl in the world to marry him. By the time they'd finished discussing wedding plans it was late. Both Eva and Jeremy had to be at work early the next morning. They said their good-nights and Mia went to the guest bedroom.

Despite her lack of sleep the night before, Mia was still on Pacific time. Once she'd changed into her sleepwear, she sat wide-eyed and cross-legged on the bed in the beautifully decorated guest room.

She picked up her phone and puzzled over the lack of messages and emails. And then she realized she'd not taken her phone off airplane mode. She swiftly restored her cell service and watched the red notification indicators explode.

Even before his car cleared the airport, Nate started kicking himself for not accompanying Mia to LA. He never should've let her talk him into staying behind. They were in this together and together was how they should have tackled her father and sister.

If he wasn't so damn busy with the studio he would circle around right this second, drop his car in short-term parking and chase after her. But he had a business to run and artists he couldn't let down. Maybe he could reschedule his day tomorrow and fly to LA tonight. Nate headed for the studio to see what could be done before he let Mia know his plans.

Two hours later he'd spoken with all the artists who were coming in to work with him the next day. Each of them was fine with a short postponement. It meant Nate was going to be working extra-long hours in the days to come, but standing beside Mia as she told her father that she was pregnant was worth it.

Nate called Mia to tell her his plans, but got her voice mail. He'd expected as much. She was probably midflight on her way to LA. She would get the message when she landed and know to put off meeting with her father until later that night.

Pleased with the arrangements he'd made, Nate headed into the studio. He got a text from his publicist letting him know his statement had gone out to news organizations denying that he was the father of Ivy's baby. An hour later his phone lit up with Javier Navarro's number. Nate was in the middle of a recording session and let the call go to voice mail. He knew it would only annoy Mia's father, but Nate wanted to pick the time and place for his conversation with Javier.

Forty-five minutes later he turned the session over to one of his assistants and headed to his office. Nate dialed Javier and braced himself for what was to come. Ivy's dad could be hotheaded when it came to his daughter.

"How dare you call my daughter a liar," was the first thing out of Javier's mouth.

Nate sighed and pinched the bridge of his nose. "I think you need to have a conversation with your daughter," he said. "I am not the father of Ivy's baby."

"She says you are."

"That's impossible, since she and I don't have that sort of relationship." Nate wanted very badly to tell Javier exactly what he thought of his spoiled, childish daughter, but he owed it to Mia to try to keep from exacerbating an already tricky situation.

"That's not how she sees it."

Nate was over trying to keep his cool and remain polite, but recognized if he blew up Mia would catch the brunt of the trouble. "Look." He paused to suck in a calming breath and even out his tone. "Ivy and I never… I don't know why she picked me, but I'm not the guy."

"What reason would my daughter have to lie about something like that?"

"I really couldn't say." He was really trying not to go there with Javier. Nate leaned back in his chair and stared at the ceiling. "I think your daughter is incredibly talented and has the potential to be a huge star. Our relationship is and always has been professional."

"Not all that professional. You've done nothing but badger Ivy the entire time she was recording at your studio."

"That's not what happened." But Nate knew he was wasting his breath. Still, he persisted. "Ivy and I had creative differences, that's all."

"Well, Ivy wants Hunter Graves to step in as the producer."

"Trent and I have already spoken about this and I understand." Nate didn't add that he'd thrown Hunter at Ivy hoping for this exact result. "I'm sure they'll work well together."

"She has a lot riding on this album," Javier said. "I hope the label is ready to get behind her."

"Of course. Ivy is very important to West Coast Records. The intention is to get behind her one hundred percent."

This last seemed to mollify Ivy's father and the conversation ended more cordially than it had begun.

After Nate hung up with Mia's father, he raked his fingers through his hair and spent several minutes calming down. He couldn't call Mia, given his mood. When he felt sufficiently chilled, he dialed her number. Once again it went to voice mail. He left her a quick message, summarizing his conversation with her father. And then he returned to the recording studio to wait for her to call him back.

That call didn't come until a little after nine. He'd just let himself into his hotel room in LA and was about to leave Mia another text when she called.

"Hi."

"Hey." Air gusted from his lungs. He was so relieved to hear her voice. "Did you get my messages?"

"Ah…" She drew the word out. "Not until just now. I'm sorry."

Nate reined in his concern. She sounded mortified, but her voice lacked the tense edge from that morning. He realized that whatever she'd been up to, she'd discovered some peace.

"I cleared my schedule and came to LA. Where are you?"

"Ah…" Again that strange little pause. "I'm not in LA. Last minute, I decided to visit Eva in Chicago."

"That's not what we discussed this morning."

"I know, but I just needed a little more time to think things through and Eva has always been the voice of sanity in our family."

Nate was torn between frustration, relief and concern. Frustration, because he wanted Mia's priorities to shift from her family to him. What would it have taken for her to text him before her flight and let him know where she was bound? But he wasn't going to react as her family would, pushing her around, telling her what she should and shouldn't do.

He was relieved because when he hadn't heard from her since dropping her at the airport, he'd begun thinking all sorts of terrible things. Didn't she realize she meant the world to him, even before he found out she was carrying his child? Why was it she refused to believe anyone would want to put her first? Surely it couldn't all be laid at Ivy's feet.

And lastly he felt concern because if she'd fled to Chicago instead of confronting her problems and going to LA, then she was a lot more out of sorts than she'd let on.

"What did Eva tell you?" Nate made his voice as calm as possible.

"Nothing that I didn't already know. That Ivy is insecure and has a knack for spoiling other people's happiness."

"So what are you going to do about that?"

"Be happy in spite of her?"

"You don't sound very convinced."

"What is wrong with me?" Mia blurted out.

He wished he was there to offer her support, but as he'd often remarked about Ivy needing to become more responsible, Mia also needed to not only claim her independence, but also accept that she deserved to be happy.

"There's nothing wrong with you. It isn't your fault that your parents put too great a burden on you at such a young age. They pushed Ivy to be a star and made you her keeper." Nate paused and listened, wishing he could see Mia face. "There's nothing wrong with you," he repeated, more quietly this time. "Tomorrow you'll fly back to LA, and then you and I will go talk to your parents together."

"Okay." It was a squeaky whisper, as if something was blocking her voice.

"I have your back."

"Thank you." She sounded clearer and more confident.

"You don't have to thank me. It's time someone took care of you. And from now on that someone is me."

Her laughter was the most wonderful thing he'd heard all day. He wished he was there to see happiness brighten her eyes and soften the curve of her lips.

"You know I love you, right?"

She tossed out the phrase with such an ease that he wasn't sure if she meant it as a heartfelt pledge or if they were just words that conveyed her fondness. She still hadn't committed to moving to Las Vegas to be with him. And instead of going to LA to confront her family, she'd run off to Chicago.

"I do now," he teased back, but his heart was a brick in his chest. "Get some sleep. I'll see you tomorrow."

Nate's presence was a solid comfort at her side as Mia pushed the doorbell of Ivy's house the next afternoon. It felt weird to not just let herself in. She'd lived here with Ivy for nearly two years, coming and going at will. But it had never been her home, and since Ivy had tossed her out four days earlier, it didn't feel right to just walk in.

Clara answered the door. The housekeeper gave Mia a tentative smile as she stepped back to let them in, but sadness overcame her features as Mia's eyes fell on the stack of boxes in the foyer.

"I'm so sorry. She made me pack up all your things."

Mia gave the woman a hug. "It's okay." The pile was small enough to fit into their rental SUV: just her clothes, her journals and a few mementos. It was a sad reflection on Mia's personal life to this point.

"How is Ivy doing?"

With a furtive glance over her shoulder, Clara shook her head. "She's..."

"Mia?" Javier Navarro stood at the far end of the foyer, radiating impatience and disapproval. "We're waiting for you in the living room."

Nate squeezed her shoulder and Mia gave Clara a reassuring smile. As the housekeeper stepped aside, Mia lifted her chin. Then, fortified by Nate's support, she headed toward her father. Javier's eyes flickered from her to Nate.

"I don't think it's a good idea that he's here."

"We have something to tell you." Mia's stomach was a knot of anxiety as she and Nate entered the living room. Only her mother occupied the space. "Where's Ivy?"

"She doesn't want to see you," her mother said.

Mia frowned. "I imagine she doesn't want to face up to what she's done."

"And what is that, exactly?" Javier asked, stepping to his wife's side.

"Lied about being pregnant for one." Mia wasn't surprised at her parents' relief. A baby wouldn't be good for Ivy's career. "It was my test she splashed all over social media." Mia glanced up at Nate. "We're going to have a baby."

Mia's mother gasped. "Why would she do that?"

Her spirits plummeted at her mother's words. She'd just announced the most amazing thing that had ever happened to her, but all her parents could think about was Ivy. Her throat tightened.

"It's a cry for help."

"Then you should be here to help her," Javier said.

Beside her, Mia felt Nate tense as the familiar scene played out. "She doesn't want me around anymore," Mia explained.

"I take it back." A soft voice spoke up from the glass doors leading out to the pool. Ivy stood just outside. Wearing workout clothes and no makeup, she looked fragile, unsure and younger than her twenty-five years. "I don't want you to leave me."

Mia glanced over her shoulder at Nate and saw his dismay. He was her future. She couldn't imagine her life any other way. But Ivy was her twin and she couldn't go with Nate until she'd made peace with her.

"Let me go talk to her," Mia said, her gaze lingering on his as she silently pleaded with him to understand.

A muscle worked in his jaw, and then he nodded to the boxes beside the front door. "I'll take those out to the SUV."

Before he could go, Mia stepped into his space and wrapped her arms around his waist. "I love you," she said, her cheek pressed against his chest.

His arms bound her to him until she could barely breathe. "I love you, too."

The words made her smile. She pulled back and looked up at him. "And I'm choosing you."

The relief on his face made her heart stop. He set his forehead against hers. "Thank you." With a quick, hard kiss he let her go. "I'll wait for you outside."

Ignoring her parents, Mia ran across the room and put her arms around Ivy. At first her sister resisted, then her body went limp and she hugged back.

"Don't leave me," Ivy murmured again, her voice muffled against Mia's shoulder.

"You know I have to go. I love Nate. I can't live without him."

"I can't do any of this without you."

"You can and you will. Stop letting Dad pressure you into doing things. Fire him if you have to. Ditch Skylar and Riley. Get clean. Forget about the stupid album. Start a fashion line. Do what you want. I'll support you."

"I'm so sorry about how I treated you."

"I know." As she hugged Ivy she felt as if she got her sister back.

"I'm glad you and Nate are together."

"That means a lot to me."

"We never hooked up, you know."

"I do."

"He's only ever had eyes for you. I saw that while we were on tour and I was so afraid he would take you away from me. But in the end I knew that you needed to go." Ivy gave her a sad smile. "That's why I leaked that you wrote all my songs. I needed a reason to fire you."

Mia was stunned. "You did that?" Her throat closed up. "For me?"

"I knew you wouldn't stop worrying about me."

"But you just asked me to stay."

"I didn't realize how lonely it would be not having you around." Ivy dashed tears from her cheeks. "Now, get out of here before I stop being nice and go all Ivy Bliss on your ass."

Mia laughed. "I love you."

"And I love you."

With one final hug, Mia left her sister and retraced her steps through the living room. She gave her parents a brief nod and burst through Ivy's front door, feeling free for the first time in eight years.

Nate waited for her by the SUV, his tall figure relaxed as she sped across the distance between them. His broad smile became her whole world as she flung herself into his arms and kissed him.

"Let's get out of here." Taking her by the hand, he led her to the car, opened the passenger door and ushered her inside. Seconds later he was sliding behind the wheel and starting the engine.

"Where are we going?"

"To the shipping store for these boxes, and then the airport. I intend to get you settled in Las Vegas before you change your mind."

"I'm not going to do that," she assured him.

An hour later they were walking hand in hand toward the security checkpoint at LAX when Nate pulled her out of the traffic flow. She gazed up at him in surprise as he gave her a sheepish grin.

"This isn't at all how I'd planned to do this, but it occurs to me they're going to make me empty my pockets." He pulled out a small box and popped the lid. Nestled in the black velvet was a diamond ring. "Mia Navarro, love of my life, will you marry me?"

Stunned to silence, she stared at the gorgeous ring and then lifted her gaze to his.

When she didn't speak, his brows drew together. "I'm not asking because you're pregnant. I'm not that guy."

"You are exactly that guy." She gave a self-conscious laugh. "Which is why I love you."

The look on his face set her heart to pounding. "Say that again," he demanded.

"Say what?"

"That you love me."

"I love you."

"And," he prompted.

"And I absolutely will marry you."

He took her hand in his and slid the ring onto her finger. "You are my world."

Mia put her palm against his cheek and leaned close. "You are mine. Forever and always."

And after a tender kiss that sealed their vows, they headed for the plane that would take them home.

* * * * *

THE DOWNFALL OF A GOOD GIRL

KIMBERLY LANG

This is my tenth book—a milestone that I couldn't have hit without the continued love and support of my family: Darling Geek, Amazing Child and Wonder Mom. Y'all are the best.

But I want to extend a huge thanks to the talented and delightful Cristina Lynn, who literally put a song on Connor's lips by allowing me to use her lyrics in this book. You can hear those songs—and a new one called 'Sinners and Saints', inspired by Connor and Vivi's story!—by visiting her website at: www.CristinaLynn.com

CHAPTER ONE

VIVIENNE LABLANC waited impatiently, trying not to bump her wings against anything or move too quickly in a way that would cause her halo to slide off, as Max Hale gave his introductory speech on the other side of the curtain.

"There are many krewes, but none like the Bon Argent. Five years ago, we decided to do something—in our own hometown style—to raise money for the victims of Hurricane Katrina. We were far more successful than we dreamed. Through the Saints and Sinners Festival—which grows bigger every year—we've raised hundreds of thousands of dollars for dozens of local charities, and I thank all of you for your continued support."

After a short round of polite applause, Max continued to laud their accomplishments, but Vivi listened with only half an ear. She was well aware of the great work of Bon Argent; she'd been involved with the krewe since its inception. Candy Hale was one of her oldest friends, and Max was like a second father. Her mother used to serve on the board, for goodness' sake, so she didn't need to be sold on the success. She did, however, need a primer on these wings.

How am I supposed to sit in these things? The feathered and bejeweled wings were beautiful, arching up to head height and hanging to her calves. Vivi frowned as she tried to adjust the buckle on her gold sandals and felt the whole getup shift dangerously. Honestly, she looked less like a saint and more like a Vegas showgirl who'd crashed the neighborhood nativity play.

The Saints and Sinners ball—and the whole Bon Argent krewe—bordered on silly at times, but the costumes and the parody of pomp and pageantry was what had made the Saints and Sinners fundraiser so fun, popular and immensely successful in such a short time.

And there were three hundred people out there eagerly awaiting the announcement of this year's Saint and Sinner. Following the traditions of the traditional Mardi Gras krewes, those identities were top secret info. As far as Vivi knew, only three people were in the know this year. Max, the head of the Bon Argent charity, Paula, the head of PR, and Ms. Rene, the seamstress who'd made the costumes for the Sinner and the Saint. Even she didn't know who would be her other half between now and Fat Tuesday.

She had a few guesses in mind.

Unlike the traditional krewes, however, who would crown a king and a queen, Bon Argent had no gender requirements to fulfill. The Saint and the Sinner were chosen for their local celebrity and reputations and could be of the same gender. Vivi had her bets on nightclub owner Marianne Foster, who'd been in the news a lot recently and would provide excellent competition before Vivi crushed her. While Marianne would be popular in the voting and bring in large amounts of money, it wasn't an overstatement or egoism to say that she, herself, was *more* popular and could raise *huge* amounts of money in comparison.

She stomped down the unkind thought. Thoughts were the precursors to words and actions, and she'd learned to keep her head in the right place in order to avoid saying or doing anything she might regret later. *It's about the money we can raise, not about winning.*

But it was *also* about winning. The Sinner had taken the crown the last two years, but this year top honors were going to the Saint, because she simply refused to lose. She'd only lost one crown in her life, and she still remembered the bitter taste of watching Miss Indiana walk away with it. It didn't matter how much she liked Janelle personally, or what a great Miss America she'd turned out to be, it still sucked to lose.

So she was competitive. It was hardly a personality flaw. No one *liked* to lose. And in this case, her competitive nature would be beneficial because it was all for a good cause.

Max was now introducing her Cherubim Court: ten local high school kids chosen by the charity's board to be her team in the fundraising.

And now it was her turn. She took a deep breath, checked her dress, and waited.

"…my pleasure to introduce Saint Vivienne LaBlanc!"

The curtain opened to a strobe of flashes from the photographers gathered in front of the stage and a very heartening roar of approval and applause from the guests. Vivi heard her sister's distinctive whistle and looked over at the table where her family sat. When she'd left the table twenty minutes ago, claiming she had an emergency phone call from the gallery, Lorelei had given her a knowing look. She waved as she watched people from the surrounding tables congratulate her parents.

Being chosen as the Saint was quite an honor, and Vivi was beyond touched by the applause that showed so many people thought her deserving of it. She'd won a lot of contests in her life, brought home quite a few crowns, but this was different. It wasn't about being pretty or popular. The downside to her pageant career was the assumption by all that she was just a pretty little face with no real substance. She'd spent years fighting that stereotype, trying to prove that there was more to her. It had been her biggest challenge to date, and the halo on her head was proof she'd succeeded. It might be cheesy and rather silly-looking, but it suddenly meant more to her than any crown she'd ever worn.

Beating the Sinner—whoever that turned out to be—would be icing on the cake at this point, and now she wanted that trophy more than anything.

Vivi removed her halo with the proper pomp, placing it on the blue satin pillow that would hold both the Saint's halo and the Sinner's horns until the competition ended and the winner claimed both trophies. She then took her seat with her court and applauded politely as the Sinner's court, the Imps, was introduced.

Max took a deep breath and looked so excited he might burst with it. "Our Sinner this year is an obvious choice, and we're so pleased he's made time in his schedule to reign over this important event."

The pronoun usage told Vivi that she'd lost her bet. Damn, she'd been so sure it would be Marianne. *It doesn't really matter,* she thought with a mental shrug. She was ready to take on anyone.

"...Connor Mansfield!"

Vivi's smile froze as the crowd broke into wild applause. *You're freakin' kidding me.*

Connor caught a glimpse of Vivi's face as he stepped onto the stage and nearly laughed at the perfect mix of horror and fury against a feathery backdrop of angel wings. Not that he blamed her; his response had been very similar when he'd heard her name called, but he'd still been safely behind the curtain.

He had to hand it to the board of Bon Argent; they certainly knew how to guarantee maximum attention from the local press—attention that could be otherwise difficult to draw amid everything else happening during the Mardi Gras season. They'd probably break every fundraising record in history.

Vivi just looked like she'd like to wring his neck, but then she always looked at him like that. Some things just never changed, no matter how long you were gone from your hometown.

But the show must go on, and everyone was waiting for them to take their seats so dinner could be served. He removed his horns and solemnly placed them next to the Saint's halo. Then he walked over to Vivi, nodded politely and waited for her to return the gesture. Slowly, they made their way to the high table. When they reached their seats a cheer went up from the crowd, and the competition of the Saints and Sinners Festival officially began. Servers appeared from the woodwork and the crowd turned its attention to the salad course.

He leaned a few inches in her direction. "You're going to ruin three years of orthodontic work if you don't stop grinding your teeth, Vivi."

Her eyes narrowed, but she released her jaw the tiniest bit. She reached for her wineglass, noticed it was empty and reached for a water glass instead. He saw her look at it carefully, then shrug before she drank. Knowing Vivi, she'd debated dumping it in his lap.

"I'd say Welcome Home, but—"

"But you wouldn't mean it." He grinned at her to annoy her.

"But," she corrected, "it would be rather redundant, considering the reception you just got."

"Jealous I got more applause?"

"No." She shifted in her chair. "I'm not an attention whore."

"Big talk from the pageant queen."

Vivi inhaled sharply and her smile became tight. "Some of us have outgrown our adolescence."

He pretended to think about that for a second, then shook his head sadly. "No, you're still sanctimonious."

"And you're still a—"

She stopped herself so suddenly Connor wondered if she'd bitten her tongue.

She inhaled sharply through her nose and swallowed. "You must be very pleased to finally be recognized for *your* achievements."

"I hate to burst your bubble, *Saint* Vivienne, but these titles aren't character references."

"Oh, really?" Vivi's face was the picture of confused innocence. "You seem to be perfectly suited for the title."

And there was the first dig. He should have known that Vivi wouldn't let that pass. Although he'd been vindicated, rumor and gossip had done their damage. Everyone believed there had to be a grain of truth in there somewhere—*which* grain it might be was the engine that drove the gossip that wouldn't die.

Vivi might have hit a sore spot with her first salvo, but damned if he'd admit that. "Sanctimonious *and* judgmental. You need to increase your repertoire."

"Maybe you should add some to yours, as well. A little decorum from you would be nice, considering the honor you've been given."

"According to you, it's not really an honor, now, is it?"

"Yet you still seem very pleased with yourself." She snorted. "You look ridiculous, you know. Black leather pants, Connor? Really? What is this? 1988?"

He'd had a similar thought when they'd been presented to him. "I agree on the pants. Very eighties glam metal. But then I guess it fits the costume."

Vivi smiled—a genuine one this time—at the server who

filled her wineglass, but the smile disappeared as soon as the server did. "I don't know what Max was thinking," she grumbled at her salad. "The Saint and the Sinner are supposed to be *local* celebrities."

"I'm literally the boy next door, Vivi. I'm as local as you are."

"You *were* local," she corrected him. "Now you're international. You're off touring far more than you're in town."

He tried to get comfortable in his chair, but the enormous black wings attached to his back made that feat nearly impossible. He didn't quite understand the mixed-metaphor approach to Saints and Sinners, but Ms. Rene had gone for a Lucifer vibe. He felt more like a giant crow. "So it's the fact that my job requirements keep me out of town a lot that you object to?"

Vivi tried to brush her hair back over her shoulder, but it only got tangled in her wings, creating modern art-inspired shapes in the white feathers. She tugged at the strands as she spoke. "I object to the creation of an unlevel playing field."

Except for that jet-black hair, Vivi had the right looks to pass as an angel—wide blue eyes, fair skin, elegant features. The fire in her eyes was far from angelic, though. Irritation made her movements jerky, tangling her hair even worse.

"How is this unlevel in any way?"

With one final tug that probably pulled some of it out by the roots, Vivi finally got the last of her hair loose. A rhinestone from her wings, loosened in the tussle, fell into her cleavage. Vivi looked down briefly, and Connor's eyes followed hers to the valley of creamy skin before he snapped them back to her face. She had a beautiful mouth, lush and full and sinful—until she opened it and killed the illusion.

"Your groupies and your fan club and all your famous friends will make sure to fill your coffers so that you win."

"But that's what this is about, right? Raising money?"

"Of course that's what's important," she conceded through a jaw clenched so tight it had to be painful, "but you have an unfair advantage when it comes to the actual contest. No one could compete with you."

He grinned at her. "I'm glad to finally hear you admit it."

"I meant," she gritted out, "that I'm a hometown girl and you're a freakin' rock star. You have a bigger fan base by default and *that's* an unfair advantage."

"Your title is 'Saint', Vivi, not 'martyr'."

Vivi's knuckles turned white, and Connor expected the stem of her wineglass to snap at any moment.

"Just eat your dinner."

He shot her a smile instead. "You could just concede now, you know."

She choked on her wine. "Hell has not frozen over."

"So it's on?" he challenged.

"You're damn right it's on." Grabbing her fork, she speared her lettuce with far more force than necessary.

Vivi could never turn down a challenge. It didn't matter what it was, Vivi went after everything in her full-out, take-no-prisoners style. He actually respected that about her. It was one of the few things they had in common. Everything *else* about her, though, drove him insane. Always had.

He really shouldn't let Vivi get to him. He was an adult, for God's sake. Vivi might not like him, but plenty of other women did, so her holier-than-Connor attitude shouldn't bother him. There was something about her, though, that just crawled under his skin and itched.

Would he have agreed to do this if he'd known up front that Vivi would be a part of it? Or would he have just sent another check and let it go?

No, he'd been thinking about home for a while now; this was just the nudge he'd needed to get him here. It gave him an excuse to do some damage control, make some new headlines that didn't involve paternity suits or sexual activities. He could take a step back and maybe take a deep breath for the first time in years.

He hadn't realized how truly tired he was. Getting everything he'd ever wanted in life was great in theory, but he hadn't known he'd be left feeling like a well-dressed hobo. He had accepted that at first: he couldn't have gotten this far if he'd been tied down to any one place or thing. There was a great freedom to it. But it came at a cost, nonetheless.

Being home—really home, not just the place he slept between shows—made him feel like the earth was solid under his feet again. The ideas that had been swimming unformed in the back of his mind seemed to be taking shape now that he was here. New Orleans was good for his mind and soul, and he could use the next few weeks to really refocus and figure out what was next. Or what he wanted to be next.

He heard Vivi's deep sigh of irritation and it brought him back to the present. Right now he had a contest to win. It felt good to come home; even better to come home to a warm welcome *and* the opportunity to do something good for his hometown.

Annoying Vivi while he did it was just a bonus.

Vivi chewed each bite a dozen times and then immediately put another bite in her mouth to keep it full. She couldn't control her thoughts, but this was one way to guarantee she would not take Connor's bait and end up saying something she'd regret later.

This just sucked. She'd headed enough fundraisers to know that Connor was a gift from the fundraising gods. The money would pour in *and* the publicity would be unreal. The rational, reasonable part of her mind applauded Max Hale's choice and envied his ability to get Connor to agree to participate.

But Connor Mansfield? *Argh.* If she had to be paired with a musical superstar, why couldn't they have picked any one of the *other* dozens of musical legends who called New Orleans home? But, no, they had to get maximum mileage by bringing Connor in, especially since he was very much the biggest Sinner in the media right now.

From the top table she had an excellent view of the entire ballroom. The guest list was a Who's Who of New Orleans' rich and powerful, and she knew every face in the crowd. And everyone in the room knew damn well that they hated each other.

Hated was the wrong word. People liked to toss it around, but she didn't hate Connor. She disliked him a hell of a lot, but *hate* implied more energy than she was willing to commit. She and Connor were just not meant to occupy the same time-space continuum. Connor was the one person who could make her blood boil just by breathing. Any conversation was just asking for an anger-induced stroke.

She felt a headache forming behind her left eye.

From the looks being tossed their way, every person in that room knew exactly how much she hated being up here with Connor and found it endlessly amusing. There were probably bets being taken right this second that they'd witness a repeat of that ball ten years ago when the Queen had slapped the King ten minutes after their coronation.

Connor had completely deserved it, but it had taken her forever to live that down nonetheless. It had even come up a few months later, in her interview during the Mississippi River Princess pageant, with the implication that she had a penchant for making unseemly scenes that would be detrimental to the title. She'd learned quite a bit about handling herself and her image after that, so in an odd way Connor had helped fuel her pageant success. Still, that night had pretty much been the final straw, and she and Connor had kept a healthy distance from then on unless forced otherwise by circumstance.

But then Connor's music had started to take off, and he'd spent more time out of town than in it. Within a few years he'd become a rising superstar and their paths had ceased to cross entirely. Bliss.

She would console herself with the knowledge that Ash Wednesday was only four weeks away, and Connor would go back to Los Angeles or New York or wherever his home base was now, and her life would go back to normal. It was a small consolation, but consolation nonetheless.

Could she put up with him for that long? *Without* blowing her top? They were adults now: older, wiser, more mature. Maybe things could be different. She risked a sideways glance.

Probably not.

Everything about Connor projected smug arrogance. He was overly sure of himself, always seeming to have that mocking smile on his face as if he was laughing at her. Even sitting there, dressed like Lucifer on his way to a Pride parade, he still managed to look confident and cocksure.

Ms. Rene had put him in black leather—not only the pants she'd mocked him about earlier, but also a black sleeveless vest and motorcycle boots. Strips of studded black leather circled his biceps, drawing attention to the powerful bulges no one would expect a piano-playing singer to have.

It was a nice contrast to her all-white satin and feather combo. But where her costume veered to the demure and saintly, Connor's screamed *sex:* the leather fit him like a second skin, leaving little to the imagination. While Ms. Rene had covered every exposed inch of *her* skin with body glitter, Connor's skin had been oiled to give him an otherworldly sheen.

He was tall, dark and dangerous personified—from the

dark hair that hung a little too long to the goatee that framed his mouth… She swallowed hard. Her love of art gave her an appreciation for beauty, but this was not just male beauty. There was virility, strength, passion. It was hard *not* to appreciate Connor on that level. Connor looked up, caught her glance, and grinned a lady-killer smile that crinkled the corners of his rich brown eyes.

It was enough to melt any woman—at least until he opened his mouth.

"Problem, Vivi?"

"Just surprised by your goatee. Lose your razor while you were on tour?"

He rubbed a hand over it. "I thought it went with the costume. Maybe made me look a little devilish, you know."

"It's as ridiculous as the pants," she lied, and went back to her dinner. Connor looked devilish, dangerous, sexy and ready to steal a dozen female souls.

And the women probably wouldn't even put up much of a fight. Women loved Connor.

Who was she kidding? *Everyone* loved Connor, praised his talents, celebrated his success. That was one of the reasons why everyone made such a big deal out of the fact that she didn't.

She wasn't a hundred percent sure why or how it all started, but in the twenty-five years she'd known Connor she couldn't remember a single time when he had not irritated her to the point of justifiable homicide.

And it wasn't like she was evil. She *liked* people. Connor was the only person on the planet who affected her in that way, and she dealt with all kinds of irritating people all the time. She was known for her people skills. Those skills just didn't extend to cover annoying man-child rock stars.

As he'd said, he was, literally, the boy next door. Their mothers were on twelve charitable committees together and did lunch twice a week. Their fathers played golf and did business together. She'd spent her whole life hearing about how great Connor was. Sometimes it was like their entire social circle existed merely to live in the shadow of his greatness. They were the same age, went to the same prep school, had many of the same friends, and folks had been pushing them at each other since puberty.

It didn't seem to matter to anyone that they didn't like each other, and that Connor went out of his way to annoy her whenever possible.

People were shallow. They let good looks and talent outweigh deep personality flaws.

Or else she was just the lucky recipient of whatever the reverse of charm was. Connor didn't care about much beyond his own universe—which he was the center of, of course—so it irked her no end that he'd been chosen this year to co-lead the fundraising drive. This was supposed to be about other people, but now it would be all about him.

Losing the Saints and Sinners competition would suck regardless, but losing to Connor would just be more than her pride could stand.

And pride was all that was keeping her in her seat at the moment. She'd need to draw on that pride to save her in the coming weeks.

Conscientious eating kept her from having to make any kind of conversation, and she used the time to mentally flip through her Rolodex and plan out new strategies. She needed to think big—beyond just New Orleans. That would be tough, though, for most of the world had forgotten about the city once the Katrina news left the spotlight.

She could involve her sorority for sure. Maybe she could go to the national level. Hell, she needed to get the whole Greek Council involved. All of her pageant connections, up to and including that former Miss Indiana, every favor she was owed was going to have to be called in. She needed to get creative, since all Connor had to do was smile and the money and the votes would pile up.

Ugh. She'd spent weeks looking forward to this, hugging the secret to herself and looking forward to everything Saints and Sinners entailed. But now… All the joy and excitement had been sucked out of it. Her heart sank as she accepted the reality that, despite her efforts, she was probably going to lose through no fault of her own. That brief moment onstage when she'd congratulated herself for the accomplishment felt foolish now. They'd probably just picked her to add contrast and interest to Connor's selection. She hated Connor just a little more.

No. She gave herself a strong mental shake. She would *not* let Connor take that from her. She'd *earned* this title.

And, while she might lose the competition, by God she was going to make it as close as possible. At least she'd keep her dignity and gain satisfaction for a job well done for a good cause.

Dignity. Hmm… How *was* she going to keep her dignity through all of this?

A wicked idea pinged and the more she thought about it, the better it sounded.

She couldn't control Connor or the contest, but she *could* control herself. She'd been chosen to be the Saint. She just needed to be saintly and gracious. In contrast, Connor would look like an arrogant schmuck *and* go slowly insane at the same time. It would be a small victory, but she'd take it nonetheless.

She set her fork down carefully and reached for her wineglass. "Connor?"

"Yes, Vivi?"

She raised the glass in a toast, and Connor's look turned wary. "To a good competitor and a good cause. I'm looking forward to the adventure, because the real winners are the people and the communities we're going to help. I'm glad you came home to be a part of it."

Connor's eyebrows disappeared into his hairline in his shock, but he recovered quickly and picked up his glass. As he touched it to hers she heard a rumble skitter over the crowd, and there was a strobe of flashes. She put on her very best I'm-so-happy-to-be-first-runner-up smile.

The look that crossed Connor's face made it all worthwhile. This might be fun after all.

It was certainly going to be satisfying.

CHAPTER TWO

IT WAS well after midnight by the time Vivi made it home. The clubs on Frenchman Street were going strong, and though it was January, the nights were mild enough that a sweatshirt provided enough warmth. All the tables on the sidewalks were packed. In some places the crowds spilled out into the street, and she had to slow almost to a crawl to avoid pedestrians the last few blocks before turning into her driveway. She'd grown up on the tree-lined quiet streets of the Garden District, so adjusting to the much more active nightlife of the Marigny Triangle had been difficult at first, but now she couldn't imagine living anywhere else. Coming home always made her smile.

Sam, her neighbor, was on his porch, drinking a beer and listening to the buskers in Washington Square. He waved and called out, "Congrats, Saint Vivi."

Lorelei had probably spread the news. "Thanks, Sam." She should stop and talk for a few minutes, but she was exhausted, her head was pounding, and her cheeks ached from all the smiling. Plus, the straps from the harness that had held her wings on had chafed against her skin, irritating her almost as much as Connor.

All she wanted to do was wash off the glitter and go to bed. She needed to be up early in the morning to work the phone lines. Another glass of wine was tempting, but sleep would work just as well against the Connor-induced headache.

But, unsurprisingly, Lorelei had waited up for her. They hadn't had much time at the Saints and Sinners Ball to talk beyond quick congratulations.

"There she is," Lorelei sang to a familiar tune. "Saint Vi-vi-enne."

Vivi obligingly did her pageant wave and wiped away an imaginary tear before dropping her purse and bags and sinking onto the couch next to Lorelei with a sigh.

"I can't believe you didn't tell me, Vivi."

"It was top secret stuff. I found out just after Thanksgiving, so I'd have time to make the necessary arrangements to my schedule. It's going to be really busy between now and Mardi Gras."

"We're all so proud. Mama and Daddy were about to burst with it."

"I noticed. But I hope *you're* rethinking your annual pledge of allegiance to the Sinners now. I'm counting on your support."

Lorelei crinkled her nose. "But the Sinners are much more fun."

"Don't make me play the sister card."

"You sure you want me? Your halo might be tarnished by association."

"Repent, reform and sin no more, my child."

Lorelei snorted. "Don't push your luck. One saint is plenty for the LaBlanc family, and it isn't going to be me. That's your job."

"Yep." They'd had similar conversations before, but for the first time she felt a small stab of envy for Lorelei's freedom before she stomped it down. Adopting a bit of Lorelei's attitude might make the next few weeks easier. She kicked off her shoes and leaned back. "Okay, just aim for temporary sainthood. A couple of weeks won't kill you."

"But it will still be painful…" Lorelei wrinkled her nose again. She liked to play the bad girl too much for comfort, but somehow it worked for her. "You know, no one has ever considered me saint-like in any way. It will be a challenge." Lorelei squared her shoulders. "And LaBlancs love a challenge."

"Amen."

"Speaking of challenges…" Lorelei started, and Vivi knew what was coming next "…you did quite well not ripping Connor's head off at the ball."

Vivi felt herself snarl. "I totally understand the choice—it's great PR, money will come rolling in, blah, blah, blah—but, *yeesh.* Is there wine?"

"I'll pour." Lorelei disappeared into the kitchen and returned with two glasses. "I have to agree that it's *brilliant* PR, but you need to be careful."

"I promise it will be justifiable homicide. I won't ask you to bail me out of jail."

Lorelei leveled a look at her. "Do I really need to bring up your coronation ball?"

"No. I've already had those flashbacks tonight."

"Good. Remember you don't want to look bad, so *you're* the one who's going to have to be gracious."

Vivi raised her glass in a mock toast. "Luckily I came to that conclusion on my own earlier."

"*That* explains your good behavior." Lorelei returned the toast. "Good for you, Vivi. You're growing as a person."

Vivi snorted into her glass and earned a suspicious look from Lorelei. "Vivienne LaBlanc, what did you do?"

The smile was hard to fight, but Vivi would stick to the truth regardless. "Nothing. Nothing at all."

The suspicious look sharpened. "*What* did you do?"

"I was gracious, kind and friendly. Perfectly saint-like."

"Exactly the actions that will make Connor wonder if you poisoned his meal."

Vivi bit back the laugh and shrugged instead. "I can't control Connor's thoughts or behavior. If he wants to look foolish and juvenile, he'll have to go there alone."

"You know that *I* find you two endlessly entertaining, but honestly, Vivi—"

She held up a hand. "Lorelei, don't start. Why do we have to go through this every single time Connor's name is mentioned?"

"Because it's just ridiculous. I like Connor—"

"I know. You started his fan club."

A pink flush climbed up her neck. "Someone had to."

"Three years before his first record came out?"

Lorelei tried to brush it off. "He's a nice guy, you know."

"You barely know him."

"I know enough. I know he's had some bad PR recently—"

Vivi nearly choked. "*Bad PR?* Good Lord, Lorelei, the man's fresh off a scandal that covered the tabloids for weeks."

"The DNA tests cleared him of paternity."

"That only means he wasn't the father and escaped child support. The rest..."

"You're taking the tabloids at face value? I can't believe that. You're always telling me not to jump to judgment of people based on rumors."

"No one is rushing to judgment. I'm just saying that you don't really know him—at least not now that he's an adult. And you know *nothing* of his sex life beyond chatter in the high school bathrooms. Who knows what he's really into?"

Lorelei shook her head. "I don't believe Connor could change that much."

"He lives a life we can't even begin to imagine."

"Still, I stand by my earlier assertion that he's a good guy."

Vivi shook her head. "I had no idea you could be swayed by good looks alone."

That earned her a cheeky smile. "At least you admit he's good-looking."

"I'm not blind. I just know that a pretty face can hide an evil heart."

"Another scar from your pageant battles, Vivi?"

One of many. "Oh, hush. I'm not saying Connor's a serial killer in his spare time. *I* just don't like him."

"Then tell me why." Expectation written all over her face, Lorelei leaned back into the corner of the couch and stared at her. "And I mean it. No wiggling out."

Vivi struggled for words. She was really too fried to handle deep conversations tonight. Charm and personality were like superpowers, and both Lorelei and Connor had them in spades. Connor, though, had turned supervillain with his, and used those powers for evil instead of good. Lorelei had never used her superpowers against Vivi or anyone else to get something she wanted. Lorelei didn't use people the way Connor did. So it probably made it hard for her to see how someone else could.

Vivi sighed because it was just too hard to put into words. "Are you trying to tell me that you've never met a single person that you didn't like? Who just rubbed you the wrong way?"

"Of course I have, but I'm not you. You like everyone. Everyone likes you. You're the closest thing I've ever seen remotely close to an actual saint, so this irrational and extremely juvenile head-butting with Connor just isn't you. It doesn't make sense." Her blue eyes narrowed and sisterly concern crept into her voice. "Is there something you're not telling me? Did Connor…?"

I do not need that kind of rumor floating around. “No. There’s nothing dark or evil lurking.”

“There were all those rumors around the time you were Mississippi River Princess…”

“And they nearly cost me the crown. But none of them were remotely true.”

She saw Lorelei wasn’t totally convinced. Funny that she’d never mentioned those rumors bothered her before now.

“You swear?”

“Hand to God.”

“Good. Because I *will* kill him for you if I need to.”

The show of loyalty warmed her. At least Lorelei liked her better than she liked Connor. “Thank you, sweetie, but it’s not necessary. If Connor needed killing, I’d have taken care of it already.”

That lightened Lorelei’s mood. “Then tell me. How bad can it be? Did he pull your hair in kindergarten? Steal your lunch money? Tease you?”

“Yes.” Lorelei frowned and Vivi shrugged. “He did sing that song he wrote about me all the way to Baton Rouge on the eighth-grade field trip.”

“Oh, well, that explains it all.” Lorelei snorted. “Connor Mansfield wrote you a *song.* No wonder you hate him so much.”

“It was called ‘Vivi in a Tizzy.’”

Lorelei raised an eyebrow. “I love you, *cherie,* but you often were.”

“That’s beside the point. No fourteen-year-old girl wants a cute fourteen-year-old boy making fun of her.”

“Ah, I see. There’s a little unrequited tween crush—”

Oh, for a different choice of words. “Stop right there.”

Lorelei grinned at her.

“First of all, I happen to know for a fact that you failed

Psych 101, so please don't try to analyze me. Secondly, we don't live in a sitcom. And third, I'm really, really tired of people shoving Connor in my face and telling me to like him. That's just annoying and it makes me like him even less."

"That's hardly his fault."

Maybe it was the wine, the late hour or just the exhaustion, but Vivi finally sighed. "Marie Lester."

Lorelei looked confused until she placed the name. "What's Marie got to do with it?"

"He used me to get to her."

"What?"

Vivi rubbed a hand over her face. *This* was why she didn't want to talk about it. "You know how sheltered and sweet Marie was, right?" At Lorelei's nod, she continued, "That's why her parents sent her to St. Katharine's. New Orleans is this big bad sin city, and they figured she'd be safe there."

"And?"

"Junior year, Connor's friend Reg asked Marie out and she said no. She considered them a bunch of hell-raisers, and she was too good for that. Connor took that as some kind of challenge and a chance to show up Reg."

"Okay…but still not really following you."

She took a big gulp of wine. "Well, Marie and I were lab partners and her parents just loved me, you know."

"Of course."

"So Connor started hanging around me, being nice and all, in order to make himself look better to Marie."

Lorelei nodded. "Because if *you* said he was an okay guy then Marie might change her mind?"

"Exactly."

"So *that's* why Connor started hanging around our house more."

"He was just using me to get to her. And to top it all off

he didn't really like her. He just wanted to prove *he* could get Marie when his friend had failed."

"It's a jerk move, but really..." Vivi shot a look at her and Lorelei trailed off. "Oh. You thought he was interested in you. Ouch. *That's* why you slapped him at your coronation."

The hurt and humiliation she'd felt at seventeen might have been dulled by time, but her twenty-eight-year-old self remembered the blow to her ego and pride. She nodded.

Lorelei rolled her eyes. "That was years ago. Teenage crap. I don't know a nice way to say this, but...get over it."

"He lied to me, used me, hurt me and made me an unwilling accomplice in his quest to use Marie in order to one-up one of his friends. I don't care if it *was* teenage crap. He was wrong. And, even worse, I should have known better. Even after years of his crap I fell for it."

"And you can't just let it go?" Lorelei shook her head. "Wow, Vivi. That's *really* mature."

"This from the girl who is still mad at Steve Milner for cheating on her."

"He left me at prom to go have sex with another girl!"

"So call me when you're over that and we'll talk again about teenage crap I need to get over."

Lorelei's lips pressed into a thin line. Vivi had made her point.

"Even if I wanted to let that slide, I haven't really seen anything in the intervening years to convince me that Connor isn't still an arrogant, self-centered man-child. If anything, his fame has only fueled it. And since Connor is still holding on to his preadolescent grudges against *me,* I'm not too worried about maturity."

It was Lorelei's turn to rub her eyes. "I think I need more wine for this to make any sense at all."

Vivi patted her sister's knee. "Look at it from a different perspective. Animosity will add interest to the competition. If Connor and I suddenly bury the hatchet and become best buddies, people will be disappointed. And I'd hate to deny Bon Argent the opportunity to exploit this for a good cause's gain."

Lorelei sighed. "I hate it when the words you say *sound* perfectly reasonable even though it's actually crazy talk. How do you even manage that?"

"It's a gift." Vivi looked down and noticed she was shedding glitter on the sofa cushions. The glitter reminded her of her purpose, and her personal problems with Connor weren't it. "So you've got my back? I need all the help I can get."

Lorelei nodded. "Blood—however crazy that blood is—is thicker than water, so I'll be as saintly as possible for the duration of your reign. I await my marching orders."

"Good." Vivi grabbed one of the bags and dug inside for a T-shirt. "Welcome to Team Saint."

Lorelei unfolded the powder-blue shirt and scowled at the angel wings emblazoned across the back. "Do I really have to wear this?"

"Yep. Every minute you can. And your first assignment is Tuesday. We're going to the lower Ninth Ward for cleanup detail."

The scowl morphed into horror. "I didn't realize you meant for me to do manual labor."

"It's good for the soul, honey, if bad for your manicure."

"I think I might have to work on Tuesday," she grumbled.

"*I* think it's safe to assume that Daddy will give you the time off."

"Fine." Lorelei looked at the shirt again, distaste written across her face. "This is *not* in my color palette. What color are the shirts for Connor's team?"

"Don't even joke about that. I'm already at a great disadvantage without my sister defecting to the dark side."

"Okay, here's the thing, Vivi. It's ridiculous, but I'll back off. However, I'm not going to listen to you moan about Connor for the next four weeks. It'll ruin my whole Mardi Gras."

Vivi just wished someone had taken that into consideration before they'd stuck her with Connor for the next month. The rest of the city may be planning on *laissez le bons temps rouler,* but her *temps* weren't looking very *bon* at the moment.

Connor spent most of Sunday morning and part of the afternoon on the phone with his manager and his agent, but the chore didn't aggravate him as much when he could sit on a balcony overlooking Royal Street with a *café au lait* and real beignets. The third-floor apartment had been sitting empty while Gabe was in Italy, and Connor appreciated the solitude it offered while still being in the heart of the French Quarter. The street musician below his balcony displayed more enthusiasm than talent, but it was as much a sound of home as the *clop-clop* and jingle of the mule-drawn carriages and the shouts of the tour guides leading groups down the street.

Sitting here in the winter sunshine, his feet propped up on the wrought-iron rail with nothing to do except let his mind wander…bliss. Until this moment he hadn't realized how stressed he'd been.

Even the doctor's orders to rest his hands and wrists seemed less onerous and restrictive today. The piano wasn't calling him, and the only workout his hands were getting involved lifting his coffee cup to his mouth repeatedly. Even after hours on the phone his head felt clear, and he could feel his muscles relaxing and the pain receding—no pharmaceutical intervention necessary.

Yep, bliss. He might just sit here all day and attempt absolutely nothing more strenuous than a solid nap.

His mother was a bit irritated that he'd chosen to stay in a friend's apartment instead of his childhood home, but this was a high-profile visit, and he didn't want photographers or fans staking out his parents' house and trampling Mom's flowers. This was just easier.

He wasn't the only celebrity to call New Orleans home, but coming straight off tour to the Saints and Sinners fundraiser right after Katy Arras and her accusations… It was best to let that all die down some first.

People would be used to having him around again soon enough, and in time, it would no longer be big news.

God, he loved this city.

Which was why he'd jumped at the chance to be this year's Sinner. Silliness aside, it was an honor, and he felt very much the hometown boy made good. He was glad his fame guaranteed big money this year for the fundraiser, even if it created an "uneven playing field" that steamed Vivi's oysters.

Speaking of Vivi…

The view from Gabe's apartment balcony contained a surprise: he had a clear view to the front door to Vivi's art gallery just a few buildings up Royal. According to Mom, who kept him fully up-to-date on all of the goings-on in New Orleans—*especially* those of her friends and their children—Vivi's gallery was doing very well, walking the line between art that was accessible and sellable yet still high-end quality.

Good for Vivi. He'd had no clue that art was Vivi's passion, but after years of hearing all about her pageant successes—Good Lord, her reign as Miss Louisiana had been one of the longest years of his life—it was good to know that she could do something other than twirl batons and look pretty. She'd always had brains; it was nice to know she'd finally decided to use them for something.

Thanks to Mom, he also knew that Vivi wasn't a surprise choice for Saint at all. If the city could canonize her they probably would. Vivi was involved in *everything;* any organization that needed a face or a volunteer had Vivi on speed dial. The only surprise was that they hadn't made her the Saint long before now. Cynically, he wondered if Max and the board had held off until his schedule had cleared so they could get the maximum impact.

The morning paper had been almost gleeful about the announcement, making sure to illustrate their "antagonistic relationship" with anecdotes that dated all the way back to their seventh-grade performance of *Bye Bye Birdie,* just in case there were people in town who *weren't* aware that the children of two of the city's oldest and most influential families were at odds like an alternate universe's Romeo and Juliet.

For years he'd held out hope that everyone would move on, but it just went to show that no matter how big he got, or how many millions of records he sold, people would never let anyone live down their past. Especially if that past was something they could still milk for attention and laughs.

But it was his time to milk the cash cow he'd become. Half-formed ideas that had been swimming in his mind were getting even more solid, and the pieces were falling into place with a rapidity that felt like fate intervening. The old coffee warehouse on Julia Street, investors like Gabe lining up with their wallets open…

If this all worked out—and it was looking like it just might—he'd be more than just a hometown boy done good. He'd be a part of this town in a way he'd never planned on before. Some of this was very new territory for him, but it felt good. It felt right. He didn't have to put down roots here; the roots were here, waiting for him to come back. He just had to make sure they didn't strangle him this time.

Mom might have thought his desire to be a musician

was an act of defiance—a revolt against the expectations of going to college, joining Dad's firm, marrying a nice local girl like one of the LaBlancs, and settling down in a mansion three blocks away. In retrospect, she might have been a little right, but other than the occasional unpleasant run through the tabloids and the time away from home she really couldn't complain. Well, she was still pushing the nice-girl-big-house-some-grandkids agenda…

Which, oddly, brought him back to Vivi.

If he was serious about spending more time here at home he'd have to call some kind of truce with Vivi. Come to some kind of understanding. The circles they ran in overlapped occasionally, thanks to their parents and shared friends. They wouldn't be able to completely avoid or ignore each other.

Fame had its privileges, but Vivi had clout. People respected her, and her opinions went a long way. It would be hard to claim he was trying to do something good if Vivi objected. Hell, you couldn't even claim to be a decent human being in this town if Vivi hated you. People might like him for various reasons, but everyone *loved* Vivi and courted her approval. As long as she hated him, folks would wonder why. And they'd assume it was all his fault.

God, it was annoying.

And while Vivi had miraculously become the most gracious and polite dinner partner he'd ever had Friday night, he doubted that graciousness would continue once she found out he was planning a return to what she no doubt considered *her* turf now.

Vivi would be fit to be tied, and he almost looked forward to telling her. *No,* he thought, walking that thought back in light of his earlier conclusions. He didn't need her approval—though it would help—but he did need her tolerance. Egging her on wouldn't help his cause.

He hadn't fully realized that he'd been staring at the door

to Vivi's gallery until the door opened and Vivi stepped outside. He started to slide back, but then realized she had no reason to look up, and probably wouldn't see him even if she happened to do so. She paused mid-step, digging through her bag and pulling out a phone.

Two men standing next to a car gawked openly at Vivi, and realistically he couldn't blame them. The black pencil skirt emphasized her legs and tiny waist, and the upswept hair showcased the line of her neck and high cheekbones. One of the men seemed to be encouraging the other to go over and speak to her. *She is way out of your league, buddy,* Connor thought. Vivi was, to quote his departed grandmother, "a prime example of good breeding and a proper upbringing."

She finished her call and set a pair of sunglasses on her face before walking briskly toward the corner and turning on to St. Ann's Street toward Jackson Square. Connor—and most of the other men on the street—watched her until she was out of sight.

Tomorrow he and Vivi would start the morning show media blitz, hitting all the local TV stations and kicking off the fundraising in earnest. After that, it was breakfast with some big donors and organization heads and a photo call. Most of his day would be spent in Vivi's company.

While she'd been polite and gracious the other night, Connor didn't believe for a second that it wasn't an act. He knew her too well to fall for that. She was out to prove something by *not* sniping at him. He wouldn't try to guess what her overall goal was—beyond not making herself look bad in the press—but he would not help her achieve it by attacking first. It played right into his plans to have her publically playing nice. It gave him her stamp of approval without her actually giving it. She probably hadn't thought that part through. Talk about steaming her oysters.

He might be the Sinner—and it might be a well-deserved title—but Vivi wasn't the only one who knew how to behave.

It would be interesting to see who broke first.

CHAPTER THREE

THE reporter with the plastic smile thought she was being very clever, but Vivi knew what was coming. Intentionally trying to fluster a guest with "gotcha" questions was unbelievably rude, in her opinion, but it was standard fare and just part of the game.

If Chatty Cathy here thinks she can fluster me, though, that girl is in for a big surprise.

She'd had every derogatory stereotype about pageants thrown in her face by reporters with more gravitas and bigger audiences and hadn't broken. It might have been a few years, but she hadn't forgotten how this was done. A couple of comments and questions about Connor weren't going to tie her tongue and cause her to say something stupid. Or scandalously quotable out of context.

The smile grew wider. *Bring it,* Vivi thought, and let her own smile widen a bit, too.

"So, Vivienne, how did you feel when Connor's name was announced Friday night? Were you very shocked?"

Vivi nodded, and the reporter brightened a bit, obviously figuring she'd hit the mark. *Amateur.* "Just as much as everyone else, I imagine. With Connor's career taking off like it has, I never dreamed his schedule would allow him to come back and do something like Saints and Sinners."

"So no problems, then, with this matchup?"

"Sort of." She waited just long enough to tease that there might be a sound bite forthcoming. "I am quite competitive, and I wish they'd chosen someone who'd be easier to beat. But then I remind myself that, while this *is* a competition, there are no real losers in it. The money raised through Saints and Sinners does so much good for the community, and everyone involved is a winner."

Answer the question, but deflect the intent and bring the interview back to the proper topic.

"And what about you, Connor?"

Vivi kept her face neutral as she turned toward him and thought, *Don't screw this up now.* Surely Connor's fame meant he had the experience to answer this? She thought of a dozen good answers and tried to think them hard enough that Connor might pick one up through ESP.

"I was pretty shocked myself to be chosen this year, but it's an honor that actually brings with it the chance to do something good for a lot of people. So, like Vivi said, we all win—although I do hope to put on a good show at least." He shot the lady-killer grin at the reporter, and now that he'd shaved off the goatee, his dimple was clearly visible. When he added a wink, the reporter blushed slightly and fumbled over her next words.

Oh, good Lord. Spare me the simpering females. Women had been falling all over themselves since Connor hit puberty, but the maturation of his features and body combined with his fame and charm… Vivi might understand the reaction, but she was still ashamed of her entire gender.

But she had to admit that Connor had done well dodging the impertinent question.

Unable to get a good answer out of Connor, the reporter had no choice but to cut to the graphic listing the upcoming events and direct people to the Saints and Sinners website. The camera turned to the station's meteorologist for the weather report and Vivi unhooked her mic.

Making all four local morning shows in two hours meant that their schedule was very tight, and there was no time to waste in idle chitchat. Connor, however, had decided to stop to sign autographs and pose for pictures. Vivi bit her tongue and waited with what she hoped looked like patience.

Finally, though, she had to step in and break up the love-fest. "I'm so sorry, y'all, but we're going to be late for our next interview if we don't leave right now."

Connor fell into step beside her as they exited the building. "Thanks for the save. It's hard to get away sometimes."

"You can't do that at every stop this morning or we'll never make them all. I know you just hate to tear yourself away, but there are other people's schedules to consider."

"And *there's* the mood swing to the Vivi I know." He sighed dramatically. "I knew that perkiness was too good to last."

Damn it, she'd already forgotten her pledge to be gracious and polite. "It's six o'clock in the morning. I need to save all my perkiness for the cameras. Sorry."

The driver had fresh coffee from a nearby shop waiting for them in the car. She nearly hugged him in gratitude—both for the caffeine and the chance to gather her thoughts and adjust her tone as she took a few sips and settled in.

"However, I don't have the skill set necessary to be your bouncer, so you'll need to either provide one yourself or else learn how to extract yourself from the fawning adulation of your fans."

Connor leveled a look at her across the backseat. "Without those people I have no career. They support me. So the least I can do for them is sign an autograph and smile for the camera. Mock me all you like, but don't *ever* mock my fans."

The words were hard and cold, and that combination got

her attention. She'd never heard Connor speak like that. "You're actually serious."

"As a heart attack."

Vivi felt about two feet tall. "My apologies, then, for insulting your fans."

Connor nodded his acceptance of her apology, then pulled his phone out of his pocket and began to tap at it. Vivi was glad for his distraction; she needed a moment to process. She'd seen Connor's posing and autographing as glory-mongering—something to feed his ego. She hadn't expected Connor to get so passionate about it. It made sense, though. He *wouldn't* have a career without fans, so he should be appreciative of them.

She just wouldn't have guessed that he would be.

Connor didn't look up from his phone. "By the way, good job deflecting that question and reframing. You've had media training."

The terminology gave him away. "As have you, it seems."

"I learned the hard way that performing onstage and doing an interview are two totally different things. I only had to screw up once before I swore I'd never make that mistake again. What made you do it?"

Was he being intentionally dense? "About the time I won Mississippi River Princess I realized I really needed it." She paused, but Connor didn't make the connection. "I had my sights on Miss Louisiana and Miss America. I had a platform to promote, a title to represent and a reputation to protect. There was no way I was going in unprepared for the job."

"I hadn't thought about that. It doesn't really look like that hard of a job."

She snorted. "I could say the same thing about your job, you know."

He looked at her like she was insane. "*You've* never done a six-month world tour."

"And *you've* never been Miss Louisiana."

"It's not all glory and encores, you know. It's hard, exhausting, cutthroat work."

She smiled sweetly at him. "So is the Miss America pageant."

Connor's eyes widened at the implication. "I'm just surprised there's more to it than showing up and looking pretty."

"Somehow your lack of insight doesn't really surprise me."

"No need to get so huffy about it."

She caught herself mid-huff and lifted her chin instead. "I really don't have the patience to school you on incorrect pageant stereotypes this morning. If you want to believe I'm nothing more than an airhead, so be it. I've been called worse by better. But just let me remind you that my reign was over years ago. My tiara-wearing days are behind me, and I've moved on to other things to be proud of."

"Like your gallery?"

"Yes." She was very proud of the gallery and happy to brag about it to anyone who would listen—including Connor. And it seemed like a safe enough topic. "It seemed to take forever to get off the ground, but it's doing really well now. We've recently been able to offer patronage to a few young emerging artists—providing studio space and a small stipend."

"Good for you, Vivi."

She couldn't tell if that was sarcasm or not. Not that she would bite back—she was determined to keep a better hold of her tongue if it killed her—but she'd still like to know if Connor was mocking her. His face was inscrutable as he leaned back against the leather seats of the limo and closed his eyes.

"Wake me when we get there."

And now I'm an alarm clock? Connor was obviously used

to traveling with an entourage to cater to him. *Don't be so touchy.* If it were anyone other than Connor, she knew it wouldn't bother her quite as much. Still, though…it was rude to decide to nap instead of make polite conversation. Not that she *wanted* to make polite conversation, but it was the principle of the thing.

Connor stretched out his long legs, taking up a bit more than his fair share of the available space, and crossed his feet at the ankles. Amazingly, he seemed to be asleep a second later, his breathing slow and deep. *How did he do that?*

But that left her crawling through morning traffic in the back of a town car with no one to talk to. She could lower the privacy screen and talk to the driver, but thanks to Connor hogging the space she'd have to contort herself in order to accomplish that.

She pulled out her phone instead, to check her mail, but her eyes drifted to the big black boots parked next to her simple black flats. *Big feet,* she thought, *to match his big head.*

The head in question was tipped back against the headrest. Shaving the goatee really did make a difference, making his mouth seem more prominent and emphasizing that strong chin. Even with his features relaxed in sleep, Connor projected attitude.

He might be a piano-playing crooner, but Connor *looked* the part of a bad-boy rock star, and that image had helped fuel his popularity. Women loved the idea of a man who looked like *that* singing love songs in a voice that could send shivers all the way down to their toes. He was practically a musical fantasy come to life.

Even she had to admit—privately, of course—that Connor was freakin' gorgeous. Broad shoulders, lean hips, a smile that caused feminine flusters every single time… A woman would have to be blind or dead not to appreciate him based on looks alone, and she was neither. She wasn't ignorant or denying of his attributes; she was just immune to them because she knew him.

Wow, it was getting hot in here. The man radiated heat like a generator. Vivi had to fan herself. She did *not* want to go on TV all sweaty and red-faced. The climate controls were next to Connor, out of her reach unless she wanted to crawl across his lap, so she'd settle for cracking a window for fresh air.

The windows on her side of the car didn't seem to open, so that meant she'd have to open the ones on the other side. But Connor's legs blocked easy access to those controls, too. *Who designed this vehicle?* She should just wake him up, but that would seem petty and she was *not* going to be petty.

At least outwardly. *Inwardly* was a different situation.

Vivi slid to the edge of the seat, pushed up, placed one knee in her seat and lifted the other leg over Connor's. She was reaching for the handle on the other side to pull herself over without touching him when the driver braked hard, jerking her forward and then backward as the car came to a stop.

Vivi lost her balance and fell back, landing hard and ungracefully in Connor's lap.

Connor had merely been dozing, but the sudden stop of the car jerked him awake a split second before Vivi landed in his lap.

His arms went around her instinctively to steady her as she slid sideways, and his first ridiculous thought was that Vivi was a nice armful. She was small, but compact: the butt pressed against his groin was firm, and the thigh under his hand lean and strong. The curves he'd admired the other day felt even better than they looked. His body tightened and his skin heated at the contact.

Vivi's head was just below his shoulder, and the light floral scent that always faintly surrounded her filled his lungs as he inhaled. He could feel her heartbeat and realized that his *other* hand had landed directly on her breast; the soft curve filled his palm perfectly. Something flashed through him, landing in his lap with as much force as Vivi had.

He moved his hand away, brushing her hair out of her face instead. "You okay?" he asked as he uncovered her mouth.

"I'm fine." She scrambled to an upright position and scooted off his lap into the seat beside him and began finger-combing her hair back into place.

The privacy screen slid open and the driver's concerned face appeared. "Sorry about that. Some idiot ran the light. You two okay?"

"I think so," Vivi answered, but her voice was a little shaky. "Connor?"

"Fine," he answered. While it seemed like Vivi had been in his lap for a long time, he realized only a few seconds had actually passed. Still, though, his body had reacted like a horny teenager's, as if he'd never touched a girl before.

This was *Vivi,* for God's sake.

He shifted in the seat, trying to find a more comfortable position while he got it back under control.

Vivi's face was flushed, and he noticed her hands were shaking the tiniest bit. "Are you sure you're okay?"

"I'm fine, really." As the car started forward again Vivi moved to the other seat. "I was trying to get across to open the window when we stopped. Sorry I landed on you."

Maybe it *was* a little warm in here. He jumped on the excuse and pushed the button to lower the window. Fresh air filled the car, dispersing both the heat and the tension in the air. "Better?"

"Much."

Vivi swallowed hard, and when she lifted her eyes to meet his and smile her thanks, he noticed how wide they were. How the pupils had dilated until the blue was a thin circle. Color still flagged her cheeks, and her breath had a ragged edge.

Vivi couldn't hold the look or the smile, and she began to dig in her bag, emerging with lipstick and a mirror. Her hands still weren't steady, and she concentrated on the task like it was the most important thing she'd ever done.

He hadn't been the only one affected by those few seconds, and it looked like Vivi was still riding the shockwave. *That* knowledge slammed into him, and the air felt warm again.

"Oh, look—we're here." Vivi spoke rapidly, with relief dripping off her words, and she had the door open before the car came to a complete stop in front of the studio. "I'm going to run in and freshen up real quick before we go on air." Then she bolted for the building like the hounds of hell were on her heels.

Honestly, he didn't blame her at all.

Vivi needed to splash cold water on her face, but that would only make her mascara run and then she'd look like a raccoon during the interview. She settled for wetting a paper towel and running it over her neck and under the collar of her shirt to cool her skin.

Checking under the stall doors for feet and seeing none, Vivi let her breath out in a deep sigh and braced her hands on the counter.

Sweet mercy.

I was in his lap.

And his hand was...

And the other was...

Oh, she knew exactly where each hand had landed. She felt branded from the touch.

His hands weren't the only part of him that had burned

into her skin. Her butt had… He'd… *She'd...* Dear heaven, she couldn't have landed in that exact position if she'd tried.

Mortified wasn't a strong enough word.

Maybe if she hadn't been ogling him just seconds before she might not now feel like she'd intentionally given him a lap dance.

That was bad enough, but worse was the realization that for a split second she'd enjoyed the embrace.

And so did he, a little voice said. The evidence had been impossible to miss.

But then she'd fluttered and stammered and… *Ugh.* She'd seen that look: he *knew.* And with his ego…

Her quick wish that the floor would open and swallow her went ungranted. Instead she dug for a comb and tried to repair the damage she'd done to her hair with her fingers earlier. After a critical look, she shrugged and let it go at presentable. Hopefully that flush would fade before they went on camera, but considering she was going to have to face Connor, she'd probably look like a ripe tomato all through the interview.

Connor was a hottie, but she was immune. She was not so shallow as to allow good looks and an amazing body sway her. She liked men with substance.

Somebody tell that to my libido.

"Vivienne?" A young woman poked her head around the door. "If you're ready, we really need to get you miked."

"Coming." Vivi checked her teeth for lipstick in a last-ditch stall for time, but she really had no choice but to follow the woman out into the hallway.

Connor stood about twenty feet away by the studio door, autographing a CD case. He handed it and the pen back to the waiting fan, then smiled as a third person snapped a photo. He looked up as the woman shooed the other two away. His eyes met Vivi's briefly before he looked away.

Great. Now I can add uncomfortable sexual tension to this nightmare. And while Connor had plenty of fans who wanted to meet him, talk to him, get his autograph or generally just slobber all over him, she didn't have anything or anyone to distract *her.* She had no choice but to stand there feeling foolish as Connor charmed and dazzled them all.

It might not be so bad if she hadn't just realized—even if only for a second—that she was just as prone to simpering and flustering as the women basking in his charm right now.

No, that was embarrassing, and knowledge she wished she didn't have, but that wasn't completely it. Facing that unhappy truth just seemed to open the gate to other, far more disturbing truths.

Mainly that Connor's life was taking off and hers had already plateaued.

Art galleries in New Orleans weren't nearly as interesting as concert tours and celebrity-studded parties in Los Angeles. She'd done dozens of interviews at this station before, but all for various charities, and everyone knew her story already.

Connor was exciting and interesting and she felt every bit the washed-up beauty queen whose fifteen minutes were over. At twenty-eight she'd already peaked, and was now just another socialite doing the rounds and clinging to past glory.

Depression hit like a brick.

She didn't begrudge Connor his success or his popularity—even she would admit that he was extremely talented—but it still forced her to admit that Connor had something she didn't: the "It" factor. Nothing really set her apart. She was just average.

Average wasn't bad, but being stuck next to someone so obviously above average was more damaging to her ego than she'd expected. Was this new simpering and flustered reaction to Connor a symptom of a larger issue?

Was she really that shallow?

Something was off. Vivi answered all the questions, shook all the hands and smiled for the cameras appropriately, but *something* wasn't right. Connor couldn't put his finger on exactly what, but he had no doubt that Vivi had something on her mind.

He was hardly an expert on Vivi's moods, but she lacked her normal sparkle—or at least the sparkle she normally gave off to other people. People who weren't him.

When she did speak to him directly—which wasn't often and lessened to almost complete silence as the day continued—her voice lacked that normal Vivi edge. Her answers bordered on a monotone, and she passed up several easy opportunities to mock him outright.

He'd been looking for ways to broker some kind of peace, but this wasn't at all how he imagined that peace would be.

It was just plain odd. Disturbing, even.

After several hours of this uncomfortable non-conversation—plus a few strange, indefinable looks from Vivi—they were finally done and the driver was taking them home. Vivi spent her time playing with her phone or staring out the window as if she'd never seen the city before.

He'd had a hard time pulling himself back under control after…after whatever it was that had happened earlier. Coupled with her dramatic attitude change, he began to wonder if he'd misread the look on her face. Maybe that hadn't been shock. Horror? Disgust? Offense? Give Vivi the choice of landing in his lap or a slime pit and she'd probably ask if there was any difference.

No, he knew his strengths and weaknesses, and he hadn't misread that look. He'd seen it plenty before. Vivi might have been horrified, but it wasn't necessarily because she'd landed on him. Or that he'd accidentally copped a feel.

Damn. He shouldn't have gone there. The palms of his hands burned with the memory and now he needed a cold shower to offset the effects of it.

Vivi cleared her throat. "About earlier…I was serious."

Connor's train of thought derailed. Surely Vivi wasn't—?

"This is a competition, but we should focus on what's really important."

Oh. He gave himself a good mental shake. "Agreed."

She slid her finger over her phone, looking at something. "You're already kicking my butt with online donations to your war chest, but I still plan to put on a good showing—in the competitions, if nothing else."

"Because that's what's important."

"Of course. You're going to bring in buckets of money and—"

Enough. "I'll match yours." The words were out before he'd even thought them through.

Vivi chuckled. "Oh, you'll surpass mine. I've accepted that."

"No. I mean I'll match yours. Dollar for dollar, whatever you raise, I'll match."

That got her attention and she finally met his eyes. "You can't."

"Worried about my finances?"

"Oh, I don't doubt you can afford it. It's just that any money donated personally by the Sinner and the Saint doesn't go into the final tally."

He relaxed back into his seat and got comfortable. This might be interesting. Could her personal dislike of him outweigh her competitive spirit? His money had never brought him quite so much pleasure before. "I can't count personal donations into my own war chest, but there's nothing in the rules that says I can't donate to yours."

"But why would you?" Vivi was too competitive to even contemplate the idea.

"It levels that playing field."

Vivi's eyes narrowed suspiciously. "What if that puts me over the top?"

"Then you win."

That brought another chuckle, only this time there was real humor behind it. That was progress. "Can your pride handle that, Connor?"

"The question is, can yours?"

She snorted. "Taking your money? Definitely. In fact, it would give me great pleasure."

"There's a first time for everything."

A flush crept up her neck. "As I've said, this isn't about us."

"Then why else would it give you pleasure to beat me?"

"The fact there's a bigger, more important purpose to this competition doesn't preclude me from gaining personal satisfaction."

He raised an eyebrow at her choice of words and watched the flush get darker. Strangely, it made his pulse kick up a notch.

She cleared her throat. "From beating you, that is. Competition is healthy and good."

"If you say so."

"I do. But I fully expect you to live up to your promise. If you try to renege on this…"

"I always deliver on my promises, Vivi. Always."

A strange silence fell and Vivi looked away. The tension still felt heavy, but it crackled a bit now that pride and challenge had joined it.

The car stopped and Vivi looked out the window, eyebrows drawing together. Reaching for the intercom button, Vivi said, "My car's at my house. I don't know why he came to the gallery."

Connor caught her hand, causing those eyebrows to furrow at him. Then, like his touch was painful, Vivi extracted her hand from his.

"This is *my* stop."

"What?"

"I'm staying in a friend's place."

Vivi looked around. "Where?"

He pointed to Gabe's building.

"But that's Gabe Morrow's building."

"Yeah. He's in Italy right now—"

"I know that. I didn't know *you* knew Gabe, though."

"We have mutual friends. I just didn't know they included you."

"Did you know my gallery is right there?" She pointed.

"I do now. I'd say you were welcome to drop by for a drink sometime…" He let the thought trail off and, predictably, Vivi rolled her eyes. "See you tomorrow, Vivi."

The cool air felt good against his skin as he stepped out of the car, and with Vivi safely away, he began to feel normal again for the first time in hours.

Something had happened today. He just wasn't sure exactly what. Or why. Or how, for that matter. But whatever that *something* was…

Vivi just had the ability to make his brain short-circuit. That was the only explanation.

But while it was nice to have that explanation, it also meant he was going to be permanently brain-damaged by the time this was done.

CHAPTER FOUR

IT NEVER failed to amaze Vivi how slow recovery was coming to some areas. If not for the tall weeds and faded Xs painted on the buildings, people might think the hurricane had come through weeks ago instead of years. It wasn't something visitors to New Orleans saw unless they specifically came to see it—all the popular tourist areas were up and running—and, unbelievably, it wasn't something *she* saw very often even though she lived in the city. More than distance separated the hardest hit areas like the Lower Ninth Ward from the Garden District and the French Quarter. Less than a third of the residents had been able to return, and the neighborhood felt empty and lifeless. She thought of her own lively neighborhood, and it only made the loss here sharper.

Vivi hauled another bag to the portable Dumpster and grunted as she tossed it in. Her shoulders and arms throbbed and her legs ached, and they'd only been at this for a few hours. There was a big difference between working out at the gym and actually working, and she was feeling it already.

Lorelei appeared beside her, water bottle in hand. Although the day was cool, sweat beaded around her hairline from the work. She had a dirty smudge across one cheek. Like Vivi, she'd layered a thermal shirt under her Team Saint T-shirt, and the sleeves were now dirty and stained.

Lorelei took a long drink and groaned as she leaned

against the Dumpster. "You owe me a massage and a manicure."

"Done." The look of surprise on Lorelei's face told Vivi she'd been looking for a chance to grumble, and that look was well worth what she'd pay for the spa. "I do appreciate your help, though. We are kicking Connor's butt."

"It's a fine butt to kick, if you ask me."

"I happen to agree," said Vivi.

Lorelei snorted, and Vivi wanted to suck the words back in.

"It *is* a very fine butt, isn't it? I didn't know you'd noticed."

"Don't you have work to do?"

"Slave-driver." Lorelei pulled her gloves back on. "I feel bad for Connor, though."

"What?"

"It's got to suck to always have a camera following you around. Here he is, trying to do charity work, and while everyone wants him to *talk* about what he's doing, none of them will actually let him *do* it."

Vivi turned to look at the circus on the other side of the street. Connor and his team were being followed by camera crews and reporters. It was good publicity for what they were doing, but it meant Connor's team was doing it very, very slowly. Lorelei had a point, but still… "Pardon me if I don't cry for him."

"Wow, you're mean. It's a good thing the Bon Argent people don't know you better or they'd pull your halo in a heartbeat, Saint Vivi."

"He told me yesterday how much his fans mean to him. He doesn't mind this."

"There's a big difference between fans who love and admire him and the press who just want something from him."

When had Lorelei developed such insights—*and* the need

to share them? "Maybe. But the two go hand in hand. He can't have one without the other, so…"

Lorelei patted her on the shoulder. "You just keep clinging to that if it makes you feel better." Grabbing an empty trash bag, she started to walk away. Over her shoulder, though, she tossed one last grenade. "But remember it the next time you wonder why everyone always thought you were so sanctimonious."

Lorelei was too far away for Vivi to rebut the accusation, and her words hung in the air like a rebuke. A very unfair rebuke. She *wasn't* sanctimonious, darn it; she just had a strong inner compass. That wasn't a character flaw; it was practically a virtue. More people needed that kind of inner knowledge; otherwise they ended up in the tabloids like Connor.

But…Connor *was* rather struggling over there, and with the press in the way nothing was going to get done, and that was what was really important. He'd mentioned his loyalty to his fans, but nothing about the press. She could throw him a rope.

Taking a deep breath, she crossed to the middle of the street. Hands on her hips in what she hoped looked like annoyance, she shouted as loud as she could, "Hey, Connor!" Cameras turned in her direction, but she brazened it out. "You gonna stand around all day like a pretty boy or are you gonna work?"

Silence fell. She raised an eyebrow and all the heads swiveled back to Connor for his response. Connor met her eyes and she swore she saw the corner of his mouth twitch into a smile before he caught it.

"It's not that my team doesn't relish kicking your butt," she said, and a cheer went up behind her from her team, "but it just doesn't seem sporting if you're not even trying."

"We're just warming up, Vivi, so don't start celebrating

too soon." He turned to the press. "Y'all have enough to run with. You're welcome to stay, but if you do I'm going to expect you to work. I've got some catching up to do."

There were grumbles, both from the media and Connor's team, but the reminder seemed to do the trick. Work gloves were pulled back on, trash bags picked back up and cameras loaded into vans. Connor joined her on the street—neutral territory between the two teams now working in earnest.

Quietly he said, "Thanks. I owe you."

"That's twice now, and I do intend to collect."

"I always pay my debts."

"Good to know. But I should warn you my favors don't come cheap."

"I should certainly hope not." He looked her up and down in a way he never had before, and something fluttery came to life in her stomach. *Damn it, damn it, damn it.* She should be past this kind of juvenile response. But there was just something so raw and sexy about Connor in his black Sinner shirt, jeans and work boots. She'd have to have been dead for a week not to feel the effect. Even with the cameras following him around he'd managed to work up a sweat, and the beads of moisture at his temples only added to that purely masculine vibe.

Focus. "And you won't be getting off quick and easy, either."

"Excellent." Connor obviously found something amusing in this—more amusing than it actually was—and Vivi felt like she was tripping over a current running through the conversation without knowing how or why. "Quick and easy aren't really my style, you know."

What on earth…? Lord, she needed a map to navigate this conversation. "Well, I didn't break that circus up to stand around and chitchat with you, so I think we should both get back to work."

There was that smirk again. "On you go, then."

Vivi stepped back to do just that and immediately tripped over a piece of asphalt knocked loose by the flooding. She landed with a thud, and a sharp pain shot through her left butt cheek. Her eyes watered as she reached under herself and removed another, smaller piece of asphalt. "Ouch."

Connor squatted, amusement and concern written equally on his face. "You okay?"

"Yes." It was embarrassing, but at least the cameras had already been put away. *Small favors.*

"That whole 'grace and poise' thing doesn't actually count as much in the pageant system as we're led to believe, does it?"

"Hush."

There was that grin again. "You're not the first woman to be knocked off-kilter by my presence..."

"Don't flatter yourself."

Conner chuckled and stood. "Should I offer assistance?"

"It would be nice," she snapped.

He extended a hand and hauled her to her feet. Vivi rubbed a hand over the spot where the sharp debris had dug in. "That's going to leave a bruise."

"Want me to rub it for you?"

Shock rocketed through her. "Why don't you just kiss it," she snapped.

His voice dropped a notch as he leaned in. "Calling in one of your favors already?"

Vivi's throat closed. She hadn't meant it like *that.* Heat rushed over her body at the thought of Connor... Of Connor's lips... His hands...

She took a big step back and tried to blot out the image, to shake off the feeling... "You wish." *Ugh.* She'd meant that to sound snappy and flip, but it came out weak and shaky.

Connor's response was another low chuckle that did nothing to help the situation. Then he was heading back to his side of the street without a backward glance, and his casual whistling floated back to her ears. The heat on her skin found a new source. *Damn him.*

This is ridiculous. She was just oversensitive after yesterday, and Connor's attempt to fluster her in the wake of that was adolescent. As was her response, she admitted.

Her butt still hurt, but she couldn't rub the ache away without thinking of Connor's offer. She went to the cooler and grabbed a water bottle and drank deeply, trying to look casual. Her brain began to function normally once she had some distance from him, and she froze in horror as the conversation replayed in her head. Dear Lord, had she really implied that…? And he'd said… And then… *Oh, my God.*

How could her face feel hot while cold chills of horror crawled over her skin? Maybe she was sick. That would truly be excellent: she could claim the earlier conversation was simply feverish ramblings *and* she could spend the rest of Saints and Sinners locked up in her house.

I should be so lucky.

This was what came of trying to be nice to Connor. At least when he was insulting or irritating her he didn't throw little *double entendres* into the conversation to trip her up and mess with her mind.

That explains it. Relief washed over her. She wasn't insane; she just wasn't used to Connor acting like that. He'd taken advantage of her politeness and gotten flirty as if she was just another simpering fan. *That* was what had thrown her off her game. Her world didn't seem quite so off-kilter now. She straightened her shoulders and got ahold of herself. No more Miss Nice-Vivi. It was dangerous.

And how dare he talk to her like she was one of his slobbering, sex-starved groupies? Anger flashed through her. There was a time and a place for that kind of banter and here and now were neither. And she certainly wasn't the right audience. Anger at Connor gave way to anger at herself when a little voice piped up to remind her how quickly she'd jumped to a full-color visual of Connor…

Ugh. Do you have no self-respect at all?

Okay, note to self: no more tossing Connor a rope.

It might end up tied around her neck next time.

Connor had hoped that the physical labor would occupy his mind—or at least focus his thoughts someplace other than south of Vivi's belt. It wasn't working.

What had possessed him to flirt like that with Vivi? After yesterday's awkwardness he shouldn't have said anything even remotely risqué, but neither the words nor Vivi's reaction should have affected him so strongly. A few stupid little remarks, and now all he could think about was Vivi: those long legs, the shapely curve of her butt covered by faded denim clinging to it like a second skin, the way her hands-on-hips stance had called attention to her breasts and the gentle flare of her hips. He'd had a handful of those curves just yesterday, and he was insanely curious to know what they felt like without the fabric separating them from his hands.

Which was totally wrong and crazy because this was *Vivi,* for God's sake. Who didn't even like him. More important, he didn't like her.

But, honestly, that was getting harder to justify as well. Vivi hadn't just helped him shoo off the press—who'd spent more time this morning asking about his next album instead of about the news they were actually supposed to be covering—she'd done so in a way guaranteed to make the biggest splash. The image of Vivi in the middle of the street calling him a pretty boy had done more than save him. She'd provided the press with a money shot and the lead to the story.

That could backfire on her and make her look foolish, but it had solved a problem *and* ensured they'd make the local news tonight. They'd probably make several blogs as well.

Vivi was too media-savvy not to know that, so it had to have been her intent. If nothing else, he had to give her props for caring about the cause.

His muscles protested as he hauled an old tire to the refuse pile. This was backbreakingly hard work, especially for someone who'd spent six of the last eight months on the road. Sweat rolled down his spine, and he was glad he'd agreed to do this in January rather than August.

The pain in his wrists and hands reminded him that he probably shouldn't have agreed to this activity at all. He went to the cooler full of water bottles, leaving his hands submerged in the icy water for a few seconds longer than necessary in order to get a little relief.

If he couldn't get his thoughts under control he'd need to be sitting in that ice water soon. And he'd have no one to blame but himself. One thing he was very sure of: Vivi hadn't intended for her words to come across with a double meaning. He'd looked back briefly once safely on his side of the street, just in time to watch all the color drain from her face before she turned bright red. At least the conversation had shaken her, too—if for different reasons.

And *that* knowledge only made his situation worse.

Vivi ignored him for the next few hours, and he returned the favor, refusing to pay any attention to what was going on in her camp until a couple of the Bon Argent board members showed up and waved them both over to inform them of some schedule changes. Vivi was polite and perky until the board members left and they were alone. Then her smile disappeared and she turned abruptly away.

"Vivi—"

She spun and cut him off. "I think it's best if we don't talk. Ever."

"What?"

"Since you can't carry on a civilized and mature conversation on appropriate topics, I'd prefer you not speak to me at all," she said primly.

Vivi was back up on her high horse. "Oh, really?"

"Really."

"Are you this condescending to everyone or just to me?"

Her jaw tightened. "I don't know why we're even attempting a conversation."

He was beginning to agree with her, but before he could say anything Vivi continued.

"You know, I'm not one of your fans, or some reporter you can charm or seduce. I'm not interested, so it doesn't work on me."

That was a slap to his ego. It was also a bald-faced lie, because she wouldn't be so damned upset about it otherwise. "If I had been trying to seduce you, you'd know. The flying pigs would have been a dead giveaway."

Vivi's lips all but disappeared as she bit back whatever she wanted to say. Finally, she pried them open again. "Is there an actual reason you stopped me? Or are you just being your usual annoying self?"

"Silly me—I was just trying to be friendly."

"Wow. Your definition of friendly is…insane."

"And *you* need to look up the definitions of *civilized, mature* and *appropriate.* What's gotten your panties all in a twist, anyway?"

Damn it. I shouldn't have brought up her panties.

The look on her face said she agreed—albeit for a different reason. "The condition of my panties is none of your concern."

That was the truth. That reminder didn't help shut down his imagination any, though. "You know, it wouldn't kill you to loosen up some. Relax a little."

"You're giving *me* advice? *You're* supposed to be my role model for lifestyle choices?" With a laugh and a snort that could only be described as disdainful, she added, "Maybe you need to look up *irony* while you've got your dictionary out."

"I think I'm doing pretty well, thank you very damn much."

That eyebrow arched up and it infuriated him.

"I can see where *you'd* think that. *My* goals, however, are a bit higher than just sex, drugs and rock and roll."

"Excuse me?"

She thought for a moment. "No. There's no excuse for you."

For the first time in his life Connor was speechless. Vivi took advantage of the moment, turning on her heel and walking away before he had a chance to gather his wits and rebut.

Vivi could be cold and cutting, and he had no idea what had flipped the switch. He'd actually thought they were making good progress today toward some mutual tolerance.

Boy, were you wrong.

This situation had just crossed into farce territory. He couldn't stop thinking about the panties of a woman who'd just as soon shoot him as look at him. And, since he appreciated and returned the sentiment, the fact he couldn't stop thinking about Vivi and her panties—and the possible lack thereof—was just insult to injury.

This wasn't a farce. It was a nightmare. The very definition of insanity.

How many days left until Mardi Gras?

CHAPTER FIVE

THREE days later, Vivi was pretty sure she was up to facing Connor again. Well, she was ready to fake it, at least.

Tonight was the Saints and Sinners jazz cruise, and the jazz cruise was corporate money night. Representatives from all the major donors would be there, supposedly to be wooed into opening up their checkbooks. In reality this was just a perk for the donors—another chance to see and be seen and get their pictures in the paper for being good corporate citizens. And she was expected to stand politely next to Connor.

I can do that. Even if it kills me.

Deep down, she was afraid it just might.

No matter how often she reminded herself how much she disliked Connor, *and* repeated her top-ten list of reasons why, she simply could not extinguish that low-grade fire in her belly that had burned all week long. It was bad enough that she couldn't seem to stop thinking about sex, but she could at least rationalize that away because, sadly, her sex life was a bit pitiful at the moment. The disturbing thing was that she couldn't stop thinking about sex with Connor, which was utterly and absolutely insane. She'd spent her entire life *not* thinking about sex with Connor because… well, it was *Connor.*

Maybe once she had small talk and donors to occupy her

thoughts, Connor would be forgotten—at least temporarily. She'd be able to make it through the evening then.

A girl can hope.

Dress, wings, shoes, glitter. She'd have to wait until she got to the boat to get dressed. There was no way she could ride in a car in those wings. There were some serious design flaws in that outfit. She'd have to grab one of the servers or someone to help, but she'd worry about that later. She grabbed a lightweight shawl because it would be chilly on the river and carried everything to the living room.

Lorelei sat on the couch, flipping through the paper. She looked up when Vivi entered. "You ready?"

There was no way Lorelei knew just how loaded that question was. "I guess."

"There's a great write-up in here about the work we did Tuesday."

"I know."

"And there's a very *interesting* picture of you and Connor."

She knew that too. What she didn't know was who had taken it. She was horrified to realize that not only had people witnessed their argument, they'd taken a picture—*and* the paper had printed it. So far no one had come forward saying they'd overheard anything, though, and she took small comfort in that much.

"What were you two fighting about anyway?"

Vivi tried to sound casual. "The shape of the earth? The color of the sky? I can't even remember," she lied.

"You're a really bad liar. You know that, right?"

To avoid eye contact, she dug for her lipstick. "He said something about me being uptight, that I needed to relax or something."

"Well, he's not wrong about that."

"Gee, thanks."

"You're running yourself into the ground."

"Between the gallery and Saints and Sinners—"

"And the dozen other organizations that lean on you to get things done, you're busy. I know. It doesn't change the fact that you're letting this town suck you dry. I know you want to be useful. I know you really want to help. But you've surpassed every goal you set out to accomplish. Everyone loves and respects you. They're in awe of you. So give yourself a break."

"I don't have time to take a break."

"Let me ask you something. Do you enjoy all the stuff that you do?"

"It's satisfying and important stuff."

"Yes, but do you *enjoy* it?"

Vivi thought for a second. The answer surprised her. "You know, not as much as I thought I would."

"That's what I suspected. Now, when was the last time you did something for yourself, just because you wanted to? Or went to a party or dinner that didn't have another purpose?"

Vivi couldn't come up with something fast enough to satisfy Lorelei.

Lorelei sighed dramatically. "See? It's Mardi Gras and this whole town is heaving with people here to party and have a good time. But not you."

"Drunken debauchery isn't my idea of a good time."

"And you know this *how?* When was the last time you were drunk or debauched?"

Never. Not even in college. There had always been the worry that it might come back to haunt her. That sounded pitiful, even to her. "I gotta go. I think I hear the car out front."

"Just think about it. You don't have to be a real saint. There's no Miss Perfect title to be won. You don't have to go full-out Sinner, either, but consider being just a little bit bad. It won't kill you. You might even enjoy it."

Like she needed something else on her plate to think about. "And when, exactly, will I fit that into my schedule?"

Lorelei put a hand to her heart and her face melted into disappointed worry. "Oh, Vivi, you're worse than I thought. This has nothing to do with a schedule. You only have one life." Then she smiled and squeezed Vivi's arm. "*Carpe diem,* girl. *Laissez les bon temps rouler.* Enjoy yourself and quit worrying so much about appearances and what other people think."

She was about to go out in public again in a set of freakin' wings. Appearances, indeed. "I'll think about it, okay?"

"I guess that's a start." Lorelei patted her arm. "Have fun tonight. Raise lots of money."

Vivi did think about it on the ride to the dock. Lorelei had a point; even she herself realized that she'd succeeded in her quest and there wasn't anything else to prove. Or anyone to really prove it to.

And for once she was very tempted. She, however, was an expert at resisting temptation. Giving in seemed weak. Anyway, if she did give in who would she be? That was the scary part.

Maybe she could take baby steps in that direction. See how it went before she committed fully.

As the car came to a stop and the driver came around to open her door Vivi shook off Lorelei's words. She had to be the current Vivi tonight and get through Saints and Sinners first.

An hour later the *Mississippi Belle* was packed to the seams as it set off, and Vivi spent far too much energy trying not to bump people with her wings. It was one thing to wear that getup at the ball, but with everyone else here in normal cocktail attire, she felt a little overdressed and awkward.

There were toasts and light snacks before the bands got into the action and people started dancing. Other than the first toast, where she had to stand next to Connor, the mingling kept them far enough apart that her embarrassment over the other day could be kept to a minimum. Connor was enough of a topic of conversation, though, to make her occasionally uncomfortable, but the heat in the room could be blamed for any tell-tale color in her cheeks.

Suddenly a buzz rippled through the crowd, and Vivi turned from her conversation with the mayor to face the stage with everyone else. "What's going on?" she whispered to the lady in front of her.

"Connor Mansfield is going to sing," the woman gushed.

She was sixty if she was a day, and Vivi felt her eyebrows go up when the woman giggled like a teenager.

Every woman alive, indeed.

Connor mounted the stage to a roar of applause. He'd removed his wings, and the black leather outfit looked far less ridiculous under the spotlights. He looked every inch the rock god, and when he sat at the piano bench Vivi got a good look at his shoulders—all oiled skin stretching over muscle as he flexed his arms and loosened up. *Mercy.* It was a mouthwatering sight.

The collective feminine sigh told her she wasn't alone in her reaction.

"I hadn't really planned on doing this tonight. Just don't tell my agent, okay? She'll expect a cut of the money," Connor joked as he ran his fingers across the keys like he was warming up. "Y'all might know this one," he said with a little smile as he started to play.

The room erupted in applause. Of course the crowd knew the song; "Whiskey and Honey" was one of his biggest hits, and it played almost constantly on the radio.

Connor leaned into the microphone and that sexy baritone filled the room.

He sat down at the bar,
And said, "Gimme what you got,
That'll numb this pain and lie to me tonight."

Vivi willed herself to smile politely and clap along, but her insides were melting. She needed something numbing herself. Connor's voice was whiskey on that low-grade fire, and the heat was building. It just wasn't fair. She'd picked the wrong night to start thinking about being a different Vivi. Damn Lorelei for putting ideas about being bad in her head. That idea kept swirling around with the other bad thoughts in her head and that was very dangerous.

She said, "Honey, what you need,
Is something we've got.
Sit right on back—"

Vivi tried to make her way to the other side of the room as unobtrusively as possible, but her stupid wings kept bumping people. Thankfully almost everyone was enthralled with Connor's performance and the interruption was shrugged off.

Then Connor launched into the chorus.

She served a little whiskey and honey.
It goes down real easy when you drink it slow.
She can stop a heart and free a weary soul.
She sang a lot like whiskey...whiskey and honey.

The whole room was singing now, and Vivi felt a stab of something between anger and jealousy. It was a nice change from the earlier confusion. This was Connor's event now. He owned it as surely as he owned the crowd. She wanted to be angry at him for grabbing the spotlight and making tonight about him, but at the same time she was jealous he was able to do it so easily. And everyone in the room was glad he did. They felt special now: the lucky few attendees at a private concert.

Think of the positives. Connor was giving the crowd what they wanted, and in return the crowd would donate money—even more than they'd originally planned.

She actually wasn't upset at Connor's showboating, or jealous of his popularity. He was right to be working the angles he had.

No, it just made her situation worse. Her personal situation. She was lusting after a man she couldn't have. Dear heaven, Connor was the one man she *shouldn't* be lusting after at all. The sound of his voice washed over her, fanning those flames and making it hard to focus on anything else.

She was pitiful. Pathetic. Insane.

She pushed open the door to the deck; getting outside would lessen the shock and sensations. The cool air helped some, but not enough.

One week down. Three to go.

She wasn't going to make it.

Three songs and his hands were burning. He was supposed to be resting them, letting the inflammation subside and heal. So much for that idea. At least he'd been able to leave it at three, turning the stage and spotlight back over to the band.

Connor held his beer in one hand, letting the cold soothe that hand some before switching and giving the other a little relief. It wasn't ideal, but it helped and did so in an unobtrusive way. The banker talking to him had no idea—which was fair, he thought, because Connor really hadn't been listening and had no idea what he was talking about.

He was dripping sweat from his performance, and the heat from the mass of bodies in the room kept him from cooling down. "Can you excuse me? I'm going to step outside and cool off."

"Sure thing. Maybe we could talk later about my idea?"

Damn. He should have listened a bit more carefully. God only knew what the banker—whose name he didn't even know—might have in mind. Thankfully he was saved from having to make even the most noncommittal of commitments by the arrival of a slightly drunk woman who stumbled over the banker and spilled her drink onto his shirt. Connor used the distraction to slip out the side door.

The air cooled him immediately and the breeze off the river helped dry the sweat. It felt good.

He wasn't the only one escaping the crowd. Small groups of people lined the railings, but it was much quieter out here. The music inside was muted by the walls, the thrumming of the engines and the splashes of the big paddle wheel. The breeze carried conversations out over the river, making the deck feel more private and isolated than it really was. Meanwhile, the lights of the city looked as lively as ever, even from this distance, and he inhaled the sights and smells of home.

He made his way toward the back of the boat, away from the windows, lest anyone inside see him outside alone and think he needed company. He threw a glance over his shoulder as he turned the corner and bumped into something. He turned quickly, and feathers hit him in the mouth.

Vivi jumped, apologizing before she'd fully turned around. When she saw it was him, the words died in an instant. She stepped away and awkwardness settled around her as he felt the tension rise. That wasn't anger, either. It was tension relating to the *other* things that had happened this week. Seemed she wasn't quite past that yet.

Oddly, neither was he. It didn't seem as cold out here now.

"Show over already?"

"Should I be insulted that you didn't stick around to listen?"

Vivi snorted. "I'm sure no one noticed *my* absence."

Like he'd been asking for the additional attention. "Why are you hiding back here?"

"It's noisy and hot inside. I needed a break, so I slipped out for a minute."

Vivi had a shawl wrapped around her, but it couldn't be doing much good, hiked up over her wings like it was. It covered her arms, but he could see her shivering. She'd been out here longer than a minute or two.

"You should go back inside. You're turning blue."

"I'm perfectly fine." Her chin lifted regally, but her chattering teeth ruined the effect.

"Seriously, you look like Angel Smurf."

Vivi set her shoulders. "Is there a reason you're out here looking for me? If not, just butt out. I'm a big girl and I'll go back inside when I'm good and ready." She'd raised her voice to a near shout, and a door opened behind them and a crew member carrying a box exited to give them a strange look before scurrying away. Vivi cleared her throat and smiled. "Thank you for your concern, but I'm good."

In other words Vivi would stand here until she began suffering from exposure just to spite him. And for some reason that pure, completely irrational stubbornness infuriated him. Connor caught the door with his foot before it closed and reached for Vivi's arm.

"What the—?" Vivi sputtered as he pulled her inside.

The door slammed with a satisfying bang. The little storage room was quiet except for the throb of the engines and nominally warmer. Her grinned at her. "At least stand out of the wind."

"You are insufferable, Connor Mansfield." She tried to move past him, but he blocked her. Her eyes narrowed dangerously. "Move, or I will kill you where you stand."

"Sorry. I can't let you be an idiot."

"What difference does it make to you?"

He paused. *Excellent question.* "If you end up in the hospital with pneumonia, you'll have to forfeit the competition."

"That's ridiculous."

"Warm up in here or go back inside. It's up to you."

"Why the hell do you care so much?"

"Because you're acting like a two-year-old instead of a grown woman."

Her jaw tightened. "But I *am* a grown woman, and therefore able to decide when I'm cold. New Orleans isn't exactly the Arctic Circle. I think I can survive a few minutes outside without frostbite."

Good Lord, were they really fighting about the temperature? He chuckled, and Vivi shot him a look.

"What's so funny?"

"You'd argue the earth was flat just because I said it was round."

Vivi's lips pressed together as the truth and ridiculousness of the situation was clarified for her. She cleared her throat and lifted her chin again. "Possibly. I do like a lively debate."

"You just like to try to prove me wrong."

She shrugged, but there was a smile tugging at her lips. "That too."

This current scene, playing out in all of its ridiculousness, proved that they really couldn't go on like this. It would make them both crazy, and it held zero appeal. "How about a cease-fire?" he said.

That got her attention in a big way, and he had no idea why.

"Excuse me?"

"Just until this Saints and Sinners thing is over. We're going to have to be around each other and the constant battling is giving me a headache."

Shock caused her jaw to drop, so he softened it with a promise.

"You can go back to hating me with a passion on Ash Wednesday."

"That rather defeats the purpose. You know that half the interest this year comes from the fact we're well-known to be adversarial."

That was true. Vivi's little showdown at the cleanup site on Tuesday had been the lead in every news item about Saints and Sinners. "I didn't say we had to become best friends. Just a small attempt at tolerance so I don't have to watch my back all the time."

Vivi seemed to find the proposition amusing for some reason, but she finally nodded. "I agree. Now, in the spirit of this cease-fire, will you please step aside?"

He bowed deep from the waist and stepped aside. "Of course."

Vivi nearly hit him with her wings again as she put her hands against the door and pushed. The door didn't open. She pushed again, harder, but nothing happened.

She turned to him. "A little help, please?"

He tried, but the door wouldn't open. A second, harder push also accomplished nothing. He cursed, and Vivi looked at him sharply.

"It can't be locked."

"It's either locked or stuck. Either way, it's not opening."

"What kind of door locks people inside?"

He was thinking the same thing. The door was smooth and blank on this side, and he couldn't locate any kind of mechanism to explain why the door wouldn't open now. "It must lock from the outside somehow."

"It wasn't locked a minute ago."

"True."

Vivi turned sharply, smacking him with her wings again. "Oh, damn it. That guy was carrying a box when he came out. I bet he came back and threw the lock."

"That's as good an explanation as any."

"This is going to be embarrassing." She thought for a minute, then sighed. "Who can you call that will come unlock the door? *Discreetly,*" she added.

"No one." At her look, he added, "I'm not exactly close friends with anyone on this boat."

That got him another sigh. "Let me think. Caroline McGee is here, and I'm pretty sure I know her number. I'll never live this down, but she'll be less likely to make a big production out of it. Can I borrow your phone?"

"Where's yours?"

"In my purse in the dining room. Why are you being difficult?"

"Because mine is in my jacket in the dining room as well."

Her eyebrows went up. "You're kidding me."

He pointed to his very tight leather pants. "No pockets."

Vivi cursed a blue streak that would have been amusing in a different situation. "Okay, this is going to be so embarrassing, but…" She made a fist and beat against the door. "*Hey! Help!* There are people trapped in here!"

He leaned against the steel wall and let her bang until she stopped and rubbed her hand. "Do you really think anyone will hear you?"

"Yes, I do."

"Everyone is at the other end of the boat. There's a band, the engine noise…"

"Then break it down." She waved a hand toward the door. "I'll pay for the damage."

"Break it down? Are you crazy?"

"Be all macho. Put your shoulder into it."

"It's a metal door, Vivi. No one's that macho."

"So we're just stuck in here?"

"People are bound to miss us eventually. We're not exactly just part of the crowd tonight. They'll come looking."

"Great. I'm going to die in a storage room." She rubbed a hand over her eyes.

"Relax. We're not going to die in here. Worst case scenario is that we have to wait until we dock and the engines are turned off. Someone will hear us shouting then."

Vivi started pacing. The wings were smacking against everything—including him—but at least she would be warming up some with the exercise.

"This is your fault, you know," she snapped.

It was his turn to sigh at her. "So much for that truce."

"That was agreed *before* you got me trapped in a freakin' closet."

"*I* didn't lock the door."

"No, but you pulled me in here. Therefore it's your fault."

He threw his hands up. "Fine. It's my fault. I'm very sorry, Vivi, and you can berate me all you like."

Vivi merely frowned at him in response.

He looked around with the vague notion there might be something in here of help, but it was just a storage closet. Boxes of dishes and glasses were stacked neatly on shelves next to bundles of cloth napkins. With no other options, he sat on the floor and leaned against the metal wall to wait.

"What are you doing?"

"Getting comfortable. You might as well have a seat."

"I'll pass, thank you." She crossed her arms and adjusted the shawl.

"The floor's not that dirty. You can even grab one of those napkins if you're worried about your dress."

Vivi shot him a withering look, and he realized the problem: her wings. The wings were hard to sit in, but it could be done. In a chair, at least. On the floor it would be impossible. "Want me to help you get your wings off?"

"No. I'll just stand."

Vivi couldn't even lean properly against something with those wings in the way. Unless, of course, she wanted to lean face-forward against the wall. Connor laughed to himself at the visual. He looked at Vivi's dress carefully, visualizing the wings' harness. Assuming hers was designed similarly to his, she'd have to strip to the waist to get them off. Her refusal made a little sense then, but he couldn't believe her modesty would go that far.

"Let me know if you change your mind."

"I will."

He kind of hoped she would. Or that she wouldn't. Being locked in a closet with Vivi—much less a half-naked Vivi—was dangerous and confusing territory. Maybe it would be best if she didn't. He would just hope they weren't stuck in here for very long.

Vivi paced and Connor stared at the walls. Time slowed to a crawl, and without a watch or his phone he had no idea how long they'd been in there. The silence and tension were palpable things, but he was bored out of his mind. "Talk about *déjà vu.*"

Vivi jumped at the break in the silence. "Excuse me?"

"Mike Delacroix's party—sophomore year. We played Seven Minutes in Heaven, remember? Although in our case, it was more like Three Minutes of Insults Followed by Four Minutes of Stony Silence." He chuckled, but Vivi's look clearly said she didn't share his amusement at the memory.

"How could I forget that? It was one of the most humiliating moments of my life."

"You've led a charmed life, then."

"Oh, shut up. I could have easily forgotten those seven minutes and lived them down if you hadn't told Julie Hebert how I threw myself at you and how awful it was."

"I did no such thing." He might have been a juvenile ass, but that was just simply untrue and he felt unfairly vilified.

"No one would believe *my* story that nothing happened, and Andy Ackerman broke up with me the next day for cheating on him."

"So *that's* what happened between you two." At her frown, he added, "You know that Julie wanted Andy for herself."

"Duh. They started going out a week later."

"Not that it makes a difference now, but I never said anything to Julie Hebert about anything. The girl was a viper."

"She still is."

"But you don't believe me?"

She shrugged, but it was tight, not casual. "As you said, it doesn't make a difference now."

"Then why bring it up?"

"*You're* the one who brought it up."

"*I* was just trying to make conversation."

She rolled her eyes again. "How 'bout them Saints?"

He took the hint. "They had a decent season. I missed most of it, of course. The NFL doesn't get a lot of airtime in Europe."

"Pity." Vivi was shifting from one foot to the other. Her legs had to be getting tired. She reached around, experimenting with the wings' position, but they didn't move much. Certainly not enough for her to get comfortable at all.

He let it continue for a few minutes before trying again. "Seriously, Vivi. Let me help you get those off."

She hesitated, and he expected another refusal.

"Fine." Her voice was pained.

It took him a second to move past the surprise that she'd agreed to his help. He levered himself up off the floor as Vivi turned her back to him. A row of hooks ran from the neckline, down her back, and ended a few inches below her waist. Vivi couldn't have gotten out of this alone if she'd wanted to. He wondered who'd gotten her into it in the first place.

He undid the three hooks above the place where her wings connected, carefully keeping his fingers away from her skin, and the shoulder straps of her dress loosened and sagged.

Vivi's hands came up to grab the bodice and hold it against her chest.

The hooks underneath the wings were harder to undo, but soon he was staring at the bare length of Vivi's spine from the wings all the way down to the lacy trim on her panties. She had a lovely back, the musculature defined without looking sharp or harsh. His fingers were an inch away from tracing that line of her spine before he caught himself. *Not a good idea. Behave like a gentleman.*

Vivi's breathing had turned shallow, causing her ribs to move only the tiniest bit with each breath. His own ribs felt too tight against his lungs, and it got even harder to breathe as Vivi pulled her arms out of the dress.

He couldn't help her get her shoulders out of the harness without touching her, and the cool softness of her skin seemed to sear his fingers. One hand clutched the fabric over her breasts as she pulled her arm through the first strap. She seemed to be holding her breath as they quickly repeated the action on the other side.

Then he released the hooks of the strap around her ribs and the wings fell into his hands. He set the wings aside as Vivi shrugged the dress straps back over her shoulders.

Red lines marred her skin, and without thinking he ran

his hands over them to soothe the pain. Vivi gasped at the touch, bringing him quickly back to his senses.

His hands were shaking like a teenager's as he quickly re-hooked the dress. Goosebumps covered her skin—from the cold or something else? he wondered. When he stepped back Vivi didn't turn around immediately, instead taking her time wrapping her shawl around her. With a casualness he didn't really feel, he returned to his former seat and tried to get comfortable again.

That was impossible, and he ended up bending his leg at the knee to camouflage the evidence that the ridiculous leather pants seemed to want to advertise.

"Thank you." Vivi's voice was as thin as air. "That feels much better."

He swallowed hard. "You're welcome."

Vivi pulled a couple of napkins off the shelf and laid them carefully on the floor. Then she sat, her back against the locked door. It wasn't an ideal position, but the only other option would be to sit next to him. At this moment he was happy she'd chosen to face him instead. She wrapped her shawl tight around her shoulders before leaning back. She wouldn't meet his eyes, focusing instead on the fringed edge of her shawl, straightening the strings into neat, precise lines.

The tension and silence were now suffocating.

How much longer until they were found?

CHAPTER SIX

EVERY breath Vivi took felt like glass cutting into her lungs. She felt drained from bouncing from emotion to emotion, but oddly electrified at the same time. It was disturbing.

Connor said he wanted her to warm up. Well, she'd accomplished that in spades. Between embarrassment and lust, she might burn to ashes long before anyone ever rescued them.

She was glad to have the wings off, glad to be able to finally sit down, but once again she was trapped in a small, enclosed space with Connor. And between the last few days of inappropriate thoughts and the touch of his hands against her skin she was primed and nearly shaking with need.

She clasped her hands together until the knuckles turned white, but she kept them in her lap where they belonged.

Connor's hands, she noted, were on his thighs, splaying out in a stretch before he curled them back into loose fists. As she watched, he did it again. She let her eyes cut to his face and saw his jaw tighten.

"Something wrong with your hands?" The words were out before she realized it.

His eyes flew to hers. "What?"

There was something in his voice, but it was a simple question so she didn't back down. "You're moving them like they're cramped or something, and you look like you're in pain."

He was quiet for a moment, examining them, then he shrugged. "It's tendonitis. I'm supposed to be resting them, not banging away like Jerry Lee Lewis."

"Then why did you play?"

An eyebrow cocked up. "Because how could I say no?"

"Easy. You say, 'No, I'm supposed to be resting my hands'."

"Gee, why didn't I think of that?"

The sarcasm caught her off guard, and it took a second for her to put the pieces together. "I see. You don't want anyone to know."

"Bingo." He clasped his hands together and let them rest in his lap. "So I'd appreciate it if you kept this information to yourself."

He seemed so serious she answered, "I will," immediately. She met his eyes to show she meant it. "But can I ask why?"

"Because."

Men. "It's an injury, not a personal failing."

"This is my career, Vivi. I don't need something—however minor it may seem—overshadowing me."

"Can't stand the shadows, can you? Gotta be the superstar."

Connor shot her an irritated look, but shrugged instead of biting back.

She regretted the words instantly. Music was Connor's life—it always had been—and now, just when he was reaping success for his work, he was facing a problem that could jeopardize that success. Being told he couldn't play music would be like asking him not to breathe. If the situation were reversed, she'd be freaking out over the possibility. She was ashamed of herself for making light of it, even for a second.

"I'm sorry. That snark was uncalled for."

"Old habits die hard."

"True. But look at it this way," she offered in her best perky voice, "*I'm* the one person you can trust not to blow sunshine up your skirt. If there was a way for me to give you grief about this, you know I'd do it in a heartbeat. But I'm coming up empty. If it's impossible for *me,* then people who actually *like* you won't be able to make anything of it either."

Connor shook his head in amused disbelief. "The fact you're right about that seems unbelievably wrong."

"See, you thought having a mortal enemy was a *bad* thing." She crossed her feet at the ankles and looked at him with all the innocence she could muster. "Any other hard truths you need hearing? I've got nothing better to do, thanks to you."

Connor's eyebrows went up. "Sounds like I owe you a hard truth or two."

Ugh. Return of high school trauma. "I'll pass, thanks."

"Scared, Vivi?"

"Hardly." She tried to wave it off like it was nothing. "I don't need you to give me a hard time. I have Lorelei for that."

Connor had the nerve to cluck at her.

I will not take the bait. It might kill her, but she wasn't opening herself up to Connor's derision. She wasn't stupid. "Any idea how long we've been in here?"

"None."

How frustrating. "You know, you'd think someone would have noticed you were missing by now."

"Just me? You're not exactly incognito tonight, Saint Vivienne."

"But you're the star attraction."

"Jealous?"

"Not at all." Oddly, she meant it. "You've earned your

adulation and all the perks that come with that. We mere mortals just do the best we can."

Connor's laugh was sharp and mocking. "'Mere mortals?' Please. Let me tell you something, since we're sharing hard truths tonight. If I have to hear one more person sing *your* praises, I just might puke."

"My praises? Yeah, right."

"'Vivi is so *giving* and *selfless* and *hardworking,*'" he gushed in a singsong voice. "'She does so *much* for the community. Don't know *what* we'd do without her…' Blah, blah, blah. I'm surprised they haven't built a freakin' statue in your honor in Jackson Square."

"Seriously?"

"Seriously. We mere mortals who lack your saintly perfection are rather sick of it."

A happy glow started in her chest. "Wow. Thanks."

"That wasn't a compliment," he grumped.

"But I'm taking it as such, and I won't let you take it back, either."

"Only you."

"Only me, what?"

Connor merely shrugged.

His attitude damped her happy glow and nearly snapped her temper. "You know, just because you don't like me, you shouldn't be so shocked that others do."

He crossed his arms over his chest. "You certainly seem shocked that folks might like *me* even though you don't."

"No, I know exactly why people like you. You're charming and glib and talented. You're also quite handsome."

"Why, thank you, Vivi."

He said it so grudgingly she wanted to smack him. "Like I said, there are plenty of reasons for people to like you. I'm just not that shallow. And I know you better than that."

"Oh, really?"

"Uh-huh. You're charming because it gets you what you want from people, and you're glib because you don't really care all that much. You're crazy talented—I won't deny that. And I know you've worked hard, so I give you proper credit there, too. I also know you can be very petty, extremely superficial and completely self-centered. Oh, and your ego is suffocatingly immense." *Wow, saying that felt good.*

"While, you, Miss Vivi, are sanctimonious and supercilious. You are dismissive to anyone or anything that doesn't meet *your* standards. And I don't know what's more insufferable—your pride or your superiority complex."

They were trading insults, but it still hurt. "You're the insufferable one. Plus, you're…mean."

"Mean?" He snorted. "Great, now we're ten years old again."

"No, when we were ten we were still sort of friends. It wasn't until puberty that you became a jerk."

"All teenage boys are jerks. It's called testosterone."

She nearly choked on her temper. "*That's* your excuse? Testosterone?"

"It's an explanation, not an excuse."

"You're such a jerk, you can't even apologize."

"Hi, Pot. I'm Kettle. I think we're on equal ground, sweetheart."

The condescending "sweetheart" broke her hold on the last strings of her temper. "Two words—Marie Lester."

"Who?"

"Wow, you don't even remember. That's pitiful." She didn't care if she sounded sanctimonious. She had reason to be. "Marie Lester—the girl from Alabama who moved here junior year."

"Oh, yeah. What about her?"

"You used me to get to her for no reason other than to stroke your ego. You made me your accomplice. And you played—" She stopped before she let the rest of that out. "That's a character flaw that can't be chalked up to testosterone."

"*That's* why you slapped me at coronation?"

"Uh-huh. You deserved it."

"And you're still stewing over that? That's some grudge you've got going on there."

"Marie was my friend, and she never forgave me."

"She moved away the next year."

"That's not the point."

"Then what *is* your point, Vivi?"

"I have yet to see any real reason to believe that's not still part of your personality. You came to me looking for a cease-fire then, too. You took me to the movies, walked me home from school…" She choked on the words. "Then I found out I was nothing more than a means to an end. And neither then nor now do you see the problem with that."

He leveled a stare at her until the silence became tense. "You're right. That was a jerk move. I will offer a blanket apology for everything that happened from the time we were twelve until we were twenty-five. Teenagers—specifically teenage boys—are a different breed. I probably was a jerk. But now that my frontal lobe is fully developed I would really like to quit being condemned based on something that happened years ago."

That was an eye-opening concession on Connor's part. Vivi was about to accept and offer an apology of her own when he opened his mouth again.

"What's your excuse, Vivi?"

He just couldn't quit while he was ahead. That was good. It worked wonders at negating all those earlier conflicting feelings and disturbing thoughts.

"I've had just about enough of this fun for tonight." Vivi pushed to her feet and banged on the door, calling for help until her hands throbbed and her throat felt scratchy. No one came. She leaned against it in defeat and let her head fall back. "This is a nightmare."

Connor stacked his hands behind his head and grinned at her. "Some women would consider being locked in with me a dream come true." Mercy, he really did look just like Satan, dangling temptation.

She closed her eyes against the sight. "They're deluded. And stupid."

"This isn't exactly my idea of a fun time either."

Vivi scrubbed her hands over her face. "God, this is going to be even worse than Mike Delacroix's party."

"*This* was an accident."

"So we *say*. We're hiding in a closet in the middle of a party. How we got locked in that closet doesn't matter beyond the humor factor. No one's going to believe that this was totally innocent, and I'm a laughingstock either way."

"You're overreacting."

"Oh, really?" His condescending nod had her fingernails digging into her palms as she kept her fists at her sides. "No one's going to believe that you dragged me in here, so I will be the assumed dragg*er* instead of the drag*ee*. If nothing happened after I dragged you into a closet, it's obvious that you're immune to my advances. Cue the laughter at my expense. If something did happen, then I'm just another one of Connor Mansfield's many groupies. Either way you win, I lose. It's tenth grade all over again. At least I don't have a boyfriend to dump me this time." She banged her head against the door gently.

"You're right, Vivi."

"Pardon me if that admission doesn't exactly fill me with the glee and satisfaction it normally would."

"We'll just tell everyone that I dragged you in here to seduce you, but you declined the offer."

"Like anyone would believe *that.*"

"You can punch me in the face. The bruise should be enough proof."

"Don't tempt me."

He stood and lifted his chin, daring her. "Go ahead. Take a shot. You can't tell me you're not dying to anyway. I'll look like a horn dog and your virtue will be redeemed."

There had to be a trap here someplace. "But why would you do that?"

"Because in the grand scheme of things one musician trying to seduce one beautiful girl really isn't news."

"Why would you decide to seduce *me?* And why now after all these years?"

There was that little smirk again. "Maybe the groupies aren't as plentiful as you seem to believe."

"Yeah, right."

"Why is it so hard to believe that I'm not *that* indiscriminate about my sexual partners?"

"Because that's not what I heard."

His jaw tightened. She'd hit a nerve. "Yeah, well a lot of people have heard that. That doesn't make it true. And the woman has been proved a liar."

"Only in that you didn't father her baby."

"I can't say for certain that I never met the woman, because I meet a lot of people, but I think I'd remember sleeping with her. Especially considering her description of the event."

"You're telling me it's inaccurate?"

"I'm not sure half of what she claimed happened is even possible. And if it is possible, it probably shouldn't be legal."

He certainly seemed sincere. "So why take the paternity test?"

"Denials weren't making it—or her—go away. Do you

know how damn hard it is to prove you *didn't* do something?"

It would be. People liked to believe the worst. Plus, Connor had no reason to lie to her, of all people. It wasn't as if he really worried about what she thought of him. Strangely, though, it made a difference to her to know he wasn't some kind of player, regardless of the rumors. She didn't like the fact that it *did* make a difference, though.

"Want to know why famous people usually date other famous people?" Connor asked.

"So you can be fabulous together?"

"No. It's self-protection in the form of mutual annihilation. When you have nothing to gain and a lot to lose, you're more likely to keep your mouth shut."

Vivi had nothing to say to that. It was a sad state of affairs, and she felt a stab of pity. It must have shown on her face because Connor scowled at her.

"It still doesn't mean anyone would believe you'd try to seduce me. I'm not famous, and everyone knows you don't even like me," she said.

"But who would blame me for trying? Vivi LaBlanc is the city's sweetheart. Smart, beautiful…saintly. Sexy. People would question my masculinity if I didn't at least try, right?"

There was a bit of snark behind the words, but not enough to completely counter the funny effect they had on her insides. She tried to ignore them. "You're laying it on pretty thick, don't you think?"

His voice dropped a notch. "You're assuming none of it is true. And I can be very convincing when I need to be. You'll be the envy of half the women in the city, yet retain the respect of all."

A shiver ran over her. "Except for the ones who'll think I was stupid to pass up the chance."

"Well, we all must live with regrets."

Connor's voice was hypnotic, and his eyes were hooded as they roamed over her. It would be too easy forget it was part of the overall act, the cover story to salvage her pride.

"You are beautiful, Vivi. Your hair… Your eyes… Your skin." His fingers followed his words. "Your mouth—including that sharp tongue—is enough to drive a man crazy." Connor's lips quirked up. "In more ways than one, that is."

Those talented fingers traced over her shoulder and down her arm. Tingles danced across her skin and her blood felt thick in her veins. It might not be real, but her body didn't know the difference and her mind was happy to play along ignorantly. The air felt close and heavy, and she couldn't hear the engines above the thudding of her own pulse. She watched the rise and fall of Connor's chest as the weight of his stare and the silence built to a crushing level that made her knees weak.

Connor leaned forward, his chest barely brushing hers each time they breathed, and his head dropped until his lips were level to her ear. The slight breeze of his breath over the lobe sent a shiver arcing all the way to her core as a hand snaked around her waist to her lower back, edging her closer. The hard lines of Connor's body seared into hers. The air turned thick, each breath filling her lungs with his scent.

"You could tempt a saint, Vivi, much less a simple sinner like me. Resistance is a battle. One I'm not sure I want to win." He paused, letting the words hang, and her hand floated up of its own accord to land on his chest. The muscle leapt at her touch and she could feel the thump of his heart against her palm. An ache started to build in her core.

"Ready to punch me now?"

The words were a bucket of cold water that doused the rising heat and left shame in its place. She shoved him away.

Connor stumbled and caught himself on the wall. Righting himself, he shook like a wet dog and focused on her face. "You were supposed to hit me. A shove won't leave a bruise."

"Just shut up." She swallowed hard. She'd never hit another human being before, didn't think she'd be capable of it, but Connor might be the one to change all of that. Not because of what he'd done, but because of her reaction to it.

She took a deep breath, but whether it was to calm herself or prepare herself to berate him she'd never know, because cold air rushed in as the door opened. The same crew member from earlier stood there with his mouth open. The shock seemed to ricochet off the metal walls.

Connor recovered first. "We thought you'd never come back."

"I j-just needed to get some glasses…" He started to step back outside.

Vivi scanned the deck behind him. Empty. Thankfully it was just the three of them. No one else was there to witness this. She cleared her throat and smiled at the gaping man. "Connor and I stepped in here to speak privately out of the wind, not realizing you'd be back to lock the door. We've been shouting, but no one could hear us."

His face reddened. "I'm *so* sorry, Miss LaBlanc, Mr. Mansfield."

"Not as sorry as we are." Connor grinned at the young man. "But no harm, no foul. We won't mention this if you won't."

The threat was subtle, but the young man caught it and nodded. "Of course. I appreciate it. I don't want to get into trouble with the captain."

Connor grabbed Vivi's wings and held the door for her to step through. The man stood there, probably in shock, but possibly a little starstruck too, as they left. The wind had picked up while they were locked away, and it blew Vivi's hair into her face. While that would normally be annoying, Vivi didn't try to right it. It meant she didn't have to look at Connor.

"You go on inside," he said as they walked. "I'll follow in a minute or two. If anyone asks, don't deny you were with me. Just don't say where. If that guy decides to talk later, a denial you were ever with me will make you look guilty." She nodded, and he handed her the wings. "Don't worry. I don't think it's going to be a problem. And if it becomes one, we'll just go back to the other plan."

"You're serious?"

"Vivi, I never say anything I don't mean. Now, go."

The noise of the party seemed ten times louder after being in that closet for so long. But no one gave her a second glance as she left her wings by the door and went to the bar for a glass of water. People spoke to her as she made her way through the crowd, but it was the same basic chatter. No one seemed to have noticed she and Connor had been rather conspicuously absent at the same time. Relief rushed through her as she pushed open the door to the ladies' room and checked her reflection. Other than a slight pinkness to her cheeks and a rather chaotic hairstyle—both of which could be chalked up to the wind on deck—nothing looked amiss.

I never say anything I don't mean. She thought about everything Connor *had* said and the statement began to sound vaguely ominous—if only because of her reaction to his words. Just replaying those moments in her mind had her nipples tightening against the silk lining of her dress and her thighs clenching in anticipation.

This is not good. Not good at all.

She pressed a hand to her belly to calm the butterflies there. She might not have a public problem, but she sure as hell had a private one.

* * *

They'd been locked in that closet for over an hour. It had felt like a lifetime, but with several hundred people on board—and the flow of cocktails probably helped—no one had found it noteworthy that neither he nor Vivi had been seen for a while. Everyone had just assumed the two of them were someplace else—not necessarily together, because…well, why *would* they be? Connor didn't bother to correct any assumptions.

When they finally docked, he and Vivi were forced back into the shared spotlight in a reverse receiving line. Though they were side by side, Vivi kept her attention on the guests, barely throwing a single glance his way.

Then, with a simple "See ya," Vivi followed the last guest down the gangplank.

Normally Connor wouldn't have given it a second thought, but Vivi had been in his thoughts a lot recently. And after tonight… Well, Vivi was pretty much all he could think about, and none of it made any sense at all.

The chauffeur dropped him in front of Gabe's building. There had been huge crowds of revelers on Bourbon, but the crowds were thinner here, and most of the people were either too intoxicated or too focused on their own good time to pay him any notice at all.

Good, because I'm really not in the mood tonight.

The kind of mood he was in was easy to pinpoint and name. His whole body thrummed with want, but it was a specific want. *Vivi.* And that didn't make any sense at all.

Why now? Why after all these years did he suddenly have the hots for Vivi LaBlanc? He'd crossed a line tonight, taken everything a step too far, and the next thing he knew he'd had Vivi in his arms, just seconds from kissing her.

While he tried to remind himself that Vivi was his self-proclaimed mortal enemy, she'd certainly shown a new side of herself to him tonight—in between insults, at least. And when he tried to remind himself that he didn't like Vivi—had never liked Vivi—his body was quick to argue that wasn't entirely true. Her confession that had stopped just short of admitting that she might have had different feelings toward him once upon a time didn't help either.

The normal litany of reasons he could usually recite failed him. Insanity was the only explanation that made sense.

He dropped his keys on the table and propped his wings against the wall. At least he wouldn't have to wear this outfit again until Fat Tuesday. Grabbing a beer from the fridge, he drank half of it in one long swallow as he went to the bathroom and pulled off the leather pants and vest. A long, slightly cooler than normal shower helped him clear his head and focus, but it did nothing to take the edge off.

Sleep was out of the question, so he pulled on a pair of sweats and went to the kitchen for another beer. He could see himself needing several tonight. And if the mental replay couldn't be stopped, he'd need another, much colder shower soon.

The intercom buzzed loudly in the silence. It was most likely a lost tourist or random drunk, but he answered anyway.

"It's Vivi."

His hand slammed the release button before the words were even completely out of her mouth. He didn't bother to question why she'd suddenly appeared, didn't really care. The jolt to his system caused by her voice honed that earlier dull edge to painful sharpness. As he opened the door to the stairwell, he heard the outside door close and the sounds of feet on the stairs. It was the sound of a slow climb, but a purposeful one. When Vivi rounded the last landing she looked up and saw him. Her feet seemed to stall, and she climbed the last flight at a snail's pace, not quite holding eye contact, but not staring at her feet either. She'd changed from the satin column of her Saint costume into jeans and a battered jacket zipped up to her neck.

She blew her hair out of her face. "Thanks for letting me in. I wasn't sure you would."

"It's one o'clock in the morning. I couldn't leave you standing on the street." That was a good enough explanation. And until he knew her reason for coming by in the middle of the night…

Connor realized he was holding his breath.

On the top stair, Vivi stopped, and he noticed her knuckles turning white as her fingers gripped the banister. She was totally still, except for the rapid rise and fall of her chest. Out of breath from the climb? Or…?

She didn't move, so Connor didn't either. He stayed in the doorway, leaning against the door frame. The silence stretched out. Finally he couldn't take it anymore. "Why are you here, Vivi?"

Vivi's eyes flew to his. *Damn.* That came out sharper than he'd intended. Then that flush began to climb out of the collar of her jacket again.

"I—I don't really know." She sighed, and he thought he heard a small curse. "You know, I probably shouldn't have come. I'm sorry I bothered you."

She turned and started slowly back down the stairs.

Let her go. It's really better to just— Even as he was thinking the thoughts his feet were moving, closing the space between them, and he was at the top of the stairs before she'd taken more than a couple.

"Vivi."

She turned, and he held out his hand. It was her choice. He couldn't make it for her, but she'd come this far and he felt like he needed to meet her halfway. She hesitated, then put her hand in his.

He hauled her up the last few stairs and pulled her body

against his. He could feel her tension, but their bodies seemed to fit together like puzzle pieces and the sensation was electric.

Vivi's eyes widened at the contact, and he knew she felt the same electricity. She swallowed hard, then he felt the slow slide of her chest against his as she rose up on her toes and aligned her mouth evenly with his.

There was the smallest moment of hesitation—one breath's worth—and then her lips touched his.

He never knew what to expect from Vivi, and this was no different. Her mouth was pliant and warm, but cautious, gently moving against his.

Every rational thought shouted at him to stop. This was Vivi, and he had no business kissing her. He shouldn't want to.

But he couldn't have stopped if he tried. She tasted fresh, sweet and, God help him, *right.* Her tongue slid past his lips, and the tentative touch awakened something primal inside him, beating down all the rational thoughts until he couldn't imagine not kissing her.

Vivi's fingers threaded through his hair as his hands splayed over her back, pulling her weight onto his chest, and he felt the change in her as the kiss turned carnal and needy.

Without breaking contact, he backed up the few feet into the apartment and let the door swing closed. The sound punctuated the moment as a point of no return. He couldn't say what exactly had changed between them, or when or why, but the wall had been crumbling and the kiss had reduced it to rubble. It defied reason, but it somehow made perfect sense.

"Vivi—"

She stopped him by pressing a finger against his lips, and he lost his train of thought when those blue eyes met his.

The clear evidence of desire he saw there just threw gasoline on to the bonfire.

She swallowed hard and her voice was barely above a whisper. "Could we not…actually…talk? I'm about to lose my nerve, and I really don't want to."

He should follow up, not just let that statement slide, but Vivi was kissing him again, and nothing else seemed to matter.

Vivi didn't want to think, didn't want to examine this too closely, because if she did, she'd realize what a fool she was. She just hadn't been able to shake his words or the feelings those words evoked. Coupled with the echoes of Lorelei's words—*Carpe diem. Be bad.*—she'd been showered and changed and on her way before really thinking it all the way through. Her nerve had nearly failed her a dozen times on the short walk from her house to here, but now…

She couldn't regret the decision. She might not be able to say why she'd made that choice, but something about the feel of Connor's mouth on her neck, the caress of his hands under her jacket to the small of her back…it felt good. There was something liberating in this—more than just seizing the day. It was new and scary territory for her, but it felt right, too.

And it felt *good.* Connor's hands were truly talented, alternating between feather-light touches that sent shivers over her to strong caresses that left her knees weak. She might as well let go. It wasn't like Connor was a stranger, even if he wasn't what she'd call a friend. That strange place they inhabited with each other seemed perfect for exactly this.

It shouldn't make sense, but it sort of *did.* Vivi didn't care. Connor had answered the door shirtless, and the skin under her hands felt as good as it looked. The heat seeped through her jacket and shirt to warm her skin. She wanted more, though, not just warmth.

As if he was able to read her mind, Connor slid the zipper

of her jacket down and pushed it off her shoulders. She felt her T-shirt rising until it stopped at her breasts. She lifted her arms as Connor broke their kiss long enough to sweep the shirt over her head. The cool rush of air over her skin was fleeting as Connor pulled her immediately back against his chest. The contact was shocking, yet Vivi wanted more, and she melted into him.

Her lips traced the ridge of muscle from his shoulder to his neck and Connor growled, the rumble vibrating through her from lips to toes. The world suddenly shifted, making her head spin, but Connor had carried her halfway down the hall before it fully registered, and a second later she felt cool sheets under her.

Connor loomed over her, those powerful arms bracketing her shoulders, holding him solid and steady, his eyes hot on her body and face. When he finally met her gaze she realized he was giving her one last chance to end this before it was too late.

She hooked a foot around his leg and slid it over his calf. She let her hands trace the planes of Connor's chest and felt the tightening of the muscles under her fingers. "It's already too late," she whispered.

The corner of Connor's mouth curved up. "But I've only just begun."

Her blood took his words as a promise, surging through her veins. And Connor made good on that promise, exploring every inch of her with unhurried, methodical intensity until she was whimpering and incoherent. She wanted to bring him to the same place, but her hands were fisted in the sheets as she tried to hang on to the last shreds of her sanity.

Not an inch of her skin went unmapped by his hands, then by his lips and tongue and teeth. He held her at the edge until she wanted to beg, but she couldn't find the words.

Connor was shaking, holding on to his control by mere

strings in danger of breaking at any moment. Vivi felt like a flame under his hands—hot and alive and dangerous. Her responses were raw, honest and almost more than he could handle without combusting himself as well. She seemed designed expressly for him: her curves slotted perfectly against him, her skin responded to his touch, demanding more. Vivi's hands contained electricity. Her mouth… Her mouth did things to him that defied words.

The need to take her, lose himself in her, was overwhelming, and only the sting of Vivi's nails biting into his shoulders kept him grounded as he slid into her. Hot… Tight… Wet…The sensations fogged his brain.

Then Vivi was arching into him, pressing her hips hard against his, seeking more, searching for the rhythm. His hands fisted in her silky hair and Vivi scored tracks down his back. His mouth landed on hers as he quickened the pace, and he felt the tremors building until she broke.

The contractions and shudders of her orgasm pushed him over the edge himself, and the world dimmed at the edges.

He vaguely realized he'd shouted her name.

CHAPTER SEVEN

VIVI lay facedown in the bed. She hadn't moved other than to brush the hair out of her face since she'd rolled away from him. Her breathing had evened out and returned to normal, but beads of sweat still pooled in the indentation of her spine. Connor wasn't much for *was-it-good-for-you?* pillow talk, but Vivi's complete and continuing silence seemed odd. Finally she sighed and rolled to her side to face him. Her brow was furrowed slightly.

"Deep thoughts, Vivi?"

"I'm not really capable of higher brain functions yet."

He'd take that as a compliment, but he was in a similar state. "That explains your silence."

"Actually, that just seemed…" She laughed quietly. "Prudent."

"Prudent?"

"It's an awkward enough situation, and we're not real good at talking without it denigrating into something else at the best of times. I'm not keen on the idea of arguing with you while I'm naked."

"You do have a point."

That earned him a smile. "Plus, it would kind of kill the afterglow, you know?"

"Well, I kind of suck at the afterglow chitchat anyway."

"See? Silence seemed the best bet."

"I think I'm slightly offended," he teased.

"Why?"

"Sex but no talking? Just using me for my body?"

"The tables may have turned, but you have to have more experience in this situation. And you just said you suck at the chitchat anyway."

He tried to keep his voice light. "It doesn't mean that I'm happy to be your boy toy for the night."

Vivi rolled her eyes. "Don't pretend you're that fragile."

"I'm a musician. I'm artistic and sensitive, you know."

She snorted. "I work with artists every day. I'm not likely to swallow that line."

"You're a hard woman, Vivi." He rubbed a hand over his face.

"I try." She smiled at him.

"That wasn't a compliment."

"Coming from you? Of course not. But I'm going to take it as one anyway."

The relaxed mood evaporated and he felt the usual tension building. It was at odds with the lingering scents of sex and sweat. "Because you want to be a hard-ass?"

Vivi pushed to a seated position and dragged the sheet up to cover her breasts. "Boy, you really do suck at this part."

"Maybe we should have stuck with the silence." His languorous, sated mood was giving way to a headache. He dropped his head back onto the pillow and draped an arm over his eyes. Vivi equaled trouble. Always.

"I tried to tell you."

"But what you haven't told me is why."

"I just did. I don't want to fight, so talking—"

"I get that." He levered himself up onto his elbows. "Why are you even here? Your feelings toward me are pretty clear, so why on earth are you in my bed?"

Vivi was quiet for a moment. "I could ask you something similar."

His pride answered for him. "What kind of man turns down sex?"

"What kind of man accepts sex from a woman he doesn't like?" she shot back.

"What kind of woman offers sex to a man she hates?"

The sharp intake of breath told him he'd hit the mark. Vivi's jaw tightened. "I knew I shouldn't have come. I should have just stayed in a cold shower until the urge passed. Or should've just kept drinking until I forgot."

"As someone who was doing both of those things when you showed up…"

She held up a hand. "Maybe now's a good time for me to leave." She edged toward the end of the bed, pulling the sheet with her as she went. "I'd say to just forget this ever happened, but I'll settle for you not bringing it up in public."

"Ashamed of yourself, Vivi?"

He caught the stiffening of her shoulders, the telltale flush of pink across the tops of her breasts. She shot him a dirty look and that supercilious eyebrow went up again. "Well, aligning myself with thousands of other groupies isn't something I'm going to put on my résumé, you know."

Argh. "What is this obsession you have with groupies?"

"Because I've seen you charm people and I prided myself on being immune to it. And then…" She swung her legs off the bed and stood, seemingly unaware or uncaring of the fact she was gloriously naked.

"Then what?"

"Then I spent time with you this week, and I started to think that maybe I wasn't completely right about you. That you'd changed or matured. I fell for it—again—and I shouldn't have." Vivi squatted, sorting through the piles of discarded clothing. "I'm going to kill Lorelei," she muttered.

That was a bit of a non sequitur. "I'm afraid to ask what Lorelei has to do with any of this."

"Nothing. This was a mistake. I shouldn't have come, so I'll just go. I'm really sorry." Her words degraded into mumbles, but he could pick up the occasional "stupid" and "insane." He couldn't be sure which one of them she was referring to.

She was right, though. They should just forget this ever happened. But he didn't want her to leave. Even though she infuriated him, his body was still primed for her touch. The edge was off, but the need was still there. How had they gotten to this point?

"Vivi, wait."

"What?"

Vivi had swallowed her pride to come here; he not only appreciated that, he understood how much it had cost her. He should—and could—offer her something in return. He crossed the space and captured her face between his hands. Her eyes widened as he leaned in and kissed her.

"I've wanted to do that since eighth grade."

"You're kidding me."

"Nope."

"Then why didn't you?"

"Because I didn't want my bleeding head handed back to me."

Vivi's lips twitched at the image.

"I've never been a glutton for abuse."

"You like to hand it out, though. At least to me."

"I could say the same about you."

That statement sent Vivi's eyebrows to her hairline, and he knew once she recovered from the shock she'd be back at his throat again. Right now he really just wanted her to come back to bed.

"I asked you for a truce earlier tonight, and it was a serious offer." *Especially now.*

"Forgive and forget? Bygones and all that?"

"The apology was also sincere. Why don't we just decide that the statute of limitations for childhood and teenage idiocy has expired and go forth acting like grownups."

"That sounds very mature." Her lips twitched. "It might be a hard habit to break, though."

"Any current idiocy can still be game. Just not old grudges."

The last of the hostility drained out of her. "I think I can agree to that."

"Glad to hear it."

Vivi looked at the clothes she held in her hands. "Now I don't know what to do."

He took the shirt she was holding and dropped it to the floor. "I'd like it if you stayed."

He sounded like the lyrics to one of his songs. It was embarrassing, but Vivi's cautious "Really?" made it worthwhile. It was a strange feeling—one he didn't understand or care to explore right now, though. His body was already recovering, simply from being this close to her.

"Eighth grade, remember?"

Vivi's smile was seductive. She stepped closer and placed a hand on his chest. The smile got bigger as she looked up at him. "You had braces in eighth grade."

"So did you."

"At least we won't have to worry about getting them locked together."

The clock beside the bed ticked closer to four. Connor was snoring softly beside her, one arm thrown over her stomach, but Vivi couldn't sleep. She was sated and exhausted; every muscle in her body felt like pudding, but her brain just wouldn't turn off and let her sleep. Not that her brain was working properly by any stretch of the imagination; it jumped from topic to topic like a flea on speed, unable to process any thoughts beyond the superficial and not following any kind of logical progression.

It was frustrating, but it was probably self-defense. Thinking too much about the last week—much less the last few hours—might cause her head to explode.

She eased out from under Connor's arm. He rolled over but didn't wake up, and she exhaled in relief. Her clothes were still a tangled mess, so she grabbed one of Connor's shirts hanging off a chairback and slipped it on. The scent of Connor's aftershave drifted up as she buttoned it.

On tiptoes, she crept into the living room. She knew the apartment well; Gabe Morrow had bought all of the art on the walls from her gallery and she'd been here many times, delivering or helping to hang. Although Connor was a temporary tenant, he'd made himself at home and his things were scattered throughout the room—it wasn't untidy, but it showed Connor was comfortable here.

But there was nothing personal—no photos or anything like that. It underscored the fact that she didn't really know much about the man Connor was now. And it also reminded her that his stay was temporary. *That* made all of this a little easier to understand, at least.

The biggest change to the apartment was the baby grand piano that now sat close to the balcony doors. Had Connor had one brought in for himself? To the best of her knowledge Gabe didn't play, but that didn't mean he hadn't decided to get a piano anyway. It would make sense that Connor would want or need a piano in whatever accommodations he took, but now that she knew he was nursing an injury, having a piano here seemed like it would be a temptation or a distraction.

She smoothed a hand over the lacquered lid. Connor's parents had a piano in the front parlor—an old upright that half the kids in the neighborhood had banged on until Connor discovered his passion and put it off-limits so they didn't knock it out of tune. Even she'd tinkered on the keys as a child while her mother and Mrs. Mansfield had coffee in another room. As she'd gotten older, she'd been able to sit in her room and hear Connor practicing next door, mastering everything from Chopin to Count Basie to Billy Joel.

She sat on the bench and ran her hands lightly over the keys without making a sound. She traced the shapes and the edges with her fingers, not really wanting to think about the repercussions of what she'd just done, but unable to escape it.

Against all good judgment she'd let her libido bring her here tonight, and that had worked out pretty well, making her now question her judgment in general. Letting go of all that adolescent angst was an excellent idea—in theory, at least. It was a shame, though, that she hadn't done that *before* she'd shown up at his door like she was desperate for his body.

Did she feel better? Definitely. Lorelei might have had a point about the joys of being bad after all. All the tension seemed gone from her body, if not her mind. If this was what being bad was all about, she now understood the appeal. How something could feel right and wrong at the same time, though, was a conundrum her brain just couldn't process. Had she used him? Had he used her? Was it really possible that years of angst and anger could disappear just like that? Was she being shallow, falling under the allure of Connor Mansfield? No, that much she was sure of. Whatever she'd done, whatever this was, it had nothing to do with who Connor was other than just himself.

Like that hadn't proved tempting enough.

But why had it happened *now* instead of five or ten years ago?

Maybe things just had their own timelines, and she shouldn't question it. Tonight felt momentous—and not just because of the toe-curling experiences she'd discovered in Connor's bed. No, she felt on the edge of something—like she'd left a part of herself behind and was moving into something new.

But that something new wouldn't—couldn't—involve Connor. He wasn't a permanent kind of guy.

How many women had Connor made the papers with? It was a veritable *Who's Who* of celebrity singles—all of them beautiful, powerful and talented—but none of them had lasted longer than a month or so. The idea of a fling had never appealed to her, though; it just wasn't something she thought she'd do. Now she seemed to be in one, and while she didn't quite understand it, she was okay with it. Connor might not be a permanent kind of guy, but he seemed to bring about excellent transitions.

Vivi felt more than heard Connor behind her, and a second later she felt his hands stroking her hair. Leaning back, she let her weight rest against Connor's thighs as he ran those long fingers through her hair, removing the tangles. She wanted to purr. Obviously her libido wasn't done with her yet.

"Do you play, Vivi?"

She shook her head. "Just 'Chopsticks.' Badly, I might add."

Connor scooted her forward on the bench and moved in behind her, his chest pressed against her back, his naked thighs surrounding hers. The muscles in those thighs felt like iron and the crisp hairs tickled her skin. His hands slid under hers, lining them up from fingers to elbows as he began to play slowly.

"I thought you were supposed to be resting your hands."

"Shh." His breath moved the hair at her temple.

It was a simple but beautiful string of notes, and as long as she remained still and relaxed, her hands moved with his.

And now that she knew exactly how talented Connor's hands were, watching him play seemed intensely erotic, and feeling him play under her hands made it all the more intimate.

Too intimate. Too intense.

She let her hands slide off his and into her lap.

Connor's fingers changed direction and tempo, and the string of notes turned into a melody. The muscles in his forearms flexed, and she could feel his chest and shoulders moving against her like a massage.

And then he began to sing quietly, his voice just inches above her ear.

Oh, it's raining,
Outside her window, inside her soul.

His voice. *Mercy.* It was a shot of straight sex, but served with a side of emotion that reverberated through her. She let her hands slide over the thick muscle of his thighs and heard the quick catch of his breath.

And her blue eyes,
Just keep cryin',
While she remembers a love untold.

The music died abruptly when Connor's hands came to rest on hers again, twining their fingers together and tracing them along the seams where his thighs met hers.

"I'm not familiar with that song."

Connor's chin rested on her shoulder and his breath moved across her neck. "It's just something I've been working on."

"It's beautiful."

She felt his shrug. "It's different. We'll see how it goes over."

"It'll be a hit. Just like the others."

"That's the hope."

"Hope? You're Connor freakin' Mansfield."

"The public is fickle. That's why there are so many one-hit wonders."

He released her hands. One arm snaked around her waist, his thumb brushing lightly over the bottom of her ribs. The other went back to the keyboard where he started to play again, soft and slow. She recognized the top-line melody of one of his early songs.

"You never know when they'll turn on you."

Connor sounded…almost vulnerable. Worried. That was ridiculous. Why would he be? Or had the sordid and tawdry headlines affected him more than he allowed others to know? "Your fans love you."

"They love an idea. An image. That Connor has little to do with me personally."

"And who's that Connor?" She was almost afraid to ask, but the quiet and the dark created an intimacy of the moment that lent itself to deep questions.

She felt his smile against her cheek. "Interestingly enough, I'd say it was the same Connor you dislike so much."

That didn't make sense. The arrogance, the swagger, the lady-killing charm. The confidence… She, too, had been reacting to that—negatively, of course—but now that they'd called their truce she was realizing and remembering everything else she knew about Connor. How kind he'd been to Lorelei when she was deep in her crush on him years ago. How serious he was about this competition—and not just to beat her. She thought shamefully about some of her own motivations. How hard he'd practiced, even amid the taunts of boys more interested in touchdowns than Tchaikovsky. How ready he'd been to put the past behind them.

Had she been judging him unfairly? Using her own adolescent grudges and his recent notoriety to prevent her from seeing Connor as a person?

Connor was far more complex than she'd realized or given him credit for. Consciously at least. The fact none of this surprised her meant she'd known it all along and just refused to recognize it. Wow, she *was* shallow.

No. Everything had been such a roller coaster since that closet door slammed shut, and in retrospect she'd gotten glimpses into Connor that had led her here tonight. *Great.* That just made tonight even more complicated. Maybe her subconscious was smarter than she gave it credit and that was why it had let her libido push her here. To force her to think. Damn it, she didn't want to think. Wasn't not thinking the whole point of *carpe diem?*

Vivi put her right hand on the keyboard and tried to remember the notes Connor had played earlier. As she stumbled around Connor began pointing to the correct keys. After a few tries she had sixteen counts' worth.

"Just repeat that phrase. Same tempo."

Connor's left hand began a much more complicated set, playing perfectly off her few notes, yet it was completely different than the earlier tune. It was incredible not only to witness but to be a part of. She played the last note, and Connor ended with a flourish.

She dropped her hands back into her lap and, surprisingly, Connor's followed. He ran his fingers gently over her wrists and arms.

"That's amazing, Connor." She felt him shrug in response. "I mean it. I felt like I was actually playing something."

"You were."

"With help, though."

"That doesn't mean you weren't part of it."

But Connor was a solo act. Still, there was something wonderful about being inside his arms as he played. The sensation of feeling him create the music… It was silly, but she wanted him to play something else. She was about to ask when she remembered he was supposed to be resting his hands.

There was a slight pang of disappointment, but it was quickly routed when Connor placed a feather-light kiss on her neck. His hands moved from her arms to the buttons of her borrowed shirt, opening them and sliding inside to caress her lower stomach and tease her breasts. His movements became more focused, his thumb rasping across her nipple, wringing a gasp from her and causing her to grip his thighs for purchase. Vivi could feel his erection hardening against her back, and her breath picked up as his did. She arched, pressing her breast into his hand when a finger slipped between her legs and slid inside.

Just like that the switch was flipped, and Vivi's focus narrowed sharply. She opened her legs wider, quietly demanding more, and Connor obliged, whispering encouragement between pressing hot kisses against her neck and shoulders.

With a groan, Connor turned her around, wrapping her legs around his waist, and leaned her back against the piano. Her elbows hit the keyboard, making an off-key chord, as Connor flicked the rest of the buttons out of their holes and spread the edges of her shirt wide.

A big hand slid up her torso, over her chest and neck, before circling around her nape to tangle in her hair. His eyes were hooded as he examined the freckles sprinkled across the tops of her breasts. A tug pulled her fully into his lap again, where the crisp hairs on his chest tickled her nipples as his mouth claimed hers. A surge of those powerful thighs had him on his feet, and Vivi clung to him as he carried her back to the bedroom and collapsed onto the bed.

She had no idea what she was doing. It scared her not to know what this was. But it didn't scare her enough to stop, because whatever this was, it was good. She'd sort out the rest later.

Connor had vague memories of Vivi kissing him as the first weak rays of sunshine began to lighten the curtains. He didn't realize it had been a goodbye kiss until the alarm went off and he woke to find her side of the bed empty and cold. He wasn't quite sure what to make of her sneaky departure, but since their first attempt at post-coital conversation had ended in her nearly walking out, he was almost relieved not to have to deal with the possible awkwardness this morning.

Almost.

Two hours later, he was seated between the director of the local humanities council and the director of an after-school program at a brunch meeting of the city's non-profit organizations. His mom was seated across from him, but she was there in her capacity as the current chair of…something. He couldn't remember which of the many organizations she was involved with. The broader purpose of the meeting was to discuss fundraising in general, but half the people in the room had known him since he was a child, which made this a little surreal, to say the least.

Vivi was about five chairs down, and other than a very quick greeting when she hadn't quite met his eyes, they hadn't spoken two words to each other. Everyone seemed very careful to keep them apart and refrained from talking to him about Vivi—which only took this to new levels of surrealism, because that *never* happened. But every now and then he heard someone say her name or heard her laugh. This was Vivi's element; she knew every single person here—as a contributing adult, unlike him—and she had probably worked with most of them at some point.

He might have been imagining it, but Vivi seemed to be avoiding him even more than usual. Either she was over-compensating, so as not to give away their activities of the previous evening, or she was having serious regrets. Either way, it irked him.

He kept half an eye on her, noting how she kept stifling yawns as the meal concluded. Once the mingling began, he eventually ended up close enough to actually speak to her—except that there were seven other people standing with them. Vivi looked distinctly uncomfortable, and she'd probably bolt if given the opportunity. She still wouldn't meet his eyes, and he was seconds from pulling her aside and finding out what the problem was.

But Dr. Robins, the head of an inner-city free clinic, put a stop to that plan. "So, how was last night?"

It took Connor a second to figure out what the man was talking about. Damn, the jazz cruise seemed like it had happened *days* ago. "It was very nice. I haven't done one of those riverboat cruises in years." Seeing his opening, he turned to Vivi. "What about you? Did you enjoy yourself last night, Vivi?"

The mimosa in Vivi's hand sloshed dangerously close to the rim as she jumped, but she recovered quickly. She shot him a warning look. "I did, thank you. Very much." Then the corner of her mouth twitched. "It's funny. I wasn't sure that I would, but I was very pleasantly surprised."

It was very hard to keep his amusement in check and his face neutral. "Glad to hear it. You left so quickly once we docked I wasn't sure."

"I was tired and wanted to get home. Plus, I didn't want Lorelei to wonder where I was."

That made sense. Since none of the people around them understood the subtext, he decided to push a little harder. "It was quite a busy evening, wasn't it? So many different things happening. What was your favorite part, Vivi?"

Her cheeks turned a little pink. "There's so much to choose from. But you're quite good on the piano, and I found myself enjoying that more than I thought I would."

He was going to ask her something else, but a woman he didn't know spoke first.

"You played for the guests last night? How wonderful for them."

Great. Vivi shot him a smile that told him she'd done that on purpose. "Just a couple of songs to help the party along."

"There's a piano here. Maybe you could play for us?"

Vivi answered before he could. "He can't." All eyes swiveled in her direction.

She wouldn't. "Vivi..."

"It's not fair, Connor." Her voice took on that clipped, chilly tone he knew so well. "You have this great talent, and it makes me look me look bad when you keep showing off like that." She turned to the crowd. "I'm doing everything I can to keep up as it is. He has an unfair advantage, you know. Don't encourage him."

He wanted to kiss her. She could have let him try to get out of it himself, but she hadn't. Vivi was actually watching his back. An unfamiliar feeling spread through his chest, and as the conversation turned, he smiled his thanks at Vivi. She nodded.

Vivi was pulled away a moment later by her mother, and when the event finally broke up a little while later, Vivi was nowhere in sight. That irritated feeling returned. Could he have misread or misunderstood something? He didn't like that idea.

"Mr. Mansfield?"

Connor turned to find a pretty hostess flashing a flirtatious smile at him.

"You had a phone call earlier. A Miss White left a number for you to return her call." She handed him a piece of paper and her brow wrinkled in confusion. "It's strange. I think she said it was about piano lessons, but that just seems crazy considering…well, who you are."

Heat rushed to his groin at the mention of "piano lessons." "Thanks. It makes sense to me."

He put his mother into a cab in almost unseemly haste, and started walking the six blocks back to the Quarter, dialing as he walked. Vivi answered on the second ring.

"You are terrible, Connor Mansfield."

"Where are you?"

"The gallery. I couldn't stay at the brunch. Between Madeline Jensen's upset that I wouldn't let you play and the fact you seemed to be doing your best to embarrass me…"

"That's what you get for sneaking out before I woke up."

"I was hoping it would be less awkward that way."

Vivi didn't seem to be feeling that awkwardness now. "And avoiding me?"

"Self-preservation."

"You are hell on the ego, Vivi."

"I think your ego can handle it. So…" She trailed off, and the silence was so complete he wondered if the call had been dropped. Then he heard her clear her throat. "So what happens now?"

The awkwardness was back. He'd never heard her sound so hesitant. "I thought you wanted piano lessons."

There was another of those long silences, and Connor wondered if he'd said the wrong thing. Then he heard her laugh softly.

"Yeah. I think I'd like that."

CHAPTER EIGHT

AT THE one-week mark he and Vivi had been running neck-and-neck in the fundraising. Well, once he counted his matching her funds plan, at least. Early in week two Vivi had pulled ahead by landing a couple of corporate sponsors on her side, but one message on Twitter pulled him back into the lead. That trick had earned him an earful from Vivi, but Vivi's tongue had lost a bit of its sting these days.

In a way he missed the battle of wills and wits, but while the tone had changed, Vivi still kept him on his toes. She was the first to call him on things, but also the first to give credit and accolades. She could be hell on his ego when she took him down a peg, but things were different now.

When it came to the actual challenges, like today's work for the food bank, Vivi was definitely kicking his butt. She could organize people like a pro, and her team always ran with easy efficiency while he looked like he was trying to herd cats.

It was almost embarrassing, but he could take it. Everyone had their strengths and areas of expertise, and no one could touch Vivi when it came to any aspect of volunteer work.

Two weeks ago he would have had something snarky to say about that, but now… He didn't have to admit to grudging admiration for Vivi's talents. He could just be impressed by them. Vivi was completely focused and no-nonsense, but she had a way of getting work and money out of people and leaving them thinking it was all their idea.

Now, *that* was a talent. And, as he was discovering, Vivi had many interesting talents.

After that initial awkwardness the day after, Vivi had slowly warmed to the new status quo. She wasn't openly advertising that change, but even the bloggers had picked up on what they called an "easing of hostilities."

If they only knew…

Connor felt better than he had in months. He might not be getting a lot of sleep, thanks to Vivi, but otherwise he was feeling grounded and sane and normal—and that probably had something to do with Vivi as well. It should feel stranger than it did, and that was strange in and of itself.

He caught Vivi's eye across the room, and she gave him a half-smile before looking at his untidy piles of unfinished work and raising her eyebrows. "How's it going over there?" she called.

"Perfectly."

She shook her head. "Doesn't look like it."

"It's like walking into the middle of major surgery. It looks like a bloody mess, but it's all under control."

"Glad to hear it. I just hope you get it finished today."

So did he. However, it might end up like their workday in the Lower Ninth Ward where Vivi's team had finally had to come help his under the mercy rule. He turned around and gave a few encouraging shouts to his Imps and was gratified to see them pick up the pace. Then he jumped a pile of canned green beans and walked over to her.

"How do you manage it?"

"They're kids. They need clear, specific instructions." She dropped her chin and gave him a look that would have done the nuns in high school proud. "And a good example to follow, I might add."

"Hey, I'm working my butt off over there."

Vivi just shrugged. "After we're finished here I'll send a few of the Cherubim over to help."

"Much appreciated."

"Well, y'all will be here until midnight if I don't."

"We definitely don't want that." At her look, he dropped his voice and added, "I was kind of planning on taking you to dinner tonight. I got reservations at LaSalle."

Vivi looked suitably impressed. "LaSalle is booked out for months."

"Fame has its perks. Table reservations is just one of them."

Vivi looked uncomfortable. "Isn't that rather public?"

"It's less public than this." He pointed to the cameras and the crowds.

"This is different."

"Ashamed to be seen with me or something?" he challenged.

"No, that's not it. I just didn't know that we…it…*that*… was for public knowledge. I thought we were staying low, under the radar."

Ah. "You like sneaking around?" He liked her discretion. It was a nice change from the view-all, tell-all of celebrity relationships. Or maybe Vivi had a streak in her he didn't know about that enjoyed the game. He could get behind that, too.

"That's not it either. It's just…" She trailed off and frowned.

"It's just…?" he prompted.

Vivi sighed and shrugged. "Dinner sounds great. What time?"

"Seven. I'll pick you up."

"No, I'll meet you at your place." At his look, she added,

"I need to run by the gallery, so I'll do that on my way." She added a smile. "I'll see you at seven."

She went back to work, leaving him feeling a little off-kilter. Vivi wasn't like any other woman he'd ever met, that was for sure. He was quickly discovering, however, that that wasn't a bad thing. It sounded cheesy, but Vivi brought out the Boy Scout in him. He found himself wanting to do the smaller things, like pick her up for dinner. It didn't make sense. He snorted. When had Vivi ever made sense to him?

Connor turned around, fully intending to get this job finished as soon as possible, and he saw his Imps standing idle, watching him. "Who called a union break? They're killing us here."

Before he could get anything accomplished, though, his phone rang. A glance at the number had him sighing. He really didn't want to wade back into the fray today. He was enjoying the interlude from his life.

Balancing the phone uncomfortably on his shoulder, he closed a box and strapped tape across the top. "What's up, Angie?"

"I've got excellent news."

His agent wasn't one to exaggerate, so whatever it was it had to be damn good. "I like excellent news."

"In light of the paternity test results, the plaintiff's countersuit has been dismissed and we have our permanent injunction."

"And in simple English that means…?"

"Katy Arras has been told to shut her lying trap."

"That *is* excellent news."

"Thought you might like that. In other good news, thanks to your current charity work and some internet search engine magic I don't understand, all that dirt is now buried on page two and beyond. It's pretty much over."

The dirt would never be completely washed away, but

he'd settle for it being lost on the internet. He might be personally vindicated, but people would still mutter about the rumors behind his back, wondering how much was really true. Those kinds of stories stuck around forever, becoming urban legends and the butt of jokes.

At least he wasn't the first. He was in company with some of the greats. "You are a doll, Angie"

"That's why you pay me the big bucks. How are you holding up down there?"

"I'm home, not exiled to Siberia."

Angie, who considered the suburbs too rustic to visit and New York the only city outside California worth acknowledging, snorted. "Well, keep hanging in there. You're getting all kinds of good press."

"And I'm having a good time, too."

"Good for you. Just don't have *too* good of a time. One Katy Arras a year is my limit."

"Don't worry. I'm being a good boy."

That caused Angie to chuckle. "Well, don't take that too far either," she warned. "Remember your brand."

"How could I forget it?" He didn't bother to hide his exasperation, but Angie ignored it.

"I'll be in touch next week. I've got some plans cooking for March and April. When are you planning to go back into the studio?"

"Don't know yet. The brain is still recovering from the tour." Angie didn't know about his hands, and he saw no reason to go into that now. She was still reeling from hearing about all of his plans that didn't involve going back into the studio.

"Keep me posted."

"I will. Right now I have boxes to pack."

"Oh, yeah, that charity stuff. Good for you. Keep it up."

He could almost hear the dismissive wave. Beyond the

PR op, Angie didn't have much use for this, and that irked him as well. He snorted. He really was finding his inner Boy Scout.

"By the way, I'm coming down there for Mardi Gras," she added.

"Good luck finding a hotel room."

"I can't just stay with you?" she teased.

That would make things very awkward with Vivi. "In a word, no. In two words, hell no. I like my privacy."

"That's typical of you. Fine," she huffed. "I'll make some calls. I do know other people."

"I'll be happy to point you in the right direction for whatever you want to do once you're here," he offered.

"That I'll take you up on. Talk to you later. 'Bye."

Connor stuck his phone back in his pocket. He didn't really want to think about March or April or going back into the studio. He'd given Angie unfettered access to his schedule for the last six years, and while he appreciated her efforts on his behalf, he'd made them both enough money for him to take a little control back. Of his name, his time, his image and his freakin' *brand.*

He wasn't ignorant of the fact that this new desire for control and his current frustration with the status quo were probably fueling his situation with Vivi. It wasn't just lust—although that did help, he thought with a small smile—it was a whole new approach to his life. The solid confirmation of that knowledge sent a mini-shockwave through him. He hadn't known he had it in him.

How novel. *I'm growing as a person.* Vivi would have quite a bit of fun with that. In fact he might have to mention it, just to see what she'd have to say about it.

True to her word, Vivi and her crew came over to help his team finish up—but true to her nature she waited until they'd conceded defeat and the points were added to her column before she did. And when she shot him a smile full of secret promise Connor was very glad he'd come home.

All of his choices seemed to be working out quite well.

Vivi slid her feet into her shoes and opened her bedroom door. Lorelei stood against the wall, facing her door, arms crossed over her chest. "Spill."

"Excuse me?"

"I've kept my mouth shut all week long about your late nights and lack of details—"

"And it's been bliss." Vivi stepped past her, but Lorelei ignored the hint and followed her into the living room. This wasn't exactly how she'd planned to tell Lorelei about the rather dramatic shift in her life, but Lorelei hadn't been home much and time had gotten away from her.

"But now you're all dressed up. Your new snuggle monkey is finally taking you out on the town, huh?"

She raised an eyebrow at Lorelei. *"Snuggle monkey?"*

"It wasn't my first choice of term, but the others were more vulgar and would have gotten you mad at me. I know you're having sex, and I'm dying to know who with."

"Like *that's* any of your business."

"No, I think it's great. You're all glowy and relaxed. Not only are you having sex, you're having some *awesome* sex."

Vivi couldn't stop the blush. She tried to hide it by turning away, but Lorelei saw and pounced.

"Whoa! *That* good, huh? I have to know the identity of this sex god."

This was not exactly how she'd pictured this conversation. Vivi searched for words, but Lorelei took it as hesitation.

"If he's taking you out tonight, it's not exactly a secret affair, you know." She paused and her eyes narrowed. "Oh, God, unless… He's not married or anything, is he?"

"For heaven's sake, Lorelei, of course not."

"Well, it *would* explain all the secrecy."

Vivi took a deep breath. "I'm going out with Connor."

"Connor who?"

"Mansfield. How many other Connors do you know?"

Lorelei looked disappointed. "Well, I read that all wrong. I didn't realize you had a Saints and Sinners thing tonight."

"I don't."

"Then why are you going to dinner with Connor?"

Either Lorelei was very dense, or this news really was too incredible to believe. "Because he asked me to."

Lorelei's eyebrows knitted together. "This makes no sense. My world is officially askew. You're not planning on dumping his meal in his lap, are you?"

"It's not on the agenda, no. And I'd never make a scene like that at LaSalle."

"LaSalle? *Wow.* Hang on. All these late nights and now…" The furrow on her brow deepened, then her eyes grew wide in shock. "Wait. *Connor* is your secret snuggle monkey?"

Oh, Lord. "Lorelei…"

Lorelei rose to her feet, blinking and shaking her head. "You're sleeping with *Connor?*"

"Lorelei…"

Her voice rose to a shout. "You're having *sex* with Connor Mansfield?"

"Let's not announce that to the entire neighborhood, please."

"Oh, my God, you *are* sleeping with him. Oh. My. *God. When* did this start? How? Why? I need lots of details."

Vivi didn't feel like sharing details at the moment, and she certainly didn't have good answers to *how* or *why.* It made her head hurt to make sense of it. This was new territory, and it kind of freaked her out when she thought about it too much.

She made a point of looking at her watch and picking up her purse. "I've got to run."

Lorelei snatched her purse out of her hand. "Oh, no, you don't. You're not dropping a bomb like that and then prancing out of here like it's nothing."

"Give me my purse."

"Give me some answers."

"This is not your business. I don't owe you any answers about anything."

"I've spent my entire life listening to you complain about Connor and how he makes your existence miserable—so, yeah, you do owe me some answers now."

Oh, how she wished she had answers to give. "Connor and I have…um…resolved many of our differences—"

"I should certainly hope so."

Argh. "And we are…um…moving past old grudges and…um…moving forward as adults."

"By knocking boots."

"Must you be so crude?" Lorelei made it sound tawdry. Maybe it was. Vivi just didn't want to think so.

"I don't see you denying it."

"Fine." She lowered her voice to a whisper, even though she was in the privacy of her own house. "Yes, I am sleeping with Connor. We are adults, and it's nobody else's business…"

Lorelei stomped back to the couch, dragging Vivi with her, and forced her to sit. "First—congratulations. I mean, *Connor.* Yum." She fanned her face. "But we'll come back to that in a minute. You keep saying it's nobody's business—and that's sort of true—but the minute you're spotted with Connor at LaSalle—and you *will* be spotted—it will be *everyone's* business."

"The media has left Connor alone recently."

"It's not the press you need to worry about. It's everyone

with a cell phone who wants to make a quick buck. You'll be on all the blogs before midnight, I guarantee it. Even if you weren't sleeping together—and I do intend to come back to that, so don't think you're going to weasel out—the world will think you are."

"Well, I can't control what people think."

"But you'll certainly care once it's your name being bandied about. And after all the recent gossip about Connor's, *ahem,* preferences..."

"Which you never claimed to believe in the first place."

"I'm not Jane Q. Public in middle America, with no reason not to believe it."

"I'm not worried about middle America. Most of them think New Orleans is a den of iniquity anyway. I'm not running for political office or competing for Miss America, so I don't care what Jane Q. Public thinks about anything. The only people whose opinions I care about know me—and Connor, too, for that matter—so it's not likely they'll get caught up in any gossip frenzy."

"Good for you, Vivi." There was genuine pride in Lorelei's voice. "I just hope it's worth it."

"It is," she answered without thinking, and as Lorelei's eyes lit up Vivi desperately wanted to suck the words back in.

"*Now* we're getting somewhere. Exactly *how* worth it is it?"

Damn it, she could feel the heat in her face again.

Lorelei sighed. "You are one lucky girl."

Silently, she agreed—and that shocked her a little.

"So what happened? What changed?"

"I don't really know. We were spending all this time together, and actually talking to him kind of made me see things—him—differently, and..." She shrugged. "*Carpe diem,* I guess."

"Wow. Just *wow.*" Lorelei leaned forward. "So is this serious? Like going somewhere?"

Vivi nearly choked. "Oh, no—no, no. It's just casual."

"And you're okay with that?" Lorelei was wide-eyed with shock.

She had to think about it, and that kind of shocked her, too. "Yeah. I think I am."

"I gotta say, Vivi, I never would have expected this."

"Me neither."

Lorelei handed over her purse. "Then enjoy it. Every single minute of it. You deserve it."

"Thanks, sweetie." The grandfather clock began to bong the hour. She was late. "I've got to go. Don't wait up, okay?"

"Since I know you won't dish the details, I guess I won't. By the way—how does it feel?"

Vivi was shrugging into her coat. "How does what feel?"

"Being the bad one, for once."

Was she being bad? Not really. Reckless? Maybe. Less than circumspect? Definitely. But she was an adult; Connor was an adult. She might be being a little bit bad, but in comparison to others, Vivi was still on the narrow path. "I have to admit that it feels pretty darn good."

"Told ya so."

Dressed as she was, it was a little too chilly to be walking, and her shoes weren't exactly designed for navigating the cobblestones and often ankle-twisting sidewalks of the French Quarter. It would take longer to drive than walk to Connor's place, but that couldn't be helped. And if she left her car on Connor's block, he wouldn't have to take her home in the middle of the night either. Although she'd spent her entire life in this city, and the blocks between Royal Street and Washington Square were far from deserted or particularly dangerous, Connor had developed a chivalrous streak that refused to let her walk home alone in the wee hours of the morning.

She'd lied when she'd said she had to go by the gallery first. She'd told herself that she didn't want to give Lorelei a chance to embarrass her in front of Connor, but that wasn't entirely true. She needed to keep things very separate in her mind, for her sanity's sake, and Connor picking her up like this was an actual date would blur those lines.

But this *was* an actual date, her inner voice reminded her. A very public one. And the thought of "dating" Connor opened up a whole new slew of thoughts she wasn't really willing to process. *No,* she told herself. Going public didn't change the nature of this. Connor was temporary. A change from the norm. A transition from the old Vivi to the new Vivi.

Right.

Connor buzzed her up, and the sight that greeted her caused her to wobble on her stilettos. *Mercy.* She was accustomed to his bad-boy rocker look, and she'd gotten used to the more casual look he'd been sporting during Saints and Sinners, but this… Connor was downright devastating in black pants, white button-down shirt and a blazer. It was completely simple, but something about it just flipped every switch in her body. This wasn't Connor the Rock Star, Connor the Sinner, or even Connor Her Arch Enemy; this was Connor the Man, all strength and assurance and everything the Y chromosome had to brag about.

"You're gorgeous, Vivi."

His compliment shook her out of her shock. A quick inventory told her she wasn't staring openmouthed or drooling. "You look pretty darn good yourself."

An eyebrow arched up. "We better go quickly, then."

"What? Why?"

"You look good enough to eat in small, slow bites, and we'll never make our reservation if I indulge."

The words carried promise and warning, and they nearly caused her to wobble again. Who cared about their reservation? Who needed food anyway? *This,* though…

She took a step forward.

The buzz of the intercom stopped her.

"That's our taxi." Connor opened the door for her and waited, but her feet didn't want to move. "You ready?"

No. "Sure."

The cab driver did a double-take when he saw Connor, and then spent much of the trip with one eye on the rearview mirror. Connor just shrugged good-naturedly and thanked the cabbie when he got effusive over Connor's music. Vivi knew it was a normal occurrence, and tried not to let it bother her that she couldn't talk to her date because the cabbie was. Connor apologized with a smile and a squeeze of her knee. And when the driver asked for a picture with Connor to add to his collection of celebrities he'd driven, Vivi got to play photographer.

Connor's life was different, that was for sure.

It wasn't until the taxi pulled away that Vivi realized she'd been so distracted that she hadn't realized where they were. "LaSalle is three blocks that way."

"I know. I wanted to show you this first."

Vivi looked around. She knew exactly where she was—Julia Street in the Warehouse District—but she didn't see anything out of the ordinary. Connor was pointing at an old three-story coffee warehouse that hadn't benefited yet from the revival of the neighborhood. "What am I looking at?"

"My new building." He held up a key ring. "I closed this afternoon, after I left the food bank." Connor unlocked the door and it swung open on rusty protesting hinges.

Vivi followed him inside, and Connor flipped on the light.

The inside was as dilapidated as the outside, but the exposed brick walls and hardwood floors held promise of future beauty. It was a huge space, and their footsteps echoed.

"What do you need a warehouse for?"

Connor's grin spread from ear to ear. "This is the future home of ConMan Records."

He seemed to think she'd have a clue what that meant, but whatever it was he was proud and excited about it. The enthusiasm was contagious. "I'm not entirely sure what that means, but congratulations nonetheless."

"It means that a lot of new doors are opening."

"Wow. You're thinking about going out on your own?"

"It's a possibility. Something I've been thinking about for a while now."

"Looking for artistic freedom?"

"That's some of it. I must admit, though, after spending time with Imps and Cherubims, I've also been thinking about doing something to encourage more music education for local kids. Some kind of outreach or something. Not sure what, exactly, but the label and the studio can be part of that."

This was a new aspect of Connor, and Vivi's chest warmed at the generosity of spirit it displayed. Connor was quick to write a check, but this would be something more than just distant philanthropy. Her mind immediately began to whirl, thinking of community programs, fundraising opportunities…

The habits of a lifetime in non-profit work, though, didn't stop another thought from barging in, and the whirl of ideas ground to a halt. "So this means you're moving home? Full-time?"

He shook his head. "Not full-time, but I'm going to convert the top floor into an apartment for me, because I do plan to be in town a lot more in the future."

Oh. She didn't know what to say to that. This fling with Connor was doable and reasonable and understandable because he was only here temporarily. Being reckless and bad could be acceptable if it were only for a short while. If she'd known he was planning on reestablishing a base here…

And they were about to be very publicly connected…

Damn it. Things had just gotten really complicated.

CHAPTER NINE

THERE was a reason LaSalle stayed booked. Sure, it was trendy, and the current hot spot created by a celebrity chef, but in Connor's experience, trendy hot spots were usually highly overrated. LaSalle, though… Another bite of the bread pudding might kill him, but letting it go to waste seemed like a cardinal sin.

Vivi eyeballed the last bite, but put her fork down and admitted defeat. "I simply can't. You're going to have to carry me out of here as it is."

"I was hoping you'd carry me."

"Then we'll just have to sit here until we can walk." She sipped at her coffee. "In my case, that's looking like sometime next week."

"Sitting is an excellent idea."

While the view across the table from him had kept the internal fires stoked, he was, unbelievably enough, having an excellent time anyway. Vivi's simple black dress clung to every curve, and the neckline was just low enough to showcase the gentle swell of her cleavage and classic double string of pearls without crossing over into a tacky advertisement of her charms. She'd pulled her hair up into some kind of fancy twist, leaving the elegant column of her neck bare.

He wanted her, but anticipation was part of the attraction

and excitement. He wasn't in a rush—well, he *was,* but he was enjoying this, too.

After so long on the road, and living that life, he'd forgotten what it was like to be in the company of a *lady.* A well-bred, well-mannered, well-spoken, real Southern lady. Of course, he wouldn't expect Vivi to be anything less, but to his amazement he was utterly captivated by it. By *her.*

Vivi was sharp and smart; she had both the business sense and the non-profit experience to converse about his ideas for ConMan and outreach to the community. They had enough in common for conversation to flow easily, yet they were different enough to keep it interesting. She never bored him, and he was someone who was bored easily. She was gracious and amusing and charming, and she wasn't the least bit impressed by him. The honesty was refreshing. His ego should be smarting, but it made her responses genuine.

Now Connor understood why his father always cringed at his West Coast love affairs with starlets and musicians. In comparison to someone like Vivi… There simply wasn't a comparison.

Vivi's smile faded a little and she looked uncomfortable again as three people on the sidewalk pressed against the window of LaSalle, pointing and waving. One even tried to put a camera against the glass for a picture. Other patrons of the restaurant looked annoyed, but Vivi's discomfort got his attention.

"Just try to ignore it, Vivi."

"How? You can't even take a taxi or eat in peace. How do you ignore it?"

"It takes practice. Mainly I just try to remember that for some people celebrity-spotting is the biggest or best thing that's happened to them today. Or maybe even this week or this month. They'll post it to Facebook and Twitter and impress their friends and that will make them happy."

"At your expense?"

"Like I said, I owe my career to a million people I've never met. It seems a little petty to complain now."

She nodded, but picked up her coffee and turned slightly away from the window.

"Come on, Vivi, I know it's been a while, but surely you remember what it's like for people to want that brush with fame. You've done the photo ops."

"Yes, but not like this. People didn't normally recognize me unless I was wearing a crown and sash. Even then, they didn't know my name or who I was beyond Miss Louisiana. I wasn't famous. My *title* was famous. That's a big difference."

"That's not true."

"Fine. Name one Miss Louisiana other than me," she challenged.

She had him there. "Uh…"

"I'll go even easier. Who's the current Miss America? Or any Miss America *other* than Vanessa Williams."

Since he'd have been hard-pressed even to come up with Vanessa Williams, he had to admit defeat. "Regardless, you're still Vivienne LaBlanc. Everyone in New Orleans knows you."

"But they don't stalk me at restaurants to take my picture."

"Would you want them to?"

"You know, that kind of fame sounds good in theory, but now that I've seen it in practice…" She looked out the window, where the crowd had grown. "Maybe not."

"I can't control the paparazzi—not the professionals and not the amateurs. They come with the territory. If that's a problem for you…"

Vivi studied her napkin. He could almost see the wheels spinning inside her head. She finally looked up and met his eyes. "Lorelei says that we'll be on every blog by midnight."

"She's not wrong."

"I never planned on being infamous."

"You will be by morning."

He saw understanding dawn in her eyes. "I didn't think this through all the way. Did you?"

He didn't have to "think this through." This was just his life. "Vivi, you yourself said that tonight would make this public."

She swallowed. "I don't think I quite realized *how* public."

Time for those hard truths he'd promised her. "Until now your comings and goings at Gabe's have gone unnoticed. Once those pictures hit the blogs, there's a good chance someone will remember that they saw you there. Other people will start looking for you. If you walk out of here with me tonight there's no going back. You'll just have to ride it out."

"And if I don't?"

He took a deep breath. "No one could really blame me for trying to charm you. And we could claim that tonight's dinner had something to do with Saints and Sinners. There will still be speculation, but it'll fade. You have quite the reputation around here as a good girl, so folks will believe you. But, of course, that will be it for us."

Connor didn't like the rock that settled in his stomach as he said that. But Vivi had to realize that truth. And so did he. It had to be said, if for no other reason than to make *him* acknowledge it. The importance of this moment had sneaked up on him. He didn't like that.

"There's no way we can sneak around when everyone's looking out for just that."

Vivi blew out her breath in a long sigh. "Good Lord, I thought this was just going to be a quiet dinner. I had no idea it was some kind of point of no return."

Indeed. Vivi had a choice to make—and he had to, in all fairness, give her the opportunity to make it. Part of him wanted to argue his case, but he resisted. Instead, he signaled for the check, putting the ball in her court. "If you're going, now's a good time. Have the *maître d'* call you a cab and be seen by that crowd getting into it *alone*."

"I understand." She fell quiet.

So did he, but he wasn't expecting the disappointment that had come with her words. Boy, this was a record even for him. He shouldn't care. They'd had their fun; they could part ways now, before ugliness set in to make the future unpleasant. But something unfamiliar spread through his stomach at the thought of Vivi walking out now. His cynical inner voice told him it would be better and safer if she did, but it didn't stop him from hoping that she might not. That hope left his inner cynic howling a protest that told *him* to get out now.

What a mess. And in public, too. He left a hefty tip—even bigger than usual—so if the server was asked about tonight she'd have a good story to tell and maybe keep from mentioning anything she'd inadvertently overheard. He pocketed the receipt, but Vivi still sat there.

"Well?"

She picked up her purse. "I'm ready when you are."

It took a minute for her words to sink in, but even as they did he kept his optimism on a short leash. The *maître d'* stepped outside to shoo the crowd away from the door and flagged down a taxi.

It coasted to a stop at the curb, and Vivi still seemed like she was going to go through with this. He wasn't holding his breath, though. Vivi had a lot on the line. When he stepped outside, the flashes seemed blinding after the tastefully dim interior of LaSalle. Vivi kept her eyes on the buttons of her coat at first, but then she stepped forward and tucked her hand under his arm.

He wasn't prepared for the effect that simple gesture would have on him.

A gasp rose from the gathered crowd. Or maybe that was just his brain misfiring in shock. Head held high, Vivi looked calm, like she *hadn't* just tortured herself over this mere minutes ago. It was a small gesture, but one that would be as good as gold for the bloggers. People started shouting questions, but Vivi let him help her into the taxi, and then, in full view of the gawking crowd, kissed him as he closed the door behind them.

"You've done it now."

She smiled. "I know."

"Why, Vivi?"

"Because you only live once. And right now I'm not ready to be done with this."

A week ago, Vivi had convinced herself that Connor's predictions were overstated and hysterical. Now—well, she wanted to be angry at him for his knack for understatement. She felt like she was living in a damn circus.

She'd had an uptick in attention after the announcement of the Sinner and Saint, but it had mostly been local. The non-local attention had really just been reflected off Connor. It had been noticeable, but small. But now…

The email address for the gallery overflowed with interview requests, questions and fan mail she was supposed to pass along to Connor. She'd had to turn the ringer off on the phone at the gallery days ago, before the constant noise drove everyone insane, and now she just checked the voice mail a few times a day. Thankfully no one had gotten hold of her personal email address or her cell phone number, so she could still do some business. The gallery itself was hopping, but it was mostly gawkers, not buyers, and she'd had to hire additional staff just for crowd control. She certainly couldn't be in there during opening hours; she'd learned that just two days after their "quiet dinner" had exploded.

Her address had gotten out very easily, and plenty of people now stalked her house, either hoping for a glimpse of Connor or hoping to get a comment from her. Her house didn't have a fence or a gated courtyard, so people could just walk up to her front door—and many had. No wonder Connor had never come to her house. After she'd found one photographer hiding in the bushes under her bedroom window, Daddy had finally hired a private security firm to keep them off her property.

Lorelei had enjoyed the attention at first, but it had gotten old fast for her, too, and she was spending more time at their parents' house—which *did* have a nice big fence to keep people away.

Lord, just the walk from the gallery to Connor's apartment was like running a gauntlet sometimes. And with people from all over coming in for the parades and the Mardi Gras celebrations, there always seemed to be a fresh onslaught.

And, coming off Connor's recent run in the tabloids, everyone wanted to know who she was—who she used to be. If one more picture of her in crown and sash hit the papers she might barf. There were plenty of photos of her that were far more current, but everyone loved the beauty queen angle. The press was having a heyday with Bad-Boy Connor and Good-Girl Vivi from past to present. There was a quest for dirt on her, but at least she knew she was safe there: she really *was* a good girl and there was no dirt to be found.

But even her reputation didn't stop folks from speculating—pretty graphically, at times—about what she and Connor were up to. Every day she hated Katy Arras and her lies a little more.

They were certainly a popular couple, regardless of the

speculation. At first, being dropped into Connor's world had been jarring. She hadn't realized how difficult it really was to be *that* famous. Everything Connor did—what he wore, where he went, what he ate—was interesting to someone, somewhere.

And that made her interesting to people as well.

She'd been offered several ways to cash in on her new-found notoriety and popularity and at Connor's insistence had hired a manager to field those offers. While many of the offers seemed like seedy and skeevy ways to cash in on her fame quickly, this circus had reignited a part of her career she'd thought long behind her. She was being asked to speak to groups—maybe even consider writing a book—on the platforms she'd promoted as Miss Louisiana, the work she'd done since then in non-profits and the arts, all the way up to and including beauty tips. It was like the whole country had woken up and decided she might have something worthwhile to say. Her fifteen minutes weren't quite up, it seemed, which was both good and bad.

What kind of world was it where fame came knocking solely because of who you dated? *Welcome to the era of the internet and twenty-four-hour news. It made people famous for sleeping with someone famous.*

Ugh. Her faith in humanity was being sorely tried.

The sad and slightly scary part, though, was that she really didn't mind. She was having *that* good of a time. Top of the list of Things She Thought She Would Never, Ever Say was *Connor is totally worth it.* Yet he was.

And that might be the truly freaky part. Connor had offered her an escape route, and she'd walked right by. She'd told herself at LaSalle that nothing had really changed beyond public awareness and a less definite timeframe, but that wasn't proving to be true. There was something *else*—

something she wasn't quite willing to explore too deeply yet—that made the circus totally worthwhile.

All in all, this was the oddest experience of her life—dwarfing even the madness of the Miss America contest—but it was also the most incredible. So, in that way, it kind of balanced out.

Either that or she was totally losing her mind.

Vivi shut down her computer and turned off the lights in the gallery's office. She'd come in an hour ago at closing time to catch up on some paperwork, but focus wouldn't come. *At least I got the bills paid.* The electricity would stay on and the staff would get their paychecks, so that was enough for tonight.

Officially, Saints and Sinners only had six days left before the winner was announced and the fundraiser came to an end with the rest of the city's celebrations. Tomorrow would be their last public event until the winner took his or her place on top of the Bon Argent float on Tuesday morning. While the final five days—Friday to midnight Tuesday—would be the busiest for the city as a whole, they would be amazingly calm for her and Connor. Everyone had other plans—this was one of the busiest weekends of the entire year—so even as the flavor of the moment for the media, thanks to Connor, she was looking at a relatively low-key weekend.

But first she had a quiet evening at Connor's planned for tonight.

An anticipatory shiver ran through her and put speed in her steps as she gathered her stuff, set the alarm and locked the doors to the gallery behind her. A glance up showed two feet propped on the balcony railing. She couldn't see Connor from this vantage point, but he could probably see her, so she smiled before she stepped into the street. The feet disappeared, and by the time she'd made it to the nondescript wooden door, the sound of the buzzer releasing the lock was greeting her.

Connor met her at the top of the stairs with a kiss that had her toes curling in pleasure. "'Bout time you showed up."

Vivi dropped her bags and left her shoes by the door before following Connor into the kitchen. She took the glass of wine he offered with a grateful sigh and took a sip. "I spent some time on the phone with a reporter from the *LA Times.* He's doing a story on post-Katrina reconstruction."

"And he called *you?*"

"Gee, you don't have to sound so surprised."

Connor schooled his features. "Sorry, it's just that doesn't seem like your area of expertise."

"I know. But people think reconstruction is all about houses, and this was more about the effects on people. Loss of community, effects on children and families, the overstretched resources of non-profits…"

Connor nodded in understanding. "And that *is* your area of expertise."

"Exactly. My new manager has been out full force getting my name in front of people."

He refilled both of their glasses and leaned against the counter. "Raymond's awesome at finding those angles."

"Well, I appreciate the recommendation. I had no idea it would explode like this."

"And you didn't even have to release a sex tape."

She snorted. "Don't think for a second that I haven't been offered a hell of a lot of money for exactly that."

"Good thing you're a saint." He lifted his glass to hers in a toast.

She sighed and took a big sip of wine. "You know, you're suddenly being vindicated just because I *am* such a saint."

"Don't think I don't know it. It's much appreciated."

Nodding at his battered blue jeans and well-worn black

and gold jersey, she untucked her blouse from her pants and started removing the heavy necklace and bracelet she'd worn that day. "So, you seem to have spent the day lounging on the balcony? Must be nice."

"Hey, I was working," he informed her. "I talked to an interior designer about plans for the warehouse, approved a licensing agreement for some music, went over the final figures from the tour with my accountant—"

"All from the comfort of your balcony?"

Connor grinned. "The job has to come with some perks, you know."

"I want to be a rock star. Think I'm too old to get my big break?"

He laughed. "Age isn't the problem, Vivi. The fact you're tone-deaf, though, is an obstacle."

She smacked his arm and frowned at him. He responded with a shrug and a grin. "I am *not* tone-deaf," she insisted.

"You are many wonderful things, Vivi, and you have many great talents, but I've heard you sing in the shower. You couldn't carry a tune in a bucket if I put the tune in the bucket and handed it to you."

He was right, but… "Wow, I may swoon from the flattery."

Connor snorted. "Because I'm the one you can always come to for empty flattery?"

"Point taken."

That was why this worked. Connor was, oddly enough, the one person she could drop any and all attempts at pretense with. It wasn't as if he could think worse of her than he had at some point in the past. It was a very strange situation—and an unusual way to find that acceptance of who she really was—but it worked for her. It made it easy.

He took the wineglass from her hand and set it behind her on the counter. Then he lifted her up, sat her on the counter, and moved between her legs. "You've had a long day. Are you hungry? Tired?"

One minute ago she'd have said yes, but Connor asked the questions with his lips against her neck, and the need for food or rest gave way to a much more simple, primal need.

His mouth found hers, and she sighed into him with a release she'd never felt with anyone before. It should be scary, but it wasn't.

It felt pretty close to perfect.

CHAPTER TEN

"IT'S six o'clock in the morning," Lorelei grumped as she pushed past Vivi to the coffeepot. "Could you stop the humming? Your constant good mood is making me ill."

"Aren't you a ray of sunshine this morning?"

Lorelei held the cup of coffee like a lifeline. "Do you not need sleep like normal humans?"

"I'm just in a good mood this morning."

"As usual."

"What?"

"I feel like I'm living in a Disney movie. I'm expecting you to burst into song while woodland creatures clean the house and make you a dress for the ball."

"Well, that would be interesting, wouldn't it? I'm rather tone-deaf, and I'm not sure that gators and nutria have the same dexterity and sewing skills as bunnies and chipmunks." Vivi winked at her sister, but refrained from more humming as she left the kitchen.

Lorelei followed. "See—I can't even get a rise out of you by making fun of you. Where's the sanctimonious Vivi I know and love?"

"Poor Lorelei. You're living a nightmare."

Lorelei made a face as she took her usual spot in the corner of the couch. "I'm glad you're happy, but do you *have* to be so chipper about it?"

"Boy, you're grumpy. Drink your coffee. I like you better when you're fully caffeinated." She patted Lorelei on the arm. "I've got to go. I'm going straight to Connor's after we're done today, so I'll see you in the morning."

"Surprise, surprise," Lorelei muttered.

"Something wrong?"

"No." Lorelei took another sip of coffee. "Actually, yes. Something is wrong."

"Okay, what?"

"You." Lorelei's stare was unsettling. "You're not quite right these days."

"Excuse me?"

"This is really not like you."

"I know. It's crazy. But it's fun. And you wanted me to have fun, right?"

"Of course. But how deep are you into this thing with Connor?"

That brought her up short. "What do you mean?"

"You have never, not once in your life, had a fling, an affair, or a one-night stand. You are a serial monogamist at best. Now you're sleeping—very publicly, I might add—with Connor. You spend all of your free time—and even time that's not free—with him. From where I stand, it looks like you're getting serious about this."

"Then why do you sound like the Oracle of Doom?"

"Because Connor isn't really a smart long-term investment. I don't want you to get hurt." Lorelei put her coffee cup on the table and leveled a hard stare at her. "Are you in love with Connor?"

The concept had been floating around in her mind, but it wasn't something she was willing to explore too deeply. "What?"

"It's a very simple question. Are you in love with Connor?"

She tried to be nonchalant. "You're jumping ahead a bit, aren't you? This is still very new."

"Well, are you and Connor on the same page at least?"

"Are you asking me if we've had a 'Where is this going?' conversation?" The mere idea of such a thing seemed totally out of the question. "No. We haven't."

Lorelei looked at her like she'd lost her mind. "And that doesn't bother you? Have aliens taken over your body?"

It did bother her a little. But Connor wasn't the kind of man she'd be comfortable having that kind of conversation with. "No. It just seems a bit premature to be talking about it."

Vivi could almost hear Lorelei's eyeballs rolling. "You've never walked blindly into anything in your life. You always have a plan. A purpose. You have to have some kind of plan cooking in there."

Why did Vivi feel like the younger sister? "My plan is to see how it goes. There's definitely something. I don't think it's love. It could be hormones or infatuation or any number of things. It's a very strong *like,* though, and I'm willing to explore that and enjoy it now, for what it is. There's no need for me to rush into this." She met Lorelei's eyes. "I'm an adult. I can handle this—whatever it is, whatever it becomes. Or doesn't become."

"Vivi—"

"Look, I've got to get ready to go. But I promise you that it's all good. I'm fine."

Lorelei didn't look convinced, but other than some deep sighs, she dropped the subject.

But Vivi was having a hard time doing the same. She couldn't keep skittering around the edges of this. At some point she was going to have to really decide. But not yet. She wanted to enjoy this as long as she could.

The street was quiet as Vivi locked the door behind her.

She started down the stone steps, only to stop short when she saw Connor leaning against his rented red sportscar parked at the curb. He opened the passenger-side door as she approached.

"This is a surprise," she said.

"I'm full of surprises," he said as he helped her in. Once he was in his seat, he handed her a small bag. "Here."

"What's this?"

"Just something I happened to find yesterday at the French Market. Open it."

She did, allowing the contents to slide into her palm. It was a bracelet, and when she held it up she saw the charm: a halo hanging off a set of devil horns.

Connor winked at her. "I thought it might be appropriate."

"It's perfect." She leaned over the console and gave him a kiss. "Thank you."

"You're welcome." Connor started the engine.

Vivi dangled the bracelet from her fingers, admiring the charm. It wasn't an expensive gift; she could tell by looking at it that it wasn't the highest quality and might possibly turn her wrist green. But that was part of its charm. It wasn't a gift meant to impress—not beyond the thought behind it, at least. And that thought caused her chest to feel a bit tight.

She had to face it: she *was* in love with Connor. While it felt good to put a name to it, to admit to it, the happy feeling was short-lived due to reality. She'd fallen in love with a man who hadn't given her even the slightest of hints about his own feelings or what might lie ahead.

The enormous folly of that slammed into her like a bag of bricks, and no matter how hard she tried, she couldn't quite shake that feeling off to focus on the day's project.

The last day of the competition part of Saints and Sinners had them at a community center in one of the poorest areas of town. The teams were painting walls, washing windows and mulching the playground as part of a larger rehabilitation project. They were halfway through the day when Vivi realized she'd forgotten they were in competition at all. For the first time in, well...*ever,* her competitive streak had remained underground. She'd been too lost in the mess inside her own head even to compete properly.

It took a real effort of will—and garnered her some strange looks from both sides—to pull Team Saint back together so they'd take the points. Only once they were safely in her column did she go back to help Connor paint the hallway.

"Hate to say it, but you lose. Again."

He winked at her. "I wondered when you'd remember."

"I can't believe you took advantage of me like that."

Connor shook his head. "I don't look gift horses in the mouth and I don't question my luck. I need you in order to get through this without looking like a loser in front of the press."

Something about the words—or maybe the tone—put her hackles up. "Is that all you want from me?"

"Given a choice, I'd rather not be here at all. We'd be at Gabe's on a rug in front of the fireplace drinking mimosas. Trust me, Vivi. What I want from you right now doesn't involve painting a wall. And it certainly doesn't include two dozen bystanders."

Well, gee, if she'd been looking for a declaration of some sort, that certainly wasn't it.

"All I ask from you is honesty. If you want something, just ask. Don't try to charm it out of me."

That got her an odd look from Connor. "What are you talking about?"

Her spurt of bravado fled the scene. She was not going to be the one to broach that topic, and she certainly wasn't going to do it *here,* of all places. She had her pride. "Nothing." She forced a smile. "You may be able to addle my mind with orgasms, but you will not be able to woo me to the dark side with your charms. I'm made of sterner stuff than that."

She waited for Connor to wink or shrug or crack off a smart comeback, but none of those things happened. Instead, Connor's paintbrush hit the bucket with a splat, and she found herself being led—almost dragged, actually—into an empty activity room, where he closed the door behind him.

Déjà vu. "That door better not lock from the outside. After our recent publicity, no one will believe we *weren't* up to something in here." It was a lame attempt at a joke and it fell flat.

Connor crossed his arms over his chest. "Explain."

"I don't know what you mean."

"I've known you a hell of a long time, Vivi, and that was a loaded statement. I'd like to know what you meant by it."

Damn. "I think you're reading a bit much into a few words."

"Again, I know you better than that."

The calm assurance caused her temper to flare. "Actually, Connor, I don't think you know me at all. Which isn't entirely surprising, since I'm beginning to think that I don't know myself very well either. My whole life has flipped upside down."

Connor had the gall to look surprised. "So has mine, you know."

"Really? I figured this was par for the course for you."

"No." He shook his head. "*This* is definitely new territory."

"I don't think we're talking about the same thing."

There was that odd look again. "What are *you* talking about, Vivi?"

"I asked you first."

"Vivi…"

"Fine." This was neither the time nor the place, but she'd led the way here and there wasn't a graceful way to turn back now. "We have five days left of Saints and Sinners. What happens *six* days from now?"

"I don't know about you, but I'll be sleeping in."

His attempt to dodge her question only highlighted the necessity of asking it. She *needed* those answers she'd blithely dismissed this morning. "Okay, ten days from now? Two weeks? A month?"

Connor looked like he'd swallowed something vile. *Well, there's my answer.* Better to get it now. "That's what I thought."

He shoved his hands into his jeans pockets. "Are you looking for some kind of declaration of intent? I hadn't really thought that far in advance."

"I have to, sadly. It feels like the whole country is watching me, so I need to prepare for the aftermath. This whole thing with you has been a departure from the norm, and I need to be ready to deal with the fallout."

"You're jumping way ahead—"

"Actually, I'm trying to fall back. I jumped ahead of myself getting involved with you so quickly. Now I'm just regrouping and preparing for what comes next."

"And what do you think that is?"

"I really don't know. So much is happening so quickly—"

He stepped closer to her and reached for her arms. "So why not wait until things calm down before we have this conversation? Can't we just continue on as we are and see where it goes?"

"If you were anyone other than Connor Mansfield I'd say yes." She pulled her arms out of his hands gently. This hurt more than she'd expected, which only strengthened her resolve that it was the right thing to do. Now, before she got any more attached and Connor did serious damage to her heart. "I stand to lose a lot more than you do if this ends badly. Maybe we should quit while we're ahead."

Connor couldn't quite believe his ears. How had they gotten here? Talk about things coming from left field… "What are you saying, Vivi?"

"I'm saying that I can't invest in something that doesn't have a future. I thought I could. I thought I could just seize the day and not worry. But I'm not a fling kind of girl, and you're not a long-haul kind of guy."

She might as well have slapped him. He felt unfairly vilified. "So you dipped your toes in the pool, decided it was too hot and are now pulling out?"

"No. I jumped completely in. But now I think the pool is too dangerous for me to swim in. You know me well enough, Connor, to know that I'm a good girl. I'm not cut out to be flavor of the month."

Vivi seemed genuinely distressed at the idea. Distressed enough to make him want to play Lancelot and soothe her. "I had no intention of getting involved with anyone when I came home. After the disaster of the last few months the last thing I wanted was to have my love life back in the papers at all. Much less with you. No offense intended."

Vivi actually cracked a smile. "None taken."

He hooked a finger through her belt loop and pulled her an inch closer to him. She didn't resist. He used a finger to lift her chin, making her look him straight in the eye. "I didn't expect this, didn't plan on it and if anyone had tried to tell me it was going to happen I'd have laughed in their face. At the same time, though, I'm not unhappy it did."

"Oh, me neither. It's been fun."

"It *is* fun. And it can continue to be fun. I know it's tough for you to deal with the carnival sideshow that is my life, but believe me when I say it gets easier. You can't live worrying about how your life is being interpreted or judged by the wider world. That way lies only madness." He saw Vivi's eyebrows draw together. "And remember you have a manager now. Damage control is his job, because his paycheck rather depends on you. Is he telling you to dump me?"

She shook her head. "I think you're missing my point."

Oh, he hadn't missed it; he'd just hoped he could sidestep it. No such luck. He wasn't going to get off that easily. He took a deep breath, rather wishing he'd let that statement in the hallway slide. "When it comes to women, I'm not used to thinking too far ahead. The only thing I can say is that I'm not ready for this to be over yet. Are you? Really?"

"Honestly?" She seemed to think about it. "No."

He let out the breath he'd been holding. "I don't have a lot of experience with women like you, but I'm not willing to give it up just yet." This was an odd place and time for him to be having this kind of revelatory discussion, but the weight in his chest wouldn't allow him to just let Vivi walk out.

Those blue eyes were wide and luminous. "So we let it play out?"

"Yeah. Can you do that? Just wait and see what happens?"

There was that silence again that had him holding his breath. He felt a bit foolish.

Finally Vivi nodded. "I think so. I'll try, at least."

"That's all I ask, Vivi." In reality, he knew he was asking a lot from her, and he was beyond relieved to see her nod. He leaned down to give her a kiss, only to have her jump back when someone knocked on the door.

Vivi's smile twisted. "They're looking for us."

"Of course they are. Come on." He tucked her hand in his and opened the door.

Vivi wasn't the only one in uncharted waters. This was completely new for him, too. Usually, though, he liked uncharted waters. They were exciting. They kept life interesting. He'd just never gone off without a map in his personal life before.

He reminded himself that he hadn't made it this far without taking chances. Vivi seemed to be a chance he was willing to take. One that might be worth taking.

And that was a new feeling.

Although few would believe it, Connor hadn't been home for a single parade in years. There just hadn't been time. Even fewer would believe that after such a hiatus Connor Mansfield wouldn't be part of the throngs of people on the streets partying—after all, that was part of the brand he'd built.

No one would believe, though, that he'd spend Saturday—the first major day of revelry—at a family friend's house on St. Charles Street, eating burgers off the grill and watching the parades from a balcony set back from the road and separated from the people by a large fence. It wasn't quiet by any stretch of the imagination—not between the crowds and the thirty or so people gathered in the Devereauxes' home—but the fence separated the public bacchanal from the family party nicely.

Angie, fresh off an afternoon on Bourbon Street, looked a little worse for wear when she returned around sunset. Angie was in her forties, her dark blond hair showing small streaks of gray like highlights. Seeing his all-business, L.A.-glam agent in jeans, with her usually perfectly coiffed hair askew and piles of colorful beads ringing her neck, was almost amusing.

"Wow! I kinda love this town," she said.

"It does have its charms."

"But to leave the French Quarter—which was almost scary at times—to come here..." She looked pointedly at the group of kids playing in the yard and the tables full of food. “It’s a bit of a disconnect.”

“This is how I remember most Mardi Gras growing up. I did the crazier stuff in high school, but as a kid… Well, all kids love a parade, right?”

“Not quite Norman Rockwell, but still very family-friendly. I wouldn’t have believed it.”

He smiled as he offered her another beer. “You might as well get comfortable and grab something to eat. We have a little time before the parade arrives.”

“And you’ll be on one of those floats on Tuesday, right?”

“Yep. The Sinner and the Saint and the whole court. Bon Argent doesn’t run its own parade, but since it’s a charity krewe, another krewe is more than willing to let us parade with them every year.”

Surprise crossed Angie’s face. “*Us?* You’ve joined up or something?”

“Of course. Membership for the Saint and Sinner is honorary, if they’re not already members, but they’ve asked me to serve on the board next year.”

“And you’re going to do it?”

Why was Angie looking at him like that? “Of course. Why wouldn’t I?”

“As your agent, I should probably know about these things before they’re a done deal.”

“It’s a volunteer position. I don’t get paid for it, so it doesn’t really require your input.”

“It’s not the money, Connor. Your plate is quite full at the moment—”

“And you would know, since you’re the one filling it,” he interrupted.

She smiled like that was a compliment. “You seem to be trying to rearrange everything to center around New Orleans.”

"Everyone needs a home base. I've decided to make my home my home base."

Angie sighed and shook her head. "This is Vivi's influence on you, isn't it?"

"What?"

"I feel like I'm staging an intervention." Setting down her beer, Angie clasped her hands in her lap and leaned forward. "I like Vivi. She's a nice girl, and a role model for many, but she's not *your* role model." She looked over to where Vivi, Lorelei and Jennie Devereaux were loading yet more food—and a King Cake—onto an already groaning table. "I know you're enjoying this, but don't screw up everything we've worked so hard for over the years."

We've. Like it had been a real joint effort. "I'm not screwing anything up. I'm just enjoying the benefits."

"Good." Angie nodded like a bobble-head doll. "Do that. Everyone should. Vivi certainly is, but you have a lot more to lose."

He was not in the mood for this. "Angie, if there's something you want to say, just say it. Quit beating around the bush."

"All right, then. I find it very interesting that out of nowhere you hook up with some local girl—"

"It's not out of nowhere," he corrected. "I've known Vivi my whole life."

Angie rolled her eyes. "Oh, it sounds all romantic, but when did you start believing your own lyrics? Step back for a minute. You yourself told me how this girl has hated you most of your life, yet she suddenly gets over it now that you're famous? That sounds a bit opportunistic to me."

"You're cynical, Ange."

"No, I'm realistic. Three weeks ago she was an aging beauty queen-slash-socialite with a small gallery in New

Orleans. This week she's on the cover of *People*. You know exactly the type of woman I'm talking about."

"I do. But you don't know Vivi. That's not her style at all."

"Really? And you know this *how?* Connor, her face is everywhere right now. She's had to hire a manager, companies are pitching reality TV shows to her, and she's suddenly a commodity on the speaker circuit… She went from nobody to somebody in record time, and all she had to do was sleep with you."

An unusual feeling, someplace between dread and anger, settled on his chest. Who or what it was directed at was a mystery. "There's a causal relationship, sure. But that doesn't imply forethought."

"But it should give *you* second thoughts, at least. Especially now that you're toying with ideas that could put your career back *years.*"

It shouldn't give him second thoughts, but Angie's earnestness forced him to consider it. He pushed it away as quickly as he could. "You're making all kinds of connections where there aren't any, and assigning motives where none exist. That smacks of paranoia."

"You're not my first or only client. After some of the crap I've seen, I sound like Pollyanna right now. I only want what's best for you, Connor."

Others might think Angie was mothering him with her concern, but Connor knew Angie didn't have a maternal bone in her body. She didn't even like live houseplants. They weren't friends. This was business.

"Or do you want what makes you the most money?"

"Honey, that's one and the same. Your success is my paycheck, but it's still your success and your paycheck. Let's not make any rash decisions you'll regret."

Right now his only regret was allowing his agent to attend a social event. Angie had soured his good mood. Her assertions were far-fetched at best, but he was too much of a cynic—or maybe he had had a little too much of spotlight-seeking women recently—to dismiss them completely out of hand.

But this was *Vivi* Angie was talking about…

The crowd on the street roared to life, and Vivi appeared a second later to put a hand on his shoulder. "That's the parade. You two coming?"

Connor had learned early on that no one in this business really cared about him—beyond what he could do for them, at least. Angie was just protecting her turf and the biggest cash cow in the herd. She had no life outside business and didn't understand anyone who did.

He stood and let Vivi catch his hand. *No.* This thing with Vivi was the realest thing that had happened to him in a long time.

Glancing over at Angie, he smiled. "I don't believe in regrets."

CHAPTER ELEVEN

RAIN came in Monday night, making Vivi worry, but Tuesday morning dawned clear. Vivi watched the morning weather report, cup of coffee in hand, and smiled when the meteorologist promised a sunny and mild afternoon. She'd both sweated and shivered through Mardi Gras in the past, but today might not be a bad day to spend in satin and angel wings.

"You're up early," Connor mumbled as he passed her on his way to the kitchen for coffee, pausing only to drop a kiss on the top of her head.

"It's a big day."

It certainly felt momentous already. Although it had been hard at times, Vivi had never spent the whole night with Connor, choosing instead to make her way home in the wee hours of the night. There'd been a couple of mornings where she'd barely made it home before dawn—which might be splitting hairs—but yesterday afternoon she'd purposefully packed a bag with the intent of staying all night. Waking up to sunshine peeking around the curtains and Connor snuggled firmly behind her had certainly felt momentous.

Connor came back with a steaming mug and read the weather ticker off the bottom of the screen. He looked sleep-rumpled and freshly rolled-out-of-bed-sexy, whereas she'd taken a couple of minutes to wash her face and brush her hair. He looked delicious, no matter what, but she didn't have quite the same confidence.

"You okay?" he asked.

She didn't have to ask about what. Connor's call had come from Max about nine o'clock last night, congratulating him on his win. Although she'd been next to Connor on the couch, and heard Connor's side of the entire conversation, she'd waited for Max to call her a few minutes later to break the news to her. They'd been a little preoccupied with other activities, though, and hadn't had much of a chance to discuss it.

"Of course. I'm disappointed, but I reconciled myself to this weeks ago. All things considered, I think I put in a good showing, and we raised a ton of money."

"That's Pageant Vivi talking."

"I've had practice at being a gracious loser."

"You can still ride up top with me, you know."

"I will not flout tradition like that. *You* will be on top, where you belong."

"But I like it when you're on top."

That statement had Vivi trying to calculate how much time they had this morning before they had to leave for the parade. Traffic would be terrible, but…

They were half an hour late. But everyone and everything seemed to be running late as well, so they spent another twenty minutes hanging around. Well, *she* hung around; Connor signed autographs and smiled for cameras with fans from their host krewe and riders on the floats. She rather wished she'd brought a book.

"Congratulations, Vivi."

Angie stood behind her, slightly overdressed for the event, with big black sunglasses covering her eyes. Vivi knew that Angie was very good at her job, but Vivi didn't like her all that much. There was something about her that was just off-putting. She was just too brusque and focused on the bottom line for Vivi's taste.

"I will say thanks, because it's over and we did a great job, but they haven't officially announced anything. All congratulations are technically premature."

"I'd say you did pretty well, regardless."

"Thank you. I was afraid Connor would simply stomp me, but I think I held my own."

"I didn't mean in the competition—but kudos to you, of course, for that."

She couldn't see Angie's eyes for the sunglasses, but the slightly mocking smile put her on alert. "Then I'm afraid I don't know what you mean."

"It doesn't really matter if you win or lose this competition. I'd think you'd be proud of yourself either way."

What was Angie getting at? "I am. Like I said, Saints and Sinners has been a great success."

"You're certainly reaping the benefits."

Okay, there was definitely a snort in there. Vivi lost patience. "Angie, if there's something you want to say, please just say it. I'm really not in the mood for games."

"You've managed to ride this little event straight into the spotlight…on Connor," she finished crudely.

"Excuse me?"

"Oh, you're quite clever, and I repeat my kudos. You certainly know how to take advantage of a situation. Nice write-up in the *Times,* by the way."

The insult and implication were obvious. Vivi felt her jaw gape in shock. "I won't deny that my relationship with Connor has opened up all kinds of new doors for me, but I'm not seeing Connor for that reason."

"Oh, honey, I'm not judging you—"

It sure sounds like it.

"I know all about how this game is played."

"This isn't a game. If you're worried about Connor—"

"I never worry about Connor. He's a pro. He knows how it works. This business creates strange bedfellows, but it's all still business in the end. A little *quid pro quo* is just part of it."

"Well, if there was supposed to be some *quid pro quo* Connor got the short end of that stick." Vivi tried to laugh it off, because outrage and insult were growing. Soon she'd be saying something she'd really regret.

"I don't worry about Connor. Saints and Sinners gave him a chance to do something to counterbalance the whole Katy Arras thing. I tried to tell him it would die down and pass in its own time, but he's not the patient type. He likes to be proactive, you know. Change the PR conversation himself."

Vivi felt a small rock settle in her stomach. So much for pure altruism. But what had she expected, really? Connor had had an opportunity to change the narrative surrounding him and he had. And he'd done a great job as the Sinner—raised the profile of the event… The fact that he'd benefitted personally and professionally didn't negate the entire experience.

Even if it did cheapen it a bit.

Vivi pulled herself back. It was a multilayered situation. It couldn't be pulled apart and overanalyzed. Even if she was tempted to do just that.

Angie shrugged and surveyed the crowds of people milling around. Vivi knew the body language and braced herself.

"Connor's a very smart guy. Hooking up with you was a brilliant idea."

That *definitely* wasn't a compliment. Vivi gathered up as much dignity as she could while wearing five-foot wings. "I like to think that Connor has very good taste." *Damn. That came out stiffer than she'd hoped.*

Angie looked her up and down. "Oh, certainly. He needed

to find himself a good girl to vindicate him. It would have been better if he'd been able to go the whole redemption route—much more press that way, and people just eat it up—but your approval was almost as good as papal forgiveness. And brilliantly played by both of you. It was like a fairy tale or something. By the time he gets back home—L.A. home, that is—everyone will be claiming they never believed that woman to begin with."

"Connor has plans here, too."

Angie's eyebrows arched over her sunglasses again, and Vivi felt the look of amused pity even if she couldn't fully see it.

"Connor's full of ideas. Half of them never work out. That's why he needs me. He always claims he's moving home after a tour, but once he's caught up on his sleep he forgets all about it." Angie shook her head. "I know Connor. I've known him since he was opening for second-string acts at crappy clubs. Whatever those plans are, I promise you that he will lose all interest very soon. He'll need to be back in the studio and back on the road."

The rock in Vivi's stomach grew and made her nauseous. She recognized the cattiness for what it was, but that didn't help allay the sick feeling. If this had come from anyone other than Angie, Vivi would easily have dismissed it as jealousy. But this had been delivered with unemotional, professional distance. Angie had no personal reason to unsheath her claws.

It was ridiculous, but that very ridiculousness gave it weight. And that weight settled into Vivi's stomach. Angie's phone rang. She answered it without so much as an *excuse me,* but Vivi was happy for the reprieve.

But she couldn't shake the sick feeling. It niggled at her, playing on insecurities she hadn't known she still had. By the time Max got everyone's attention for the official announcement, she felt green around the gills.

Vivi made her way to the float, where Connor met her at the makeshift stairs. It was similar to their pageantry on the night of the ball. They climbed slowly to the top and took their places behind the velvet pillow holding the Saint's halo and the Sinner's horns.

Max started his speech—a rundown of how much they'd accomplished with their various community projects and the amount of money raised. Even through her unease, Vivi felt a moment of pride at the amount. A huge cheer went through the crowd and Vivi tried to enjoy it.

"Team Sinner!"

There was another roar of approval, and Vivi shot an apologetic look at her team of Cherubim. Connor noticed and leaned down.

"Don't worry about them. Both courts get excellent seats at my next concert, but the losing team gets backstage passes as well."

The forethought and kindness of the gesture lightened the rock. Connor wasn't in this for just selfish reasons.

Max signaled her, and Vivi picked up her halo and presented it to Connor, who hoisted it above the float like a pirate flag. He then placed his horns back on his head. Vivi curtseyed, and Connor climbed to the top tier of the float, his Imps right behind him, and took his place on the enormous throne with the Saints and Sinners crest above him. She and her Cherubim would man the lower tier.

The float began to inch forward. She looked up at Connor's throne and found him staring at her. Once he'd caught her eye, he gave her a wink and a small wave. Then, a huge grin on his face, he leaned back, propped his feet on the railing, and stacked his hands behind his head. He seemed to be genuinely enjoying the moment.

Whatever Angie's problem was, Vivi wasn't going to convict Connor of anything on hearsay alone. And if Angie was wrong on one front, she was probably wrong on the other, too.

The drumline of the marching band began their beat, and they were officially under way. The sun came out from behind a cloud, and the excitement of the kids around her was palpable.

Today was a day to celebrate—even if she was celebrating a loss. And for now she had beads to throw.

Connor dropped his and Vivi's wings by the door with a mental sigh of relief. Cool-looking or not, twelve hours in them was more than enough for any man. The chafing…

As if she'd read his mind, Vivi chuckled as she kicked off her shoes and dug a pair of sweatpants out of her overnight bag. "I told you to wear something underneath the harness. I learned my lesson after the last time."

Connor carried the three-foot Saints and Sinners trophy they'd presented to him at the end of the parade to the coffee table and set it down. "Think it's big enough?"

"No need to brag about it," Vivi grumbled.

He shook his head at her. "You are a poor loser."

"I am not. I just like trophies."

He shot her a disbelieving look.

"It's true. I do like trophies. Because you get them when you win."

"And you like to win," he added.

"I am a serious competitor," she corrected.

"And a poor loser."

Vivi shook her head at him. "Whatever. I will not lie and say I didn't want that trophy. Unhook me, please?"

She turned her back to him as she asked and looked out the French doors at the street below. The crowds in the

French Quarter had reached their peak tonight, and even through the thick window glass he could hear the noise of the party a block over on Bourbon. Even Royal Street—with its lack of bars—was busy. If he could muster the energy, he *might* go out on the balcony and toss some beads to folks in the street, but right now even that seemed beyond his capability. In two hours, at midnight, the police would begin to clear the streets and Mardi Gras would be over.

The hooks of Vivi's dress opened under his fingers, but unlike the last time he'd done this, he found the soft cotton of an undershirt instead of soft skin. She was probably still sore from the harness, and it would have solved the chafing problem nicely. "You're lucky your dress covers you enough to wear something under the harness. How could I possibly wear a shirt under this getup?"

Vivi pulled her arms out of the dress and let it drop to the floor. Clad in only the undershirt and a tiny pair of lacy panties, she stretched and groaned in relief. It was a lovely, erotic view he was almost too tired to fully appreciate, but he was still disappointed when Vivi's legs disappeared into the purple sweats. Then she dropped to the couch and let her head rest against the arm.

"I'll call Ms. Rene in the morning and offer some advice for the next time she wants to put someone in wings. But not right now. I'm just too exhausted to move anymore. I just want a glass of wine, a seat that doesn't move under me and a little quiet."

Connor peeled the leather vest off and started unwinding the leather straps from around his arms. "Amen to that. I was almost afraid you'd want to head out for the last couple of hours."

"No way. It was a fun day but, mercy, it's been a long one." She sighed. "I don't want to see or talk to another human being for several days."

"Including me?"

"You may stay—but only if you bring the wine over here," she conceded. "I'm not moving from this spot until tomorrow. Call me a party pooper if you wish, but stick a fork in me 'cause I'm done."

He grabbed the wine and two glasses and set them on the table next to Vivi. The leather pants were off next, and he felt much better immediately. Tossing them into the pile with Vivi's dress, he went to the bedroom and grabbed a pair of jeans.

As he returned, Vivi shot him a sly look. "However, please don't let me stop you from enjoying yourself out there."

"I may not leave this apartment for at least a week." He joined her on the couch, lifting her feet out of the way to sit before placing them in his lap. "But if anyone asks, it was your idea to stay in for the rest of the night. Connor Mansfield should be out there partying hard, not safe on his couch and contemplating sleep at ten o'clock."

She frowned at him, a little crinkle forming between her eyes. "That makes me sound like a drag on your social life."

He poured, and handed a glass to Vivi. "One of the greatest things about dating a saint, I've discovered, is that everyone expects you to rein me in, reform my wicked ways and get me accepted back into polite society."

Vivi stiffened, and the wineglass paused halfway to her mouth. "Really? Is that what I'm doing?"

The clipped words came from left field. "Huh?"

"I'm reforming you?" She removed her legs from his lap and pushed up to a seated position. "Bringing you back into the 'right' social circles because you're a good boy now?"

"You don't actually have to do anything, you know. It's the appearance that counts."

"I see." She swung her feet to the floor and put her glass

back on the table. "Are you saying that getting involved with me was part of some larger PR stunt?"

For someone claiming exhaustion a few minutes ago, she certainly seemed to have energy to spare now. "What? No."

"But you do admit that being with me has cleaned up your image some?"

What did it matter? "Yes, but I'd already decided to try to make peace with you before we became anything at all."

"Why?"

"We've been through this, Vivi."

"No, I think we skipped this. When, *exactly,* did you decide you wanted a cease-fire?"

He thought. "I don't know. That first weekend, maybe? Why?"

"Actually, that's my next question for you."

"Why would I try to get past the ridiculous antagonism of our youth?" To his surprise, she nodded. "Because we're adults."

Vivi scrubbed a hand across her face. "And what brought you home this time, after so many years?"

Okay, new topic. He was too tired to keep up. "I was asked to do Saints and Sinners. Same as you. Vivi, what are you talking about?"

"I just want to know why you agreed to be the Sinner. For someone fresh off a paternity and sex scandal, proclaiming yourself a sinner seems a bit counterintuitive PR-wise."

"What better way to get past it all? It showed I had a good sense of humor and—"

"Made you look good, too?"

"Yes. Is that a problem, Vivi?"

"It kinda is, yeah."

"Why?"

"Because that's not what this is supposed to be about."

"I'm sorry that my motives aren't as pure as you'd like

them to be, but that doesn't make them evil either. Bon Argent wanted to make money and increase their profile. Mission accomplished. Big round of applause. Everybody wins, right?"

Vivi was biting her bottom lip so hard the skin was turning white. She'd be drawing blood soon. "So was I…was *this*...part of your not entirely evil plan, too?"

"You're not making sense, Vivi."

"Actually, it's making perfect sense now. I can't believe I didn't see it before. Saint Vivienne was just the icing on your redemption cake. After all, if sweet Saint Vivi is on your side, you must be just a misunderstood and unfairly vilified sinner. It's so obvious now. I can't believe I fell for that 'bygones' and 'let's be adults' crap, much less slept with you. Lord, I am *such* a fool."

"Have you lost your mind? Where is all this coming from?"

"You used me."

"I didn't use you."

Vivi rolled her eyes. "It's Marie Lester all over again."

"Really? We're going back *there?*"

"You haven't changed at all."

"Only you seem to see it that way. I just wanted the war to end. I want to live in this town in peace, and I can't do that when we're always sniping at each other. I get enough hassle elsewhere, thanks. I never claimed otherwise."

"And sleeping with me?"

"I thought that was a mutual attraction. I didn't know I'd have to prove my intentions after the fact."

Vivi's eyes narrowed. That wary, distrustful and disapproving look he knew so well was back. It cut him to the quick and angered him at the same time.

"You don't believe me. Wow. That's just…" Even after everything, Vivi so easily thought the worst of him. Shaking his head, he walked over to Gabe's bar in search of something stronger than wine. "Have you been stewing on this the whole time, Vivi?"

"No."

The relief that rushed in at her denial was short-lived.

"Maybe at first, but I got swept up in you and everything else and didn't bother to think about anything. You know, I could've handled just being a fling. But a pawn in your overall career plan? That's just wrong. Maybe I might have been willing to play along if you'd just been honest with me from the start. It didn't have to be like this."

Her words hit him like a slap. "Until right now, I thought 'this' was pretty damn good."

She didn't say anything.

"Oh, get off your high horse, Vivi. *You* showed up at *my* door in the middle of the night. And *you're* the one who keeps coming back."

If looks could kill, he'd be dead on the floor in a puddle of blood right now.

"You don't see me hurling accusations about your motives simply because it worked out so well for *you*."

Her jaw dropped. *"What?"*

"I'm not the only one who's benefitted from this. Being Connor Mansfield's flavor of the month seems to be much more beneficial than first runner-up in Miss America. Just when you thought your glory days were behind you..."

"Shut up! You know, I kinda felt bad about all that attention, but now...not so much. It's only fair that I get something out of this, too."

"Wow, it seems *I* should be the one fluttering about my wounded virtue and being used, not you."

"You have no one to blame but yourself, then. I was willing to just hope for civility during Saints and Sinners. You, though, started spouting all that garbage about the inherent foibles of teenage boys and asking for forgiveness—"

"*Forgiveness?* Honestly, sanctimonious doesn't even *begin* to describe your attitude. Your superiority complex is unbelievable. Either you're fooling yourself, or you're working hard to fool everybody else, because you're nothing but a fraud."

Vivi was one of those rare women for whom anger was a good look. Pieces of her hair had come down from its ponytail, curling perfectly around the curve of her cheeks—which were flushed pink and brought out the blue in her eyes. Anger snapped in the air around them, and her chest heaved with it. But her eyes were clear—no false tears there.

Those eyes raked over him in cold disdain before her lip curled into a snarl. "Screw you, Connor."

Lips pressed together like she was dying to say more, Vivi pulled her sneakers out of her bag and shoved her feet inside. Then she began gathering up the few things of hers scattered around the apartment and tossing them in on top.

"Oh, that's mature," he said, mostly to her back as she stomped around.

She made a rude hand gesture in return.

"And, oh, so ladylike. If people knew the real you they'd think twice before relying so heavily on your opinions and judgments of other people."

She grabbed her coat, shoved her arms inside, and then spun around to level a steely look at him. "At least people *can* rely on me. They can trust me. I'm honest, and I care. That's a lot more than I can say about you." Vivi looked him up and down, then shook her head. "You're a great musician, Connor, but you're a lousy human being."

Hitching her bag over her shoulder, Vivi grabbed her wings and slammed out the door. A moment later he heard the security door at the bottom of the stairs slam shut as well.

Connor couldn't remember a time when he'd been this angry at another person. Oh, he could remember plenty of times being this angry with Vivi, but this level couldn't be reached with anyone else. He splashed another two fingers of Gabe's excellent and expensive Scotch into a glass and tossed it back in one swallow.

So much for that. To think that Vivi could harbor that much distrust and old grudges after everything that had happened recently. And to automatically believe the absolute worst about him. It was insulting. Infuriating.

And it hurt, too.

If anyone had been played for a fool it was him. He'd thought… Well, he'd thought this was more than it had actually turned out to be, and that just rubbed salt in the wound.

He'd brought it on himself, though. He should have known getting involved with Vivi would be a disaster. And, hey, he'd have been right. In less than forty-five minutes they'd gone from lovers to enemies. And now he was beginning to think she'd always been his enemy, and this was just a grand plot on her part to inflict some new misery into his life.

And when she'd stormed out the door…

Damn it, Vivi had just stormed out into the biggest street party in the country in the middle of the night—alone. Between the drunks and the type of people who preyed on the drunks it simply wasn't safe.

He wasn't that big of a jerk.

He stepped out onto the balcony, searching for her in the crowd below, but she was already gone.

Vivi locked the gallery door behind her and reset the alarm. She dropped the stupid wings to the floor in disgust. There was no way on earth she was fighting her way through that mess out there to get home.

Of course she hadn't planned to go home tonight at all.

But somehow she'd managed to end up in a shouting match, saying really horrible things, and she had no idea how she'd got there.

The details were a bit fuzzy—the result of letting temper and pride rule the day instead of her brain.

That had been ugly, but those were things that had needed to be said. Connor hadn't changed a bit, and she'd been foolish to pretend otherwise. Angie, whatever her catty reasons for doing so, had been honest with her. Her own willingness to dismiss that information only made the foolishness worse.

There was a bottle of champagne in the fridge in her office, a Christmas gift that she'd never taken home, and that knowledge drew her to her office like a magnet. She didn't feel much like celebrating, but alcohol would dull the current pain. Connor's words had sliced her, but the realization that he just might be right about her deepened the cuts and poured salt in the wound.

She had no one to blame but herself. She'd fallen for Connor's line. The shame came from how easily she'd done it simply because it was so attractive. She'd thought she was breaking new personal ground—growing as a person, trying new things—but that just seemed like a weak excuse now.

She hated feeling weak. And she hated Connor a little more for being the one to ferret out that weakness and exploit it.

The cork popped out with ease, and Vivi didn't bother looking for a glass. Drinking straight from the bottle—even if it was champagne instead of something harder—seemed to fit her mood. She hugged the bottle to her chest as she curled into the corner of the couch in her office to berate herself and mope. From the depths of her bag she heard her phone chime as a text came in.

Whatever it is, I'm not interested.

Then, with a sigh, she dug the phone out anyway—only

to stop short when she saw Connor's name. The message was brief: *At least let me know you made it home.*

What had she expected? An apology? Of course not. And she couldn't—*wouldn't*—read anything into the message. No matter how much she tried to convince him otherwise, he just wouldn't believe she could handle herself on the bad streets of their hometown. Obviously he thought she was weak, too, and it fueled both her anger and her self-flagellation.

Ignore it. She certainly didn't owe Connor anything. Even as she thought it, though, her thumbs were moving over the screen: *I am safely indoors.* There was no need to offer the information that she'd only gone as far as the gallery—just in case Connor decided he wasn't finished with the conversation.

She spent a restless, miserable night on the couch, and when the cathedral bells began to chime for the first Ash Wednesday services she dragged herself home through the nearly empty streets.

Surprisingly, Lorelei was already up. From the pained look and dark bags under her eyes to the aspirin in her hands and the careful, unsteady walk, Lorelei was a living picture of a bad hangover.

"Mercy, Vivi, what happened to you? You look worse than I feel."

Vivi took a deep breath. All the justifications and condemnations she'd arrived at during a mostly sleepless night scrambled to the tip of her tongue, ready to flay Connor.

She burst into tears instead.

CHAPTER TWELVE

Good to his word, Connor didn't leave the apartment for several days. He told himself that he needed to work, and he did, getting more accomplished in those days than he had in weeks. Months, probably. It was amazing how productive he could be when he didn't have all kinds of distractions.

His first major accomplishment involved firing Angie shortly after she appeared on Wednesday afternoon. Her somewhat smug acceptance of the condensed and sanitized story of Vivi's departure and her less than enthusiastic response to his decisions about his career clearly showed they'd reached the end of their usefulness to each other.

But throwing himself into his plans only kept the demons at bay for a while, and it didn't taken long for the walls to close in on him. He'd had such a high profile the last few weeks that any absence led to speculation, and his first couple of forays out into the public quickly hit the star-watching blogs—complete with questions about Vivi's sudden absence and what it might mean.

Vivi's words and Vivi's absence haunted him. After a few days he realized she'd been partly right. He'd fired Angie rather than continuing to let her use him as a cash cow, and it had forced him to recognize Vivi's hurt at the possibility he'd used her in a similar fashion. The kernel of truth was there—however small—and had the tables been turned he'd probably feel the same way.

But the fact she'd assumed the worst, rushed to judgment and condemnation… That was just messed up. They might not have the best track record, but that quick jump to believing the worst was uncalled for. *She* was the one who'd made noise about where they were going until he'd started to think that way as well. Now that that had bitten him in the ass, he was discovering he was more than just a little bitter about it.

He was honest enough with himself to realize that the strange hollow feeling in his chest had Vivi's name all over it, and the black irony of the situation didn't escape him. The one woman he'd never thought he'd want to have was the one woman who turned out to be the person who'd made him the happiest. The one woman whose opinion seemed to matter the most didn't like the man he was.

Vivi didn't want him, didn't need him, and didn't trust him. He sat at the piano, his hands wandering aimlessly over the keys, and realized that it mattered a hell of a lot more than it should. Because, if nothing else, the last few weeks had given him a whole new perspective on Vivi—a new appreciation for the woman she was.

And she didn't think he was worth it.

It was a blow to his ego and his pride.

Unable to focus, he took his coffee to the balcony. Two days ago, he'd rearranged the furniture so that all the chairs faced the other way. It gave him a different view, but more important it kept him from staring at the door of Vivi's gallery as if life was a bad, broody music video. He'd seen her a couple of times entering or leaving the gallery, but she never looked up in his direction.

While Vivi hadn't dropped out of the public spotlight, she was definitely keeping a low profile, refusing to comment on Connor's whereabouts or their sudden lack of public togetherness. As far as he could tell Vivi, had simply decided to pretend he didn't exist.

And why did that bother him so much?

He'd made a heap of money singing about this moment, this feeling—even if he'd never truly experienced it before, never wanted to get emotionally involved with anyone before, *ever.* And now he knew why. It sucked. Once he got over it, though, he'd probably make a boatload more money from the songs he would write. He snorted. The whole music industry was predicated on the misery of failed relationships.

Damn it, he didn't *want* to suffer for his art or any of that crap. It was pathetic and ridiculous and shameful, but he wanted Vivi. He wanted that feeling of ease and contentment that came from being with her. He missed her smile and the way she rolled her eyes at him when he said something stupid, and the way she grounded him in reality when he started believing his own press releases.

He wanted Vivi to want him the way he wanted her. He wanted Vivi to love him.

Because he was in love with her.

He sighed and let his head fall back. Great timing figuring that out.

Or maybe it wasn't.

He might have been a little slow getting to this point, but she'd hated him for twenty-something years and managed to come around—*and* she'd come far enough to admit she wanted more. She'd only had a few days to hate him this time, and she didn't know that he was in love with her. He might be able to salvage this.

How was a damn fine question, though.

It wasn't like he could just call her. Even if she deigned to take his call, this was news that needed to be delivered in person. But he had no idea where she was. If he went to the gallery to look for her someone would notice—and the chances of *that* working out well were slim to none.

Which meant his best bet was to call Lorelei.

It took him forever to find her number, and by the time she answered he was feeling more confident about the possibilities.

"It's Connor."

"I know." The clipped words, followed by silence, undermined that confidence a little. She'd always been an ally, but now… Whatever Vivi had told her, it had turned Lorelei against him as well. He'd really screwed this up.

"Do you know where Vivi is?"

"Of course."

Sisterly loyalties were obviously stronger than he'd thought. This was going to be worse than pulling teeth. But this was nothing compared to the reception he expected from Vivi, so it would be good practice.

"Could you tell me where she is?"

"I *could,*" she stressed, "but why on earth would I *want* to?"

"Because it's really, really important that I talk to her."

"Let me save you some time, Connor. She doesn't want to talk to you."

"I just need to tell her something. Please, Lorelei?"

"Why don't you give me the message and I'll pass it along."

He wanted to bang his head against something hard. It would probably be easier in the long run to sit on her front porch until she came home. It would be very public, and possibly very messy, but it might still be preferable to this.

No, if it got ugly, he didn't want it on the blogs. "It's not that kind of message."

"Then, no. I'm not going to let you hurt her more. You've done enough damage."

"And I want to fix it."

"Really?" Lorelei's voice held interest for the first time in this conversation and it buoyed his hopes.

"Yes. That's why I need to find her. To apologize and tell her that I—" He stopped himself. If he was going to say the words, he should say them to Vivi first. He rubbed his temples, feeling like a complete idiot right now. "There's something she needs to know."

Lorelei thought for a moment, and he hoped that meant he was winning her over. When she spoke, he heaved a sigh of relief. "She's got a ton going on today—"

That figured.

"—but she should be home by five-thirty or six, maybe?"

He didn't want to wait that long. "Where is she now, Lorelei?"

"It's that important, huh? All righty, then." He thought he could hear a smile. "She has meetings this morning—Arts Council, maybe?—then a luncheon of some sort. She'll be at your mom's at three, of course—"

"My mom's?"

"Oh, how quickly we forget. It's the third Thursday of the month. That's the Musical Association meeting."

Of course.

"That'll work. Thanks, Lorelei."

Her voice turned deadly serious. "Don't screw this up. If you hurt her, I will strangle you with Mardi Gras beads and throw your body in the bayou. Understand?"

"Perfectly."

She laughed. "I'm actually looking forward to this meeting now. Good luck."

Lorelei hung up, and Connor felt optimistic for the first time in days. Vivi would be tougher to win over, but Lorelei wouldn't have provided the information if she didn't believe

Connor had something to say that Vivi would *want* to hear. That boded well.

He had a couple of hours to figure out what he was going to say and how he was going to do it. He knew the when and the where, but beyond that… His brain went blank.

Lorelei's words came back to him: *Don't screw this up.*

He had to do this right.

For the first time ever, he had a bout of stage fright.

Vivi wanted to care about what Mrs. Gilroy was saying about the annual Musical Association Ball, but honestly she couldn't manage to pay attention—much less dredge up enough of a damn to offer anything to the conversation. From the looks Mrs. Gilroy kept giving her, Vivi had to guess that she was surprised she had so little to say.

But the truth was Vivi didn't care about centerpieces or invitation lists. She didn't care about the budget or potential donors. She didn't even care that Mrs. Mansfield had promised her famous *petit fours* after the business meeting.

She just didn't care. About anything.

She'd tried the time-honored tradition of ice cream and mindless TV, but that had only provided time for self-recrimination and painful moping. Coming face-to-face with the fact she was sanctimonious, supercilious, uptight and everything else Connor had called her was downright depressing. She deserved every bit of the pain she was feeling and had no one to blame but herself that she'd screwed this up so bad.

So she'd gone the opposite route, covering herself in work in the hopes it would keep her busy enough not to think and possibly redeem herself at the same time. Even adding three new committees to her schedule hadn't filled the empty spaces. All it did was occupy her time and exhaust her enough to sleep at night.

But it didn't mean anything or fill her with any satisfaction. She felt like a fraud.

She didn't want to go home, but she certainly didn't want to sit here in Connor's mother's parlor under the gaze of twenty women who all knew she'd been involved with Connor and were dying to ask questions that etiquette mandated were none of their business. Mrs. Mansfield kept giving her long, inscrutable looks from her seat under a picture of Connor at his high school graduation.

I should have just skipped this meeting.

Her mom, showing clairvoyance, patted her knee under the table and gave a small squeeze of support. On her left Lorelei, unbelievably, looked enraptured by the discussion of the possibility of a "Winter Wonderland" theme. Aside from the ridiculous fact the Musical Association Ball would be held in the sweltering heat of August, same as it had been for the last thirty-five years, Lorelei hadn't given the ball a second thought since her presentation seven years ago. She only came to these meetings because Mom expected her to, so this newfound interest in the Association's business was a new development.

Vivi gave herself a strong mental slap and sat up straight in her chair with the intent of listening to Mrs. Gilroy and coming up with something constructive to add. Like it or not, *this* was her life. Connor had been an interlude, a fling, a stray outside of the norm. Like all experiences, it had something to teach her—mainly about the dangers of straying outside the norm.

But the norm was very hard to find now. Not giving a damn about Connor beyond the fact she couldn't stand him *was* the norm, and it was nearly impossible to get back to that state of being. It was the first challenge of her life that didn't hold excitement or appeal. She didn't even want to try.

Her best hope was that time would help. She'd overheard

Mrs. Mansfield tell Mrs. Raines that Connor would be going back to L.A. sooner than expected to take care of some business. To Vivi, that had felt like a slap, but she knew that not having Connor around, staying just yards from her gallery's door, would be good for her in the long run.

If that didn't work… Moving to a different city herself was an option under serious consideration as well.

Through the jumble of her thoughts Vivi heard the magic words "meeting adjourned." The ladies of the Musical Association headed for the sideboard *en masse.* Vivi leaned toward her mother. "I'm going to leave now. My allergies are giving me a splitting headache."

Lorelei turned toward her and frowned. "You don't have allergies."

"Well, something is giving me a headache."

Mom stepped in. "Go home and lie down, Vivi. I hope you feel better."

"Good afternoon, ladies. I hear my mom made *petit fours.*"

The silence that fell in the wake of Connor's entrance was total as the matriarchs of New Orleans society swiveled their heads to Connor and then to Vivi.

"Connor, sweetheart." Mrs. Mansfield swept forward to give her only son a hug. "This is certainly a surprise."

On cue, everyone started speaking again—slightly louder than necessary in an uncomfortable attempt to seem normal. Her mom's lips pulled into a tight line and she stepped closer to Vivi. Lorelei was grinning like a fool. Everyone else was ignoring her—except Connor, who seemed to be trying to stare her into the floor even as he greeted the women who pressed forward to see him. The ice that had formed around her feet at the sound of Connor's voice felt impossible to break, and Vivi's pulse jumped as adrenaline surged through her veins.

Connor's voice sounded unnaturally loud. "I remember when Mom used to make me come and play for Association meetings. I thought it might be fun to do it without being forced."

"For once." Mrs. Mansfield smiled with pride. "That would be wonderful."

Connor moved to the piano, and the women seemed to be back in their seats instantly. Only Vivi remained standing. Leaving now would only call attention to herself and embarrass her. She gave the universe the chance to grant her wish and let the floor swallow her, but when that didn't happen, she sank carefully into her chair with what she hoped looked like poise.

The need to strangle Connor felt comfortably familiar, and actually helped tame her racing heart. She felt her mother's hand slide under hers in support, and then, unbelievably, Lorelei did the same from the other side.

Connor played a quick progression of notes. "Trust my mom to keep it in perfect tune."

Mrs. Mansfield looked ready to burst with pride and pleasure.

"This is the Musical Association, so I should probably play some Chopin or Liszt. If I remember correctly, Mrs. Gilroy loves Rachmaninoff." He played a few bars.

Now Mrs. Gilroy had the same expression as Mrs. Mansfield. Vivi focused her eyes on an oil painting above the piano and took slow breaths.

"But I'm a bit out of practice on the classics, ladies—sorry. I'm actually here to get your collective and esteemed opinion on a new piece I've been working on."

Vivi could feel the pleasure of the members. *Spare me.* Connor had these women eating out of the palms of his very talented hands. She knew the feeling.

"It's actually a song inspired by our own Vivienne LaBlanc."

A gasp fluttered though the crowd.

"We've spent quite a lot of time together the last few weeks, as you know."

I hate him. Did he have to have the last word, humiliating her in front of people she'd known her entire life? *If I ever get out of here, I'm moving to a cabin in Wisconsin.*

"It's funny how coming home can bring you full circle. One of the first songs I ever wrote was for Vivi. We were in junior high and, while the rest of the class enjoyed it, it didn't go over very well with Vivi herself."

No, I'll kill him first, and then move to Wisconsin.

"I hope she likes this one a bit better."

Vivi was so focused on not looking at him, not completely losing it in front of all these people, that the music didn't register at first. Then shock moved through her. Sixteen notes that she knew by heart. The sixteen notes that he'd taught her that first night they were together.

She remembered sitting inside the circle of his arms while he helped her find the keys, and then the way he'd made the music around her. The memory brought a physical sensation that bordered on pain. Her eyes began to burn, and she quickly swallowed the lump forming in her throat.

Look at me, what do you see?
A man, longing to be free.

Connor's voice rolled over the room like a rich blanket, and pain streaked through her soul.

Free to be, true to you,
To the end.

Vivi could feel twenty pairs of eyes on her, but she refused to take *her* eyes off the painting above the piano.

I'll listen close and understand.
To the end.

The music grew louder and Connor's voice grew stronger.

I dare you to hold me.
One touch and you'll never know lonely again.

Although she didn't want to, Vivi couldn't stop herself from risking a peek at Connor. His eyes bored straight into hers.

Again and again, we'll just be—
To the end.

Vivi's feet finally unfroze, and she moved quickly to the door. She was nearly blinded by the tears in her eyes, but she made it down the porch stairs without falling and headed for the gate.

Connor caught her before she had it open.

"Vivi, where are you going?"

"Anywhere but here. I can't believe you just did that."

Connor's eyes went wide. "That? *That* was my attempt at an apology."

Vivi had been hit with too many things in the last few minutes. She said the first thing that came to mind. "You had to do it in front of the Musical Association?"

There was an awkward pause. "Well, you don't have a piano at your house." He half smiled at her. "And I didn't think I could get you to come to Gabe's. This was the only place."

His earlier words finally filtered through. "Wait. That was an apology? To me?"

"Yeah. It's still a little rough in places, but I generally do better with words set to music."

"An apology?" She couldn't quite wrap her head around it.

"For being a jerk. For not being honest with you—not at the beginning, and not the other night."

She couldn't quite keep up. "About what the other night?"

"If I'd been honest, I'd have told you that I love you."

The world swam for a moment. When it righted, Vivi couldn't believe she'd heard him correctly. "That doesn't make sense."

He nodded. "You're right. And yet the weird thing is that it still manages to be true. I don't know why I didn't figure that out years ago." Shrugging that off, he reached for her hands. "Of course, you've never accused me of being particularly intelligent."

"But…"

"I don't understand it either, Vivi. All I know is that you are the strongest woman I've ever met. You're smart and beautiful and you don't let anyone—including me—stand in your way. You care and you have a good heart. You make me want to be the kind of man who deserves that kind of woman."

Her breath caught in her chest and her lungs squeezed her heart in a vise. His words made her actions the other night all the more inexcusable. "I'm the one who owes *you* an apology. I was way out of line and I overreacted."

"All things considered, though…it's understandable."

"I'm still really sorry."

"Me, too. Old habits die hard."

"Yeah." Then she looked up at him. "But is it weird to say that I'm happy anyway?"

"Not at all." He rubbed his hands over her arms. "You know what would make *me* happy, though?"

"What?"

He cleared his throat. "I said something kind of big and important a second ago, and you haven't said it back. The suspense is bordering on painful."

Her heart gave another small squeeze. "For someone who's made a lot of money—and made a lot of women swoon—with love songs, you're a little unknowledgeable of the particulars. If I didn't love you—hadn't loved you—I wouldn't have cared what you said or did."

"Really?" Connor looked quite pleased.

She returned the smile. "Really."

"Good, because I'm realizing I'm a bit of a sore loser, too. At least when it comes to losing you."

Connor's mouth found hers, and Vivi felt whole for the first time. It didn't make sense, but that didn't make it any less right.

The sound of applause brought her back to reality. Heat rising in her cheeks, she peeked over Connor's shoulder to see the entire Musical Association membership crowded on the Mansfields' front porch.

"Do you always draw an audience?" she asked.

"It happens." Connor laced his fingers through hers and squeezed her hand. "You know, there's a whole other verse to that song. Want to hear it?"

"Maybe later. If you hadn't noticed, I was on my way out when you stopped me."

Connor's smile dimmed slightly. "Oh? Where are you going?"

"Wherever you're willing to take me."

That brought back Connor's smile, and it carried a promise that sent shivers down to the soles of her feet. Opening the gate, he pulled her through without so much as a fare-well glance at the ladies on the porch.

His car was parked at the curb, and the lights blinked as they approached. Opening the door, Connor gave her a quick kiss and a wink. "Then you better hold on to your halo, Saint Vivi."

"Saints and Sinners is over," she told him. "You even got the trophy."

"Forget the trophy. I got the girl. And that's far better."

Her heart turned gooey and melty at his words. Connor helped her into the front seat and then got in the other side. As the engine roared to life he reached out to take her hand. He was right: it might be crazy, but it still made perfect sense.

"I was right. There were no losers in this competition."

"I wholeheartedly agree."

A thought flashed across her brain and it must have shown on her face, because Connor looked at her funny. "What's wrong, Vivi?"

I can't. I shouldn't. But he was the one who'd brought it up.

"If we're both winners, and you only wanted the girl anyway…?"

"Yes…?" he prompted.

"Can *I* have the trophy?"

Connor was laughing as he kissed her.

* * * * *

NINA SINGH
MICHELLE MAJOR
MILLS & BOON
True Love
KATE HARDY
MELISSA SENATE
MILLS & BOON
True Love
THERESE BEHARRIS
STELLA BAGWELL
MILLS & BOON
True Love